He Was Her Destiny. . . .

In the dark of an abandoned woodcutter's cottage, Michael made a place for them to lie with his saddle blanket. He did not ask for an explanation; her body, warm in his arms, communicated with its own eloquence. He was hungry, ravenous for her after weeks of waiting, weeks of imagining this moment of surrender. He pulled her roughly to the floor beside him and, taking her face between his hands, kissed her mouth long and hard.

"I love you, Michael," Fiona breathed. In spite of everything, the simple phrase sounded right. It washed over her suddenly, an immense wave of truth. The dream, the Prince—they were her destiny. But so was Michael Cameron. . . .

Dear Reader:

We trust you will enjoy this Richard Gallen romance. We plan to bring you more of the best in both contemporary and historical romantic fiction with four exciting new titles each month.

We'd like your help.

We value your suggestions and opinions. They will help us to publish the kind of romances you want to read. Please send us your comments, or just let us know which Richard Gallen romances you have especially enjoyed. Write to the address below. We're looking forward to hearing from you!

Happy reading!

Judy Sullivan
Richard Gallen Books
8-10 West 36th St.
New York, N.Y. 10018

A Dream of Fire

DRUSILLA CAMPBELL

Q

PUBLISHED BY RICHARD GALLEN BOOKS
Distributed by POCKET BOOKS

Books by Drusilla Campbell

A Dream of Fire
The Frost and the Flame

Also published by RICHARD GALLEN BOOKS

An Elegant Affair   *Roman Candles*
  by Kathleen Morris   by Sofi O'Bryan

Waters of Eden
  by Katherine Kent

A RICHARD GALLEN BOOKS *Original* publication

Distributed by
POCKET BOOKS, a Simon & Schuster division of
GULF & WESTERN CORPORATION
1230 Avenue of the Americas, New York, N.Y. 10020

ISBN: 0-671-43468-3

First Pocket Books printing August, 1981

10 9 8 7 6 5 4 3 2 1

RICHARD GALLEN and colophon are trademarks
of Simon & Schuster and Richard Gallen & Co., Inc.

Printed in the U.S.A.

For my clansmen—
Arthur, Rocky and Matthew.

Book One

———

FAERY KIN

Chapter 1

The Isle of Skye, Scotland, 1735

On the night they took her mother away, Fiona Macleod had a dream.

From the march of a black wood, she saw a wide flat moorland, bounded by a river and the sea beyond. The plain was winter-drab; the sky opaque, leaden. The wind off the sea bore ice on its breath, and the slumbering Fiona shivered from its kiss. She was alone save for the ubiquitous rooks, perched, like harbingers of doom, on the uniformly round stones scattered about the moor as if tossed aside by a giant indifferent hand. With the toe of her boot, she nudged a stone. Animated by her touch, it rolled around, revealing a mangled face. Soundlessly, she screamed, looked frantically around her. All the stones had turned, and now a thousand faces, torn and bleeding, stared at her. Accused her . . .

The sound of voices in the yard below awoke her abruptly. Chilled and groggy, Fiona pushed aside the coverlet and raised herself on her knees near the foot of her narrow bed. Leaning her high forehead against the tiny dormer window of her attic bedroom, Fiona peered out at the small yard surrounding the cottage that she shared with her mother.

Everything she saw—the garden patch, the stack of peat beside the clothesline, even the surrounding stone wall crumbling with age—had lost its comforting familiarity. A storm was coming from the western sea. The moon seemed to dance drunkenly behind fleeting clouds, spotlighting the dozen or so villagers who were milling about in the yard. Although she was some ten feet above them and safely hidden from view, Fiona shrank fearfully from the steaming mob: the anger-heated bodies sweating in winter woolens; the muttering voices—outraged and churlish; the savage faces contorted with passion and brutality. Fiona's childish limbs shook with terror. Who were these folk, and why had they come here with their anger in the middle of the night?

The home where eight-year-old Fiona and her mother had lived for as long as Fiona could remember was a typical Scottish crofter's cottage in the village of Dunvegan, on the Isle of Skye. The cottage was made of rough stone, white-washed, with a half-dozen small square windows set into the thick walls. A snug thatch roof, held down by heavy stones, protected the two rooms and the attic loft where Fiona slept. Situated on a rise to the east of Dunvegan, the cottage looked out on a panorama that stretched from the castle to the village and across the moor, to the point and the pipers' village of Borreraig, where Fiona's Aunt Mathilda Duncan lived. On fine summer days the cottage looked cheerful, welcoming. But on this chill December night, it seemed to Fiona that her home had suddenly been occupied by malignant spirits. A persistent wind nagged at the thatch and whined in the eaves, providing a sinister accompaniment to the threatening voices of the gathered villagers.

Here and there in the faltering moonlight, Fiona saw faces she knew. There was Rachel Macdonald, the pious and overbearing wife of the village storekeeper, to whom Janet Macleod was much in debt. Mistress Macdonald stood right below Fiona's window, facing the cottage door; beside her Fiona thought she recognized the schoolmaster's assistant, Miss Catherine. It was hard to be certain though; her face was in shadow. Several townspeople, including Mistress Macdonald, carried unlighted torches and as Fiona watched spellbound, a light was produced and passed among them. The scene leapt into flame. Illuminated by the satanic light of her torch, Mistress Macdonald leered with cruelty. Fiona reached behind her and lifted the edge of the comforter, wrapping the warm softness around her shoulders. She was trembling uncontrollably.

Fists pounded on the door, and Fiona heard the voices of her mother and Aunt Mathilda Duncan, arguing in the house below. Then she heard the bolt being lifted from the door, and saw her mother step into the lighted courtyard and confront the nocturnal visitors.

Janet Macleod was a large woman, over six feet tall and statuesque. In the orange-gold light of Mistress Macdonald's torch, her red hair flamed out in the wind; to Fiona's eyes, she seemed to be ablaze. Sharp-featured, some people called the widow Macleod. But to her daughter and only child she was beautiful, and never more so than on that winter night. Her broad shoulders did not stoop with fear; her noble features did not melt with pleading.

At first, Fiona thought they would talk as grownups always did; an agreement would be reached. But before she could think more about this, she felt the hostility of the mob swell into a murderous rage. The voices grew louder, and Fiona heard the word *witch*. Not once, but many times.

"Why are we wasting time?" a voice demanded impatiently.

"Get on with it!" cried a woman in the rear.

Suddenly—Fiona froze in horror—she saw Mistress Macdonald begin to claw and pull at her mother's arms and shoulders. The crowd pushed forward, grabbing Janet's skirt and hair, shoving her ahead through the garden gate. She grabbed at the arbor, but someone pried loose her fingers. Janet thrashed and screamed, but the mob only intensified its antagonism. There was just time for the hapless widow to turn and raise her eyes to the attic window where her little girl watched. Their eyes locked in one instant of anguished clarity, and then Fiona saw her mother shake her head fervently from side to side. As she repeated the action, someone in the mob pushed her roughly onto the moonlit track that led from the cottage to the Post Road below.

"Come back, Mama!" Fiona cried. Too late. Her mother and the mob had dropped below the lip of the hill.

She scrambled off the bed and down the ladder to the ground floor. As she reached for her cloak, which hung on a wooden peg by the door, Aunt Mathilda's strong arm arrested her.

"Don't go out there, Fiona!" As plain as her sister Janet was beautiful, Mathilda Duncan's gaunt face was immobile, as if carved from stone.

"They've taken Mama! Mistress Macdonald was there, and Miss Catherine too, I think. They took her down toward the . . ." Fiona tugged at Mathilda's sleeve. Her aunt was a grownup. Couldn't she explain everything, couldn't she bring Mama back? "Come on, Aunty. Make them . . ."

"I can't make them do anything, child. I am as helpless as you."

"But, I must . . ."

"You must stay here and pray God they have forgotten you," Mathilda said huskily, her blue eyes wet with tears. "Oh, Lord," she moaned, "Why have you visited this curse upon our family? Take pity now on this wee lassie."

Forgetting the urgency of the moment, Mathilda relaxed her grip. When she recovered her senses, Fiona was out the door and into the yard.

An icy rain had begun to fall, and in the east the sky was lightening just perceptibly. It would be a long dark morning on the Isle of Skye, but Fiona was oblivious to the sharding rain that soaked her flannel nightdress. She had almost reached the gate, when her aunt grabbed her again.

"Don't speak! Don't make a sound!" Mathilda hissed, trying to drag the protesting child back to the cottage. "If you value your life, be silent, child!"

"Let me go!" Fiona screamed, wrenching away. In seconds, she was racing like a fawn down the hill toward the Coach Road. The steep path through the heather was littered with rocks and pitted with holes; nevertheless, Fiona moved swiftly through the thin dawnlight. She knew this path as well as any bit of land anywhere. She had skipped up and down its length a thousand times, in moments of carefree play. Now her feet seemed to fly. In a few minutes, she reached the Coach Road and leaned against an oak to catch her breath. She felt her courage ebbing. Her flannel nighty was drenched with rain and clung to her like an icy second skin. She crouched beneath the broad canopy of the oak tree, pressing her face against its trunk. At that moment, the comforting sensation of the rough-ridged bark was all that seemed real to Fiona. Everything else was like a continuation of the nightmare that had visited her earlier in the night. Her mouth was dry. She stuck out her tongue to catch the cold rain and tasted salt on her lips. She was crying.

"Why, Mama? Why?"

"Fiona . . ."

At the sound of Mathilda's voice behind her, Fiona jumped to her feet and ran down the road in the direction of the mob. She could hear their voices ahead, and sometimes she caught a glimpse of them. They were traveling east on the Coach Road, moving away from Dunvegan toward the wide rocky strand that marked the termination of the loch. There were few trees to hide behind as they approached the water, but Fiona was not afraid that one of the villagers would catch her. She was possessed by a terrible calm, and moved with the natural stealth of a wild creature raised in the Highlands of the misty isle.

Above the rocky strand was a rising arc of sand, terminating at a grassy knoll crowned by boulders. Fiona crouched there, almost shielded from the wind and rain, completely concealed from the mob. Higher up was another graceful rise, of moorgrass and bracken, littered with boulders and stones. Below, the beach too was covered with stones—a million times a million of them—worn smooth and round between the palms of time.

Janet Macleod could feel her heart beating in her throat, strangling her. She thought her chest would burst with fear and breathlessness. Hooking one foot behind her she staggered, and fell to her knees on the stones. She wanted to rest, but she had to keep moving. The mob was driving her toward the water.

A man's boot rammed her thigh.

"Get up, witch!" yelled someone.

"Rise, harlot of Satan!" commanded Mistress Macdonald.

Janet heard herself yelling over the sound of waves and rain. Her beautiful hair clung to her skull like a shroud, and her skin, white with terror, was stretched taut as a mask. She tried to reason with her captors. "I have done nothing! I am one of you. You must believe me, I am innocent . . ."

She felt the first one on her shoulder. She wondered what it was that came so unexpectedly, that bit her skin so cruelly. The next one grazed her forehead, just above the ear, and when she touched the spot her fingers came back bloodied.

"My God in Heaven . . ."

They were stoning her!

The stones were coming faster, but no more hit her head. It was as if the mob had planned it this way. They wanted her to suffer as long as possible. They wanted to drive the Devil's spirit out of her through torture. If she were innocent, a white dove would fly from her lips in time to save her. If not . . .

A stone slammed into her knee; she screamed with pain and buckled. Another hit her breast, and yet another the base of her spine. She looked around for escape, but saw only the twisted faces of her assailants, their arms raised, their fists clenched. Behind her, the breaking water noisily stirred the stones in their bed.

The rain had extinguished the torches. Now one of the townsmen prodded Janet with the blackened end of his brand. Still warm, it left a tattoo on her shoulder. And the stones kept coming, driving her slowly backward into the water. The blows came faster; the aim of the mob grew careless. A mist of blood and salt and rainwater almost blinded her as she tried to shield her head from the furious missiles; but in that instant she looked back over her shoulder and, through the rain of stones, saw a child standing on the bluff. She remembered Fiona then.

"Forgive me, dearest bairn. Forgive me," she whispered as the rocks and stones pounded and broke against her, forcing her to stagger deeper and deeper into the icy water. "Forgive me," she whispered as her bloated woolen skirts spread wide and dragged her downward, until the brine silenced her cries and blacked out forever the vision of her child.

Chapter 2

Fiona regained consciousness a few hours later, by slow perplexing stages. She stubbed her toe on a jut of root and realized that she was being dragged—by the arm—along the Post Road east of Dunvegan. It was morning—dew gleamed faintly on the bracken, and the road was puddled with last night's rain. With a belated sensation of pain, Fiona yelped, "My toe!" Her aunt turned around.

"You've come to your senses, then?" Mathilda's face was chalky.

"What's the matter, Aunt?" Fiona asked, her injury forgotten for the moment. "You're hurting me."

Mathilda tightened her grasp on the child's thin wrist. "Hush, Fiona, hurry along. There isn't much time."

Obediently, Fiona quickened her pace to match her aunt's; but she was not to be silenced so easily. "Time for what?" she asked. "Where are you taking me?"

Mathilda paused and looked searchingly at her niece. "Do you feel all right, child?"

"I stubbed my toe." Now that they were standing still, Fiona had begun to feel sorry for herself. She was cold and tired, her wrist was bruised, her head ached and her toe was throbbing. She began to cry as Mathilda dragged her forward again along the Post Road, pocked by stones and cut by icy rivulets, through the treeless open country at the end of Loch Dunvegan. "I stubbed my toe!" Fiona wailed again, but Mathilda paid her no heed. She glanced quickly over her shoulder, prompting Fiona to turn also. A hundred yards back, coming over a little rise of land, was a small band of men and women. Though Fiona counted only five persons, she was frightened, for they carried sticks; and though their cries were unintelligible, she heard anger in their voices.

"What do they want, Aunty?" Even at a distance, Fiona felt the mob's hostility. She tried to run, but fatigue made her clumsy. She stumbled.

"God bless you, child!" cried Mathilda. She dropped to her knees and embraced Fiona tightly. Too tightly. The older woman's panic was communicated to the child.

"What do they want, Aunty?" she asked again, her voice rising hysterically.

Mathilda didn't seem to hear. She shook herself, stood up and, grabbing Fiona's wrist again, dragged the little girl along the road. Sharp-edged stones cut Fiona's bare feet and ankles. She looked down and saw blood on the hem of her cloak. "I want my mama," she began to cry. "I want my mama!"

Mathilda stopped again. This time she gripped Fiona by the shoulders, squeezed tight and shook her. "Come to your senses, bairn. Don't speak of her. Whatever you do, if they catch us, don't speak of your mother."

Fiona wasn't listening. One thought, one single overpowering need, obsessed her. "Mama!"

Mathilda didn't hesitate to think. Her hand went back, then out across Fiona's cheek. In the shocked instant that followed, she grabbed her niece's hand and continued to stagger along the coach road.

No one had ever hit Fiona before, and the force of the blow, coupled with astonishment, left her mute. Her cheek burned where Mathilda's flattened palm had struck, but she was too surprised to cry out. Then, suddenly, she remembered the dream of the moor littered with bloody stones. Was it possible, she wondered, that this new horror was an extension of that other?

Oh, please, God, her young heart prayed, let this be a dream too. I want to wake up now. Please!

Instead, she heard her name called in a tone that dashed her hopes.

"Fiona Macleod, halt where ye go!" The voice was unmistakably Mistress Macdonald's. Mathilda and her niece stopped and slowly turned to face the outraged villagers.

With the dawn, Mistress Macdonald's myrmidons had shrunk to four; but her own righteousness spurred her on. As she spoke, Mathilda Duncan put her arms around Fiona and hugged her tight.

"Give her up, Mistress Duncan," Mistress Macdonald ordered. "Let us be done with this tainted blood once and for all." Drunk with the power of fanaticism, the shopkeeper's wife towered over Fiona and her aunt.

"Mama," the little girl whimpered, hunkering down at her aunt's feet. "Come back to me, Mama."

"Give me the infected brat. Give her to me!" Mistress Macdonald's voice was like the cry of a diving kestrel. Fiona covered her ears.

"Infected with what? No worse poison than runs in you, Mistress Murderess!" Mathilda raised her arm in threat. "You leave this child be. I will go to the laird himself if you make more trouble for her. I swear I will tell him what you and your friends did to my sister."

The mob grumbled. The villagers began to think of their own families, waiting at home. They too had wee bairns, like Fiona. Adam Ferguson, the tanner, shifted his club from hand to hand, remembering Janet Macleod's eyes just before she went under. Those wide accusing eyes; he knew they would haunt his dreams for the rest of his life.

"We didn't do anything," he whined, passing a fat damp palm back and forth across his lips.

Mathilda turned on him. "You lie, Adam Ferguson. You killed my sister! You threw the stones that drove her down bleeding. You and Mistress Macdonald and . . ."

Fiona stirred at Mathilda's feet.

"The child should be put away for her own good," Mistress Macdonald said grimly. "She's faery kin. A halfling."

Mathilda laughed. Fiona started up at the bitter sound. "You, Miss Catherine," her aunt said, "you're the schoolmaster's assistant. Do you believe in all this talk of faery folk and halfling children?"

Miss Catherine stammered. "Those two wee ones did disappear, Mistress Duncan. You cannot deny that."

"Exactly!" cried Mistress Macdonald. "How do you explain the disappearance of those poor bairns?" She looked to her followers for encouragement, but they had grown silent.

"If you're talking about the two little girls belonging to the laird's gardener, my sister had nothing to do with their disappearance. They wandered off into the woods and were taken by gypsies most likely." Mathilda's voice was firm and confident. Still huddled at her aunt's feet, Fiona listened well.

"The gypsies could not have taken those children. They were camped on Patterson's Field, a good five miles away. It was your sister took those bairns, and gave them to the faery folk. The magistrate found her bonnet near the place where they were sleeping."

"But she lost that bonnet weeks and weeks before, when she went berrying. The brambles were right there where the children slept. The bonnet means nothing, and everyone knows that but you and your . . . ." Mathilda gestured toward the mob. "Poor dolts," she said scornfully, "why would my sister kidnap two children?"

Mistress Macdonald smirked. "The faery folk used her. Those children were protected by charm stones hung about their necks so the faeries couldn't touch them. But your sister could, being half human. She was in league with the wee folk and did their bidding." Mistress Macdonald's expression grew cunning. "You are fortunate not to carry the bad blood yourself, Mathilda Duncan."

"If you think you could have driven me into the sea, you are mistaken."

"But you will give me the child." Mistress Macdonald's outstretched hand grazed Fiona's shoulder. She shuddered deeply and leaned into her aunt's warm skirts.

"Give the witch-baby to me!" demanded Mistress Macdonald.

Fiona erupted suddenly to life, and dashed through the space between the two women. "No witch!" she screamed, turning to the crowd like a wounded bobcat. "No witch!" she screamed again. There was a single tree near the road, a windbent oak. She scrambled up it before anyone could stop her, then crouched in the "y" of branches and glared at the villagers.

No one moved toward her; all were momentarily paralyzed by surprise.

In that moment of frozen time, Fiona recalled everything. It was as if a closed door had opened on a forbidden room. She remembered the mob in the yard and her mother's hair like a flame in the wind. She saw Mistress Macdonald throw

11

the first stone and Miss Catherine smile and point when her clumsy lob drew blood. Fiona saw and heard everything again, but her mind was like a stage and the events of the passed hours were as remote as theatrical events, on which a final curtain might drop at any time. Then she recalled her mother's face in those last moments, and rage and terror engulfed her. Her trembling shook the tree.

Miss Catherine's heart was moved at the sight. By daylight, Fiona was no more a witch-baby than Miss Catherine's own sisters. Was it possible they had been mistaken about Janet Macleod as well? Miss Catherine's mind recoiled from the thought, but it persisted. "Mistress Macdonald," she began, touching her elder's sleeve respectfully, "perhaps it would be best if . . ."

Adam Ferguson was thinking how the child's eyes reminded him of the mother's. He turned away and retched.

Mistress Macdonald knew that she was losing her followers. She tried to fire them again with her zeal. "As God is my witness," she cried, her arms outstretched like a priestess, "this child is evil as the mother was evil, as those before . . ."

Miss Catherine interrupted with uncharacteristic independence. "She's only a child."

"Satan is speaking through you, Catherine Bright," Mistress Macdonald said thunderously. "He dwells in you now, and makes you disbelieve your own righteousness."

But Miss Catherine shook her head. Slowly, she stepped back, away from Mistress Macdonald. Her cheeks were pinched with concern, and her dark eyes flashed from left to right nervously. "I never meant to hurt your sister," she whined.

"We didn't hurt her," said Adam Ferguson, coming forward now to tug on Mathilda Duncan's arm. "She lost control. That's how it happened. We were only trying to frighten her." He wanted desperately to go home.

"It was you who lost control," replied the dead woman's sister. She stared at the group with loathing. One by one, they were deserting Mistress Macdonald. Some kept their eyes downcast; one dared to whisper as she turned away, "I am truly sorry, Mistress Duncan. I always liked your sister."

Mistress Macdonald stood alone. The others were hurrying back to their homes and forgetfulness. Before departing herself, their leader shook an angry finger at Mathilda Duncan. "Keep that brat away from Dunvegan Town, or you will both regret it!"

Mathilda watched the retreating villagers until they disappeared from sight. Only then did she begin to relax. She turned to the child still trembling in the tree.

"Come down to me, Fiona," she said, trying to modulate her sharp voice to the gentle sounds she imagined a mother would make. She held out her arms; and with an eagerness that surprised them both, Fiona jumped from the tree and ran to her aunt's embrace. Simultaneously, they burst into tears. For Mathilda, who had tried so hard to sound unafraid in the face of Mistress Macdonald's wrath, the tears were a necessary purge. Then, and never again, she wept for her dead sister and the orphan child left behind. But there was no time for the luxury of grieving. Mathilda straightened her tired back, and wiped the child's tears with the hem of her skirt.

"Enough, Fiona. Give me your hand. You will live with me and mine now."

Around noon the overcast thinned. In the pleasant warmth of the sun, Fiona and Mathilda stopped to drink from a burn, and fanned themselves with ferns. They were traveling west now, into the sun. The Post Road had become a narrow track, extending out along the peninsula to the village of Borreraig, on Dunvegan Head. The path was muddy and irregular, but rough walking was no hardship to either of them, for they were accustomed to the hard Skye life and expected nothing else. As if to prevent her heart from breaking, Fiona's mind had mercifully gone blank again. She had forgotten the memory of her mother in the black water, and even the recent encounter with Mistress Macdonald. As they walked, she counted stones in time to a childhood rhyme.

She must be told, Mathilda nagged herself. She has to know the whole truth now.

By two in the afternoon, they had traveled half the distance to the point, and stopped at the village of Castle. In a hostel there they bought tea and fresh bannocks, the edges burned black from toasting on the stones of the fireplace. As they rested beside the path, Mathilda watched Fiona stuff herself and checked a reprimand as the child slurped and gulped her tea. These were signs of a healthy bairn, and Mathilda's heart swelled with gratitude. At least Fiona was safe . . .

But she must be told, Mathilda reminded herself.

"Can you see the castle?" Mathilda pointed across the loch strewn with rocky islets to the place where the massive keep of Dunvegan Castle was half hidden among trees. "Do you know who lives there?"

"My lord Macleod," answered Fiona promptly, hoping she and her aunt were going to play the school-game of question and answer.

"He is an honorable man, Fiona." The comment was uttered automatically; though she had never been introduced to the laird—nor did she ever expect to be—Mathilda's fealty to him and his family was genuine. "Long ago, our family broke from that branch of the Macleods. We stayed loyal to the clan, but apart. We were always apart. Do you know why, Fiona?" The girl shook her head, and Mathilda sighed. Her task that afternoon would not be easy.

Fiona was as innocent as Janet Macleod had wished her to be. She had heard no word of what the villagers sometimes called "the family curse." Mathilda wondered if it was possible that Fiona shared some of the dangerous talents ill fortune had lavished on Janet. It was true that the curse sometimes skipped generations; and there was never more than one person affected at a time. Mathilda was normal herself. She prayed silently that Fiona had also been spared.

Mathilda collected their tea things and returned them to the hosteler's wife. Then she took Fiona's hand and they walked on toward the distant point. As they walked, Mathilda spoke partly to Fiona, partly to herself. She knew as she talked that much of what she said was beyond Fiona's ken; nevertheless, the child seemed to listen attentively.

"There is a story, an old legend," Mathilda began, "that tells how, long long ago, a chief of the clan Macleod fell in love with a faery princess and got her with child. The infant was found squalling under a bridge to the north of Dunvegan. It was wrapped in a flag of crimson silk marked with faery runes."

"Have you seen this flag, Aunt?"

"I have not. But I am told the laird keeps it in the castle to this day, though the color be faded and the edge frayed."

"What became of the infant?"

"It was sent away from the castle and brought up out of sight of the family, for they said it was an abomination." Mathilda looked at her niece—her thick amber-colored hair stirred by the wind, wide copper eyes bright with curiosity. "It was long ago, and you are the last of that halfling line, Fiona." She went on without pausing. "You haven't any peculiar . . . abilities have you, child?"

"I don't know what you mean."

"Like your mama. You know. She was a healer and she had a knack with growing things."

There had been other talents less easily explained; but when Fiona again shook her head in complete innocence, Mathilda decided it was best to leave still waters undisturbed. She did not want to speak of the strange dreams her sister sometimes had, foretelling disasters. Like the time—she was no more than six or seven—she had dreamed Farmer Scott's barn was burning. Janet had awakened and run through the night in her gown to the farmer's door. She was seconds too late. As she stammered out her warning, a spark danced from the chimney to the thatch of the barn. People had begun to talk about Janet Macleod then.

These supernatural powers of her sister's were deeply troubling to Mathilda. Her plain-thinking logical mind was affronted by this proof of another—and to her more frightening—order than the one she understood. Nevertheless, she had to know if Fiona bore her mother's taint. If she was so gifted, she would have to be protected—like the villagers of Dunvegan, the townspeople of Borreraig were prone to superstition.

"Your mother wanted to protect you, so she did everything she could to keep you away from the villagers. That's why you two lived apart, that's why she never took you to the kirk. The folk said your mother was godless, that she had *oogly* powers; they said she was dangerous, though you and I know . . ." Mathilda's words trailed off in search of some conclusion.

What did anyone really know about Janet Macleod? She had been strange since childhood. Her will had seemed stronger than that of mortal folk, her mind uncanny; and she was eerily beautiful like some exotic plant that had grown wild amid the haunted emptiness of Skye. Though it shamed

Mathilda to admit it, she understood why the villagers' distrust of Janet had grown stronger with each year; even to her sister, Janet could be frightening.

It was cold on Dunvegan Head. Mathilda shivered in her cloak, and hurried their pace up the path. To the left the hillside rose sharply; to the right it pitched into the sea. At night, it was not difficult to believe that the island was haunted by wee folk, as the myths and legends said. Mathilda could almost feel their presence behind each dark rock. Fiona put her hand within her aunt's; they walked much more quickly now, sharing an eagerness to rest beside a reassuring peat fire, the kettle-steam sizzling the grate.

"You should never have been born," continued Mathilda after a while. She was encouraged by the sound of her own voice and did not stop to think how her words might wound her niece. "But at least you were conceived in love, and there was nothing *oogly* about that poor soldier boy who fathered you. If he had lived, he would have married your mother and taken you both away to his people on the mainland. Everything would have been different then. He would have protected you both." Mathilda walked silently for a few paces, but from the expression on her face, Fiona knew that she was still troubled. At last she stopped walking and, bending to her knees, took Fiona's face between her work-worn palms. "You don't have dreams do you, child? You cannot tell the future?"

"No," said Fiona unhesitatingly. The darkness did not frighten her, but she was tired and unhappy. She longed to sleep. By now she had forgotten the disturbing dream of the previous night. "No," she said again and yawned—and thought that she told the truth.

Chapter 3

Nine years passed. Nine long years, during which Fiona grew up, without friends or companions her own age, into a seemingly self-sufficient but lonely lass of seventeen. In the rough stone crofter's cottage on the outskirts of Borreraig where she lived with her Aunt Mathilda and Uncle Rob—a cottage nearly identical to the one which she had formerly shared with her mother—Fiona lived a retired life, rarely speaking even to her aunt and uncle, and even more rarely venturing into the village of Borreraig. Outwardly, she seemed content, apparently accepting and even welcoming her reclusive existence. Never, either by word or look, did she indicate any memory of her early childhood with Janet Macleod, or of the terrible events that had made her an orphan and forced her to flee her native village of Dunvegan. But though she gave no sign, hardly a day passed that Fiona did not recall—and grieve for—her mother. Distant impressions—the lurid vision of Mistress Macdonald's face contorted by rage and the cry of zealot voices over the rumble of the sea—these and other vague memories warned Fiona to shun village gatherings and keep her own counsel. Only a dozen times in nine years had she actually walked in Borreraig. Now, as she hurried along the path, a letter grasped tightly in her hand, she was conscious of spying eyes behind lace curtains, and even the dogs barked at her as if she meant the village harm.

Borreraig was hardly a village at all compared to thriving

Dunvegan Town, which could be seen across the loch. The nearby castle of the laird Macleod was also visible, rising out of the forest park that separated it from Dunvegan. There was no forest to shelter Borreraig, hardly any trees at all, and the village jutted out from the barren head—a cluster of huts and yards connected by a narrow hilly pathway—like a nobbled growth. In winter, when the wind from the west tore at the cottages and beat against the shutters for days and days at a time, the hardy residents of Dunvegan Head went about in thick layers of coarse clothing that bundled the bodies of both men and women into a kind of pudding sexlessness.

Fiona despised the winter months, feeling fat and awkward in her woolen swaddling, out of sorts with her wild environment. She was a fey creature, who loved nothing better than to trek the Highland country of Skye barefoot, alone except for the few sheep her Uncle Rob kept grazing high up where the grass grew in bright green bogs all summer long.

Rob kept the dogs—Bridey and Shay—with him. He was a lazy brute of a man, who liked to doze on the flat rocks that bridged the grass from the gray sea while his dogs did all the work of tending the small flock. It was hard work to keep Highland sheep, and Rob avoided work whenever possible—though he boasted of being a hard laborer. Fiona, on the other hand, loved shepherding, loved to be alone with the animals on the craggy hills of the Highlands. The misty island of Skye seemed to communicate with her, telling her she belonged to it and it to her. In her uncle's cottage she was an alien; here she was at home. On sunny days, she felt a comforting tranquility in the Highlands, a peace and joy unlike anything else in her life.

It was good to know those warm days were near again. As she hurried down the path to the Borreraig school, Fiona added an inadvertent series of skips, hops and jumps that were in keeping with her age—at seventeen most girls were merry—and yet quite alien to her nature. If there was any merriment in Fiona, it had thus far been hidden, even from her. Her habitual expression was solemn, her thoughts gloomy, and her nerves were always on edge. It was as if her customary vigilance absorbed all her energies, leaving nothing in her to laugh with.

She hated coming into Borreraig. But she had not dared refuse when Uncle Rob told her to walk to the postmistress's

house after tea. A letter was a major event in their isolated
life, and Fiona was curious about this small change in their
routine. She stopped a minute to read the writing on the
envelope. Mathilda Duncan had done her duty by her niece's
education, drilling her in the three R's until she knew them as
well, and perhaps better, than any of the children who had
the benefit of attending the village school; so Fiona had no
trouble deciphering the sender's name: Loughlin Shields,
Solicitor.

Fiona had no idea what a solicitor might be, so she tucked
the letter away in the pocket of her faded blue pinafore and
thought no more about it. Her clothing—the pinafore, the
made-over dark brown skirt and jacket, the darned tartan
plaid that circled her shoulders—were uniformly old and
drab. Even when new, these garments had done no more than
accent Mathilda Duncan's plainness, but on Fiona, her aunt's
hand-me-downs seemed to acquire a certain style and grace.
At the threshold of womanhood, Fiona was already, like her
mother, an imposing figure: tall, proud in bearing, and with a
larger-than-life quality that fascinated some observers—and
intimidated others. Her hair captivated the attention at once.
It was a rich amber color, far brighter and stranger than the
carroty-red and straw-blonde that were typical of the region.
On the London stage, or in the salons of Paris, her melancholy brown eyes flecked with gold, topaz-hued skin and
sensual unsmiling mouth might have been admired, along
with her exotic tresses, as the endowments with which Nature
sometimes chooses to bestow on her creatures a more than
mortal beauty; but the women of Borreraig, spying on Fiona
as she passed their cottages, whispered behind their hands
that looks so dramatic were suspicious in a country girl.
Occasional glimpses of the solitary Fiona, as she made one of
her infrequent journeys into the village, were enough to keep
the Borreraig gossips busy for months, nattering over the old
halfling legend.

As she approached the school, the usual taunting began.
Fiona could hear the nasty little-boy voices even before she
saw the three brats ducked down behind the peat bin where
the schoolmaster couldn't find them.

"Halfling . . . halfling . . . faery kin . . ." They chanted
the words in a jeering sing-song. "Halfling, halfling, witch's
blood . . ."

She stood over them now, looming grimly. Their eyes were wide with terror.

"Hugaboo!" shrieked Fiona, and jumped at them, waving her arms. The fact that they actually feared her and she could see it in their eyes had been enough to enrage her so she couldn't pass by, ignoring them as she had counseled herself to do. "Hugaboo!" she screamed again and they screamed too, falling all over each other and making a great commotion.

The schoolmaster appeared—on the run—from behind the school building. "You wee foxes! I've been after you to fill the waterbucket and now I find you . . ." He saw Fiona. "You!" he screamed at her, dragging the boys by their collars as he backed away. "Get out of here, you! Go away!"

For just a second, Fiona stood her ground wanting to explain—as she had at every previous encounter with the villagers—that she was nothing extraordinary, no faery kin. But she knew it was useless. They wouldn't believe her and, to tell the truth, she wasn't sure herself sometimes. She kept having the strangest dream . . .

When the schoolmaster yelled, "I'll get the dogs after you!" Fiona took off, flying down the path. She didn't stop running until she reached the bottom of the hill.

Out of breath, and angry with herself as well as with the teacher and his students, Fiona stopped to rest at the edge of a deep inlet, where the fishermen of Borreraig would beach their boats in a few hours time. The air smelled of dead fish and seagulls were everywhere. Just up the hill, Fiona could hear the evening students, who worked for their parents during the day, learning their numbers by noisy rote. She closed her mind to the sound. The schoolhouse and its hostile inhabitants were behind her. Now there was only Uncle Rob to worry about encountering between the inlet and home.

In recent weeks, her uncle had begun to lie in wait for her, hopping out from behind bushes and boulders unexpectedly. Once last week he had crept up behind her as she scrubbed the laundry, and cupped his beefy paws over her breasts. As she screamed out, he slapped her hard. "Shut up," he snarled. "Don't give me no cause to hurt you!"

The memory of Rob's threat, the feel of his greedy hands were still fresh to her. Angrily, she heaved a rock at the water. How much worse could things get, she wondered? She knew the answer. Mathilda was very sick, would probably die soon, she reminded herself. Then Fiona and Rob would occupy the remote crofter's cottage alone. Shuddering at the thought, she determined to leave Borreraig soon. In Edinburgh she could get proof that the cottage was hers, a gift deeded to her after her mother's death by her Aunt Mathilda; then she could throw Rob off the place if he misbehaved.

She would have to go soon. In the meantime, an instinct that experience had taught her to trust told her that somewhere ahead on the beach, Rob was waiting for her. She saw him vividly in her mind's eye, stretched out on one of the monstrous slabs of rock at the base of the path from their cottage to the beach. His round coarse-featured face would be bright red from the sun's dying heat; his heavy black beard would glisten with sweat as he rubbed his crotch and shaded his eyes to look for her along the beach.

I can distract him with the letter, she thought. Or take the upper path.

If she took the alternate route, she would almost certainly be late arriving. Aunt Mathilda would be anxious and Rob would likely cuff her for staying out late and avoiding his rendezvous. Better to go straight along the beach, she decided. It was cooler now than it had been in town. She wrapped the plaid around her more tightly and hurried on.

At the Galtrigill Inlet, a shadow crossed her path. She stopped, paralyzed.

"Uncle!" she cried, looking up. But it wasn't Rob. It was a kilted boy, not much older than herself. He carried a set of bagpipes comfortably on his shoulder. "Beg pardon," she said hurriedly, walking once more. "I mistook you." She could feel the stranger's eyes on her, though she kept her own gaze on the rocky strand until curiosity got the better of her. A pace or two beyond him, she looked back; the young man had not budged in his tracks. Lit by the sun, his handsome face was questioning and his wide eyes regarded her quizzically. Somehow, she had known he was looking at her. She took a few more steps, then turned once more. Still the stranger stared, and did not move.

She whirled around, hands on hips like a fishwife. "What's your name, boy?" she demanded furiously.

"Owen Hamilton," he replied. There was laughter in his voice.

His gaiety challenged her. "Well, Mister Owen Hamilton, didn't anyone teach you manners? Don't you know it's impolite to stare? Well, then, take your pipes and your fancy kilt and go back where you came from. I don't know who you are, but Hamilton's no Skye name. So go back where you came from!"

Ignoring her command, he came closer. "You're the halfling, aren't you?"

Without thinking, she grabbed a handful of stones and began to pelt him. "Don't call me that!" she yelled. "Just go away and leave me alone!"

He walked through the rain of stones and grabbed her wrist. Her hand opened unwillingly and dropped an egg-sized stone. She kicked his shins and he jumped back; but he tightened his grip on her wrist.

"What's the matter with you?" he demanded. "You wanted to hurt me." He shook her. "Calm down. I never meant to insult you. I only asked . . ."

She squirmed again in his grasp.

"If I let you go, will you promise not to throw anything?"

With her free hand she brushed her hair back from eyes, glaring at him all the while. She nodded sullenly, as if to signify that she was consenting only under duress.

"Well," he wanted to know, "are you that girl?"

"And if am—what then?"

Owen laughed. "If you are, then I believe the tales they tell." He caught her as she ducked to grab another stone. Again, his hand on her wrist made her drop the weapon. "You are a witch!" he exclaimed. "And not to be trusted, I'd say." Then regaining his good humor, he asked almost playfully, "What makes you so mean, lass?"

She heard the concern in his voice. Abruptly her eyes filled, and her face went scarlet with humiliation. She sank down on the beach and, covering her face with her hands, she sobbed.

Owen had been orphaned for many years, and though unaccustomed to the society of young women, he possessed an instinctive gallantry, which asserted itself as he dropped to his knees beside her. They were strangers; still, he wanted to put his arms around the beautiful halfling girl and comfort her. He knew somehow that she would not reject him—and she didn't. She wept against his shoulder; as he cradled her in his arms, he felt her body throb with grief. Finally, she grew still.

When Fiona withdrew from Owen's embrace, she was shy. Never had she behaved so extraordinarily. She knew some explanation was due, but where to begin? When she looked at him, her chagrin was intensified. Not only was the young gentleman well above her in station, he was also handsome. It crossed her mind that she had never looked at anyone whose features and expression gave her greater pleasure. Shyness overcame her, and she could not speak a word. Soon even the silence was embarrassing. She owed him an explanation, an apology. She would have to say something, or this wonderful young man would carry more foolish gossip about her to the village. Here was her chance! If she could just make this Owen Hamilton understand, then maybe he would tell others that she was just an ordinary Skye girl. "You called me halfling."

"And I apologize," he said quickly. "I had not known it was an insult. I would never hurt you, miss. I swear, I would rather cut off my arm than see you weep again for some careless word of mine."

"I am just like anyone else. There's nothing special about me." She was trying to be pleasant, but a belligerent tone had crept into her voice, as if she were daring him to contradict her.

There's nothing special about me, she repeated to herself. But the phrase lacked conviction, even to herself. And she saw from his face that Owen didn't believe her. But she also saw that he wanted to, and that it hurt him to know that she was lying. All at once, the yearning for a comrade of heart and mind with whom to share her feelings became a painful need. She told Owen Hamilton the truth. Sitting beside him on the twilit strand, she unburdened herself of the terrible secret—how Mistress Macdonald and the others had killed her mother because of an old story that maybe wasn't true. Maybe was . . .

When she spoke to him of her dream in a faltering whisper, Owen began to understand that she had never before spoken of these things to anyone. He was honored that she had chosen him as her confidant.

"It comes once a week for months on end and then,

23

suddenly, it's gone for a year. Maybe more. And it's always the same. I'm on a moor covered with stones. Then the stones are bloody heads. The moor is red with them."

"What does it mean?" asked Owen. He was not yet eighteen years old, and despite a superficial appearance of sophistication he was essentially a country boy, with country superstitions. He had come to Skye from the Arran Isle ten years before, but he still found the misty isle disquieting. Villagers had told him that this point of land, Dunvegan Head, was haunted. They spoke of a girl, the kin of faery folk. And this was she!

As he listened to her secrets, he saw how beautiful she was, and realized that he was enchanted, not in any *oogly* way, but in the way of a man with a maid. What if she was a halfling? He only loved her the more. For Owen Hamilton too had a secret, one that he hardly dared admit to himself . . .

"I've stayed too long," Fiona said, noticing the darkening sky all at once. She clambered to her feet, ignoring Owen's outstretched hand. "I have to go. I'm late."

"Don't go. Not yet."

"I must," she said without moving. "I have stayed too long."

"You said that before and it's not true. I wish you could stay much longer."

"You're teasing me."

"I'm not. On my honor I am not." He was grinning at her almost comically.

She stared at his expression, not sure exactly what it meant. He wasn't laughing at her, she knew that. Then what was it, if not mockery? Strangely, she was laughing too. She couldn't remember the last time she had even smiled.

"Are you my friend?" she asked.

"Forever." Laughter again.

"I must go home. I have a letter to deliver and I'm late already."

"When can I see you again?"

"Tomorrow." She pointed to the sharp hill ahead. "I live just over the other side. I will take the sheep up between those two outcrops in the morning. I'll be up there all day."

"And I must be at the piper's college all morning. But in

24

the afternoon, I can have all the time I want. Watch for me, Fiona. I'll be there."

Reluctantly, they parted, each looking back at the other several times with shy smiles.

Suddenly, Fiona called, "Owen, who's that?" Her voice was trembling as she pointed toward Dunvegan Head, where a dark figure was silhouetted against the red-orange finish of the day. "He's watching us!"

"The man you see is Michael Cameron, my guardian." Owen spoke with a pride and an awed respect that made Fiona peer again into the distance at the man who was so obviously observing them. "He was my father's best friend. He came for me when I was eight. I never knew my parents. I was raised by an aunt until Michael came back from a sea trip saying he'd promised my father he'd look after me, if anything should happen."

"Why does he stare so?" She shook herself. "He makes me feel all strange, standing there watching. Why does he do it?"

Owen didn't answer right away. As he stared silently at Fiona, she thought she saw pain flicker across his face. Just moments ago there had been smiles and laughter between them; now, suddenly, their hopeful springtime had clouded over. An inexpressible sorrow darkened her feelings. Urgently, she repeated, "Why does he stare so?"

"I think he worries about me." He longed to say more, but could not. Fiona fancied him strong, depended on him . . .

"Why, Owen?"

He smiled at her and said, in a laughing voice, "Why, indeed? Perhaps he envies my good fortune. After all, I found you."

They rushed back into each other's arms, unwilling to part although Michael Cameron still watched them from the cliff above. It did not occur to Fiona to doubt the rightness of what she felt for Owen at that moment. Instinct told her to believe in him and take the friendship he offered, to love him perhaps. But there was another instinct too, a troubling one. It was that sadness that had come on her when she saw Michael Cameron watching them. Somehow the sorrow she felt was connected with Owen's guardian. She didn't know how she knew this, but she did.

Fiona arrived home long after dark. Climbing up the steep

hill from the beach, the cottage—barely ten feet square—was a dark shadow, as if one of the boulders precariously perched further up the steep mountain slope had broken loose and rolled down to rest on this barren terrace of land. By the time Bridey and Shay began to bark, she was close enough to see the faint glow outlining the shutters; and she knew that inside the cottage Rob was waiting for her.

Both he and Mathilda jumped on her the minute she stepped into the cottage.

"You alarm me, staying out past dark. Shame on you, lass. Shame. Your uncle and me deserve better by you." Mathilda's voice was weak as she spoke from a roughly made wooden bed that was pushed against one wall of the cottage among a collection of baskets, tools and other working implements. Even in the cottage, lit only by the fireplace and a dim lamp, Mathilda looked ghastly. The constant pain of the last year had lined her face like an old woman's, and her hair had thinned and gone white. She wore a grimy ruffled bedcap, which seemed to call attention to the ravaged face with its huge sunken eyes circled in black.

"Where were you?" Rob demanded, trying to grab her arm. She ducked aside.

"I was on the beach."

Rob looked suspicious. "Where on the beach? I was down there too. I didn't see you." He grabbed again, and this time his hand closed around her wrist. He jerked her close to him.

"Rob, be kindly to the . . ."

"Shut up," he growled without looking at Mathilda, adding under his breath, "Shut up and die."

Fiona heard him and glared, with undisguised hatred in her expression. "Take your hands off me!"

"And if I don't?" He snickered.

Without taking her eyes off his face, without raising her voice, she replied, "Then one night I'll cut out your heart and feed it to the rooks."

Angrily, Rob dropped Fiona's arm and shoved her away. "You watch your cheek. Where's that letter, lass? Give it me, then make the tea and brown up some of them bannocks. I've come home with a fierce hunger and found the cottage cold and you off traipsing . . ."

"Dreaming most likely," carped Mathilda. "It's all very

well for you to dream, while others are busy working and dying, but you might recall that I depend on you."

Mathilda went on and on; indeed, it sometimes seemed to Fiona that the conversation between them these days amounted to little more than one long scold. In the beginning Mathilda had been kindly—even loving—to her unfortunate niece; but as the years passed and hard times were succeeded by worse, her good-hearted nature seemed to dry up. The illness that had come up on her in the last year, and which no doctor could heal, had brought steadily worsening pain—and with it the end of Mathilda's last feeble efforts to provide Fiona with mothering. Mathilda's now constant pain occupied her night and day.

As Fiona busied herself with preparing the tea and bannocks, she was aware of her aunt's labored breathing from the corner, and also of her Uncle Rob, on a stool beside the fire, slowly, laboriously, reading the letter she had brought him from Loughlin Shields, Solicitor. But her primary thoughts were of Owen Hamilton. Her mind was so distracted from her domestic tasks that she put a double dip of tea in the pot, and remembering how proud and strong Owen looked in his Hamilton tartan kilt, the jaunty tam on his dark head, she forgot the bannocks and burned a pair of them on the grate over the fire.

Rob didn't notice her distraction. He had finished reading the letter from Loughlin Shields, and now he was going back to make sure he understood the message completely. When he had reassured himself as to its meaning, he went over to Mathilda and shook her roughly.

"We go to Dunvegan Town at the end of the week. The solicitor will see us then."

Mathilda began to whimper. "But, Robby, I can't go all that way. Not in my condition. Didn't you tell him he had to come here?"

"He writes that we have to go to him to make it all legal. Then he'll take the papers to Edinburgh, and the deed'll be done."

Mathilda again complained that she couldn't go, but Rob walked away from her. His eyes were on Fiona, working at the hearth. She, lost in thoughts of Owen Hamilton, was unaware of his attention at first. When she noticed him staring, a silly half-grin painted on his lumpy face, she was instantly suspicious.

"What's happened? What's in that letter?"

"Something that's going to fix you up just fine."

"Me?" Fiona went to her aunt and knelt beside her. "What's this all about, Aunty?"

Mathilda began to cry, and turned her head toward the wall.

Fiona shook her. "Tell me. Why are you going to Dunvegan? What's it got to do with me?"

Mathilda wouldn't turn back to Fiona. She sobbed, "Ask him. Ask him what it's about."

Rob took his time answering. He knew he didn't have to say a word to Fiona if he chose not to; but he wanted to see her face when he told her she was going to lose the cottage. Fiona had arrogant ways, which had grated on Rob from the day she arrived. He knew she thought she was too good for him, too much the Macleod lady to soil her hands about his small farm. When he had embraced her like the loving uncle he had tried to be in the beginning, he had felt her cringe in his embrace; she still turned her face away from his whenever he came near her. Rob was sure she would become more agreeable when she realized that as soon as Mathilda died, the cottage would be his and she would have to please him or be thrown out. There was no one in Borreraig to befriend her; she would have to please him.

"Your aunty is going to sign the cottage over to me. That way there won't be any confusion." His smile was sly and humorless.

"But the cottage is mine! You deeded it to me long ago, Aunt Mathilda, so that I would always have a home."

"But that was before she got sick. Don't you see how that changes things?"

"No. Nothing is changed. I still need a home . . ."

"So do I, Fiona. We'll just have to share." He smirked.

"You talk about me like I'm dead already."

"How could you do this, Aunty?"

"You want me to die quick smart, don't you, Rob?"

"The cottage is mine, Aunty. You promised!"

"You made a promise to me too, Mathilda. Don't forget that." He didn't even bother to deny that he was eager for her to die.

"Don't make me dependent on Rob, Aunty. Please. I pray . . ."

Mathilda's gaze darted back and forth from Fiona to Rob. As illness had made her seem smaller and more vulnerable, good health gave them a kind of giantism that intensified Mathilda's sense of her own helplessness. She heard the threat in Rob's voice. He was a great lumbering brute who could do anything he wanted. Out here on the Head, there was no law that could keep him from beating her senseless— as he had promised to do if she refused to sign over the cottage. On the other hand, Fiona too seemed oversized and threatening. In an instant, Mathilda recalled a dozen separate incidents in the past nine years, all of which had made her wonder about her strange niece. Questioned, Fiona had always denied having portentous dreams or other *oogly* powers, but Mathilda had never quite believed her. There was something otherworldly about Fiona, something that spoke of more than mortal knowledge. Though she could not admit it to herself, Mathilda was afraid of her niece, as she had been afraid of her sister, Janet. She could see Janet in Fiona's expression as the girl knelt beside her. She remembered loving her sister intensely when they were young. The thought brought burning tears to her eyes, and she began to weep hysterically.

Fiona knew there was no sense trying to talk further with her aunt, so she turned away from the sickbed and finished the tea preparations.

Behind her, she sensed Rob's ugly leer, but he said nothing as she handed him a steaming mug of sweetened tea and a half-dozen bannocks on a dented pewter plate. Mathilda stopped crying but refused tea and food. Turning to the wall, she began to breathe regularly, and after a time snored gently. The fire in the grate burned low. A watchful silence occupied the corners of the cottage.

"Fetch more peat, lass. It'll likely be cold tonight, with that wind."

Fiona had been too concerned with other matters to notice how the west wind had shifted slightly to the north during the evening. It carried sand and ice that rasped across the slate roof and bayed longingly at the eaves. She banked the fire with squares of peat, and when the kettle boiled she washed and dried the tea dishes, and put them away on the mantel of the fireplace with a few other bits of cracked pottery. Rob watched silently, taking out his whisky jug from time to time.

At last, Fiona could stand the silence no longer. "You're an evil man, Robert Duncan! If you take this house away from me, I swear I'll be revenged on you, if it takes the whole of my life. Do you believe me?" She had to wonder at the sound of her voice: calm, even gentle, while her heart was hardened with flint-like hatred.

Rob brayed sleepily and nodded his head. He knew she was only a girl but he feared her all the same. He tried to shake off the feeling. Why, he could handle her just like he did his old Mathilda. In the meantime he was warm and sleepy, his belly full of toast and tea and the nip or two of whisky he had taken as Fiona cleared the dishes. He staggered off the stool, knocking it over, and then fell upon Mathilda's bed, shoving her against the wall. He was asleep almost instantly.

Although Rob's snores told her there was no more danger from that quarter, at least for the moment, Fiona could not relax. Every sound from the bed was like a sentry's alert. She knew she could kill her uncle if she had to, and she asked herself why she didn't do it now, as he slept, and be done with him forever. She even went so far as to finger the dirk Rob had left on the hearth in its sheath. She drew out the efficient short-bladed weapon and watched it flash in the firelight. What would it be like to kill someone, she wondered. The thought horrified her, and she quickly returned the knife to its sheath. But catching sight of her uncle—his fat belly heaving up and down in deepest sleep, his flaccid lips open to the ceiling—she was again filled with hate.

It was stifling in the cottage, and despite the harsh weather she had to get out. When the door opened, a rush of cold air invaded the room. Rob stirred and muttered something, but Fiona was outside and couldn't hear. She leaned against the door and let the wind scour her face until the skin tingled and her drenched clothing clung to the outlines of her body. It was as if this willful force of nature could in some way purge her of the hate and fear that were poisoning her.

Chilled and shivering, she finally returned to the cottage and climbed the pole ladder to her bed in the loft. Before removing her clothes, she watched Rob's sleeping back to assure herself that he was really asleep. Just in case, she pulled the pole ladder up after herself. Lying in bed she was slow to warm, slow to sleep; but the wind had done its work where Rob was concerned. She lay dozing—both in and out of sleep—and dreaming of Owen Hamilton through the night.

They met on the high moor the next day, as they had planned.

Owen Hamilton came toward her through the purple heather, kilted in his clan's red and blue, his pipes slung comfortably across his shoulder. Fiona thought for an instant that if there were any true magic in the world, it was this that she was feeling now as she waited for her friend. She laughed and waved to him from the sheltered place where she had spread her plaid. Merriment made Fiona more beautiful. She could feel it as Owen drew near, and she thought again about magic. This is it, she thought.

She had brought an extra slice of bread and butter, and Owen was happy for it after the uncommonly steep climb.

"Do you come here often?" he asked her as he finished his slice.

"Spring and summer mostly, though I wouldn't mind doing it even more often. I like it up here. Would you laugh at me if I told you the island speaks to me?" She sneaked a look at him out of the corner of her eye. He wasn't laughing.

"I'd believe anything you said, Miss Fiona." Owen spoke the truth. What had begun the day before as curiosity and a hesitant admiration had flowered into full-blown adoration on this second meeting. Fiona was more beautiful than anything he had ever seen—or dreamed of seeing. Her voice was lyrical; he knew the sound of it had caught in his memory like the pibroch and he would hear it always, no matter what happend to either of them after this day.

"Where would you choose to be?" she asked a little later.

"Apart from here, nowhere, Miss Fiona," he replied, with a seriousness that made Fiona giddy.

She stifled her unaccustomed giggles with her fingers. Unwittingly, she had become coquettish. "Be serious, Mister Hamilton. Where would you choose to be?"

"Well," he said, after a minute's serious thought, "if I could always come back here, then—and only then—I would like to join forces with the Young Pretender and help win Scotland away from the filthy English." Owen's face lit up as he spoke, and without thinking further, he began to tell her

31

all his hopes and dreams. As she had confided in him the day before, he now told her things he had barely spoken of to himself. All the while Fiona listened, her head resting comfortably against a large sun-warmed boulder. From time to time, she looked about to count the sheep grazing on the moor, but her mind never wandered from the excitement of listening to Owen.

"In war the piper is always the first to die, because he leads the army in. But it would be worth it to die for such a cause as freeing Scotland from the English."

A horrible thought crossed Fiona's mind. "Are you good enough on the pipes already? Would Michael Cameron let you go?"

The light died in Owen's eyes so suddenly, like a candle abruptly snuffed out, that Fiona thought she saw it happen. "No, he would never permit it. I might be MacCrimmon himself, but I will never lead the Highlanders." He stared at a tuft of new grass near his hand; absentmindedly, he began to tear it up, one graceful strand at a time. His head was turned away, but Fiona could see how pale he was; and the familiar shuddering sorrow of the previous day returned to her and settled down across her shoulder like a familiar hated cloak, unendurably heavy.

Later, he apologized for becoming so depressed. Fiona thought he was more than unhappy; she had seen her aunt in pain so many times, she recognized the signs. As they climbed the narrow sheep trails looking for strays, she saw him wince at almost every step. How can one who looks so strong suffer such pain, she wondered. Somehow she knew that he was altered since yesterday, was no longer the bonny hero of her nocturnal dreams. Could it be that she had infected him with her taint already? Or did this handsome lad carry within him his own doom, a doom that was perhaps known to that guardian of his who had troubled her yesterday's happiness?

"You should go; it's almost tea time," she said finally.

"I want to stay with you."

"You're ill, I know it! For your own sake, you should be home. All afternoon you've been in pain and trying to hide it!"

"Nonsense. I've got a little headache—nothing more." Owen laughed. "I must remember how tenderly you care about my health, Miss Fiona." He took her hand and raised the palm to his lips. "I want to stay with you," he whispered again.

"Oh, Owen," she sighed, as his arms embraced her. "Thank God you aren't sick! I couldn't have stood it if you were sick! I know I shouldn't say it, but I feel for you as if you were a part of me. If you suffered, I would feel the pain, I know."

His lips on hers were the only reply: breathlessly tasting her, they caressed her mouth and cheeks and hair as if he could bear to leave no part of her untried.

"Go," she whispered urgently, gently pushing him away. She was torn by the conflict inside her. She dared not be alone with him like this, and yet how could she live without his touch? She must be with him forever or die!

"When will I see you again? Tomorrow? Tonight perhaps?"

"I can't get out at night. I . . . ."

"Fiona, when? And where?" He pulled her to him again. She felt a new urgency in his embrace.

"There's trouble at home. I don't know when I can see you. Perhaps we should stay apart." His mouth on hers stopped the words, and they clung together like doomed survivors. All at once, through the fabric of his jacket, Fiona felt how thin Owen's shoulders were; the cloak of sorrow weighed heavily on her shoulders, now grown as real as the love she felt for Owen.

She tore apart from him and ran down the sloping moor, crying for the sheep and batting them gently with the end of her staff. She came to rest at last, and looked back to where Owen still stood watching her. She waved her arms farewell; but before she turned she saw him raise his pipes to his mouth.

Down the long slope of moor between the granite crags and the sea, the sound of the pipes followed Fiona like the voices of the ancients who were said to dwell in the remote niches of the rocky cliffs.

Chapter 4

Two days passed.

Fiona kept away from the high moor, grazing her flock on a low sour slope south of Dunvegan Head rather than risk a meeting with Owen. She was confused about her feelings; she was elated and yet prone to tears at the same time. She thought of Owen, dreamed of Owen, worried about Owen all day long.

Her uncle ignored her, completely involved in his own plans. Fiona could not read Rob's mind, but she could guess at his conniving thoughts. She knew that if Mathilda signed over the cottage to him, her own safety on Dunvegan Head would be jeopardized. Her aunt's failing health, already exacerbated by exhaustion and loneliness, would be aggravated by the trek to Dunvegan Town. It seemed unlikely that Mathilda would survive another winter, and when she died Fiona would be left at the mercy of her Uncle Rob . . .

She remembered that Owen had sworn no harm would come to her, promising that if all else failed, she could ask his guardian, the mysterious Michael Cameron, to assist her in finding safe lodgings somewhere. According to Owen, his guardian was a man for whom nothing was impossible, who liked nothing better than the challenge of outwitting a foe.

Owen had sounded confident, but it was not so simple for Fiona. The cloak of sorrow lay heavily on her shoulders as she thought of her young lover. As he spoke to her that day on the high moor in the exuberance of his love, she only half believed his fancies of happily-ever-after. She tried to see the future as her lover pictured it—the two of them living safely and happily under the protection of the enigmatic Michael Cameron—but she could not. She had always lived under a cloud of gloom and sadness, and not even Owen, with his repeated reassurances, could dispel it.

During the day Fiona was absent from the crofter's cottage from early morning until almost dark. Evenings she sat before the peat fire busying herself with handwork until Rob fell into bed beside Mathilda. It was lambing season now, and Fiona had brought home two newborn lambs without mothers and made a nest for them near the fire. They readily took the milk she offered, their small bodies trembling with eagerness once they got the idea. Rob took no notice of Fiona's doings. He had no interest in the sheep, the cottage or the land, apart from his urgent desire for ownership. Idly, Fiona wondered what he planned to do once Mathilda was dead and the land was his. If she left him, he would be helpless to run the place himself. With a pang of sorrow that surprised her, Fiona realized that he would probably sell the cottage and land and move into Dunvegan Town or Borreraig. If the house were mine, I would stay here forever, she thought, as she rinsed the milkbottle and put it to drain on the mantel above the fire. The night before Mathilda and Rob were planning to leave for Dunvegan Town, she prayed that some miracle would keep Mathilda from signing the cottage over to Rob, that God—if His mercy and love extended to halflings—would give her both her home and her lover. She fell asleep thinking of herself as Mistress Hamilton, imagining that the lambs whimpering in their box beside the fire were babies, hers and Owen's.

She awoke in the wee hours of the morning, before dawn. Rob was already stumbling about in the dark, lighting the lamp and adding peat to the fire. She heard him scratch and yawn, then cough up a clot of mucous. The morning noises—though she had heard them a hundred mornings before—made Fiona queasy. She realized she must try one more time to persuade her aunt not to sign away the cottage. She thought again of what would happen if Mathilda died and left her in the care of Uncle Rob. She couldn't let it happen . . .

Despite Mathilda's illness, Rob had refused to hire a pony cart to take them to Dunvegan Town. Instead, he insisted that Mathilda could walk as well as anyone.

"He hopes the trip will kill me," she groaned to Fiona, when they were alone for a few minutes. Rob had gone out to check on the dogs, who were barking ferociously down by the chicken pens. Fiona was folding bread and butter sandwiches for the trip inside a checkered kerchief.

"Don't speak of dying, Aunty. What will I do without you?"

"La, child, you'll get on well enough. I have no fears for you." Mathilda smiled feebly. She was sitting on the edge of her narrow bed running a comb through her sparse wisps of hair. "But if something does happen to me, try to understand about Rob. He's not a bad man, but his life hasn't been easy." Mathilda looked up at Fiona, and the girl wondered if her faded blue eyes were blind to what her husband was.

"I know about Rob, Aunty. While he snores in the sun, I watch his sheep. When he's too hung over to get out of bed, I do the morning chores. I know all about Rob Duncan." She didn't try to keep the bitterness from her voice. "You mustn't sign over the cottage to him, please, Aunt Mathilda. You promised . . ."

"I know. I know." Mathilda wrung her hands and began to rock back and forth on the narrow bed.

"The house is mine, Aunt."

"You're only a child."

"I will soon be eighteen."

Mathilda peered closely at her niece, surprised. Fiona realized that Mathilda's mind had begun to go; in her illness, she had lost track of the years. "Eighteen?"

"Yes, Aunt. I love this house, this point of land. Don't give it to Rob; he'll only sell the land and drink the revenue. What will happen to me?" Fiona had finished packing the lunch and was helping Mathilda into her shoes. She noted that the heels and soles were still in good condition; it had been many months since Mathilda had left the confines of the cottage and its yard. She had not visited Dunvegan Town in years.

"I haven't any choice, lass. Your uncle would fly into such a rage if I changed my mind. I hate to think . . ." Mathilda's voice trailed off. She was recalling the way Rob had spoken to her the day before while Fiona tended the sheep.

"You know what I'll do if you fail to sign," he had said. Yes, she knew—only too well. Though she tried to put a positive face on the situation, Mathilda was no fool; illness had clouded her mind but not her knowledge of her husband. She knew the fate that Fiona could expect if she were left alone with her uncle. Still, Mathilda dared not refuse Rob. She reminded herself again and again, but without much effect, that though it would be hard on Fiona—alone, without property, in the care of a gross-mannered uncle—such situations were not uncommon. Only the rich, the titled could expect fate to harmonize with their wishes.

Fiona had begun to cry, softly. She didn't want to cause further pain for Mathilda, yet to let the cottage go was unthinkable. "You must let me keep it. I want to live here, raise my family here."

"What?" Mathilda was instantly alert. "You can't have a family!"

"But, Aunty . . ."

"No! You must clear your head of such a thought. You may not have children, never, Fiona. Never." Mathilda was greatly agitated as she stood up. She donned her coat without speaking, hefted her bundle to her shoulder, and prepared to open the outside door. With her hand on the doorknob a thought stopped her.

"Where would you get a husband, anyway?" Mathilda's eyes narrowed suspiciously.

Ignoring the question, Fiona cried, "Why may I not marry? I want a normal life. I am a normal woman!" She positioned herself between Mathilda and the door.

"You're not normal at all. Have you forgotten what you are?"

"That halfling business. But it's all an old story. And suppose it isn't—why can't I marry and have a normal life?"

Mathilda tried to shove past her niece, but Fiona wouldn't permit it. "You carry tainted blood. Isn't that enough? But you are the last of our line. With you will die whatever evil poisoned your mother. That will be the end of it."

"You mean I may never love? Or have children? You want me to live like a hermit until I . . . . ?"

"That's right. Until you die you must be alone, or else you'll bring more evil and trouble in the world." For a moment, Mathilda's ravaged face was touched by sorrow. She had truly loved her niece before her own pains and troubles distracted her. But Fiona must never marry or bear children. That was plain truth.

Fiona's strength of will seemed to ebb suddenly. She still blocked the door, but seemed so feeble in her grief that even Mathilda could have pushed her aside now. But she didn't. Instead, she stared at her niece, seeing for a moment her dead sister, Janet. Didn't she owe it to Janet to protect her halfling daughter? Didn't that protection include providing the girl with a home that was hers alone, a safe haven from the evil that Mathilda was sure would come?

"Stir yourself, old woman," called Rob from outside. His gruff accents reminded Mathilda what would happen to her if she refused to do his bidding in Dunvegan. With a cry of exasperation, she shoved the weeping Fiona aside and opened the door.

As Fiona stood on the stoop a few minutes later, she could just make out her aunt and uncle slowly progressing up the hill and across the high moor to Borreraig.

Her heart, which at first had rebelled against the finality of Mathilda's harsh words, now began to accept the truth of her aunt's warning. Fiona knew that whatever enchantment had controlled her mother and made the villagers despise her resided in herself as well, though perhaps less powerfully. She had no special gifts—unless her finely developed intuition could be called a gift—but she did dream repeatedly of the bloodied moor. Fiona sensed that somehow her future and that fateful moor were bound together. Her aunt was right: her blood was tainted. She must never love. Never marry. Never have children of her own . . .

That day she tended her animals with special care and affection and cleaned the cottage and yard with particular thoroughness. But she was like a sleepwalker, mute and dispirited.

In the afternoon, she saw a movement on the high moor and thought it might be Owen Hamilton coming down to her; but her eyes had played a trick on her. The moor was empty, and she told herself she should be glad. It would be best for him, for her—for everyone—if Owen Hamilton would disappear as though he never existed. "I hope I never see him again," she said to the sea and rocks, but she knew that she was lying.

In the evening, she cared for the lambs, then ate some of the porridge that had been soaking since the morning. Outside, the dogs were yapping madly, but she ignored them. Enjoying her privacy, she slipped out of her clothes—the same brown suit and faded pinafore that she had worn for several days—and washed herself with warm water. Clean, really clean, for the first time in more than a week, she savored the feeling. It was almost as if she had scrubbed away some of her unhappiness along with the dirt. During the day, she had gathered wild herbs, tying them together with a bit of string looped around her neck. The sweet-smelling fragrance of the sachet pleased her and, instead of going to bed, she got her comforter from the loft and wrapped it about her shoulders as she sat on Rob's stool beside the fire.

She tried to make plans, knowing she must leave Borreraig as quickly as possible. Her original plan had been to go to Edinburgh—a trip that would take many months on foot—and prove her right to the cottage. Now she must leave simply to escape Rob. But where could she go? She had no family, no friends . . . The barking dogs distracted her; she went to the door to hush them. She drew back at the sound of a boot heel on the gravel in the yard.

"Fiona!" Owen rapped at the door.

She had to make a decision, one that could change her whole life . . .

For a brief moment, Mathilda's warning, the arguments yea and nay, were clear before her. She was divided into three parts: a mind, a body and a heart. And all of them cried out for Owen. I must have this bliss, she thought, though it will end when they come back. "But I will then have you to remember," she whispered, as she opened the door to him.

"I saw them leave and knew you would be alone. I waited on the moor, but you didn't come back. I've been worried, I have to talk to you. May I come in?" He looked adorable in his yeoman's trousers and coat, his shiny brown hair—blown mad by the west wind—hanging in his eyes. The wind had brought a ruddy color to his cheeks, and he was grinning at her: half shy, half scared, knowing only one thing for sure—that he was happy, happy, happy.

"You should have seen them, your aunt and uncle. They were walking so slowly. She on her cane and he a half-mile ahead, looking fierce as February. I wager it will be some time before they return." He put his arms around her quickly, as if he didn't dare think too much of what he was doing. His lips touched hers, at first with timid gentleness, and then with passion. He tangled her hair in his fingers and moaned, "I love you, Fiona. I will love you as long as I live."

"Hush, Owen. My dearest love, don't speak of it." For them there could be no future, but she no longer cared. It was as if the meaning of life had been concentrated in this one night. Whatever might happen at dawn, Fiona wanted this evening to be as perfect as possible. Her heart, deprived of love for almost eighteen years, wept now; her aching arms reached for Owen and she led him up into the loft.

Nothing in Fiona's experience had prepared her for this night. She had grown up wild, watching the coupling of sheep and dogs and even chickens. Nothing had prepared her for such tenderness . . .

Rob and Mathilda had never shown her what sweetness could exist between lovers. Their mating had stopped at the onset of Mathilda's illness, but Fiona could remember all the times in childhood when she had buried herself under the comforter in her loft and pressed her hands against her ears to keep from hearing Rob's fierce grunts and Mathilda's martyred sighs.

A broad shaft of moonlight from the tiny loft window slanted across Fiona's pallet, where they lay side by side exploring each other's bodies. A dozen different emotions kept their touching light, their eyes wide with the wonder of one another. Shy, awed, adoring, loving, needing, wanting: Owen Hamilton was all of these and more. Though he lacked experience as a lover, the intensity of his feeling guided his movements with sure instinct. Fiona felt a pride that was new to her. As she slipped the comforter off from around her shoulders, she was conscious for the first time of the perfect roundness of her breasts and the slimness of her waist.

"You're so beautiful," he whispered, touching a nipple so it peaked like a mountain of Skye. He lowered his gaze to the shell of soft hair between her legs and then back to her face, quickly, as if to assure himself that his beloved was as willing as her body proclaimed. As he slipped off his clothes, Fiona saw for the first time how thin he was. A pall fell across the moment, as if a cloud had obliterated the moon and brought a dark chill to the loft.

With a trembling hand she touched the manhood between his legs, as if this masculine power and strength could ease the sorrow. Falling back on the comforter, she opened her legs and drew him close. It was only in this way, she knew, that she could forget for a time the terrible sense of doom that now accompanied all her thoughts of Owen Hamilton.

Book Two

THE PAGAN BRIDE

Chapter 5

When Fiona awoke just after dawn, Owen was resting on his elbow staring down at her face. As naturally as if they had been married for years, they reached for each other without words. Afterward, they slept again, nested together like spoons. But Fiona's sleep was fitful. In and out of her dreams came Mathilda, exhorting, "You may not love!" As she prepared breakfast, Fiona knew that she must tell Owen, but just when she thought she had found the courage to speak, she thought of the prospect of life without him. Life without love or friendship of any kind. And so she said nothing, savoring the time they had together in the cottage before the crackling fire.

"We're like some old married couple, eh?" said Owen, as he finished his third cup of tea. He sat on Rob's stool, wearing only his boots and pants.

She blurted out the truth. "But we may never marry."

"What?"

Fiona had been caressing the lambs in their box beside the fire. She kept her head turned away so that Owen would not see the glistening tears in her eyes. "It's the bad blood. I daren't marry for fear—if we had a child—it would be passed on. Better the halfling story dies with me." Her voice caught in her throat. Almost instantly, Owen was beside her, his arms around her.

"Forget the halfling business!" he urged. "It's all a story, a faery tale. You're as normal as anyone, Fiona. I don't want to hear this talk of tainted blood." He sounded sure, as if he'd thought the whole thing out for years. Yet it was only the experience of the previous night that had convinced him that Fiona was no faery, but a woman.

Fiona didn't try to argue. She didn't expect him to understand. He had not watched Janet Macleod driven into the sea by a frightened mob. Though they would part forever soon, she wanted nothing to spoil the few remaining hours.

"Will you be my bride?" he asked, caressing her cheek, pushing her heavy amber hair back from her face. "Will you marry me today?"

"Owen, I canna . . ." Her heart screamed against the unfairness of the world, as her eyes again filled with tears. He rubbed them away with his thumbs.

"Don't say anything." He pulled on his shirt and jacket. "I will be gone an hour, perhaps two. Wait for me here. Will you promise?"

She nodded dumbly. An inner voice demanded that she tell him they must part now, before it became any more difficult, but her heart and body protested. She couldn't—wouldn't—say good-bye a moment before she had to.

As he parted from his love, Owen's heart was as heavy as Fiona's, but for different reasons. Should he have told her his own secret, that the headache he had dismissed so lightly the other day, and which had returned this very moment to blind him with pain, was no mere passing ailment but a terrible signal of doom? Should he turn back now and tell her about the curse of the Hamiltons, the mysterious way in which all the males of the line died suddenly before achieving their majority, and that no one knew why? Should he repeat to her the story related to him by the aunt who had raised him on the Arran Isle, of his young father dying of consumption and his mother seeming to catch the disease by sympathy, following her husband to the grave soon after giving birth to himself? Thank God, his own lungs were healthy—but then, every Hamilton male seemed to die of a different complaint; the untimeliness of their passing was the only similarity. Of course, Michael Cameron—strong as an ox himself—said it was all morbid nonsense, that believing the old superstition, the Hamilton men had all willed themselves to die and that he, Owen, must will himself to live. But Owen had seen the concern in his guardian's eyes whenever one of his headaches came on, and despite Michael's hearty blustering about "women's megrims and vapors", his look belied his words. Owen knew that he was doomed, knew that his guardian knew it too; and was resolved that Fiona should never, never know—until he died in her arms, as he foresaw he would. But at least she would be spared his mother's dread, and no *oogly* magic would enable her to take on his illness as his mother had taken on his father's. He must use what little life remained to him to ensure her own happiness, to take her mind off the fancied halfling curse, which seemed to have less basis in reality than his own doom. And so, although the feeling that she was, like himself, set apart from others—even if in her case it was all imagination—drew Owen to Fiona, he determined she should never know that their bond was anything more than the natural magnetism of two young lovers, ordinary creatures responding to love's mysterious call. There would be time enough for her to grieve if the curse were fulfilled; and if it wasn't, why add to the sorrow that seemed to dog her even in their happiest moments? No—he would devote all his energies to eradicating the sorrow she already bore, would not add one jot or tittle to its increase. He must believe what Michael said, though it was only a pretense; he must conquer the pain in his head with his will. She had said she couldn't bear to think him sick; well, then, she wouldn't! Already, as he approached the high moor, Owen felt the pressure on his brain start to ease. When he returned to Fiona, she would see only her bonny bridegroom. Always . . .

Meanwhile, Fiona busied herself about the cottage, awaiting Owen's return. She took the lambs out into the yard, where they staggered around on their new legs and bleated miserably. One careened toward her, falling helplessly against her feet. She picked it up gently, and placing it some distance away from her, said, "You have to get along without me. You have to depend on yourself, little lambkin."

Owen was gone almost two hours. She had begun to worry about him, and found herself looking up the hillside toward the high moor every few moments. He finally appeared, holding a basket of wildflowers awkwardly in his arms. She ran partway up the hill to meet him. Yellow buttercups, white daisies, magenta foxglove, he strewed them at her feet.

"Will you be my bride, Fiona?" Amid the flowers, he knelt before her. In the sky, a pair of kestrels swept the air in harmony and on the ground, the lambs huddled together with low baas. Owen reached up and pulled Fiona gently to her knees beside him on the grass.

He gathered the scattered wildflowers and placed them in the bright tangles of her hair. Lacing the daisies stem to stem, he made a wreath that rested lightly on her temples. She tried to interrupt him, but he silenced her with his fingers on her lips. Finally, when she was garlanded with flowers like a pagan goddess of spring, he took her hands in his and said, "Now, before God the Father and whatever *oogly* creatures dwell in this land, I marry you, Fiona Macleod. I give my heart and trust to you as long as we both shall live." And longer, he added silently, thinking that somehow his love would endure beyond the grave.

Her eyes never leaving his face, Fiona said softly, "And I before God and the Blessed Virgin marry you, Owen Hamilton. No matter what happens, I love you. Will you remember that?"

"Always," he whispered as he kissed her.

After their pagan wedding, Fiona resolved not to think of what lay ahead. Mathilda and Rob would be gone several days—perhaps as long as a week—and during that time she would totally dedicate herself to her lover. But the warm spring days passed too quickly, and their precious nights in her loft were all too short. A sense of impending parting gave to their love a special poignancy, as if they knew they must live now, in the fullness of their youth and passion, before it was too late. Fiona fancied that, despite his disclaimers,

Owen admitted in his heart the truth of the halfling story, and was prepared to renounce her upon the Duncans' return; while he, sure that any taint of blood lay wholly in himself, hoped against hope to elude the doom of the Hamiltons. It was true that the terrible pressure on his brain seemed to have lifted since the fanciful afternoon he had betrothed himself to Fiona—could it be that love conquered all, in very truth? No: his father had loved his mother perhaps as dearly as he loved Fiona, and yet the Hamilton curse had overtaken him, and Owen's mother as well. At least he would spare Fiona the dark days of anticipation his mother had suffered; and if he lived, after all, no faery nonsense would ever keep him from cleaving to his bride.

One afternoon Fiona and Owen took the new lambs up to a high pasturage where they had previously discovered a ewe, heavy with milk, bleating over a tiny withered corpse. They watched the orphan lambs fight for the teats and suck hungrily. Then, hand in hand, Fiona and Owen walked over the crest of the steep-sided hill and across a deep wide valley cut by rivulets of erosion; then they climbed over huge black rocks to the peak of Dunvegan Head, where Fiona had never before ventured. Far down to the left was a steep-roofed stone residence, set well back from the cliffs in a stand of oaks. Though smoke rose from the chimneys at either end of the roof, there was no sign of life about the house.

"My guardian is preparing to leave for Edinburgh in a few days time," Owen said. "Prince Charles Edward Stuart has come."

"The Young Pretender?" A thrill of fear went through Fiona. "You won't go with him, will you?"

Ruefully, Owen shook his head. "No. I canna be a soldier. But I will be here near you, Fiona. It appears that fate intends for me to be a lover, not a fighter."

Fiona could see that Owen would have welcomed a chance to prove his manhood as a soldier. She remembered his dream of piping the Young Pretender into battle, and the terrible sorrow—which for the past several days she had done her best to ignore—came heavily down on her again.

"Does your guardian know where you are today? Have you spoken to him of me?"

"No. We rarely see each other and when we do he is preoccupied with his plans for supporting the Prince. Besides, I gather that my guardian does not believe in love. He would laugh if he knew we were pledged to each other."

They walked on, away from the high rocks and back toward Fiona's cottage. They spoke little, preferring to communicate by smiles and unexpected laughter. This strange merriment, which had characterized their relationship from the beginning, still came as a shock and a surprise to Fiona. She wondered how she had borne her life before Owen had taught her to find amusement in everything and nothing. Married in the eyes of God, she had no ring, no legal documents to prove their bond; but this bond of laughter was sanctification enough for her. "You have taught me how to laugh, Owen," she told him later, when they were back at the cottage. "For that alone, I will always bless you."

They had finished making love only moments before and Owen was half asleep, the comforter draped carelessly across his body. How pale he is, she thought. A mist of blue ringed his eyes and shadowed the hollows of his cheeks. He looked so tired that she let him sleep, though to relinquish him even for a moment was exceedingly painful to her. She slipped down to the floor of the cottage and busied herself with domestic duties. Twice that afternoon she put aside the rags she was twisting for a rug and stood brooding at the base of the pole ladder, her face puckered with concern. Something had happened that morning, and although she had tried to dismiss it at the time, she now saw the significance of Owen's recurring headaches.

He had insisted on helping her drag a heavy sack of peat into the cottage. As he came toward her across the yard, he suddenly stopped in his tracks; his eyes bulged out, and he made a sound as if someone had punched the wind out of him. She ran to his aid just in time. His legs gave way at the knees and he collapsed against her.

"Great God!" cried Fiona trying to keep from falling backwards as his full weight hit her. "What is it, Owen?" Was he breathing? His hairline glistened with sweat. She tried to see his face. "Where do you hurt, my darling?" She felt him shake his head against her shoulder. A few seconds later, he stood up.

Apart from his eyes—which seemed different somehow—Owen recovered completely in a few moments. Sheepishly, he dismissed the incident as nothing.

"Not much of a pagan bridegroom, eh?"

They both laughed. Fiona stilled her anxious questions; he would say more when he was ready.

Late in the afternoon, after making some tea, she shook him gently awake. Although he hadn't eaten for several hours, he shrugged her hands off and turned away.

"It's a headache, only a headache," he muttered against the pillow. "Let me sleep. It'll go away."

Hours later, Fiona fed him tea and rashers. He pretended to feel better, but fear clutched at her heart.

I must tell him now, she thought. He should be in his own home, not gallivanting all over the hillside with me. I will tell him good-bye, send him home, and then . . .

"Shall I stay with you tonight?"

Tell him now, she commanded herself. But she only nodded silently and drew him to her. One more night together—what harm could it do?

In the morning Owen seemed greatly improved. She tried to tell him it was all over between them, but her mouth would not form the words. After breakfast, he wooed her back to their loft.

"It's not safe!" she argued, laughing, already excited by him. "Mathilda and . . ."

He silenced her words with his mouth. Locked in this embrace, drunk on the taste of each other, they fell backwards onto the pallet. There was a new quality between them, a passionate urgency that made their hands tremble and their breath come short as they fumbled with each other's clothing.

Later, when she walked with him up the path, he told her, "A single hour apart is too much, Fiona. Let us meet tomorrow by the same boulder where we had our meal together that first time. Say yes, Fiona. I must see you!"

"You need to rest."

"I can sleep another time. Tomorrow I must be with you."

"Very well. In the early forenoon, I will be there." She would tell him then.

Owen had been gone less than an hour when Fiona heard Bridey and Shay begin to bark excitedly. She stood in the cottage yard and peered down the hill toward the beach. The path twisted steeply through boulders and across a rough running stream that flowed from the high moor to the sea, and at first she didn't see anyone. She was about to go back inside the cottage when she made out some movement far below. It was her uncle. But where was Mathilda?

A terrible thought occurred to Fiona. Her aunt had signed over the property to Rob Duncan and then died suddenly rather than face the long walk home. Fiona had decided this must be the case when she saw her aunt straggling up the path several hundred yards behind her husband.

When Rob came near Fiona saw immediately that he had been drinking heavily. The air around him reeked of cheap whisky. Fiona stepped forward, but before she could speak his arm flew out. He hit her hard with the back of his hand, sending her sprawling in the dirt of the cottage yard.

"Get me something to eat," he roared as he stumbled across the threshold. She could hear him bumping into things inside, swearing angrily at any inanimate object that put itself in his way.

Ignoring Rob's order, Fiona ran down the path to help her aunt. When she came close enough to see the old woman clearly, Fiona gasped in horror.

Mathilda's face was purple, and swollen so fat that her eyes seemed to have disappeared into the grotesque mask. As she tried to climb the path, she had to stop every third or fourth step to catch her breath.

"Don't say anything, lass," Mathilda cautioned. "Just go up there and tend to your uncle. Do what he asks you, don't make him cross. I'll be all right."

"He beat you." Fiona made a fist. She wanted to kill Rob Duncan; at the very least, she wished she could beat him until he suffered like Mathilda. "Oh, Aunty, what can I do for you?"

"Nothing. Just tend to the man before he goes after you. Hurry up now! Go on!" She gestured her niece back up the hill; reluctantly, Fiona obeyed. She had gone only a few steps, however, when she was stopped by Mathilda's laughter—an eerie hacking cackle, as if the part of her that laughed were already dead.

"I didn't sign, Fiona. All this—and he still couldn't make me sign."

Chapter 6

After parting from Fiona at the downslope, Owen slipped between some trees and climbed further up the mountain to a high position he had visited before, from which he could see the whole area of Dunvegan Head.

To the north, up the Minch, he looked for Ardmore Point; but strata of mist concealed it, and also the islands to the west. The sea of the Minch looked calm enough, but Owen knew better. Michael Cameron, his sea-captain guardian, had taught him to distrust the Scottish waters. At the thought of his guardian, the boy looked southward from his aerie. He could make out two thin columns of smoke rising in the still evening air, but the house was not visible. Owen considered leaving his post and going home; he knew he owed it to his guardian to spend some of this last time with him.

Last time . . .

No, he could not leave his watching post. The moor began so high and steep that it was hard to say where the mountain stopped and the moor—part gravel, part grass and lichen—began. In some places, a purple shadow lay across the land where the heather blossomed. Lower down, the magenta and foxglove were in early bloom, raising their droopy heads from the bracken. Near the rocky beach, the land was almost flat, but boggy and useless. Tears sprang to Owen's eyes as he took in the loveliness of the scene that evening. Sometimes, when he thought of being robbed of life, he felt so angry, cheated, that he beat the walls or ground with his fist. But now a kind of resignation—not a happy feeling, but a peaceful one—descended on him. The tears in his eyes were a reflex; he blinked them away. He had no intention of bawling his eyes out like some pitiful lamb, separated from its mama.

Instead, he secretly watched Fiona in the cottage yard, taking down the wash that had been drying since morning. He loved her so completely, and yet was resigned to leaving her forever. He had thought of telling her that he was dying, but what was the sense? She would ask him how he knew; had he seen a doctor? If he told her of the Hamilton curse, it might only strengthen her belief that fate was against her, and cause her mind to revert to that halfling tale that he hoped their lovemaking had laid to rest.

Owen observed the arrival of Rob and Mathilda. Fiona's uncle was obviously drunk; his head sank onto his chest and he lumbered unsteadily. A little later, his wife appeared on the beach at the base of the path. She moved slowly; every movement told Owen that she was in pain. He watched Fiona and her aunt embrace; then slumped down among some rocks to rest.

Long after Fiona and her aunt had joined Rob in the cottage, Owen remained crouched amid the boulders. He was hungry and stiff, and the pain in his head had not gone away but had become a dark regular throb. It was a clock by which he could almost count the hours remaining to him.

Still, he didn't want to be parted from Fiona. Though he could not see her, he liked knowing she was near. Fiona! His heart cried her name like music. He longed for his pipes, that he might play for her one last time. He turned away only when it had become so late that the mist dividing the islands had swept across the land, laying damp fingers in every hole and hollow.

Once he turned his back on the cottage, Owen Hamilton did not look again. Going home, he walked as slowly as old Mathilda had, stopping many times to catch his breath and steady himself on a boulder. Mercifully, the pain spun a veil of fancy around his thoughts. Owen saw himself leading a grand army of Highlanders in parade before Fiona. Ahead of the generals, ahead of Prince Charles himself, Owen—in full Hamilton dress—piped the valiant home from victory over the English, his pipes resting easy against his shoulder, his eyes merry and free from pain.

All was quiet in the Duncan cottage. Mathilda had taken to her bed immediately. Rob was asleep too, but would likely awaken soon. Then what? Fiona made Mathilda comfortable and then—more to keep herself busy than from hunger—she prepared a meal, rashers and bannocks and tea.

As she worked about the cottage, Fiona kept her mind as calm as possible. If there were trouble later with Rob—and she expected there would be—she would need all her wit; he would be mean and stiff and still half drunk when he awoke. Mathilda appeared to be asleep also. Fiona knew it was for the best, and yet she yearned to question her aunt and learn the full story of her refusal to sign over the cottage to Rob. She shook her head and took up the broom; methodically sweeping the floor. The dull routine was hypnotic—she felt herself calm down, grow more patient.

Mathilda watched Fiona surreptitiously, the blanket almost covering her eyes. If the girl knew she was awake, she would be pestered half dead with questions—an ordeal that Mathilda felt utterly unequal to. She heard Rob snortle in his sleep, and there was the noise of tumbling baskets as he shifted his position in the corner.

Mathilda resisted an impulse to laugh out loud. She had fixed Rob Duncan, all right! After all these years, she was finally having the last laugh. And ever since it happened, Mathilda had felt—apart from the injuries inflicted by Rob— better than she had in almost a year. She had begun to think that despite the terror of what she knew was growing in her, she was going to be all right for a while longer. Again, the desire to laugh almost overcame her. This newly discovered vigor doubled her victory over Rob.

It had begun as they walked to Dunvegan Town that first day. The trip had taken more than the usual two days because she had had to walk so slowly. At night they slept near the path and boiled tea over the fire like a pair of gypsies, resuming their journey on the following morning. Mathilda had plenty of time to think on that long walk. She realized, finally, that she could not betray her niece and her sister by signing the cottage over to Rob. It had been the walk that decided it for her. Mathilda remembered how she and Fiona had walked the long way to the cottage after Janet's death. Mathilda had sworn to herself then that she would love and care for the poor halfling child. Now, nine years later, she resolved to keep that promise—no matter what.

They arrived in Dunvegan Town and got word that the solicitor would see them the following day. Rather than take rooms at an inn, Rob insisted that they sleep outside again. He would not even let Mathilda buy rolls from the baker or fresh milk. His stinginess intensified her resentment. There she was, a dying woman, about to give him an orphan child's inheritance; and her own husband would do nothing to make her comfortable. The place he had chosen for them to sleep was in a swale; beneath her blanket, Mathilda could feel the damp creeping into her bones. She would hobble like a centenarian in the morning!

Finally—counting her miseries one by one—she became so indignant that she told Rob she would not give him the cottage. As soon as she spoke, she regretted her candor. Rob roared, sprang off his bedroll and in a fit of anger shook her shoulders until the bones ached. They were deep in the country and there was no one but a passing fox or coin-eyed owl to hear Mathilda cry out. Rob beat her until she was sure her face must be utterly destroyed. Her back and shoulders and hips and thighs were covered with bruises, but it was the destruction of her face that finally brought Mathilda to her knees in submission. "I will sign," she swore, covering her face with her hands, pressing her forehead to the earth at Rob's feet. "Don't hit me any more. I promise."

The offices of Loughton Shields, Solicitor were crowded. The sturdy country folk stopped talking and gawked when Rob led in Mathilda. She kept her face averted, but everyone could see where a dozen hard blows had cut the skin around her eyes, broken her nose and swelled her cheeks. The embarrassed Duncans found places on one of the benches that lined the solicitor's anteroom and sat down. Rob returned the curious stares with a defiant glower, as if to say, what I did to this woman I'll do to any of you. Eventually, the conversations interrupted by their arrival were resumed. Mathilda began to relax. She told herself she was lucky to be alive.

When their names were called, Mathilda and Rob went

into the solicitor's office. They had expected to be alone with Shields. Instead, seated comfortably off to the side, was a handsome man wearing the Macleod kilt. Mathilda recognized him immediately, though she had only seen him once before. His silver sporran was engraved with the Macleod crest: a bull's head of two flags on either side, and above, the clan motto: *Hold Fast*.

"My lord Macleod," she said, curtseying low before the laird.

Rob followed her example but was visibly annoyed. To him it seemed like bad luck that the head of the clan Macleod, the laird of Dunvegan Castle, should appear so unexpectedly. Rob knew that Mathilda looked bad, and if the laird noticed there would be no way of keeping his nose out of their business. Rob hung his head and muttered his business to the solicitor, making a bad impression on everyone.

When the solicitor had heard Rob's speech, he turned to Mathilda and said, "As I understand it, Mistress Duncan, you are wishing to reassert control over the property on Dunvegan Head once owned by your father, deeded by him to your sister Janet. Following her demise, it went to you. As I understand it, there are letters in Edinburgh properly witnessed in which you request that the land be transferred at your death to your niece, your late sister's daughter, Fiona Macleod."

The laird, who had been affecting indifference, looked up when he heard the clan name. "Are those facts correct, mistress?" asked Shields.

She nodded her head.

"Can you speak, mistress?" Shields asked with concern.

"Yes, sir, I can speak." Mathilda had wanted to keep silence. She was deeply mortified by the sound of her voice—several of her front teeth were missing and her lips were so swollen that speech came painfully.

"Who did this to you, Mistress Duncan?" Shields was looking hard at Rob as he spoke.

The laird, who had been watching with growing interest, chose this moment to enter the proceedings.

"Robert Duncan!" Rob looked at him reluctantly. "Did you beat this woman to make her sign away her right to Macleod land?"

The question came too quickly for the slow-witted Rob to

prepare a credible reply. He made a gruff sound in his throat, and went back to staring at the plank floor.

"Speak up, man!" roared Loughton Shields. "When the laird asks a question, he demands an answer. Did you beat your wife in this way?" Wife-beating was common enough in the Highlands, and everywhere else Shields had ever traveled. It was permitted by the law but, only within certain limits. Clearly Duncan had transgressed those limits. Still, if Norman Macleod had not been present, Shields would have ignored the wounded woman and accepted her signature in silence. There was no sense butting into the marital affairs of these Highland peasants; some of them were scarcely human.

"Did you inflict serious bodily injury on this woman?"

Mathilda had tried to keep silent, but finally her desire for revenge overcame her fear of what might happen later when she and Rob were alone. "He did it!" she cried, first to the laird and then to Shields. "Forgive me if I break my marriage vows by speaking true. But he did it! Last night he made me sleep out in the woods, so no one would hear when he did it. He used his fists, m'lord." She looked at Rob. The expression on his face made her cringe.

The laird saw her fear. He was badly upset. "Enough!" he cried with disgust. "I have heard all I want of this!" He and Shields eyed one another. Shields began to speak.

"Your petition is denied, Robert Duncan. I will not bear your wife's signature to Edinburgh."

"Furthermore," the laird continued, rising from his chair and placing himself directly in front of Rob, "you are to take your wife to some hotel or other decent lodging place here in Dunvegan, call a doctor to tend her and permit her to rest fully. When she is recovered sufficiently to travel, you are to hire a pony cart to take her from Dunvegan Town to Borreraig." The laird and Shields exchanged glances again. "See that you do this woman no more harm, Robert Duncan. The law is lenient in affairs of matrimony, but there are limits. Do you understand me?"

When there was no answer from Rob, the laird bellowed, "Answer your betters when they speak to you, Duncan, or you'll find yourself in serious trouble! Do you understand?"

Rob nodded churlishly. He understood.

Remembering the hangdog look on his face as they left the office, Mathilda's heart sang with vengeful glee. It had been worth it. The long painful walk from the Head, the beating, the mortification in public had all been worth the sight of Rob Duncan brought low and denied his heart's desire.

"Are you awake, Aunt?" Fiona asked in a whisper near the bed. Rob was still asleep and she wanted him to stay that was as long as possible. "Can you talk?"

Mathilda nodded wearily. Much as she wished to avoid it, there were things that must be said. "Come close, Fiona. I haven't much strength to speak."

She seemed so feeble that Fiona began to weep. "Forgive me, Aunty. I never dreamed that you would suffer so on my behalf. Thank you." She continued to cry, wetting the edge of the comforter in her fist. Her knuckles were white.

"What's done is done, lass. Don't waste our time with tears." Mathilda stretched out a withered hand and grabbed Fiona's shoulder. Her grip was surprisingly strong. "Don't concern yourself for me. To tell the truth," Mathilda supressed one of her cackling laughs, "I feel better than I have since way back last year when I had that first attack. I want you to know that, so you can rest easy at night after you go."

"Go?"

Mathilda nodded, pursing her lips together. "Rob daren't touch me now." Fiona tried to interrupt, but Mathilda dismissed her question hurriedly. "There isn't time to explain why he's afraid, he just is. Still, there's no telling what he might do to you. You mustn't live here with us anymore. It isn't safe!"

"You're an invalid, Aunt. What would you . . . ?"

"An invalid who just walked miles and miles to see Rob Duncan shamed." Mathilda smiled crookedly. "I will survive. I know my own strength now, never fear. I'll be getting up tomorrow. I'm itching to be about the place cleaning. You've done well enough as a housekeeper, lass, but you never get into the corners." Instantly, she was serious. "But you must not stay here. Go now, while Rob sleeps."

"Where? I thought before of leaving, but could think of no destination. You are my only family, Aunt Mathilda."

"Aye." Mathilda's expression was sad for a moment. Then she said, "This is not a time to think of family, Fiona. Think of yourself. Go to Edinburgh and get the proof you need that this is your cottage, all free and legal. Father wanted Janet to have it because he could see how strange she was; he thought she needed something. I feel the same about you. You are a strange one, though you don't really know it yet."

From his corner, Rob muttered something about "justice" and snorted loudly. Mathilda started, her voice grew shrill. "There isn't time for this. Just go. Go!"

Fiona hurried up to the loft. She made a quick roll of her few belongings, including the dried remains of her pagan wedding wreath, which she had thrust into a leather pouch pilfered from Rob. She jumped silently down from the loft. As she slipped into her coat, Mathilda gestured frantically.

"He's waking up! You must hurry, in case he thinks to follow after and bring you back. But wait, look up there on the mantel, behind the statue of the Virgin. See that chink in the brick? Put your fingers in and dig a bit. It should come loose."

Fiona discovered a cache only a few inches square. It was full of gold coins.

"There must be better than one hundred pounds there," said Mathilda. She had got out of bed, and came to stand at the mantel beside Fiona. "Most of it came from that young soldier boy your mama loved, but over the years I've been able to save a little too. Take it. Take it and guard it—and guard yourself!"

Fiona scooped the coins into the leather bag containing her wedding wreath. It seemed fitting that her two most valuable possessions lay together in a bag she had stolen from her enemy.

The women embraced. There were tears in Mathilda's voice when she said, "Believe me, Fiona, I feel all right—I may survive the brute yet. Don't fret about me, lassie."

Fiona bent down to pick up her bedroll. At the same instant, Rob erupted into consciousness.

"And where do you think you're going, me wee darling?" He still reeked of drink, but he moved agilely. He saw the bedroll. "What have we here, eh? Ducking into the night are you, little witch-baby?" There was an evil yellow light in his eyes as he came toward her. "Ungrateful halfling bastard! Haven't I treated you nice? Haven't I . . . ?"

"Rob, keep away from her!"

"Shut up, woman." He made as if to hit her, then realized at the last minute that he dared not risk the laird learning of it. But Fiona was a different matter. "Now maybe I ought to give you what you deserve, lassie. I got something to settle with you."

As he reached for Fiona, she swung her bedroll in a wide arc, hitting him across the shoulder and head. He reeled and fell back heavily against the hearth, his head crashing against the stones. Rob Duncan was unconscious, though perhaps only for a few minutes.

It was long enough for Fiona to escape.

Chapter 7

As she approached Cameron House, Fiona's confidence faded. It was nearly ten, and by custom the Skye folk were asleep by now. She made up her mind that if no lights shone in the house, she would look for a sheltered place, open her bedroll and sleep. In the morning, she was certain Owen would be eager to help her get to Edinburgh. Perhaps he would come with her? She was a halfling, to whom love was forbidden, but perhaps . . .

Surrounded by a high privet hedge enclosing a garden and several tall conifers, Cameron House was imposing. It was clearly the home of quality folk, and not the sort of place where peasant girls were welcome unless they carried washing or came to clean the grates. Fiona found the garden gate and gently pushed it. It creaked alarmingly, and she heard a dog bark in the distance. A cobbled path bordered by rhododendron and azalea bushes led to a porticoed entrance. Owen lived in a mansion compared to her own one-room dwelling. The slate shingle roof was typical of Skye, but never had she seen anything like the elegant crow-step design worked on it—such a roof belonged on a palace in Edinburgh. At either end were chimneys with two pipes each; below were the windows—dormers upstairs and on the ground floor large rectangles shuttered on the inside. All were dark but one, through which she saw a ribbon of dull gold where the shutters met.

Did she dare knock?

She was cold and uncomfortable, despite her warm coat and the heavy plaid covering her head and shoulders. Enviously, she imagined Owen and his guardian within that lighted room. Their boots would be resting on the hearth of a turf fire and she pictured them sipping something warm, talking pleasantly of things to come. Fiona longed to join them, but God only knew what her welcome would be—it must be nearly midnight. She knew Owen would be glad to see her anyway, but what of his guardian—stormy Captain Cameron? Would he usher her in and send the housekeeper up to warm a bed for her, the cook to prepare a hot supper? Or would he glower, refuse to admit her to see Owen and send her home to Rob quick smart?

Commanding herself to think no more, she lifted the heavy iron knocker shaped like a ram's head. Inside a dog barked, and then another. After what seemed a long time, the door was opened by a middle-aged man, with heavy pleasant features and kind eyes.

"Who is it, Muddy?" asked a deep voice from inside the house. The voice was impatient and sounded tired. It belonged almost certainly to Michael Cameron.

"The friend of young Owen," the man called Muddy replied, staring at her. "Fiona Macleod." How did he know her name?

The disembodied voice inside sighed. "She may as well come in then."

The entry was beautifully furnished. Fiona had never guessed that such lovely tables and chairs existed before. And the walls! She let her fingertips slip luxuriously along the silk-papered surface until a voice interrupted her reverie. "I am Michael Cameron."

He stood at the door, blocking her view of the study. Tall, broad-shouldered, with thick brown hair worn straight and tied at the back of his neck, he was younger than Fiona had expected. He looked around thirty-five, and handsome. A heady little pain gripped her behind the ribs as she looked at him. Suddenly, she felt terribly embarrassed, gawky and out of place.

He was tall and dark with blue-black eyes fringed by heavy lashes. She could not interpret the expression in his eyes, but she knew that something was wrong. There was something grim about Michael Cameron as he stood in the doorway. His body was lion-tense, his mouth unsmiling.

"Your visit is ill-timed, lass."

"Where is Owen? What has happened?"

Without speaking, Cameron moved from the doorway, and she saw into the drawing room.

A daybed with a back curved like a snail's shell had been drawn near the fire.

"Owen!" With a frightened cry she ran to her lover. He lay on the bed, covered by a brown satin comforter. Behind her, she heard the door shut.

They were alone.

"What's happened to you? Why are you so pale, so . . . ?"

"Hush, Fiona. Let me speak." His voice was faint and calm, telling Fiona all she needed to know. She lay her head on his chest and wept. "It's all right, lassie. I'm not afraid."

She raised her tear-stained face to his. "You mean you knew before?"

"Aye, but I couldna tell you. You were so joyous."

They stared into one another's eyes, lost themselves in each other's depths. For a long time, neither one could speak. Fiona took Owen's hand in hers and clasped it tightly, as if to prevent him from being taken to the spirit world, away from her.

"You must not die." She began shaking her head from side to side, her eyes filled with tears. "Don't leave me alone, Owen. What will I do without you? Oh, my love, my love!"

The door clicked open. Fiona turned and scrambled to her feet. "Can't you do something?"

Cameron shook his head. "I'm having some wine, Miss Macleod. Will you join me?"

"How can you be so callous! Do something!"

"There is nothing I can do except remain calm. I suggest you try to do the same." He poured a glass of claret and handed it to her.

She returned to Owen's bedside. "Drink some of this, Owen. It will make you feel better."

The boy laughed softly. "Not likely, dear. But thank you."

Fiona knelt by the daybed. Michael Cameron came and stood beside her. She didn't look at him, her cares were all for Owen. His skin was white and clammy, beads of sweat stood out on his brow.

"Can I do something for you, laddie?" Captain Cameron asked.

Owen nodded and whispered, "Aye."

He spoke so softly that his guardian had to kneel beside Fiona to hear him.

"Take care of Fiona for me. Help her!"

"I don't need help, Owen. Don't worry about me." The thought of being in the care of Michael Cameron filled her with conflicting emotions. She wished he would go away and leave them alone.

"Don't argue, Fiona. You need the help, you know you do." His hands squeezed hers lightly. "Will you help her sir?"

"Of course, Owen. I will help her."

The boy sighed and closed his eyes. "I feel easier knowing that. Now I'll have some wine, Fiona."

She helped him sit, and he had a taste of the claret. Then he turned his face toward her breast and sighed.

Michael Cameron rose from beside the chaise and went to pour another glass of claret. Leaning against the rosewood sideboard, he watched the young lovers. Once, Fiona turned to look at him, and their eyes met and locked a moment. But it was impossible for her to know what he was thinking.

Around midnight, the man called Muddy came into the drawing room with a tray of bread and cheeses. He placed fresh turf in the grate and checked the shutters to see that they were tightly shut. Then he went out.

A little while after this, Owen started up from Fiona's embrace. He looked at her, his eyes clouded with pain. With great effort, he reached up to touch Fiona's lips. "My pagan wife," he whispered.

Then he was still.

Later, Muddy helped her upstairs to a room that had been readied for her.

"If you need me, lass," he said, "just ring the bell and I'll come right away."

"Thank you." She took her bedroll from him and mutely laid it out. On her knees, with her few pitiful possessions around her, Fiona looked like a lost waif. Muddy's heart turned toward her.

"You'll be all right, then?"

"Aye." She nodded slowly, her eyes downcast.

When he was gone, she undressed quickly—she was shivering with cold and shock—and pulled her flannel nighty over her head. Her movements were stiff and unnatural; she was dazed by grief. Climbing into the bed, she pulled the goose-down comforter about her, and closed her eyes.

Owen's face was before her: cheeks ruddy from the west wind, sea-blue eyes gleaming with good humor. Her eyelids stung from the image.

Without warning, her bedroom door opened. "What in damnation did that boy mean when he made me promise to help you? What kind of help do you need? Are you with child by him, lass?"

She saw Michael Cameron by the firelight. His chiseled features looked almost cruel as he came toward her.

"Go away!" she said sitting up in bed, pulling the comforter about her. "I don't want your help."

"I didn't ask that. I made my promise and I mean to keep it. Now answer me: are you with child?"

"No!" she cried.

"Then what?"

"I have to go to Edinburgh. Owen thought you'd let me go with you." Quickly, she told him of her situation at home, and of the documents she needed from Edinburgh.

"Damn you, wench! You mean you took his last days to buy a ticket to Edinburgh?" Michael shook a fist at her.

"Never!" she returned. "I loved him." She began to sob.

Michael looked as though he did not believe her. "Well, be that as it may, we leave for Edinburgh tomorrow. We'll go by pony to Dunvegan, then get a coach to Kyleakin and take the ferry to Mallaig." He stood only a foot from the bed. The air between them was charged with tension; Fiona could feel him seething with repressed anger and shivered. Michael Cameron frightened her.

"I said I don't need your help!"

"And I say you'll take it!" He grabbed her by the shoulders and pulled her to him. For just an instant, Fiona felt a return of the dynamism between them. But now she could read his blue-black eyes: he despised her and was immune to the chemistry between them. Angrily, he threw her back against the pillows, turned and strode to the door.

"I am a Cameron, a man of honor, and I keep my word. I will help you because, whatever you are, he loved you." He opened the door. "But keep away from me. I want no part of you."

Book Three

MADAME ZARTHOS

Chapter 8

The trip from Dunvegan Head to the port of Kyleakin at the easternmost point of Skye took nearly a week. The Post Road was rutted by frequent travel and rainstorms, and it was not uncommon for landslides to block it altogether. They went as far as they could each day, sleeping at night in inns and taverns. Fiona shared the interior of the carriage with the bundle and bedroll she had carried from home as well as Captain Cameron's and Muddy's belongings. Muddy was the coachman, and Michael rode beside them on a formidable black horse. Sometimes Fiona grew lonely and sat beside Muddy on the outboard, letting him talk to her about whatever took his fancy.

"Won't be long before Prince Charlie's here," he told her one day. "And when he comes!" Muddy whooped with joy. Apart from the little told to her by Owen Hamilton, Fiona knew nothing of Scottish history and the age-old rivalry—hatred rather—between the Scots and the English. Once, Muddy told her, Scotland had been a free and independent nation; then the English had stolen the crown and forced the rightful Stuart line into exile in France.

"Where is France?" she asked timidly, embarrassed by her ignorance.

Vaguely, he waved his right hand. "Off there, across the channel. It's a long way, make no mistake. But Prince Charles will come to win back the throne for his father, and when he does he'll bring a regiment of Froggy soldiers with him!" Muddy laughed, as if the carnage of war were a game.

The long trip was not unpleasant for Fiona. She was glad of the change of scene; it was easier in places distant from Dunvegan Head to forget about Owen Hamilton. "I will love you for as long as I live," he had said. And he had kept his word. Somehow his promise made it easier for her to leave the island. "I will come back someday," she said aloud. She hoped Owen could hear her, in the spirit world where he must now dwell.

The carriage and its accompanying rider followed the track that led through the middle of the island. The scenery was breathtaking: crowned by yellow moss, steep rock-topped mountains pointed at the sky, their flanks scored by streams and waterfalls dropping hundreds of feet into icy lakelets. There were a few humble cottages with plants growing wild in their thatch roofs. Despite the poverty, these stone hovels wore an air of pride. Even the most dismal places had a garden, and geranium-filled pots blooming by the doorway. I must remember this, she thought. Intuitively, she knew that memories of Skye—its haunted moors, the harsh grandeur of its mountains and valleys—would strengthen her in days to come. They rode through glens that looked as if some giant hand had scooped them out, then strewn the bouldered debris far and wide. On bright days, the sunlight reflected off the water—the ubiquitous lochs, burns, waterfalls, rapids, springs and lakelets. In the sunshine Skye was a charmed land, but under gloomy skies it brooded vengefully, as if the spirits that lurked in the mountains, the water and the glens resented the human inhabitants.

On such days Fiona brooded too. She seemed to have been hurtled out of her simple and predictable existence into another—and dismaying—realm. She sensed that she had no control over events, and could predict nothing.

As they sped eastward, Fiona came to believe that she hated Michael Cameron with all her heart. He took all his meals alone and never rode with her in the carriage, preferring to assist Muddy at his coachman's duties or gallop ahead on horseback. He rarely looked at her, but when he did his dark gaze was unfriendly.

Early one morning, as they came down out of mountains a few miles west of Kyleakin, they were hit by a squall of rain and hailstones that made it impossible to travel. Rather than allow himself to be pelted and soaked with rain for thirty minutes, Michael broke his resolve and sat inside the carriage with Fiona.

He felt like a damn fool. After making a point of avoiding the lass for many days, he was now sitting almost knee to knee with her in the small coach. He tried to cross his legs and inadvertently touched hers.

He tipped his head apologetically, but wouldn't look at her. He felt ridiculous, but he could hardly tell her that. Still, he had not been gentlemanly with Fiona, and he regretted it. The edge was off his grief now, and he could think more clearly about her relationship with his ward. It was spring love between the boy and girl; Fiona had no mercenary intent; if she had, he would have seen it by now. And Muddy, who was no fool, liked the lass.

Michael leaned back against the leather seats. They were dry and cracking with age. If he slept, he would awaken with a crick, and the rest of the day would be a disaster.

Damn!

He could do nothing but stay awake, toe to toe with Fiona Macleod.

It was difficult for Michael Cameron to believe that Owen had been of an age to love. The lad had been eight years old when Michael had first learned of his existence, and to his guardian Owen was always somewhere between eight and twelve years of age.

The boy was the son of Michael's best friend, Angus Hamilton. They had played together as boys on the Arran Isle, and had sworn eternal brotherhood at fifteen. Two years later, Michael had sailed off on his first sea voyage, with his Grandfather Cameron's fleet. Angus had longed to go with him, but already the coughing fits had begun. It was then that Angus had confided to Michael the tale of the Hamilton curse.

Michael refused to believe it. "You've only caught a cold,

man, a winter cold," he assured his friend. "You'll be with me on the next trip, I know you will."

Angus shook his head. "No, but if Bessie Macdougal will have me, knowing she may not have me long, mayhap we'll have a son who'll live to go with you some day. This curse can't last forever—perhaps it will die with me."

Soon after Michael sailed for the new world, Angus had married his Bessie and within a year word reached Michael that both were dead of consumption. He hadn't known there was a child then, hadn't learned it until much later, when he returned to his birthplace after nine years at sea. He had seen the bairn, who at eight was already the image of his father, at the kirk with his Aunt Jane, Bessie Macdougal's unmarried sister. The Macdougals were poor folk, and though she was fond of the boy, Miss Jane knew that Michael Cameron could provide much better for him; besides, the lad needed a man to take his father's place and teach him a man's ways. So she'd given the boy up to Michael, who'd become his legal guardian and taken him off to the house he had built himself on the Isle of Skye. Michael had soon come to love Owen as if the lad were his own son. But Captain Cameron was a busy man. In recent years, he and Owen had seen little of one another. Now that it was too late, he deeply regretted that time apart.

Michael watched Fiona Macleod surreptitiously, and saw what had attracted Owen to her.

She had a high broad brow framed by red-gold curls, which were tied behind her head like a schoolgirl's. He liked her eyes, liked the glints of gold in them. They were wildfire eyes, he thought, and then checked himself for thinking such foolish romantic balderdash.

But he couldn't stop looking at her. She was staring out at the wretched weather, her chin resting in the palm of her hand. Although her face had a sad girlish cast to it, her lips were pursed with a stubborn determination that both attracted and amused Michael Cameron. Yes, he could understand poor Owen's passion.

Owen chose a little fighter, he thought with approval.

Fiona felt him watching her, and wished with all her heart that he would turn away. She cursed the weather that had brought them together, but she blessed it too. After he'd made such a point of avoiding her . . .

Their knees touched and she jerked away as if bitten by a

viper. Putting her chin in her hand, she stared out at the storm, pretending to be fascinated by it.

What was it about Michael Cameron that got under her skin? He kept staring at her until she thought her face would burn.

Owen, she thought, I don't care if he is your guardian, I can't be dependent on him. He thinks ill of me, and I'd rather go alone than in his company.

Gradually, a plan formed in her mind.

From the Skye town of Kyleakin, Michael arranged for a boat to take them quickly south to Mallaig, a prosperous fishing village on the mainland shore of the sound. The sound was narrow and the days fair. During the whole of the voyage, Fiona watched the bird-filled cliffs of Skye off the starboard. The giant sea birds were resting now, but in the fall they would leave Skye and go south, just as she was doing.

"And like them, I will return to Skye in another year." Brushing a tear away, she reached inside her bodice and withdrew the leather bag in which she kept her gold coins and the petals saved from her pagan wedding wreath. As she tossed the petals back along the foaming water, she swore, "I will come back, Owen. I will come back."

They put up for the night at Mallaig's best inn, The Lavender and Lily.

"We'll be in town a day or two, lass," Muddy told her. "The Cap'n's got a thing or two that must be done, and I'll be kept busy collecting what we'll need for the trip to Edinburgh." They were standing in the doorway of Fiona's room. Muddy peered over her shoulder into the small cubicle she shared with two other female travelers. "You'll be all right, will you, lass?" He looked at her closely. "Not pining too much are you?"

"I'm well enough, Mr. Mudd. I thank you for your concern."

When Muddy had gone, Fiona took the precaution of dropping the bar across the door before emptying the contents of Rob's leather pouch on the counterpane of her hammock-bed. Counting the coins, she discovered that she possessed the almost unbelievable fortune of seventy-nine pounds. Bless Aunt Mathilda, she thought. With this sum she could get herself to Edinburgh without anymore aid from the unpleasant Captain Cameron.

She tied the leather pouch inside her camisole, threw on her cloak, and left The Lavender and Lilly, heading in the direction of a livery stable she had sighted when they had arrived at Mallaig some hours earlier.

"Do you have a carriage that's going south?" she asked.

"Where south?"

"Edinburgh," she replied, blushing under the liveryman's scrutiny.

"The Big Smoke is it? Well, now . . ." He stroked his bristled chin and narrowed his eyes at her. "Why would a pretty young lassie such as yourself be wanting to go all that long way alone? There's dangers on the road for a lady unattended: highwaymen and bandits who'd as soon cut your throat as look at you."

She swallowed. "It doesn't matter. Have you a coach for hire?" Fiona held herself very straight and dignified. Despite her shabby cloak and worn boots, she hoped to pass for quality, and thus intimidate the inquisitive stableman into compliance.

"As it happens, I don't. A gentleman was in here yestereen wanting the same as you: a coach to Edinburgh. I fixed him up with one of the best, and young Jock MacDonald will go along to tend the horses. Tell you what, lass, I believe I can arrange for you to travel with this party. It'd cost you less, and the man who did the hiring told me a young woman would be traveling with them. She might be thankful for your company."

"No," said Fiona quickly. She hesitated, then asked nervously, "Are there other livery stables?"

The man looked cross. "Twenty pounds, lass. That's all I'll take from you if you ride along with Mr. Mudd and Captain Cameron. 'Tis a bargain, ye canna do better than that!"

She was backing out of the stable, shaking her head. "I'll try elsewhere first," she said. "I thank you kindly, though."

The stableman grunted and slammed the door.

Fiona spent most of the morning and early afternoon in a fruitless effort to find transportation. At one stable they told her to go home to her parents and forget about the city; in another she was told the price would be forty pounds.

Forty pounds! That was better than half her money! And the liveryman said she would have to pay two-thirds of it in advance. How could she trust the driver not to abandon her in the Highlands, after lining his pockets with her gold? Only hours before she had thought herself rich; now she wondered. Her visits to two more stables proved equally unsuccessful. But the more fate conspired to throw her into the company of Captain Cameron, the more determined she grew to refuse his help. No matter what, she was going on alone!

But how? Dared she risk forty pounds to reach Edinburgh? And once her mission in the city had been accomplished, how could she afford the return trip to Skye? Depressed, she walked about the town staring idly into shop windows and pondering her dilemma. She had visited every stable, and to no avail. Was Captain Cameron her only hope?

Mallaig was built on the side of a cliff facing west across the sound of Sleat to Skye. A steep narrow road twisted up from the dock, which was crowded with fishing boats. On either side of this cobbled road were old stone buildings—shops and plain-faced houses mostly, with a few churches, stables, tanners and bakers. At the top of the cliff, the road cut through a broad green meadow where some bright wagons were encamped, then dropped down, skirting the dunes until it disappeared into the forest. It was the road to Edinburgh. She supposed she might walk it, but . . .

The sound of a noisy argument from the wagons caught her attention.

"If you want your wages Sunday, then you'll do as I say." The speaker, a woman, had a harsh, shrill voice. "I'll pay you not a . . ." A baby began to cry; its enraged wails filled the air. Curious, Fiona walked toward the voices. Over the squalls of the infant she heard another female voice, responding to the first. This one spoke in a thick foreign accent and pronounced her words peculiarly. Fiona couldn't understand what she said, but the shrill voice was wholly intelligible to her. "So get out then, you nasty Froggy! You'll soon be sorry. But don't come sniveling to me . . ."

A messy young woman, carrying a bundle of clothes and bedding over her shoulder, came around the corner of the nearest wagon, almost at a run. Although the meadow was spacious, she pushed past Fiona, muttering in a strange language. The baby was still bawling; its cries seemed to be getting louder. Fiona heard the crash of something heavy falling, then loud angry cursing from the shrill-voiced woman.

Fiona came around the wagon and her eyes widened in amazement. Before her was an immense mountain of a woman. She was dressed in a voluminous dark garment, a kind of tent with holes cut for the arms and neck, which bulged with rolls and folds of pale tan-freckled skin. On her head she wore a kerchief that almost concealed a fringe of thin pinkish hair. Tiny beige eyes snapped when they saw Fiona.

"What do you want?" she screamed over the noise of the baby.

Fiona opened her mouth to speak, but couldn't say a word. She stared around her at the mess. The interior of the cluttered wagon was visible through the door: piled and stacked chaotically were baskets, clothing, cooking utensils and a dozen exotic items that Fiona could not identify. On the ground beside this jumble of goods was more of the same, including the iron pot that had clattered over a moment ago. The ground still steamed where boiling water had soaked it. Jutting out from under the wagon was a reed basket containing the squalling baby.

"I asked what you want! If you're another one of those wretched Frogs, I'll . . ." The woman raised a huge dimpled fist.

Fiona found her voice. Dropping a curtsey she said, "No, mistress. There's no French blood in me!"

"Thank the Virgin for that!"

"I heard your argument. And the baby. May I hold it?"

"Keep it, for all I care."

"Beg pardon, mistress?" asked Fiona as she pulled the basket out from under the wagon and lifted the wet unhappy child into her arms.

"Oh, never mind," sighed the woman.

"Is there food somewhere? And fresh clothing?"

Fiona's questions outraged the woman anew. "And how would there be, I'l like to know? You think I can be everywhere at once: mother, cook, manager?"

"Manager?"

"These wagons were my husband's," The woman crossed herself mechanically. "But now he's gone, and they're all I've got to hold body and soul together. Three wagons full of halfwit mummers, and precious few of them can speak the language. Damn Frogs." With one hand, she lifted the iron pot back onto the fire and struck a few twigs around the peat to help it catch. Cradled in Fiona's arms, the baby had stopped crying, and it was pleasant there at the top of the sun-drenched cliff, with the gaily decorated wagons like wheeled wildflowers that had sprung up in the meadow overnight. "You're good with that brat. He's never quiet unles he's asleep."

"This is your son?" Even as she asked the question, Fiona knew it was impossible. There was clearly no drop of maternal feeling in the fat woman.

"God save us," the woman cried, crossing herself again. "If it were mine, I'd drop it in the loch. It's me daughter's. She left it with me when she ran off. It wasn't bad enough the Lord called my dear Pierre . . ."

"Pierre?"

"Yes, yes, I know what you're thinking! He was a Froggy too. But different he was. Different." A large silver tear dribbled from her eye and was lost in the folds of flesh. "Poor Pierre, it would kill him if he knew that his only bairn, that pretty daughter he was always going on about, had got a child and then run off. And that actor, that useless man she took to bed, wasn't even a Catholic." She blessed herself once again. "Well, I'm too old for keeping babies, and now that wretched nursemaid girl has gone off and left me with twice the work—the cooking, the tending, the keeping . . ."

"I'll take her job," Fiona volunteered eagerly. She had sized up the situation at a glance, and decided that this paltry band of mummers was the answer to her prayers. Michael Cameron would never suspect her of joining a band of players! "I'll tend the child and see that things are tidied. I can cook and . . ."

"Can you tell fortunes?"

"I've never tried. Is that necessary?"

The woman was eyeing her shrewdly. It seemed impossible that only moments before she had been in tears. She wiped her nose on her sleeve. "That Froggy girl wouldn't do it. Said it was a sin. But the townfolk like a fortune teller, it brings in good money. You got scruples against fortune telling, you-whoever-you-are?"

"No," answered Fiona quickly.

"Seems you're mighty eager to be joining our little band. You're not in trouble of some kind are you?" Pointedly, she stared at Fiona's belly.

"I am not with child, if that is what you think, mistress. Nor have I any argument with the law. But I must go to Edinburgh somehow and—" the protective lie came out without calculation— "I haven't any money."

"What makes you think we're going to the city?"

"I only guessed you might be heading in that direction. The rumor is that Prince Charles Edward Stuart will be there one day soon and . . ."

"Pooh, that Pretender nonsense. Froggy lies, it's all Froggy lies. But you're right in thinking we travel south soon. I cannot pay you though, just your keep." The manager looked cagey. Fiona knew she was being taken advantage of because the woman sensed her need. But she needed the position too much to risk it by arguing.

"There'll be the cooking, the wash, keeping the wagon tidy and all, as well as the bairn and the fortunes. Dry nights you sleep under the wagon. Fair enough?"

Well, thought Fiona, hardly fair. But it would do.

"I'm Mistress Lejeune. Who be you?"

It had been in Fiona's mind to give a false name, just in case Michael Cameron came looking for her, but at the last moment she changed her mind. Surely he would never seek her in the care of Mistress Lejeune.

"Fiona Macleod."

"Ah, the music of a Scottish name after all these Froggies. We'll get along just fine, Fiona; like and like, eh?" Mistress Lejeune laughed voluminously, a huge masculine-sounding belly laugh. "Now you can start the tea and see to the brat."

When Michael realized that Fiona was gone he sent Muddy to look for her, but the man came back alone after several hours of searching and questioning.

"She was trying to find a way out of town," Muddy said. "She stopped at every stable and livery."

"She must have found something else; she'd be back by now." It was after dark, and the only sounds in the village were some drunken sailors singing to carnival music.

Fiona's disappearance worried Michael. She was too inexperienced to look out for herself. The next morning, he sent

Muddy out once more, and he himself walked along the waterfront asking questions. But he learned nothing of Fiona's whereabouts. The girl seemed to have vanished without a trace. Leaving Mallaig that afternoon, Cameron and Muddy had the Edinburgh road all to themselves, save for a dilapidated column of painted wagons advertising Lejeune's Country Diversions. From the driver's seat of the lead wagon, an immensely fat woman with pink hair waved after them cheerily.

Chapter 9

Lejeune's Country Diversions were just that: entertainments for country folk. There were four wagons in the caravan. The first and largest was occupied by Mistress Lejeune, Fiona and the bairn. The next housed a French couple, André and his wife Mélisande, as well as their three acrobatic children. While the imps delighted village audiences with bold leaps and rolls and Catherine wheels, Mélisande and André mimed scenes depicting virtue rewarded and great historical moments. They accepted Fiona's presence with the caravan without a word, although the French girl sometimes cast a wistful furtive glance in her direction.

In the next wagon rode Manfred Gott and his brother Willy. They were the strongmen who awed audiences by lifting wagons off the ground and upending saplings. Fiona did not care for the German Gott brothers. With their bulging muscles, which they oiled heavily before each show, and their flat Teutonic features, they seemed more like freaks to her than Danny, the Irish midget, and his little wife, Cindy, who rode in the last wagon. Cindy and Danny were the troupe's

Shakespearean actors. The village folk liked nothing better than to see Cindy in the role of Lady Macbeth. Her thin reedy voice piping "Out, out, damned spot" was sure to bring hoots and hilarity from every audience along the Edinburgh Road.

When Fiona fell behind with her chores, Danny or Manfred generally offered her assistance. She always accepted Danny's help eagerly, but with Manfred it was different. His doting servility made Fiona uncomfortable, but in the close company of the Diversions it was impossible to avoid him. Mistress Lejeune worked her hard—unfairly so; but so happy was she to be free and on her way without the help of Michael Cameron, that it was easy to accept the fat woman's harshness. She rode in the front wagon when the weather was inclement; otherwise, she was made to walk beside. "No need to overload the horsies," Mistress Lejeune told her. When the baby cried or needed feeding, Fiona was there to care for it. The poor infant was clearly starved for affection, and Fiona was touched when he came to recognize her, and smile and raise his tubby arms to be picked up. At mealtimes, Fiona cooked for Mistress Lejeune and then cleaned and cleared away the mess. She did the washing and kept the interior of the wagon so spotless that her employer could find nothing to complain of.

But for Mistress Lejeune, Fiona soon discovered, life was meaningless without complaint. She found fault with everything Fiona did. If the child whimpered, Fiona was accused of shirking. Her culinary talents were also found wanting—there was river sand in the teakettle; the potatoes were not thoroughly peeled. "I taste dirt, girl, dirt!" the fat woman cried, spitting a mouthful of stew into the fire.

The troupe stopped in every little village. First, the wagons were parked in a field. Then the acrobatic children would run off into the village, doing wintles and whirlygigums, causing a stir and exciting the townfolk. With this promotional stunt, the Lejeune Diversions were guaranteed a sizable audience. Most of them paid for their entertainment with food—chickens, potatoes, fish or grain, a minority paid coin. Fiona told fortunes in Mistress Lejeune's wagon, the curtains drawn so the interior had a nasty otherworldly atmosphere that enhanced the gullibility of the superstitious villagers.

Though she had no gift for reading palms—or crystal balls or tea leaves or the bumps on heads, Mistress Lejeune taught

Fiona enough about each of these techniques so that she appeared authentic to the naive. For her part, Fiona enjoyed her role as Madame Zarthos, the Hungarian seer. She copied the Gott brothers' accent, and by using her powers of observation was usually able to make some pronouncement that convinced the client she indeed possessed the gift of prescience. As she became skilled in her new trade, it occurred to Fiona from time to time that fortune telling was an apt profession for one called the halfling.

The weeks followed one another in a seamless pattern of entertainment and travel. Fiona was more or less content. She was moving toward Edinburgh; that was the main thing. Gradually, her grief over the loss of Owen Hamilton lessened. His face, his words, the touch of his satin breath on her cheek—these were familiar still; but the intensity of her feeling was gone. As his memory faded Fiona was saddened, but it seemed that the harder she tried to remember, the more rapidly he slipped from her. But then, her whole Skye life seemed somehow unreal to her now, as if her past were only a dream . . .

When Fort William, one of three British fortifications in the Highlands, was a scant day's travel to the east, Mistress Lejeune called the members of her troupe together and told them how she planned to make the most of their visit.

"We'll make a parade of it," she announced gleefully, "right through their wretched midden town! The bairns'll dance ahead to clear the street and get the folk's attention." She sniggled, "We'll make a pocketful of siller off them damn Englishmen. Oh, and it do give me pleasure to cheat a Royalist!"

And so Lejeune's Country Diversions paraded through Fort William. The midgets Cindy and Danny shook tambourines and called out greetings to soldiers and townsfolk alike, bidding them come to the edge of town that night for a show they wouldn't forget. In a threadbare red and black harlequin costume, André juggled colored balls, while his wife, Mélisande, walked ahead, splendidly dressed for her role of Salomé. Their children whirled at their side like dirvishes.

Fort William was larger than any town they had visited thus far, and certainly larger than any of the towns on Skye. It was a compact little fort town, built beside a loch, with mighty Ben Nevis leaning over it like a symbol of the monstrous hand that had scooped up the Highlands. Tall narrow buildings made of stone and blackened by sooty chimney smoke walled the narrow street on either side. Fort William was an important trading center. Its position at the confluence of three important bodies of water made it central to the economy of the Highlands and highly valued by the English. From shop fronts, corners and barrows, vendors hawked food, drink and clothing; while herds of sheep, goats, pigs and bearded Highland cattle filthied the mud and cobble streets. Fiona was dazzled by the varied sights. If Fort William was like this, how much grander and more crowded must be Auld Reekie—Edinburgh!

To encourage the townspeople and the more sophisticated soldiers and traders to visit the Diversions that night, Mistress Lejeune lit the oil in all the lamps and bade Fiona hang them on the wagons so that, amid the shadows of the dark field, the wagons formed a brilliant terrestrial constellation. The niggardly manager even hired a piper to play for dancing, as an added lure. At first the crowd was sparse, but there was a contagious feeling of carnival in the air, and soon the space around the wagons was packed with merrimakers—townspeople and redcoats—chortling over Danny's diminutive Hamlet and challenging the Gott brothers to ever greater feats of strength. Fiona, with the baby cradled near her behind a curtain, was a grand success as a fortune teller. As had been the case in less metropolitan areas, the men and women who visited Madame Zarthos wanted to hear only good news. Fiona was happy to oblige with promises of weddings and babies and fame or fortune to come, so not a man or woman left her wagon without feeling encouraged. Fiona never thought of her predictions as lies. It seemed a harmless game to cheer folk with optimistic tidings of the future, and the role of exotic Bohemian gypsy was fun to play.

As the hour grew later, the crowd became rowdier and the number of soldiers increased. Rising hostility between redcoats and Scots showed itself in drunken arguments and threats. The Gotts became bad-tempered as the soldiers jeered at them and mocked their heavy accents. Danny had to be restrained when these same soldiers made lewd suggestions to his little wife. Madame Lejeune smoothed out each disturbance and encouraged the sodliers to spend and spend and spend. Under her brightly colored veils and shawls and geegaws, Fiona—Madame Zarthos—smothered her yawns and longed for sleep.

She had just dozed off in her chair when a noise at the wagon door awakened her.

"Now you're a pair of swankies, you are!" Mistress Lejeune was saying. "Just the sort who'd like to know a bit of what's in store for them, eh, General?" Fiona peered through a crack in the side of the wagon and saw Mistress Lejeune nudge one of the young soldiers suggestively. "And what about that lady you left behind? Don't you wonder what she's doing while you're on Highland duty?"

The two soldiers looked at each other.

"Go on," said one to his friend. "What harm is there? Ask her what your Dulcie's doing just this minute. Go on, mate. Have a go." He nudged his younger comrade in the ribs and, pointing to where an enterprising vendor had parked his barrow to take advantage of the crowds, added, "I'll meet you over there afterward, and we'll have another pint or two."

Later, Fiona remembered that it began as just another fortune-telling session. She knew the name of the soldier's sweetheart and was prepared to mention his lovely Dulcie, when everything changed.

She was looking at his hand, noting the dirt caked in each line and the callouses, when an image appeared in miniature between his thumb and little finger. She saw a young woman with flaxen hair.

"Dulcie," Fiona whispered.

The girl was weeping over a red soldier's coat with shining brass buttons.

"What about Dulcie?" slurred the soldier. "You see something there about her?"

Fiona could not answer. Her gaze was transfixed by the images she was seeing. First Dulcie and the red uniform, then the body of the soldier himself lying amid a rubble of stones, his face half blown away. She tried to look away, but the powerful vision held her mesmerized, as one by one the stones about the soldier turned, revealing mangled faces like his own. The dream . . .

"Hey, you," the soldier said, wrenching his hand away. "What's the matter? What do you see? What about Dulcie?" He stood up, swaying slightly, and hit his head on the roof of the wagon. "Zoons!" he bellowed, staggering drunkenly back into the chair.

Fiona sat like a woman of stone, unable to speak. She no longer needed the soldier's palm. In her mind she saw him screaming from the far side of death, him and a thousand others. It was the dream, the nightmare that had dogged her since childhood. But what did it mean, and why had it suddenly intruded on her waking moments?

"Damn you, old harridan. What about Dulcie? Speak up or give me my money back."

Fiona didn't move.

The soldier thrust his face in front of hers. The reek of whisky almost knocked her over.

"What about Dulcie?" he demanded, shaking her. "You said her name. You know something. What do you see?" His hands went to her throat.

Gradually, the mist was rising from her vision, but she was uncertain where she was or what was happening to her.

"Help," she croaked. As she struggled to get away from the soldier, the table between them toppled over. The candle fell to the floor and rolled, still alight, toward the tin of lamp oil.

Instantly, the wagon was ablaze. The soldier dropped his hands and ran. Still dazed, Fiona fell to the floor of the burning wagon.

Chapter 10

She was conscious of heat, and her nose burned with the stench of smoldering wool. Her skirt was afire! She tried to beat out the flames, but her muscles refused to cooperate; helpless panic paralyzed her entire body. She tried to pull up, but her jellied legs toppled and she fell back.

The baby cried from the back of the wagon.

I must get to the bairn, thought Fiona. Like an insect, she crabbed along the floor of the wagon in her smoldering skirt, gasping for breath in the smoky wagon. Her cheeks and forehead were sizzling. Across her mind flashed the image of a goose turning on a spit, its skin split and oozing warm juices.

Suddenly, she felt hands on her ankles and she was dragged roughly along the floor of the wagon. Immense hands grabbed her waist; then, all at once, she saw the stars twinkling above her.

"The baby!" she struggled to say. "Get the baby."

Her cries were stifled in the dirt as someone rolled her over and over on the ground. The sharp-edged bracken scraped her singed face, and she screamed; but no one heeded the noise. A bucket of icy water was thrown over her face, drowning her cries.

Mistress Lejeune towered over her like one of the furies.

"Is the baby all right?" Fiona asked faintly.

"No thanks to you, Miss Fiona Macleod. If it was up to you, we'd all be up in flames."

"Who rescued me?"

"Manfred here. If not for him, you'd likely be charcoal by now. Now I suppose you think I'll let you lie around like Lady Muck recuperating. If you think that's how I'll reward you for burning down my best wagon . . ." A large crowd had gathered around, and began to take sides in the argument. "Do you know what it will cost to get that wagon fixed? Do you?" The crowd grumbled about the cost of things and moved in closer.

"The soldier was drunk, mistress, and he dinna like what I had to say." Or didn't say. Fiona recalled the entire experience vividly now. Why couldn't she have gathered her wits and said something pleasant about his pretty little Dulcie? She had been entranced by the vision of his death, and shocked into silence by the startling apparition of the dream.

"Next time, you tell him what he wants to hear! You understand me, lass?"

Fiona shook her head and rose to her feet unsteadily. "No," she was saying. "I can't tell fortunes anymore." A wave of nausea swept over her. She dared not tempt whatever *oogly* spirit brought the bloody pictures to her mind. Above all she wanted to be alone, away from the pressing onlookers. Perhaps then she would be able to understand.

"How do you expect to pay me back for all of this?" Mistress Lejeune reached for Fiona, who ducked away. "I'll thrash you so you'll wish . . ."

The sympathies of the crowd swung to Fiona, who looked beguilingly pitiful in her charred clothing. Her face was bright red and scratched raw in places. But Mistress Lejeune ignored the crowd and lunged for Fiona, a length of rope coiled tightly in her fist like a whip. Fiona was dimly aware that the French acrobat, Mélisande, was crouched beside her making the sign of the cross over her inert body, and mumbling fervently in her native tongue, as if to ward off the menacing lash by prayer.

"Schtop that!" Mangred Gott stepped between Mistress Lejeune and Fiona. "No hurt lassie."

This interference brought the old Virago's blood to full boil. "You stupid sack of . . ."

Gott snared both her wrists and held them easily in one hand. "Fiona work wit me and Willy. Forget fortunes."

Fiona looked at the German strongman. Only now did she realize that his hands and face were badly burned. The crowd seemed to like Manfred's idea. Mistress Lejeune heard their approving murmurs and her rabitty eyes turned cunning. She was instantly alive to the commercial potential of the hulking strongmen and this slight girl working together. But it would not do to show how well the idea pleased her, so she snarled a few more insults at the German. Then—with apparent reluctance—she grudgingly agreed to try the new act.

"But she still cares for the bairn and does me cooking and cleaning. And the washing too," insisted the fat woman. "You understand me, lassie?"

What could she do? Was now the time to use Mathilda's gold hoard? Fort William was a big town, from which Edinburgh coaches left several times weekly. Half dead from exhaustion, Fiona lay back on the ground and shut her eyes. While Mistress Lejeune grumbled, Mélisande treated and dressed Fiona's wounds.

Later she would think more about leaving the Diversions. Now she was too tired to think of anything but her pain.

"I'll do it," she said to Mistress Lejeune. Then, turning to Manfred, she tried to raise her hand, but weakness overcame her. She managed to give him a radiant smile. "You saved my life, Manfred. God bless you."

Finally, even the effort of smiling grew too much; she fell into a deep sleep. The crowd dispersed, leaving the carnival in a subdued mood. Madame Lejeune stood daydreaming of silver and gold, while Manfred tended his wounds. Danny and Cindy stole away to their wagon with the baby. André, the harlequin clown, was drunk in his bed and had ignored the uproar, but his Mélisande was preparing a bed for Fiona under Lejeune's wagon. Only Willy Gott had not gone about his business. He stood in the shadows of the wagon and watched Fiona with cold narrowed eyes, until long after the last lamp was extinguished.

Lejeune's Diversions stayed in the neighborhood of Fort William for almost two weeks, awaiting the completion of repairs on the damaged wagon. During this time interest in the carnival evaporated, and finally Mistress Lejeune put away the extra lamps and sent the piper off with only half his promised wages. Day after day, the fat old woman stormed from wagon to wagon, cursing her ill fortune. "You better make me money, lass. Or else!" she warned Fiona. She continually referred to the Scots lassie as a jinx, and one morning, as Fiona scrubbed a kettle on her hands and knees, Mistress Lejeune came at her from behind and began kicking her violently in the buttocks. After that, Fiona tried to stay out of the old woman's way. The very sight of her seemed to send Mistress Lejeune into paroxysms of rage. "Jinx," she screamed. "Bad luck!"

Bad luck. Those words troubled Fiona almost as much as the physical abuse she suffered. Michael Cameron had called her bad luck too. Was it possible that he and Mistress Lejeune were right, that she carried with her some . . . taint that brought ill fortune to those about her?

She would have believed it except for one thing. She did not *feel* unlucky. In fact, she felt almost the opposite: charmed. This feeling had given her the confidence she needed to set off for Edinburgh alone. It was a peculiarly contradictory state of mind. Though nothing in her past could be pointed to as fostering a happy outlook on life she nonetheless felt a strange new optimism when she looked to the future. Even her feelings about the vision of the bloody moor had begun to change since the fire.

She had given much thought to this vision in the days following the accident. Though she went to bed each night with aching muscles from the hard labors demanded of her by the unrelenting Lejeune, during those hours of automatic work her mind was free to think, to go over one hundred times and more, the details of her vision. It was always the same. Always the moor, the stones, the mangled faces dripping gouts of blood. On the night of the fire, the picture had enlarged to include the dead soldier and his weeping lover, but it had remained essentially the original picture: the moor, the stones and the faces had all been there. But the addition of the soldier had made a crucial difference in Fiona's attitude. She now knew that her vision pertained to an actual event. The faces were those of real men—not visitations from the faery world—and the moor was a real spot, somewhere on this earth, where all these things would indeed come to pass. It was a prophesy, this dream, a clairvoyant glimpse of the future. A prophesy that had been entrusted to her.

But why? Why was this dream visited on her? Why had it all begun on the night of her mother's death? The explanation darted across her mind so quickly that she almost missed it. Then she nearly discarded her brainstorm as superstitious nonsense. Impossible! But she kept coming back to this answer as if it were conclusive: Janet Macleod had dreamed the dream herself. And on the night she was driven into the sea, the vision was given over to her daughter.

There must be a reason, she thought, and for the first time the vision ceased to be a burden and became an honor, a trust. It had come to her from her mother, and was in a sense her true inheritance. But Fiona knew she would never bequeath the moor and bloody stones to her own daughter; somehow she foresaw that she herself would witness the realization of the dream's apocalypse.

For now, though, she had to go on with her life—with reaching Edinburgh and doing her business there and then returning to Skye; the vision would stay with her or vanish. Despite its lack of substance, the dream was a reality; and she could not control it any more than she could control the color of her eyes or the flash of her temper. The vision had been part of her mother; now it was part of her and she must accept it, welcome it even, as a treasured legacy. Before long, she knew, the prophesy would be fulfilled.

Somehow, Fiona found time to practice her new act with the Gott brothers. Mistress Lejeune was always there to watch the rehearsals and offer her own suggestions.

"Put the lass up high, Willy. And you there, don't look so terrified! You think the man will drop you?" The fat woman clutched her quivering belly and laughed as if she'd made a great joke. She knew—and so did Fiona—that Willy Gott would gladly have dropped her if he thought his brother wouldn't kill him for it. Willy, the elder brother, was several inches taller than Manfred. He was a huge wide-chested man, with a thick head of wiry black hair and a beard to match. With Manfred, Willy had found a life that perfectly suited his primitive saturnine nature; now everything was being threatened by Fiona.

As the carnival wagons moved south from Fort William through the Great Glen—as if crossing a land for giants at the dawn of time—Willy's jealous resentment of Fiona became noticeable to everyone. She was afraid of him, and began making clumsy mistakes when they practiced their act together.

In dry weather, Fiona still slept beneath Mistress Lejeune's wagon. One night, the carnival was camped on an exposed barren hillside. A dense fog lay about the scene. Fiona shivered in her bedroll, unable to sleep, turning from one uncomfortable position to another. An argument had broken out in the Gott's wagon around midnight. She heard her name come up several times, heard Willy spit it out like a curse. The brothers were quarrelling about her.

Fiona blamed Manfred's puppylike devotion for the situation. She did nothing to encourage him, but his unspoken passion seemed to grow without sustenance and was apparent to everyone in the company, including his sinister brother.

As she lay beneath the wagon listening to them argue, fear clutched at her heart. Though she did not understand the words, their significance was clear. So long as she stayed with the Diversions she was in danger . . .

Mistress Lejeune had big plans for the Diversions' season in Stirling. She told everyone repeatedly that the English soldiers at Stirling were too cosmopolitan to be impressed by the company in its current shabby state, so she put them all to work—even Fiona, who was already overtaxed from childcare and housework and practicing the new routine with Willy and Manfred—washing and waxing and generally refurbishing the old wagons until they looked presentable.

One evening, the fat woman beckoned Fiona into her wagon. Mélisande, the Frenchwoman who seemed to have an unspoken sympathy for Fiona, was there as well. Since the fire, Fiona had been conscious of the French girl's increased solicitude for her, the lovely face composed and unexpressive yet somehow disturbing.

"Sit down, Fiona," said Mistress Lejeune with surprising cordiality. "You look tired, lass. You aren't sleeping well?"

"No, mistress," said Fiona sullenly.

The fat woman laughed. "You don't like the ground, eh? Do you lie awake and dream of feather beds?" She laughed some more, nudged Mélisande and said something in French. "I think I can arrange for you to have a bed. For a few hours anyway." Mistress Lejeune scratched her chin, grotesquely spotted by three or four coarse gray hairs. "You look all right, I suppose." She directed a question to Mélisande, who seemed reluctant to answer, but finally shrugged her assent.

"Melly says you'll do. Well, what do you say, Fiona?"

"I don't understand," she said. There was a dangerous atmosphere in the wagon; but she couldn't identify it. Mistress Lejeune had seemed mean and cruel to Fiona before, but now she seemed downright evil. And Mélisande . . .

For some reason Mélisande made Fiona think of Michael Cameron. She recalled something he had said to her in Mallaig. They were perhaps his final words to her, though neither had known it at the time. They were walking up from the wharf to The Lavender and Lily. There was a girl, a woman, in a doorway, and she said something to Michael Cameron that made him laugh and throw her a gold coin. Then he said to Fiona—and his tone had been unkind— "Watch out you don't end up like that one!"

She wondered now what he meant by those words.

"Oh, and we are a country kitten, aren't we?" Mistress Lejeune spoke playfully, but her small eyes gleamed within their caves of folded flesh. "Let me just tell you a wee story about Mélisande here." She patted the Frenchwoman's knee. "She and André could hardly earn their keep or hold the lease on their wagon with that snooling act of theirs. It's Melly here, pretty Melly, who brings home the Royalist gold. Isn't that right, lassie?" Again she patted Mélisande's knee with a proprietary air. Then, glancing slyly at Fiona, the old woman realized that the country girl was still in ignorance of her plan. This enormous naiveté made her furious. She roared. "She spreads her legs for soldiers, you stupid jurr. And so shall you!"

Chapter 11

Fiona looked back and forth between Lejeune and Mélisande as if seeing them for the first time. "No," was the only word she could say. She said it again and again as she stepped back to the wagon door. Madame Lejeune continued to grin at her; she seemed delighted by the startling effect of her words. Mélisande stared after her too, but her expression was astonished and fearful. She looked back and forth between Fiona and Mistress Lejeune as if unable to believe that anyone could disregard an order from the older woman. Still shaking her head and murmuring no, Fiona jumped out of the wagon.

She had no idea where to go. She wasn't thinking of anything except escape from Lejeune and her lewd proposition. She leapt down a slope of hill just beyond the wagons, stumbled and fell—right into the arms of Manfred Gott. Twisting, she felt his lips brush her cheek and hair, almost gagged on the heavy odor of the oil he used to burnish his muscles.

"Oh, no! No!" she cried, sobbing and turning in Gott's iron embrace. He was speaking too; but his words, gutteral and alien to Fiona, were lost in the curls of her hair. "Let me go, Manfred. Don't hurt me. Please, don't hurt me!" She pulled away and stared up at him, mutely pleading. He saw something in her eyes that destroyed his ardent confidence. With the cry of someone in pain, he pushed her away, turned and ran into the shadows of boulders and trees. Fiona fell to the ground. Like galloping hooves, her heartbeat resonated through her whole body, and even the ground seemed to tremble beneath her. An instinct warned her that she was still in danger. She looked around.

Willy Gott was standing only a few feet from where she lay. It was clear he had seen everything.

"Take one step nearer and I'll kill you," she warned, rising to a crouching position. It was no idle threat. She was ready for anything. Having perceived the several dangers around her, she realized how much she valued her life and independence. "I mean it, Willy. I have a knife." It was a lie, of course. But Willy could not know it; and Highland women, like their menfolk, enjoyed a reputation for bold fighting. He would be wary. "You put a hand on me, I'll slit your gullet."

It was dark; she could hardly see his face except for its ugly expression. She didn't need to see more. She could feel him resenting her, hating her across the space of rock and grass and heather as if a current of heated air stretched between them. She stayed in her crouch position, her hand at her waist, until he turned at last and left her, going down the slope in search of his brother.

The path lay across ridge after rolling ridge, bare of all but the hardiest plants. Mosses—chartreuse and red and leaf-gold like Fiona's hair—grew in brilliant profusion among the piled rocks and boulders, the noisy roiling streams. In many places the track was in such bad condition that Willy and Manfred were enlisted to move boulders and uproot encroaching saplings. The troupe complained loudly of the hard land, but Fiona loved the wild country and was reluctant to part from it. She was, after all, a Highland lass, a Macleod of Skye; the land was all she knew and now each step was carrying her away into an alien city.

She tried not to think of what lay ahead for her in Stirling. The present was gruesome enough. She worked all day and sometimes half the night, driven by Mistress Lejeune. The cruel manager seemed to relish watching Fiona faint from exhaustion, too weak to eat the food she herself had prepared.

It wasn't only Mistress Lejeune. Willy never took his eyes off her during their rehearsals. Disoriented by his scrutiny, she fell twice in one day and sprained her ankle painfully. As she performed her housekeeping tasks, she was constantly aware of his malevolent gaze. Another time, after slipping away for an early morning bath in a pool surrounded by boulders, Fiona saw Willy watching from above as she dried her long hair in the air. Sickened, she knew that he had watched her as she bathed.

Manfred was watching her too. His huge bovine eyes began to nauseate her, and the sickly sweet smell of the oil he rubbed in his skin would not leave her nostrils. Her own skin was coated with it after their rehearsals. More and more, it sickened her to touch him. As he tried to lift her to his shoulders one night at practice, she shrank from his hand at the last moment and fell, injuring her back.

Lejeune continued to work her like a navvy, until Fiona wept from the pain. The fat woman seemed to take pleasure in the injuries Fiona sustained during practice with the Gott brothers, and allowed no rest for her muscles and bones to heal.

"Stop sniveling, jurr!" she snarled, aiming a sharp kick at Fiona's ribs as she knelt scrubbing the floor of the wagon. "You better bring me good money in Stirling, lassie, or I'll take my whip to your butt and beat you till you bleed! I'll have no more of this bad luck you bring, you understand me?"

"I want to leave. You can't make me stay here!" Fiona scrubbed as she talked; if she stopped work for even an instant, Mistress Lejeune would give her the boot again.

The old woman grabbed her by the throat of her drab blouse and jerked her to her feet, pulling Fiona's face close to hers. "First you pay me every penny you owe. Every penny. Plus a little more."

I can buy my way out of this, Fiona thought. All ideas of frugality were banished by the grinding pain in her lower back and the fear of what Mistress Lejeune might do to her if she remained any longer with the Diversions. "How much do I owe you?"

Mistress Lejeune's eyebrows shot up. Suspiciously, she asked, "Why do you want to know all of a sudden, eh? Thinking of cheating me, I suspect." Her laugh was flat and humorless. "Well, never you mind about that. Just please the soldiers. Maybe in a year or two I'll reckon up your debt."

Fiona discarded the hope of buying her freedom. No

matter what she had to give Lejeune, the grasping harridan would want more and more. Her greed was insatiable. And she had not abandoned her ugly scheme of forcing Fiona to prostitution in Stirling. Fiona's only hope lay in escape.

It was now Highland summer.

The mountains and glens burst with life and the irrepressible exuberance of nature's bounty. It was a season of sunny mornings and long damp afternoons, and nights luminous with star and moonlight. Fiona liked to take her bedroll away from the wagons to where the dense fern growth provided a soft sweet-smelling cushion. On such perfect nights, as Fiona lay on her back trying to count the stars, she believed in her faery kinship. Though far from Skye, even here, near the edge of the great plain, she felt the Highland spirits alive and all about her. It was as if the land itself were trying to tell her something.

One night, as she lay thus distracted, Fiona became conscious of someone nearby, hunkered down in the grass.

"Who's there?" she demanded in a loud whisper. "Say your name." Instinctively, she grasped for a rock or heavy stick with which to protect yourself. "Say your name!" she repeated louder.

Mélisande crawled quickly toward her through the bracken. The sky had begun to lighten with the early dawn; Fiona saw the young Frenchwoman clearly. She had been beaten terribly—undoubtedly by Mistress Lejeune.

"Forgive me," Fiona said softly, gathering Mélisande into her arms and rocking her gently. "If I could do something to make this up to you, I would. I swear I would."

Mélisande stirred. "Tell her I talked you into staying. Den maybe she leave me alone for a while." In the ravaged face, dark eyes pleaded eloquently.

With a deep sigh of resignation Fiona said, "Very well. I'll say so. I will speak to her first thing tomorrow." As Mélisande wept gratefully against her breast, Fiona remembered her Aunt Mathilda's bruised face, after Rob had beaten her on the way to the solicitor's office. Mélisande looked even worse.

"Why?" Fiona asked, gently touching the purpled skin about the girl's eye. Only a mad woman would attempt to disfigure anyone as lovely as Mélisande. Now she was pitiful, like a small mistreated animal cringing to survive. "She did this to you? But why?"

Mélisande could scarcely move her swollen lips. "She want me to tell you. She said you maybe try . . ." It was obviously painful for her to speak. Fiona hushed her into silence. She didn't have to be a fortune teller to understand Mistress Lejeune's intent. The woman was truly diabolical. Fiona suspected that some of Mélisande's wounds would not mend; she would be permanently scarred by her beating, and all because Lejeune wanted to warn Fiona against leaving.

"But why you?" Fiona asked. "Why didn't she attack me directly?"

The Frenchwoman shrugged. "She say she let soldiers take care of you. But I theenk she maybe afraid. Something about you . . . *Je ne sais pas, moi.* But me, I am easy victim; she not afraid of me." Fiona sat very still and upright, watching the morning spread across the Highlands. She could see a long swath of hillside across a misted glen; in another day they would be out of the Highlands. She counted the days until Stirling. Somehow, she must elude the awful fate Lejeune planned for her there.

Stirling was not what any of them expected. The monstrous castle perched on its rocky pedestal towered over a town silenced by fear. At a crossroads where they stopped to water their horses and refresh themselves, they met a pair of young men decked out in Highland finery, their polished blades flashing in the sunlight, and even the brass of their sporrans gleaming.

"You won't find much to profit you in Stirling Town, mistress," one of them told Lejeune, doffing his cap politely. "The soldiers there are scared half out of their wits by our bonny Prince and his army. 'Tis said the army lies but two days' march from here."

Fiona, filling water bottles at the spring, heard the whole conversation. The talk of Prince Charles and liberty brought Owen to her mind. She tried to remember his face, his touch, but he had been so far from her thoughts lately that it was hard to revive his fading memory. But she had loved him. And now she recalled his hopeful expression as he spoke of the Young Pretender who would restore the Scottish crown and defeat the German House of Hanover, which had stolen the throne of England. How thrilled he would be, how ready to do battle if he had lived. If only . . .

"He raised the standard at Glen Finnan but a few weeks ago, mistress," said one of the young men. "Since that time he and his army have been moving south while the English along the way shutter up their doors and windows and pray to God to protect them from a true Stuart with a sword in hand." The more he talked, the younger the clansman seemed. His enthusiasm touched Fiona, reminding her again of Owen; Mistress Lejeune, however, only laughed.

"What do you bairns know about it? Every year since I can remember there have been rumors like this drivel you're spouting. In the end, it all comes to nothing. So save yourself the trouble and hie thee home."

Drawing themselves up straight and tall, the young men covered their outraged dignity with condescension. The taller and more confident boy said, "This time you're wrong, mistress. But by the time the truth gets through the fat on you, the Prince will have taken Edinburgh and crossed the border into England." Laughing, he shouldered his bundle and continued with his friend down the road toward the encamped army.

Chewing thoughtfully on her lower lip, Mistress Lejeune watched after them in silence. Then she yelled for Danny. "Unhitch the horse from your wagon and ride ahead. Find out what you can about these Prince rumors."

Danny returned to their encampment on the edge of the plain the next day. At first, Mistress Lejeune refused to believe his narrative. But the more she hammered questions at him, the more securely he stuck to his facts. The unbelievable seemed to have happened.

Prince Charles Edward Stuart, the Young Pretender, had arrived in Scotland at Borradale, aboard the French ship *Du Teillay*. On the 19th of August at Glen Finnan, the standard of the Stuarts was raised, and the clans of the Highlands officially called kith and kin to arms against the British.

At this point in the story, Mistress Lejeune began to rub her hands together with growing enthusiasm. All those soldiers, redcoat and Highlander alike, meant lonely men in search of diversion. "How many has he with him?" she asked Danny.

"Mistress, it's hard to say. There's all the Clanranald

Macdonalds as well as the Keppochs. And Lochiel has brought seven hundred Camerons. The talk in public houses is that the English have put a reward on him. Thirty thousand pounds!"

Talk of money reminded Mistress Lejeune of her own financial problems, and her mood turned nasty. "Well, so what! Princes can do me no good if they keep the town closed up like a Chinese box." "So what is the truth, Danny? Is there siller to be made in Stirling, or do we spend the summer starving?"

The midget shrugged and looked uncomfortable. He didn't know and told her so.

Lejeune's Diversions spent another night camped at the crossroads. Mistress Lejeune took the closure of Stirling Town and the curfew imposed by the English as a personal affront. Hour after hour, she paced the ground beside her wagon cursing and raging at the ill fortune that plagued her.

"You! Jurr!" she screamed at Fiona. "You brought all this bad luck! I'll make you pay . . ." An upward gust of wind carried the rest of her words away. As Fiona looked up, her hair blew wildly around her face. A terrible blue-black cloud, a monster that covered half the sky, had appeared in the southwest. Directly overhead, the sky was blackening, but in the distance it shone with an eerie electric blue light. The wind was icy cold. It stung Fiona's eyes. The awning of Mistress Lejeune's wagon flapped noisily in the air. "Get that!" screamed Mistress Lejeune, diving at the awning cloth as it began to tear. A moment before, the only sound in the camp had been the old woman yelling at Fiona. Now, like a disturbed ant colony, the area had come abruptly alive with confusion. The horses were rearing and screaming as the sky grew blacker. André tried to calm them, while Mélisande gathered the children into their wagon, trembling with fright.

Here was Fiona's chance to escape. She ducked behind Lejeune's wagon and across the track, into a stand of pine. The ground was soggy from underground springs, so she couldn't run but had to move carefully from ridge to ridge. Once or twice she stopped, listened. Was anyone following? The sighing trees, bent halfway to the ground by the storm, made a noise that sent shivers up her spine. There had been few trees on Dunvegan Head, and she had never heard the sound of a storm high in the pines. She didn't like it.

97

She came out into a field as the first crack of thunder shattered the air. Lightning followed quickly, revealing the sinister form of Willy Gott, standing only a few feet in front of her. Fiona turned hastily and ran along the edge of the pines. Time and time again, she slipped on the rough ground. Glancing behind, she saw Willy gaining on her. Fiona's heart bruised her with its beating; the ice and rain stung her face as she forced herself to move faster, faster. Willy came panting behind her, his hand brushed against her skirt. She heard a great intake of air, and then Willy landed against her with a force that knocked the breath from her lungs. "Let me go!" she screamed over the storm's thunderous rage.

Willy's hands were on her throat. If she turned her head, she would look directly into his eyes. She did it, and the quickness of her movement, the half-demented way she opened her eyes and fixed them on him, was unnerving. His fingers slipped. She felt a burning on her neck then a jerk; and at last she was free.

She scrambled to her feet and ran—almost flew—beside the ribbon of pines, disappearing at last into the storm's false night. In an abandoned shepherd's hut, she sought protection from the rain. Huddled on the floor with her arms clutched tight about her drawn-up legs, her forehead resting on her knees, she sobbed tragically.

It was true she had her freedom, but the gold from Aunt Mathilda Duncan was gone. Willy Gott had it now.

Book Four

THE PRINCE AND THE
HALFLING

Chapter 12

The claymore was heavy in the Prince's hands. The muscles of his well-developed arms strained painfully as he hefted the murderous six-foot sword. Once the weapon was up, he drove it deep into the straw dummy that O'Sullivan and Macdonald had erected for him, reluctantly.

"Why waste your time learning to use that antique?" O'Sullivan wanted to know. "Already you are the master of pistol and sword. Surely you do not need this primitive . . ." In his arrogant fashion John O'Sullivan sought for a definitive term of disparagement for the claymore. He shrugged finally and gave up. "It is beneath you, Sir."

At the time, Charles had not cared to explain his true reasons for learning the claymore. He knew that O'Sullivan could not understand the symbolic importance of the two-handed Highland sword. A man could only strike once with it; it was unwieldy and exhausting to hold. Still, this was the weapon of his forbears, and he would learn it.

Again he drove the claymore into the straw; the clumsy figure tumbled.

"Dead, Sir!" cried O'Sullivan, coming forward to retrieve the broad sword and right the dummy. "Well done!"

With a dip of his blonde head, Charles acknowledged the polite applause of Sir John Macdonald and his old tutor, Sheridan, behind him. Though it was late afternoon, the September air was muggy; the Prince was perspiring from exertion. A servant stepped forward and dabbed his face with a soft cloth. Charles pushed him away. He didn't mind sweating and straining, and wished his servants wouldn't treat him as some sort of china doll. Not far away, his army was sweating and laboring in their camp, and what was good enough for his men was good enough for the Pretender to the throne, as well.

A table and chairs had been set beside his tent. The Prince invited Sheridan, O'Sullivan and Macdonald to join him for refreshment. Sheridan—looking old and tired as he had for the twenty years Charles had known him—was wheezing asthmatically, and begged to be excused.

"I am just as pleased he didn't stay," said O'Sullivan the instant the old man was out of earshot. "John and I need to speak to you, Sir. Privately."

"Don't waste your time on the claymore, Sir. We've been about this business too long already."

"Every moment in Scotland is taken away from the conquest of England." O'Sullivan, thinking his words might be taken as a slight on the country the Prince admired, added, "Besides, the Scots are already loyal."

The Prince nodded his head and raised his glass to be refilled with wine. Yes, the Highlanders were loyal. His army was made up of loyal clansmen. And what did it matter if Macdonald and Macleod had refused to join the campaign, when Lochiel, with his immense influence, had brought three hundred strong men willing to die to see the Scottish crown restored? The Prince was remembering how the clans had appeared when the standard was raised at Glen Finnan: the ragged kilts and shabby coats could not disguise the pride of the Highland Scots. As O'Sullivan and Macdonald pampered him with praise and guarantees of success, Prince Charles recalled his words to the clans that day in mid-August.

"I want you to win, not for my father's sake or mine, but for yourselves, so that you may always be free of slavery."

With a dramatic flourish he had drawn his sword; his cries filled the glen and echoed off the dales and bluffs. "Gentlemen, I have flung away the scabbard. And with God's help, I will make you a free and happy people!" There was a thunderous response from the clansmen and their chiefs, and a thousand bonnets sailed into the sky.

It had been a glorious moment for Charles Edward Stuart, a glorious moment in a campaign that had, thus far, been disappointing. If only they had not missed the opportunity to engage General Cope. But a spy had leaked word of the Jacobite plan to the British general, who forced a march evading the Highlanders. No matter if Cope looked like a fool to every man of courage in whatever army; the Prince's troops had been weeks in the Highlands thirsting for battle, and without once drawing swords they had reached almost to Edinburgh. Walking through the camp one night, disguised, Charles heard the complaint of a pair of foot soldiers. What kind of an army is never tested in battle? they asked each other bitterly. They wanted to prove themselves in the fray—and so did their Prince. Macdonald and O'Sullivan could wait for more glorious English battles; they were tested soldiers with proud careers behind them. But Charles and his army wanted to engage the British right here in Scotland. Now. A victory would fan the flames of Jacobite loyalty. The clans reluctant to join his cause before the battle would do so afterward with alacrity. King Louis of France would send the troops he had promised.

"Although frankly, Sir," Sir John was saying, "I would feel much more secure with greater cannon power. When I fought with the Spanish in . . ."

"Lord George and Perth tell me cannons aren't suitable. They say the Highlanders have their own way of doing battle with the English." Prince Charles came back to the present long enough to order a second bottle of wine and a dish of cold fowl.

"Beg pardon, Sir, but I cannot agree with Lord George. In my experience horses and firepower . . ." Macdonald and O'Sullivan had a generally low opinion of the Highland chiefs' generalship.

"He also says that horses are useless. Half the Highlanders can't ride anything but ponies." He considered what Lord

George had told him and then went on. "They are a breed of soldier entirely unlike any you've encountered, Sir John."

"When I was in New Spain with the Spanish cavalry . . ."

"These clansmen are tough and independent. They go on foot and are proud of it. They fight with their hands, and with short knives called *skene dhus*. With the claymore if their arms are short and mighty." The Prince laughed and made a pair of swipes through the air with an imaginary broadsword.

Quick to seize any opportunity to praise the Young Pretender, O'Sullivan hastened to say, "You handled the broadsword mightily, Sir. It's a true Highlander you are!"

Charles Edward Stuart had been raised to be King of England. His exiled father, James, provided his son with the finest courtly and martial education available to the French nobility. The twenty-five-year-old Prince had been schooled to one thought since early childhood. One day the Scots would rise against their English oppressors and win back the crown for the royal House of Stuart. It was his destiny to be King.

Destiny. It was a word that came to the Prince's mind more and more frequently since his arrival in Scotland. A sense of destiny so strong as to be virtually invincible dominated his waking moments and governed his every action as Prince. He knew that his aides, the generals and even his personal chaplain, Abbé Butler, had strong doubts that their enterprise could succeed. Though the English were much engaged with fighting in Flanders, they could muster men enough to defend London, some of his aides reminded him. They were forgetting one thing. Scotland and parts of northern England teemed with Jacobite sympathizers. The army of the Highlands would swell with these numbers, needing only their Prince at the fore to give them courage and inspiration.

The trouble is, thought Charles, as he took a brief walk about the camp that night, no one here understands that it is my destiny to be King. Suddenly, staring out across the empty stretch of plain, he was assailed by loneliness. He longed for Franco.

Resuming his walk, he calculated the number of days before his close companion, Prince Gabriello Franco, would arrive in Edinburgh. It would be three weeks at the least.

Plenty of time for the Prince to occupy the city and find a discreet lodging for his friend. Charles was hungry for battle and regretted missing his chance with Cope so much that it made his teeth ache to think of it. It would have been fun to swagger before Franco, who was greatly fascinated by battle, though he preferred to comment on it from a safe distance rather than participate.

As he walked, Charles thought how it might have been if General Cope had been truly engaged—ambushed. This was a happy time for him; he forgot the practical worries of money and arms and intrigue, and lost himself in private fantasy. As he walked, his face showed no change of expression, but in his head he was a conqueror!

It rained every day that early autumn. There were frequent storms of towering blackness, like the one that had thrown the Lejeune Diversions into confusion. These atmospheric giants had a way of boiling up out of a clear sky, and in a matter of minutes the day would be night and the wind would rise and howl its prelude to thunder, lightning and torrential rains. One afternoon, a few days after his walk about the camp, Prince Charles went for a long ride on horseback. He was charmed by the parklike countryside and, distracted, lost track of both time and weather. His first warning was the dark chill that dropped over the land. Looking up, he saw ahead of him a monstrous black cloud edged in gold. The wind began to stir the pines; a hawk rocked and drifted on the currents of cold air. Its piercing cry became the wind bending the branches of the pine tree.

Then he saw her.

She was ahead of him, coming over the brow of the hill. Her back was to the storm, and though a dusk lay over the land she stood out clearly, as if she carried her own radiance. The approaching storm, the time of day, his horse's nervousness—everything dropped from the Prince's conscious thoughts. He was transfixed by the image that approached him from the country lane.

She was tall and proud and had hair the color of autumn leaves, flaming out against the distant cobalt sky. She walked without looking behind her at the cloud, as if the mightiest storm was nothing to her. Under her spell, the Prince cared nothing for the elements himself. He could think of nothing but the vision of this flamboyant Highland lassie, who seemed to personify all the hopes and youthful exuberance of Scotland and the Stuart cause.

He leapt from his horse. At that moment the storm broke; a black wind tore out of the sky. Above them—the Prince and the halfling—the clouds collided, their thunder like the roar of mighty beasts. About them, the crackling air smelled of ozone as the rain began.

Chapter 13

At the same time, in the city of Edinburgh, Captain Michael Cameron was taking a sumptuous high tea at the home of his aunt, Lady Flora Jane Campbell. Also present at the table, which was laid with damask and gold-edged china ornamented with the Campbell crest, was Miss Abigail Gunn, Michael's cousin twice removed. Michael found the meal and surroundings agreeable, and his feeling of well-being was enhanced by the appearance of the cook, bearing a dish she had prepared just "special for the Cap'n." It was brandy trifle, a favorite of Michael's since childhood, when it was forbidden to him because of the high alcoholic content.

"You're a bonny wee lass to remember so well," he told his old aunt with a wink. She responded with maidenly giggles, and blushes of obvious pleasure.

"I canna take the credit, Nephew. Though now I wish I had thought of it. It's Annie here deserves your smiles, not I, Michael."

Now it was the tubby middle-aged cook's turn to blush.

Rubbing her hands on her apron, she dipped a curtsey and scrutinized the floor. She was glad to escape the dining room; leaving the grand folk to their talk of revolution.

Prince Charles and his progress toward Edinburgh had been the favorite topic of conversation that evening—as on most others recently. It now appeared, barring some unforeseen event, that the Prince and his army would enter Edinburgh in three days' time. To Michael—and to most of the others with whom he talked—it was disturbing that the rebel army had been permitted to cross half the country without a show of force from the occupying British troops. They would enter Edinburgh as an untested army. Other things he heard disturbed him more, however. From what he understood, it was just as well the army had not been involved in skirmishes with the well-trained English soldiers garrisoned in Scotland, for a battle would surely have proved disastrous for the untrained and poorly equipped Highland forces. During the past weeks in Edinburgh, Michael had heard nothing to encourage him about the Jacobite cause. His Uncle Lochiel had joined with Prince Charles; and Michael knew this should make him optimistic, but strangely it did not. He had heard disturbing rumors about the Prince, and had begun to doubt his competence. It would take more than a charming manner and an elegant physique to wrest the throne away from the Hanovers. It would take a miracle, and Michael doubted if Prince Charles could provide that.

"Michael," Lady Flora Jane was saying, "You're too distracted this evening. It won't do!" She pouted, picking up her fan from beside her plate and pointing it at him. "That's the trouble with war: it distracts the gentlemen! I remember back in fifteen, when Papa was determined to be gallant. The whole household went amok, while he daydreamed about Stuart Kings!"

"La, Aunt," said Abigail Gunn, chiding the older woman gently, "you mustn't blame Cousin Michael for finding us dull. How can womenfolk hope to compete with the excitement of battle? I know I certainly don't expect to." She smiled at Michael and offered to refill his teacup.

"Thank you, no," he said quickly. "I'm afraid I will have to ask you ladies to excuse me somewhat early tonight. I have paperwork that requires my attention. Were it not for that, I would of course be delighted to spend the evening with two such charming gentlewomen." He spoke the words, smiled the smiles, automatically. He played the chivalrous gentleman perfectly. It was a role he had learned to play early in life, and which he found loathsome but definitely useful. He was attached to his aunt and would not have hurt her feelings, but just now—though his manner gave no indication—he was cross with her for calling him to Edinburgh to meet Abigail Gunn.

"It would be such a great favor to her dear mama and me," Flora Jane had written to him months before. Without other business in the city he might have avoided meeting his eligible cousin, but as it happened the letter was timed conveniently. And so he had appeared in Edinburgh and met Abigail, and had instantly known that if he ever married, it would not be to Abigail Gunn.

Reigning over the dinner table now, she was talking about a woman's preference for home and hearth while men were just as naturally drawn to wilder occupations. Michael continued to smile and nod his head courteously, but in his mind he was counting the days until he could escape the city and his cousin. He disliked Abigail Gunn with an intensity that he found surprising. As a matter of course, he distrusted everyone he met; early in life he had learned that this made living safer and business more profitable. But the distrust he felt toward Abigail was something new to his experience, and he could base it on nothing. She was the daughter of a distant relative; a woman of impeccable grace, a beauty to everyone's eyes but his. Something about her—perhaps it was the faint blue tracery of veins that showed beneath the surface of her thin white skin, or the immense size of her round blue eyes—made him think of a creature that had lived all its life in dark places, and was only now facing the light.

She offered him another slice of trifle but he refused it, and excused himself rapidly from the table. Abigail stared at the door as he closed it behind him. She'd like to scratch his eyes out! How dare he slight her in this way? She was Abigail Gunn, the daughter of Aeneas Gunn! Michael Cameron should have been grateful for her attention; instead he clearly could not wait to escape her company.

Flora Jane reached over and patted her hand. "There, there, child, don't feel bad. The Jacobite cause has got him all distracted. You mustn't take it personally."

On second thought, Abigail wondered if Michael had been anxious to escape Aunt Flora Jane and not herself. That made more sense. The old woman was garrulous and addlepated in the extreme, making the hours in her company stultifying and tedious for Abigail. Aeneas Gunn had told his only child she would be driven to distraction by the old woman; but he told her something else as well: "She's rich as anyone in Scotland, and she's got no one to give it to. You act the part of 'loving Abigail,' and she'll make you rich."

"La, Aunty," Abigail said, laughing shortly. "You are sweet to make all this effort on my behalf. But I'm afraid Captain Cameron is not much taken with my company." Abigail looked sadly down at her hands. The nails were perfect lustrous ovals, of which she was particularly proud. "If you could say something, Aunt Flora Jane, something to encourage him . . ." She let her voice drift off hopelessly; a glistening tear rested in the corner of each eye.

Instantly, Flora Jane was beside her young relative, patting and fussing over her. "My dear child, I had no idea you were being hurt by this, but now I understand perfectly. Of course I will speak to him. Abi, dear, he shall not be allowed to forget his responsibility to the family!" With that she picked up Toby, her lap dog, and marched purposefully from the room.

She found her nephew at a broad table in his sitting room. The mother-of-pearl inlays in the surface were almost entirely obscured by several disorderly piles of papers and documents. He stood when she came in and reached for his coat, which was slung over a straightback chair.

"Don't bother with that. Stay comfortable as you are," she said. Then, after gesturing Michael to be seated again, she ordered a servant to place a comfortable chair next to the desk for her.

"My goodness, Aunt Flora Jane, you certainly have this all worked out. I'll bet there is brandy in your plans as well." The disturbance irritated him; but when he saw that Abigail did not accompany his aunt, he began to enjoy the interruption. He laughed aloud as a servant brought brandy and coffee into his study just as he had predicted. There was even a nibble for Toby. When he had helped himself to a glass of wine, he said, "I am suspicious, Aunt. You mean to get something out of me, I think."

"Why, Michael, how can you!" It was so near the truth that Lady Flora Jane instantly blushed bright.

Michael saw and laughed again. When he spoke his manner was firm but gentle, as if he were enacting the part of lover and father at once. "You must tell me what you want, bonny Flora?"

His flattery kept the high color in her cheeks. When she had gathered her wits, she said, "I must speak to you about your cousin Abigail." Trying to sound firm, she was not very successful.

He laughed again, but this time the sound was without humor. Flora Jane did not notice. She was busy speaking her mind.

"You should know that it is your duty as a Cameron, as my sister's son, to think about the future. I've known you all your life and never, not once, have I seen you shirk your responsibilities. Not until now."

"Go on."

Something in his tone made her look up, but the face she looked into was impassive. She saw neither anger nor censure, and felt free to continue her lecture as if time had turned back and Michael were a rowdy boy again.

"Now it's true that Abigail isn't as young as you might wish. But at twenty-five she has many good years ahead of her, and she deserves to spend them as a wife and mother. She has a right!"

"Surely we both know that life is no respecter of rights," he chided her gently.

"You're speaking of the fact that I never married myself. Well, since you mention it, I will tell you that I was once engaged to be married. But my young man was killed in a storm crossing the channel on Jacobite business, and I would never have anyone after that."

He took her hand. "I'm so sorry, Flora Jane. I didn't mean . . ."

"Of course you didn't, you dear boy. It's all right. It happened a long time ago, and I've mostly forgotten it. But I don't want what happened to me to happen to Abigail. Even more, I don't want my favorite nephew, my own most precious sister's son, to end up like me—old and tired and with no one to talk to in the middle of the night." She began to sniffle. When she had used the hanky she wore tucked under the sash of her dinner dress, she said. "I'll have a wee nip of brandy now, if you don't mind, Michael."

Forward behavior was entirely outside Lady Flora Jane's character as Michael knew it, and he was surprised by her emotionalism. Indeed, he was deeply touched. He had to find some way to explain that would neither hurt her nor hide the truth in any way. But how to begin? Flora Jane helped by saying, "She'd make a fine wife, Michael."

"I agree completely. But not for me, Aunt. I'd kill her—if she didn't get me first." The unkind words were spoken without the guidance of thought. Flora Jane looked stung to the quick.

"You dreadful man! I have never heard such hateful sentiments from you before, Michael. Frankly, I am astonished." She reached for the brandy decanter and poured herself a second, somewhat more generous, drink.

"I spoke hastily, Aunt. But now that it is out, I will own my words. We are unalterably incompatible, and if I brought her into my life I would destroy myself. It is as simple as that."

"How can you say this? What reason . . . ?"

"Trust me, Aunt. I have seen more of the world than you, and the territory of manners is more familiar to me." Michael stared at the glowing brandy as he held it to warm near the candle. He remembered Fiona Macleod.

"My cousin Abigail," he continued after a moment, "thinks only of herself. She's mean-natured and greedy."

But Fiona was not. In the weeks since her disappearance he had become convinced that he had badly misjudged her, and in so doing had betrayed Owen's love and trust. Unlike Abigail, Fiona had an open and generous nature, which he should have recognized immediately. He often wondered what had become of her, and wished her safekeeping wherever she was.

Lady Flora Jane's hands fluttered and twisted about the lacy handkerchief. "What shall I tell her? I brought her here to meet you. I was virtually certain . . ." She shook her head from side to side. "I am a meddling old woman! I ought to be put outside and forgotten. I deserve no better. Michael." She reached over the empty brandy decanter. Clutching his hand she begged, "How can I tell her? What shall I say?"

Flora Jane was unsteady on her feet as he helped her rise and walked her to the door of his study. Under his hands she felt frail and bent, like a stick that might break in the wind. Before kissing her goodnight, Michael told her what to tell Abigail.

Abigail Gunn stayed awake until almost midnight, expecting a visitor to her rooms. She hoped it would be Michael, but even Lady Flora Jane would have been preferable to sitting almost three hours in the same chair before the same fire with the same thought drumming through her head, over and over like an evil incantation.

He'll never let me come home without a husband.

Aeneas Gunn was adored by his daughter. Mary Gunn had become an invalid when Abigail was born, and Aeneas was left to raise the child. In a few years, it became Aeneas's habit to take his daughter with him everywhere. They became a familiar sight as they rode through the countryside, the fair-haired child perched on the saddle before her dark angry father.

No man crossed the path of Aeneas Gunn without first considering seriously how to avoid it. Perhaps this was why no young gallant had ever come courting at the Gunn home. Abigail believed this. But sometimes, late at night, she admitted to herself the truth—that she wanted no other man but her father. She would gladly have gone on as always with him, almost alone in the huge house, a willing slave to care for his every need. But Aeneas Gunn had become a gambler in recent years, and his luck was almost always bad. During her teens and early twenties, Abigail had watched him strip the house of all its valuables to pay his gambling debts. And then he sold his land, which his father and grandfather before him had owned and loved and worked to profit. Finally, when the house stood on a plot too small for serious cultivation, when all the horses but one were gone, and the servants had long since abandoned them, Aeneas called Abigail to him and told her to get a wealthy husband. "I don't care how you do it. Just see he comes back with you." Even more important, he told her, "Get the old woman's money when she dies. Be nice to her and she'll make you her heir. Get a husband and the legacy—or don't bother coming back."

It was as cold-blooded as that.

Michael Cameron was the only man she had ever met who exuded power as her father did. And, like her father, he communicated it to her physically. She felt bigger beside him, more alive. She had just begun to hope that she could please herself as well as Aeneas.

But no one came to her room that night. A deep chill pervaded her body. Even after she had wakened the night girl and made her put warm bricks between the sheets, the bed felt clammy. Abigail drew her knees up to her chest, and felt her hardened nipples press painfully against her thighs. When she was a girl, she had aroused herself by lying so while thinking erotic thoughts of Aeneas. At first the thrilling images in her mind, the brazen words she whispered in the dark, had seemed sinful, and she had tried to force them away; but since she could never do this successfully, she eventually gave up trying. For once, though, she wasn't thinking of Aeneas as her hand stole under her nightdress and caressed her thighs and buttocks. It was Michael whose lips she felt parting the folds of skin, whose tongue stroked and cajoled the moisture from her. Afterward, it was Michael who lay like a pillow in her arms . . .

The next morning, Aunt Flora Jane called Abigail into the upstairs sewing room for a little talk. The bright day filled the closed room with sleepy warmth, and there was a heady aroma of stocks in bloom at the window. Lady Flora Jane was seated on the floor, surrounded by lengths of piece goods.

"Dear child, I have had the most marvelous idea! Come, come, bring a chair. Seat yourself and listen while I tell you of my plan!" Flora Jane, in a bonnet of blue satin trimmed lavishly with Belgian lace, cleared a space, pushed aside bolts of woolen fabric in shades of mulberry and forest green, to make room for Abigail. The young woman was struck to silence by the array of colorful fabrics: bolts of velvet and silk and even cotton. She saw a roll of silk in the drab Gunn tartan.

Flora Jane saw her looking at it. "Do you like it? I had them send it up from Princess Street. They say it is the very latest thing. Shall I order them to make it up?"

"I don't understand, Aunt," said Abigail. She truly didn't. She had come to her aunt expecting the worst news: that Michael Cameron would have nothing to do with her. Instead she encountered this! Could it be a trousseau?

"Tut, tut, of course you don't, my dear. So I shall explain!" Lady Flora Jane clapped her hands together gaily and began the story she and Michael had agreed on. "I went to Captain Cameron last night and we discussed his reasons for not wishing to marry. I assure you, we were tactful. Your name was never mentioned. I must say, after hearing him out, I respect his reservations. The man would drive you mad with his independence and foolish habits." Her sigh was almost audible. "I felt quite dreadful when I realized the mistake I'd made. I knew you'd live to curse my name if you wed him. I couldn't bear that! I started to think how cruel I was to bring you all the way to Edinburgh without cause. And I asked myself what I could do to make it up to you somehow." Lady Flora Jane paused to catch her breath, but not long enough for Abigail to interrupt. "And then it came to me! There will be a marvelous social season in Edinburgh this year, with our own dear Prince Charlie here. And I thought of the eligible young officers and clansmen who will be all about the city. Among them, I know we will find a young gentleman worthy of a woman of quality like yourself. In the meantime, you must be fitted out with the most stunning wardrobe in Edinburgh. Who knows, you may be romanced by the Prince himself. They say he is a bonny one!"

113

Chapter 14

Abigail thought about Lady Flora Jane's scheme all that day and the next. Aeneas Gunn had sent her to Edinburgh charged with two missions: to win a suitable husband and to woo an aging and extremely wealthy old woman. To Abigail's mind, Lady Flora Jane's offer virtually assured the accomplishment of both goals.

In her dressing room on the third floor of her aunt's narrow, many-storyed Edinburgh townhouse, Abigail examined her reflection in the gilt-edged mirror, as she rubbed French creams and emolliants into her skin. She was dressing to see Prince Charles enter the King's Garden beside Holyrood House. Through an open casement near the dressing table, Abigail heard the drone of the pipers practicing for the great moment of the Prince's entrance.

She stared at herself in the mirror. She knew she was a beauty. Such extreme delicacy of coloring was rare, and considered to be a mark of good breeding. Her features were small and regular, apart from her eyes which were florin-sized, and blue as Scotland's bells. Abigail had been peering at her reflection for years. She knew each feature and line; the slightest imperfection showed to her as if magnified. Now she saw how the skin across her cheekbones had grown taut, and lines—invisible to all eyes but her own—were sketched across the planes of her forehead. She was haggard, a sure sign of a woman past her prime of life. At twenty-five Abigail could no longer count on youth to conceal too many frowns and false smiles, too many nights spent weeping or railing at life.

The face in the mirror twisted angrily. The maid—a tubby country lass with neither skill nor the desire to serve—jerked the comb as she dressed her hair. Abigail swung around and hit the girl with the flat of her hand.

"Watch yourself, or you'll be back downstairs peeling potatoes!" Aghast, Abigail looked at the clutch of fine blonde hair gathered in the comb. She must be going bald like Flora Jane. She was withering up, becoming an old woman before her time. The unfairness of it all swelled her breasts, and she wanted to burst from fury.

She would have any man she wanted!

She would take every penny from Lady Flora Jane!

Aeneas would let her come home and he would praise her, love her and hold her again.

Abigail knew in that moment that she would stop at nothing to get what she wanted.

By eleven-thirty that morning, Abigail and Lady Flora Jane were ensconced in a plush open carriage beside the road through Kings' Park. The pampered Toby, a jaunty white cockade decorating his hair, sat fat and happy in his mistress's lap. The September day was cool but bright, and the women were dressed with appropriate elegance in narrow peaked caps and gowns of heavy velvet—black and gray with accents of mulberry lace for Abigail, for Flora Jane dark brown with blue—lavishly flounced and bustled. Around them were ornate open carriages occupied by well-dressed members of the aristocracy and the burgeoning merchant class. The eligible daughters and worldly wives in particular, had made special efforts to catch the attention of the Prince. There was a profusion of bright parasols and feathered hats all along the road.

Around and about these gaudy flowers, pushed and shoved the wilder, weedier residents of Edinburgh. There were no British soldiers, of course. They were all in the dark castle that loomed over the city. The gates were dropped and the commander had sworn never to relinquish his command. Meanwhile, the entrances to the city were left unguarded, and the rabble and common folk were enjoying their holiday

115

from supervision. There were frequent cries of pickpocketing and thievery from the crowds as their numbers swelled and became excited. At several different points along the line, pipers began to play. The result was a joyous cacophony that further stimulated the throng. Even Abigail, who considered herself too well-bred for public displays of emotion, found herself clapping with the music. But the staccato slap of Lady Flora Jane's agitated fan was out of time, and put Abigail's teeth on edge.

To distract the old woman, she said, "I only wish that Captain Cameron could be with us. Don't you think he would enjoy the crowds, the excitement?"

Lady Flora Jane spoke loudly, to be heard over the crowd noise. "He was invited, I assure you, but has no taste for political demonstrations. Besides, he'll be with His Highness later on." She couldn't keep from sounding smug with pride and reflected glory.

"Are they friends?"

"Goodness, I don't think so. Michael's friend Lord George will arrange the introductions and all. I think he's gone off to see Lord George now. Michael's oldest friend, you know." She was distracted by a cheer from the crowd on the south side of the park. Like everyone around them, the women stood up to see the Prince as he approached.

To a homely town like Edinburgh, a hive not noted for its fashion trendsetters, Prince Charles Edward Stuart's appearance that afternoon was almost too magnificent. His blue velvet bonnet trimmed in gold lace sat jauntily on his head, a white cockade lending a royal accent. He wore a tartan shortcoat, red velvet breeches, blue sash, knee-high military boots and silverhilted claymore with unaffected ease, and did not seem to notice the excitement he aroused as he rode into the park on a white horse. To either side of him rode powerful allies: the Duke of Perth and Lord Elcho. The young Prince kept his eyes straight ahead, and his expression was deadly serious. His solemnity awed and silenced the enthusiastic crowd. Everyone who saw him that day was struck by two things: his perfect princely appearance and his grave modesty.

Prince Charles was followed by his several advisors, also on horseback. But between the two groups of men walked a woman, alone. Abigail craned her neck to see the tall copper-haired girl, gorgeously attired in royal Stuart tartan. She walked without looking from side to side, her face as impassive as that of the Prince.

"Who is that girl?" asked Abigail loudly, in order to be heard above the noise of crowd and pipers. Whatever Lady Flora Jane answered, Abigail never knew; for just at that moment, the crowd stilled, and her question rang out loud and clear.

The girl in the procession—now less than a dozen feet away—turned her head, and the women looked at each other. Abigail hated what she saw. The high-colored girl was beautiful in a way that made her seem pallid and almost invisible by comparison. Envy stirred in Abigail and became hate.

Lord George Murray, in his tent just outside the city, was already well into his cups. With him was his friend, Captain Michael Cameron.

"I ask you: how can a man claim to conquer a country without fighting one battle? Not one battle has he had!" Lord George paused to take a drink. He wiped his mouth with the back of his hand. "And what about his advisors: O'Sullivan and Macdonald? One would have my men in Spanish armor, the other is more Frog than Irish, and a schemer into the bargain. The both of them are in this for their own hides." He took another drink and said, "I wonder at tying ourselves so tightly to these foreigners. Who are they, really?"

"Friends or foes?" asked Michael with an ironic tilt of his brow.

Lord George hated those he called foreigners. More than twenty years before he had been exiled to France for fighting in the rebellions of '15 and '19. He believed it was the divine right of the Stuarts to rule. There was a price on Lord George's head throughout the British Isles. Then, on a secret mission to see his father who was dying, he was offered a pardon from the King. He took it gladly and came home to Scotland at last.

Lord George Murray had been back on his lands near Blair Atholl for less than a week when Michael met him. The brave and dynamic warrior became something of a mentor to the boy over the succeeding months that they were together. Since then, Lord George had become settled and somewhat rigid in his ways. Michael had become known for honesty and bold ventures. He kept himself aloof from personal attachments that might make him vulnerable, but his own mortality was not important. He took risks, but always fought to win. In short, he was much the man his mentor had once been. But there was one difference and Michael and Lord George were both aware of it, though neither spoke of it. Lord George was a patriot willing to die for his beliefs. Michael Cameron was in it for profit.

Lord George continued in the same vein. "I hate the sight of that Abbé Butler person he's got with him for a chaplain. The way he prances and minces on his toes in those fancy black tights, I'd swear he's musical."

Michael wondered at the use of the word.

"Oh, you know," Lord George made a ridiculously awkward coquettish movement with his hand and wrist. "Musical."

Michael had heard the same of the Prince and said so. "I hear he has no taste for women."

Lord George made the sign of the cross. "Forgive me, Michael, but that would be too much to bear just now. And I withdraw my comment about Abbé Butler. I wouldn't want it said that I spread dissension among our band. Not now, when we need all the talent and luck we can muster." He finished his glass, and stared at the empty bottle. For a moment Michael thought he was asleep. Then the older man went on, "There's a woman traveling with him now."

"I'm glad to hear it. French, I suppose?" Michael stood up and made preparations to leave.

"No, she's as Scottish as you and I. That's the trouble." Murray stroked his cheek thoughtfully. "I canna tell you how it was they came to meet, but I do know that one moment she wasn't there and the next she was. Whatever passed between them, it took no more than an afternoon."

"An enterprising young woman!" laughed Michael, his hat in his hand.

"But not so easily classified, my friend," retorted George Murray. "Their relationship is distinctly odd. Distinctly." The men shook hands at the awning of George's tent. The general looked up and saw a cloudless midafternoon sky. "I'll say one thing. The weather's a deal better here than further back along the road. Perhaps our luck is turning. When do you meet with His Highness?"

"This evening just after six. At Holyrood House." A young liveryman in a tattered Sutherland brought Michael's horse.

"I pray you find our Prince well, and not too puffed up from his triumphant entry." Lord George gestured up toward the dark presence that was Edinburgh Castle. "Until the British are out of there, we are not triumphant. Merely tolerated."

When he left Lord George, Michael walked up the hill and through the city gates to the part of Edinburgh that was entirely within the shadow of the giant fortress. Here, it was impossible not to feel the brooding presence of the immense stone structure. The fact that the castle belonged to the English despite Charles Edward Stuart's residency at Holyrood Palace seemed to underscore the strange ineptitude of this latest Jacobite rebellion. Michael would meet with the Pretender later that day, and as he wandered in and out among the alleys and wynds of Edinburgh City, he tried to decide what his answer would be when Charles made his inevitable request for help.

Edinburgh! Michael both loved and hated the place. It was filthy, and stank both day and night of what locals euphemistically called "the flowers of Edinburgh"—the human excrement that was nightly dumped unto the streets. Though townspeople burned special brown paper to neutralize the odors and scavengers cleared the streets most mornings, the cramped little city still reeked foully, and pedestrians watched the cobbled pathways carefully.

The city was gloomy, with narrow ten and twelve-story buildings built hard against one another. There were no gardens such as surrounded Lady Flora Jane's home outside the walls, no parks or distinguished public buildings such as Michael had seen in other capitals. The main street—Cannongate—was crowded with townsfolk: sweeps, fishwives with heavy creels, water carriers, peddlers pushing barrows, curtained sedan chairs and livestock—pigs, goats, cattle, a few of the curlhorned sheep that had recently been introduced to the Highlands.

One has only to visit this city to know Scotland is a backward country, Michael thought. Would matters be improved if the Hanover dynasty toppled? Would the Stuart influence make Edinburgh as gracious as Paris? Would the abysmal poverty of the people be eradicated; would the sunlight of a new day reach and warm every dark corner?

Michael shook his head as he walked along, his hands shoved deep into the pockets of his fawn trousers. War, he thought, was simply war, and nothing could be guaranteed except that innocent folk would die. Knowing this, was there any good reason for him to support the Pretender?

When he passed out of the city walls, Michael Cameron was no closer to an answer than when he had entered an hour before.

That evening, at Holyrood Palace, Michael was ushered into a large cold reception room with walls three storys high and highly polished green marble floors. At a great height were narrow windows, cut in the three-foot stone through which bands of late afternoon sunlight were streaming. But the brilliance was too far up to warm the room. As he approached the Prince, Michael chafed his hands together and thought longingly of his gloves, tucked neatly into the pommel of his saddle.

Prince Charles was seated at a dark carved table. A servant hovering nearby brought a chair and, after the proper civilities had been observed, Michael was seated opposite the Prince. They chatted for a moment about trivial subjects of common interest: hunting, horses, the sea.

"I have need of a man like you, Captain Cameron."

"Thank you, Sir." Michael found it easy to sit like this, legs crossed casually at the knee, slumping comfortably against the flexible wicker-backed chair. It was too easy to treat this Prince as merely a good-natured acquaintance. Though there was a picture-book quality of princeliness about Charles Stuart, Michael did not feel the charisma he knew most Kings and Princes must possess in order to rule successfully.

"As you know, King Louis has guaranteed French troops to support the clans and other loyalists in our just cause. But those men and arms are doing me no good in France. The French captains fear running the British blockade. Louis holds them back, waiting for the perfect moment." Michael looked the Prince squarely in the eyes, tried to read what that blue gaze told him. Beneath a monstrous arrogance, he discerned uncertainty and fear.

120

Careful, he told himself.

"I am told by Lord George Murray that you are an astonishingly able captain, virtually fearless when the stakes are high enough." The Prince paused. "Do you agree with that assessment of your character, Captain Cameron?"

"I am that. And more, Your Highness."

Charles laughed. "How Scottish all your answers are. You are a man of few words, Captain."

Though this had not occurred to Michael before, it seemed as true as any other judgment on himself. Prince Charles was a different type, however; he talked of this and that, taking a long time to reach what was, finally, his point.

"I will reward you well for breaking the blockade and bringing me the men I need. When I am King . . ."

"Your father will be King first will he not, Sir?" Michael could not resist the offhand comment.

"Of course, but after that. When I am King, I will see to it that you are given money enough for a dozen new ships. I will have you for director of my navy!"

This peacock Prince was laughable. Pray God his father lives a long time, Michael thought.

"Well, Sir," said the Prince in summation, entirely oblivious to the effect his grandiose and slightly bombastic words were having on Michael Cameron. "Will you help me and in so doing aid both yourself and your countrymen?"

Michael considered for a moment. Would it be worth the risks to help the Prince? What he finally decided, he did for his old friend George Murray, and not from any sense of personal conviction.

"I will sail to France for you, Your Highness," he said. George would be pleased and, if the Jacobites won their conflict with the Hanovers, Michael would be a rich man. He didn't want to be Secretary of the Navy or anything else, but a friend in London could be a great help in touchy matters of trade.

Prince Charles was visibly relieved. He needed this cool, chiseled-featured man from Skye. A great deal depended on Captain Cameron. With his support finally settled, the Prince relaxed a little and became lighthearted. He could see that his cheerfulness irritated Captain Cameron, but that was immaterial to Charles. He had grown accustomed to the fact that there were some men in the world who simply did not like him, and only attempted to disguise the fact because of his rank and their dependency on his good favor. Charles told himself he didn't care if Cameron liked him or honored him or even knew his name.

The Prince had his mind on someone else.

"Cameron," he said, prompted by the wanderings of his mind, "You have an aunt of some position here in the city. Is that correct?"

"My aunt is Lady Flora Jane Campbell, Sir."

"I dislike the name!"

"Forgive her for being a Campbell, Your Highness. I assure you she is a devoted Jacobite despite her name." Prince Charles and his crusade appealed to Lady Flora Jane's romantic nature.

"I accept your assurances, Captain. And wonder if I might confide in you."

Now Michael was truly puzzled. "What has my aunt to do with this, Sir?"

"In a few days, a friend of my family will arrive from France. He is an Italian Prince whose Stuart ties go back some considerable time. He must have a residence that is apart from the army and from me. It must be some place reserved and respectable. There is also a young woman."

Chapter 15

From her room in Lady Flora Jane Campbell's home, Fiona could see down the hill to Holyrood Palace where Prince Charles was in residence. Beyond, she saw the abrupt rise of the rock-crowned hill, known—for reasons lost in antiquity—as Arthur's Seat. Homesickness and a yearning for Skye overcame her when she let her gaze linger on this unexpected bit of Highland scenery thrust up from the midst of the plain. She yearned for a day, uninterrupted by Princes or problems, when she could vanish into the folds of that hill and lie amid the heather and larkspur and stare up at the clouds going by.

But that was impossible. There *was* the Prince, and there *were* problems . . .

She stepped back from the window and surveyed the bedroom to which she had been brought in the early afternoon. It was beautifully appointed in dark wood and sumptuous fabrics. Michael Cameron's home on Skye had had a similar elegance; but her stay in that home was now so distant, nearly crowded out by memories of more recent events, that she could remember neither the look of the room nor of Michael Cameron himself.

Even Owen had, in only a few months, become a dim memory. She tried to recall his face now, as she stared at the plush swirled carpet at her feet. She screwed her eyes tight and made fists of her hands, but the image of her former beloved was persistently elusive. In the end, her eyes smarted with tears; she threw herself on the satin-covered bed and sobbed.

After a while, she convinced herself that weeping was a waste of energy. She stopped, wiped her eyes on the hem of her woolen skirt, then proceeded to pace the bedroom floor, her mind trying to sort through the confusing tangle of events that had dominated her life since the fateful meeting with Prince Charles.

Coming over the rise, the storm to her back, free at last of Lejeune's Diversions, she had been ready to dance, to romp along the road. Her thoughts had been wild and free; yet she was not astonished by, or afraid of, the man she encountered on the road before her. Nor had there been any doubt in her mind who he was. Since that meeting, she had wondered how she had recognized Prince Charles Edward Stuart when she had never before met the man, or even seen his picture. He was dressed as a common Highlander in kilt and broughams and shortcoat; all that had denoted his royalty had been the blaze of Stuart tartan. Scotland was full of Stuarts, however. It might have been any Highlander caught in the storm that cracked and boomed about them. Yet she recognized the Prince.

And her destiny . . .

A deep frown creased Fiona's smooth brow. She thought sometimes she must be half-crazy. Still, in the privacy of her own thoughts, she could not ignore the fact that when she saw Prince Charles she knew him, and knew also that it was her destiny—decreed for her by fate or enchantment or the will of God—to be with him until the Jacobite cause was finished.

In a way she was still afraid to understand, the Prince and her dream were connected. Again she recognized a kind of supernatural power in herself, which permitted her to know, beyond any doubting, that this was so. During the past several days of traveling with the Prince's entourage, the thoughts of what lay ahead—the dying and disappointment—threatened to overwhelm her. It was like being caught up in one of the tremendous storms that had ravaged the countryside that summer. The forces were so great and terrifying that it was no good looking for cover—nothing would protect her. No good crying out—no one would hear.

Was it possible—as it seemed—that the fate of the Scots was her personal responsibility? She must warn the Prince that his cause was destined to fail; she must urge him to return to France and await a more fortuitous moment. But when she tried to answer the question that she knew must come—"How do you know all this?"—she was struck dumb. Who would believe a girl and her dream, who would listen to her talk of destiny?

A polite little servant, with masses of flaming hair and a smug brown-freckled face, informed Fiona that tea would be served in the front downstairs drawing room in a half-hour. Fiona had already met Flora Jane Campbell. At this tea she would meet the others in the house. Somehow, she would have to be agreeable despite the worry in her mind; somehow, she would have to keep from making a fool of herself in Edinburgh society.

She brushed through her thick russet-gold hair, tied it at the nape of her neck as befit a girl of seventeen and touched her lips and brow with *eau de cologne*. In the oval mirror that stood in an ornate oak stand near the door to her dressing room, Fiona could see that the Stuart tartan dress the Prince had provided for her was becomingly simple. Nevertheless, she knew she would feel awkward and unattractive in the company that awaited her. Passing through the grand double drawing room doors, she was shown into a splendid room overlooking the garden and filled now with bronze afternoon sun, which highlighted every brightly waxed surface, every stroke of gilding and crystal facet.

"My dear," said Flora Jane Campbell, coming to her with hands outstretched. "You are rested now, I trust, and prepared to share with us some of the astonishing details . . ."

"Fiona!"

She looked up and saw Michael Cameron standing near a walnut desk. The Cameron tartan kilt and grey shortcoat emphasized his manly physique, and he was even more handsome than she remembered. He had been signing something, and the quill in his hand dripped ink onto the blotter as he stared at her.

"You know each other, Nephew?" Lady Flora Jane asked with surprise.

"After a fashion, yes. We know each other."

Fiona conquered the desire to run from the room. Somewhere, she found the dignity of demeanor she needed to get through the moment. She held her head erect, her expression impassive, and stood immobile, like a statue. Michael Cameron could not take his eyes from her.

Lady Flora Jane seemed to know how difficult it was for Fiona to behave normally in such an unfamiliar setting. For a while there was polite conversation about the weather, the food, the entertainments planned for Prince Charles's stay. Fiona was grateful for the inconsequential chatter. She listened carefully, nevertheless, hoping to learn all she could.

Prior to this moment, Fiona had spent her life in cottages and wagons, always under primitive conditions. The attractiveness of the drawing room, the richness of its appointments, the assured manner of Abigail Gunn as she poured tea from a silver service and the incredulity of Michael Cameron's expression all conspired to leave her tongue-tied and anxious. She felt herself a simpleton.

She glanced at Michael Cameron.

He was staring at her. She blushed and looked away, but could not forget the expression on his face. Puzzled, angry, worried: she was not sure which of these words best described the way he watched her. Perhaps none of them were accurate, but she was too shy to look at him again.

Outside the double doors there arose a commotion. Michael was just going to investigate, when the doors opened and in strode the Prince.

Abigail and Flora Jane bowed deeply to the young man who was now, in the name of his father James, the head of government in Scotland. Michael Cameron dipped his head politely but somewhat coolly, while Fiona sat still, a plate of cake and tarts on her lap, a teacup balanced precariously in her hand. She tried to stand, but there was nowhere to put the plate and, besides, she couldn't curtsey holding a teacup. She blushed at her own awkwardness. The Prince was looking at her; when he spoke it was as if no one else were in the room.

"I had thought you would be different seen here, in a conventional setting. But I was wrong. I was wrong." The handsome young Prince shook his head in wondering disbelief. He had expected—half hoped, really—that seeing Fiona in civilized surroundings would dispel the strange power she possessed to move him. Instead, he found that nothing had changed. Despite crystal and silver and plush elegance, Fiona Macleod still seemed to carry with her, like a crown, the spirit of the Highlands, of all the Scots themselves. "I salute you, miss!" With a flourish he doffed his blue velvet balmoral cap, and bowed like a courtier.

This unlikely behavior from the man who would one day be King had a confusing effect on the gathering in the drawing room. Michael Cameron turned away. Lady Flora Jane was delighted and giggled like a schoolgirl; fiddling nervously with the ringlets of her high white wig, she called for more tea and cakes, and begged the Prince to be seated. Abigail Gunn breathed deeply several times to overcome her outrage that someone like Fiona should be given special honors by the Prince. She saw Michael Cameron looking at Fiona with a puzzled expression. This further outraged her. Fiona got all the attention although she, Abigail, was just as bright and fair as the Highland girl: "I had not expected to find you here, Captain Cameron," said Prince Charles a little coolly. "After our conversation, I thought you would be on the road. I pray you will not tarry long about my business."

"Little would be accomplished by my hasty departure, Sir.

My ship is in Campbelltown and will not be seaworthy for several days. Furthermore, had I left immediately upon your arrival in Edinburgh, I fear I would only have drawn attention to myself. I prefer to travel unnoticed. I am sure you understand and agree, Sir."

"It is wise to be careful, of course. I agree. But this is a time that calls for bravery and daring, Captain Cameron. That is why I asked you to assist us." There was a pouting note of censure in the Prince's voice. "Perhaps your reputation is a trifle exaggerated?"

"Oh, my, no, Your Highness," put in Abigail, seeking to ingratiate herself with Michael. "If my cousin Captain Cameron is assisting you in any way, you may be sure the Jacobite cause is in the best of hands." She smiled at Michael, and he dipped his head in recognition of her praise. Abigail thought of saying something more in an effort to win a greater response from him, but she had no opportunity.

Lady Flora Jane rang the bell beside the tea table. "I'll just have some brandy sent in, Sir, and then you and Captain Cameron may be alone together. I'm sure you have much to discuss that is not the business of womenfolk." She stood up and straightened her bustled skirt. "Come along Abi, Fiona, we will . . ."

"I would prefer Miss Macleod to remain here with me, Lady Flora Jane," said the Prince.

Flora Jane looked doubtfully from His Highness to Fiona, but said, "As you wish, Sir."

She and Abigail were at the door when the Prince added, "I cannot thank you enough, Lady Flora Jane, for your hospitality to my friends. Prince Gabriello Franco will arrive sometime tomorrow. I must say again how grateful I am to you for your willingness to share your home with not one but two strangers. I shall remember your kindness."

Lady Flora Jane's face turned rosy with pleasure. "It is the least I can do, Your Highness," she said, curtseying out of the room.

The praise was enough to take her mind off the peculiarity of the Prince wishing to share his campaign secrets with a girl. Abigail, on the other hand, was not so easily distracted. For some time after leaving the drawing room, her thoughts remained there, centered not on the Prince or on Captain

Cameron but on the girl, Fiona, for whom Abigail had already developed a passionate dislike.

When the women were gone, Prince Charles spoke to Michael forcefully. "There is no time to lose, Captain! Quite frankly, I cannot understand your diffidence in this situation. Unless I have men and arms from France, I cannot possibly move into England."

"You mustn't go!" Fiona's words, spoken without thought, astonished even herself.

"I beg your pardon?" The Prince looked at her, disbelieving his own ears.

Michael, too, stared incredulously.

"There is danger for you, Highness. And for all the Highlands. All of Scotland."

The Prince laughed and touched her lustrous hair briefly, affectionately. "Your concern is laudable, Fiona. I bless you for the way you care for me and for my people. Of course there is danger. But I am not afraid. Nor am I less than equal to the challenges ahead. We have both luck and courage, and a righteous cause. You must not fear."

Ruefully, Michael added, "It will take more than luck and courage to defeat the British."

"And that is where you come in! Luck, courage and French soldiers fighting beside brave Scots. That's what we need! With those ingredients, we cannot fail. It is my destiny to sit upon the English throne, but I cannot do it alone!"

Michael cringed at the word destiny. It had a romantic quality that worried him. A soldier, a King, must be hard-headed and rational. Now here was Charles Edward Stuart, claiming that destiny combined with luck and valor would be enough to make him King. It boded ill for Scotland.

Michael looked down at Fiona. Whatever she was to the Prince, she had not forsworn honesty. Were they lovers? Was this story of Fiona's mystical talismanic quality merely an elaborate lie to conceal an illicit liaison? He tried to believe this. It was, after all, the simplest solution.

But Michael remained unconvinced. Looking at Fiona, he saw nothing of the worldly woman who beds a Prince for entertainment and advancement. Had it been Abigail whom he suspected, he would quickly have concluded they were lovers. Fiona, on the other hand, was innocently candid in her expressions; she was just a girl come down to Edinburgh to establish her rights in a matter of property, as she had told him so many weeks before. Just a girl and nothing to him—despite what she had somehow become to Prince Charles.

Book Five

THE CAPTAIN'S LOVE

Chapter 16

Late the following day, Lord George Murray paid a visit to his friend Michael Cameron.

Michael was glad for the distraction offered by the visit. After retiring to bed the night before, he had been unable to sleep until, near dawn, he heard the rain begin; its gentle voice had lulled him into drowsiness and, at last, a fitful sleep.

He had been thinking of Fiona, wondering what to make of her strange appearance. The girl's beauty and composure upset him, made him doubt all his memories of her. It was not so hard to understand why Prince Charles saw in her a symbol of all the Highlands. She was unmistakably a Celtic lass, and when she spoke her voice carried the music of the far islands in every inflection. There was something, Michael had to admit as he tossed and turned sleeplessly, beguiling about Fiona.

She is nothing and no one, he told himself repeatedly, as if the repetition itself might hasten sleep. But instead, it only seemed to make him more wakeful and, eventually, cross-tempered as well. When he finally slept, he dreamed of her. He saw her in a Stuart tartan running down the slope below his home on Skye. Her hair flamed out wildly in the wind. He felt a surge of desire . . .

When he awakened the next morning he had slept only three or four hours, but it was sufficient time to refresh him. He thought back over the concerns that had occupied his waking and dreaming hours the night before. By the cold gray light of day, it was easy to regard it all as nonsense. Without difficulty, he dismissed Fiona from his mind and greeted his friend Lord George.

The two men talked in Michael's sitting room on the third floor of Flora Jane's home. It was a gray day; a hard cold rain had been falling since before dawn, and the chill now seemed to seep into their very bones. Even their mood was affected. As the morning wore on, Lord George became increasingly bellicose.

"A King may not put himself above Parliament!" the clansman declared, hitting his fist into the palm of his hand. "I've no taste for dictators, Stuarts or no. I tell you, Michael, the man has no idea of how to govern. He only cares for battle—and God knows we have no proof how his skills will be in that!"

"He thinks the war will be won by luck and gallantry."

"Aye. Meanwhile, the Macleods and Macdonalds remain true to Duncan Forbes and the British, and the rest of the clans cannot make up their minds. We have few weapons, virtually no intelligence of the other side; our equipment—such as there is—is old and unreliable. An order was sent out for all Edinburgh to turn over their firearms to the army. The result? Twelve hundred muskets when we need twelve thousand!" Like all men of strong conviction, Lord George did not readily reveal his doubts. Today, however, his concern showed clearly. "You know how I feel about the Stuarts," he continued. "You know no man lives more loyal to the cause than I, but how can we teach this strutting Prince that there is more to governing than ostentatious proclamations?"

There was the sound of a large carriage arriving in the courtyard. Michael went to the casement and looked out.

After a moment he said, "I believe our Italian guest has arrived. Shall we go down to meet him?"

The men exchanged meaningful glances, and without further discussion went downstairs.

Prince Gabriello Franco was very young—no more than

twenty-two or -three—with a smooth unbearded face and large liquid-brown eyes. His mouth was perfectly shaped, with a slight pout to the lower lip. Though tall, he was slender and epicene; and his elegant clothes—dark velvet breeches to the knees, a gold embroidered frock coat and lace cravat, shiny boots and dark hose—were of the finest quality and the closest fit. His long wig was curled in heavy ringlets. Had he been a woman, he would have been described as pretty.

Michael and Lord George stood back from the reception group formed by Abigail and Lady Flora Jane. Fiona was there as well, though hanging back somewhat shyly. Just once, the two men glanced at one another. From that point on their eyes stared straight ahead, as if they dared not look at each other again lest their true feelings be revealed.

Prince Gabriello Franco spoke perfect English, but with a heavy Italian accent.

"Lady Flora Jane," he said, taking her hand and holding it to his lips a moment. "You are so kind to open your charming house to me. I doubted what manner of homes a city gray and dirty as this one might have, but let me say I am entirely content. I know I shall be quite comfortable here."

"Your Highness, you must treat this house as your own home. Whatever you need, it will be my pleasure to provide. Indeed, I will be honored to have you here for as long as you wish to remain."

Franco laughed lightly. "Ah, dear lady, you are completely gracious. However, I assure you I will not be staying long. As soon as Prince Charles has occupied London, I will be going there. Meanwhile, having heard so much of Scotland from His Highness, I could not wait. I had to come here to see for myself."

"I hope you enjoy it here, Your Highness," said Abigail. "With my aunt, let me say how honored . . ."

"Miss Gunn, I believe?" Franco smiled with his eyes as he held her pale hand to his lips. Abigail blushed; his gaze was bolder and more appreciative than any she had encountered before. "I trust we will be companionable here. I have much to learn of Scotland, and perhaps you can educate me." He turned to Fiona, who was standing a little apart from the others, in the shadow of the vaulting central stairway.

"Perhaps now you will be good enough to introduce me to this young woman and the two gentlemen on the stairs."

Franco reached for Fiona's hand. Without premeditation, she pulled it away. A frown of displeasure crossed the Italian's beautiful face. Sneering slightly, he ignored her insult and went to the stairs, where Abigail introduced him to Lord George and Captain Cameron. For a few minutes pleasantries were exchanged; then the foreign Prince was shown to his suite of rooms in a far and extremely private wing of the house.

"I'll just go along with him to make sure the servants behave themselves," said Abigail to Lady Flora Jane. "They've had so little experience with royalty."

And you have, I suppose, Lady Flora Jane almost said aloud. She was fond of her niece Abigail, but there were times when the young woman's behavior startled her. Her eagerness to follow after that prissy young Italian was not seemly. Though Flora Jane adored fine manners and all the fuss and flurry of royalty, she had not been misled by Prince Gabriello Franco. Like most Scots, she disliked elaborate verbiage, and flattery without basis. Though she had never met a man like Prince Gabriello Franco before, she knew better than to trust him. She wished Abigail did not appear so thunderstruck by his appearance; it bespoke a silliness, an unreliability in the young spinster that was unsettling to Lady Flora Jane, who was considering making her niece her heir.

"Well, Michael, I have gone from being a lonely idle old woman to being the mistress of Edinburgh's most elegant hostelry." She laughed, wrinkling the skin around her eyes until the bright orbs almost disappeared. She could tell from her nephew's expression that he was not impressed by the Prince; she liked him the better for that. And Fiona too.

"Come, dear girl," she said, taking Fiona's arm. "Let us leave Captain Cameron and Lord George to discuss their business. You and I will have the altogether more enjoyable task of arranging flowers from the garden. Come along, darling Toby!" Lady Flora Jane took Fiona's arm and propelled her out of the entry.

When the women were gone, Lord George walked to where a servant waited patiently, his coat and cane in hand.

"I will be off, Michael. I must try to find out what General Cope is up to. This army of mine cannot hold together much longer without a fight." Lord George sighed. In the pallid light of the doorway he looked gray and lined.

"A victory you mean."

Lord George sighed again. "Aye, 'tis a victory we need. But I'm not at all sure that is what we will get!"

In the garden room at the back of the house, Fiona and Lady Flora Jane stood side by side at a high table, arranging a mass of garden flowers in several crystal and china bowls. The blossoms had been picked before the rain and kept in jugs of cool water awaiting Lady Flora Jane's careful ministrations. Though she had no general love of domestic duties, there were a few that pleased the old woman. Flower arrangement was one of these, and consequently the garden that surrounded her house was, in the summertime, like a bouquet. Pansies, dahlias, roses and a dozen other floral varieties bloomed profusely, rooted in the black Scottish soil, watered by the dependable almost daily rain, nourished by the long hours of daylight.

The garden room was Lady Flora Jane's haven; she went there to work with the flowers and to think as well. Surrounded by nature at its loveliest, she could generally still her most turbulent thoughts and answer questions that, in other rooms at other times, would thoroughly perplex her. She was troubled this day.

Speaking to Michael, she had called her home Edinburgh's most elegant hostelry. She had been making a joke, of course; but there was some truth in her words, if not in her manner of expression. She was not sure she liked filling her house with strangers. Prince Franco, in particular, would grate on her nerves if she were forced to socialize with him too often. Knowing this, she resolved to leave the Italian Prince to his own devices; better, she would encourage Abigail to act the hostess where he was concerned. Ruefully, Lady Flora Jane admitted that her niece would know how to make the most of the opportunity. With this thought she was reminded of her lack of an heir.

Wealth was a burden for Lady Flora Jane Campbell. Upon the early death of her sister, Michael Cameron's mother, she had been left as the only heir to her father's enormous estate. He had always stated that his girls were equal to anyone's sons in honor and blood; and on his death bed his only advice had been that she not let her wealth be taken from her by cunning. As she snipped the long-stemmed yellow roses and passed them to Fiona to remove the thorns, Lady Flora Jane recalled the day her father died. She remembered clearly how he had raised himself on his elbows to emphasize the point. "Give the money and the land away if you wish, Flossie. That is your right. But beware of those who try to steal it from you with their smiles."

Lady Flora Jane had never forgotten her father's good advice. She wondered now if she had been on the verge of making a terrible mistake with Abigail Gunn. The young woman's eagerness to ingratiate herself with Franco struck Lady Flora Jane as conniving and flighty; and she didn't like the way she danced off up the stairs, ordering the servants about as if she were assured of being lady of the house one day.

"Watch your finger, lass," she cautioned Fiona as she passed her one especially daggered stem. "And if you will hand me that crystal vase, I shall put all of these in water and then you may take them up to the drawing room and put them on the harpsichord. You have an easy way with blossoms, Fiona. Did you have a garden at home?"

Fiona laughed and then quickly apologized lest her new friend think her rude. "Our only garden had potatoes in it, m'lady. But above our cottage the hillside bloomed with wildflowers from May until October. You might say, I suppose, that we had no need of cultivated flowers."

"Ah, I remember the house where I grew up. There were wildflowers there too." Sometimes, I wish I had never left the west, she thought. "What business brings you to Edinburgh from such a place as Skye?"

Fiona was happy, even eager, to talk about what had brought her to Edinburgh. She left out some things—Uncle Rob, her dream, Madame Lejeune's sordid proposition—but she did not hide the truth about Owen or her resentment of her own dependency on Michael Cameron. Despite its unorthodoxy, the story touched Lady Flora Jane's tender and romantic heart. "I will inform my solicitor of your needs. I am sure he will find the documents you require and set one of his clerks to copying them, so you will have what you need when you leave Edinburgh. But I hope that will not be too soon. I enjoy your company in the house, Fiona. You may stay with me for as long as you like."

The invitation might have been dangerous, had Lady Flora

Jane not been so sure of who and what Fiona was. She was wise enough to know that the girl's story had been edited; she could even use her imagination and intelligence, both of which she had in good measure, to fill in some of the missing details. Nevertheless, Fiona impressed the older woman greatly. She could not precisely define what quality set Fiona apart from the common run. Perhaps it was her innate dignity. Or was it the look of flinty determination that Lady Flora Jane saw in the amber eyes whenever Fiona spoke of her home and what she required to secure it forever as her own? Determined yet dignified, unquestionably beautiful—Flora Jane acknowledged that Fiona was all of these and much more.

Fiona took the vase of roses up to the drawing room as she had been directed. As she passed through the entryway, she met Michael Cameron, his gloves and coat in hand, preparing to go out for the afternoon. She nodded politely, curtly, not wanting to speak to him; but he followed her into the drawing room and shut the panelled rosewood doors behind him.

"I will not belabor the point, Miss Macleod," he said in his sternest voice. "However, in the best interests of my aunt, I must remind you that she is not a young woman; and should you decide suddenly to disappear without a trace as you did at Mallaig, you would cause her a great deal of concern and possibly even endanger her health." Fiona turned, facing him, with her back to the harpsichord. She tried to interrupt, but Michael held up his hand to silence her. "I really do not care to know, nor is it my business to know, what happened in Mallaig. Nevertheless, Lady Flora Jane is my legitimate concern. If you do anything . . ."

"How dare you!" Fiona interrupted angrily. "Please remember! I did not ask to be put in your charge in the first place. I did not ask to be brought to this house. I emphatically did not wish or ask to make your acquaintance a second time. But now I am here, and your aunt—who is a gracious and kindly lady—has offered to extend her hospitality as long as is required for me to obtain the documents of ownership I am seeking." She narrowed her luminous eyes and spoke slowly, emphasizing each word as though she were speaking to someone with the wit of a child. "I repeat that I have requested none of this assistance and concern. You may think what you wish of me—that is your right, for I am nothing and no one to you. But your implication that I would hurt a gracious lady like your aunt is unfair, Captain Cameron. Unfair!"

"You must admit, Fiona, that you have not brought happy times to my family. Owen . . ."

"I loved him! If I brought him pain, if I hastened his death, it was in no way intentional. God will punish me if I am at fault; but *you*, you have no right to accuse me!" Now her eyes filled with tears, but Fiona blinked them back and bit her lip to keep from saying more.

Michael wondered, Why am I trying to hurt this girl? Fiona could not be blamed for anything that had happened. He was a rational man, who had tried all his life to avoid sentimentality and the romantic daydreaming he associated with old women like his aunt. He knew there was no one who in and of himself carried bad luck. Still, the lives of some were dogged by ill fortune. They dragged it after them like a disease, infecting everyone they came in contact with. Was Fiona such a person?

They stood across the drawing room from one another without speaking. The rain had stopped at last, and the room was bright with sparkling watered sunlight. For Michael it was a moment of sudden unwished-for clarity, in which his own thoughts and motives, as if previously obscured by clouds and rain, became instantly clear. He recognized what he had hidden from himself, that Fiona attracted him against his will; that his ostensible disdain for her was only meant to hide the fact that he wanted her, and resented his ward for loving her first.

Chapter 17

For Fiona as well, the moment brought clarity where before there had been confusion. Michael Cameron did not hate her, did not truly blame her for anything that had happened. He did not even doubt her reasons for becoming involved with Prince Charles. She saw in that moment of vision, when the light in the drawing room had an almost crystal brilliance, that his stern reprimands, his outrage, were intended to disguise his true feelings. What these feelings might be, she could not tell; but she saw in his expression the beginnings of an acceptance that she had not known since Owen had loved her for herself alone, requiring nothing more.

The meeting in the drawing room, though it was over in only a few moments, had an exhilarating effect on Fiona. There was a strange feeling in her stomach, a kind of weightlessness that verged on nausea, and yet was pleasant. As the day lengthened the sensation diminished; she regretted its passing and wondered what it meant.

Like most of the houses in Edinburgh, Lady Flora Jane Campbell's was tall and narrow, with only a few rooms on each of the four floors. On the ground level were the kitchen and laundry rooms, the garden room, the scullery and the servants' quarters. On the second floor were located the receiving rooms, and on the third and fourth the bedrooms and sitting rooms. Fiona's room was off the long third floor corridor, as were Abigail's, Lady Flora Jane's and Michael's. Many years before, Lady Flora Jane's father had built an addition, a clumsy-looking two-story wing intended to provide him with a retreat from domesticity. Prince Gabriello Franco had been given an elegant suite of rooms there, in deference to his elevated position.

It seemed a good arrangement to Michael, although that evening, as he sat alone in a downstairs drawing room enjoying one whisky too many after the rest of the household had retired, he wished the Italian Prince were somewhere else entirely. Michael was devoted to his aunt, and found himself unwilling to leave her alone with both Abigail and Franco in residence. He doubted that the elderly spinster had the sophistication to deal with two whom he instinctively knew to be cunning and greedy. He poured another finger of whisky, thought better of it and poured the amber liquid back into the decanter on the low table before him. The color made him think of Fiona.

No question, he must get away from her. The scene in the drawing room that afternoon had unnerved him, made him doubt his convictions in a way he hadn't since youth. He was not falling in love with her, of course. That was impossible. He was not averse to marriage and supposed that at some point he would wed a suitable young woman who would provide him with children and a comfortable home without otherwise much disturbing his bachelor life. But to think of marrying Fiona—a peasant with a short quick temper and a will to match his own! A man would have to be a fool—or a boy like Owen—to love a woman like that, he told himself. It didn't matter that she was beautiful. Michael had traveled throughout Europe and knew dozens of women of equal beauty. But there had been something absent in them that he perceived in Fiona and, despite his resolve, he did not think he would soon get the young Skye lass out of his thoughts.

The hour was late. He climbed the steep central staircase, taking special pains not to awaken the sleeping household. At the head of the stairs, as he turned toward his room, he heard something that made him stop and approach Fiona's door. She seemed to be talking to herself. Then she cried out.

It was a sound so small and helpless that had he not been standing right at her door, Michael would not have heard it at all. It was followed by another cry, and then the words, "over, it is over!" were followed by bitter racking sobs. Without pausing, Michael pushed open her bedroom door.

She did not see him at first. She was sitting up in the large platform bed, clutching the satin coverlet to her breast, sobbing helplessly.

"Fiona." He stood in the middle of the room, holding his candle high, helpless and awkward as a boy, wishing he had not come, knowing he had no choice.

When she saw him, she reached out her arms; and he went to her, not as a lover, but to console her and drive away the horrible imaginings of the night. Sitting beside her on the bed, he held her close until, at last, she could stop crying.

"I'm sorry," she said, as if she had disturbed him.

"Don't apologize. You had a terrible dream." She shuddered in his arms, and he tightened his embrace. The skin beneath his hands was silken, and her hair smelled of grass and limes. "Sometimes it helps to talk about it. Can you do that?"

She was dazed, still under the spell of her dream, fighting her way up toward the candle of consciousness. She wanted to speak, to tell him of her ominous dream; but she had kept it within her for so long that the words came haltingly. She heard herself stammering illogically and stopped her explanation.

"You have a dream that repeats itself. Go on, Fiona. If you speak of what you see in this dream, I believe it will lose its power to affect you. It's not so unusual, you know. From time to time, I would suspect most people dream the same thing over and over. It means nothing unless you let it weaken you."

"You have had such a dream?" She was incredulous. Always Fiona had assumed that her experience was unique. To hear otherwise was like receiving a reprieve from destiny. The feeling of relief was short, however. As she described what she saw in her dream—the moor, the stones, the bloodstained faces, the dying soldier and his young lover— she watched Michael's face closely. After a few moments, she knew that he no longer regarded her recurring dream as commonplace.

"It means something. I know it does," she said lamely, when she had finished with the details.

She hung her head and looked at the strong long-fingered hands that held her own. The moment of relief was over. She had told her dream, and knew beyond certainty that it was not exorcised. She wished she had kept silent.

"Dreams mean nothing, lass. You know that, though perhaps it doesn't feel that way right now. You're a Skye child: superstition was bred into your bones. Rise above it, Fiona. Dreams and such mean nothing." He went to the sideboard and poured a glass of water for her. When he came back to the bed, she had covered herself with a wrapper and was gazing morosely at her hands. Her expression was sorrowful.

"Do you know who I am?" she asked him, looking up and into his dark eyes directly. "Have you heard of the halfling? The witch Janet Macleod?"

"You are her daughter?" Now it was Michael's turn to be incredulous.

"Aye. I am the halfling they speak of in Borreraig and Dunvegan Town. I am the faery kin."

"Nonsense!" Michael laughed aloud, but grew quickly silent when he saw the expression on Fiona's face. "Forgive me," he said, still wanting to make light of the matter, "but I cannot believe in such things as faery folk and halflings, Fiona. I am a grown man, and if I seek trouble I need not look so far as the supernatural."

She said nothing, but her eyes were eloquent.

"You believe these fanciful stories because you were taught them as a child. You suffered because of the ignorance of the Skye folk, but you need not perpetuate their foolishness. Fiona! It is the eighteenth century. Talk of halflings belongs to the Dark Ages!"

Still she would not speak, and her face showed that his words did nothing to dispel the belief of a lifetime.

Michael touched the cascades of bright hair. It crossed his mind that such extraordinary wild beauty as Fiona's did seem to have an otherworldly quality. It was probably this that had set the townspeople against Janet Macleod. He was glad Fiona had escaped Skye for the larger, less flammable world, and he wanted to tell her this. He yearned, too, to hold her until the lines of concern were gone from her face, the tenseness from her body.

She drank the water he offered and thanked him.

"Will you be able to sleep now?" he asked.

"I think so. The dream does not repeat in the same night. A small blessing, but a true one nonetheless."

"Then I will leave you." Again he felt awkward as a schoolboy, and was irritated with himself for this uncommon feeling.

He bowed stiffly from the waist and hurried into the hall. As he was closing Fiona's door, he looked up and saw his aunt, her head enveloped in a huge frilly nightcap, peering out from her own room.

"It is nothing, Aunt," he hastened to reassure her. "Fiona has been dreaming. I will tell you more in the morning."

Chapter 18

The next morning, Michael and Lady Flora Jane breakfasted alone in her private sitting room. She fed Toby bits of bacon as she scolded her nephew.

"Your behavior last night might have seriously compromised the poor child, Michael. I need hardly tell you that, regardless of your reasons, you had no business being in her bedroom alone, without a chaperone. You should have called me. As a woman, I . . ."

"I offer no excuses, Aunt. I simply did what seemed called for at the moment. The child was suffering."

Lady Flora Jane's kindly face creased with concern. "She is ill?"

Michael considered his answer. "Not ill in the sense you mean it. But she is badly troubled by some experiences in her life, which I believe you should know about before I leave."

He told the story of Janet Macleod and the persistent faery kin myth that was familiar to everyone who lived within the territory of the clan Macleod and Dunvegan Castle. He didn't bother to relate the details of Fiona's dream; it was sufficient to tell Lady Flora Jane that it repeated and that the girl believed it was portentous.

"Poor child! What a dreadful history. It is no wonder that she struck me as most unusual." Lady Flora Jane shook her head sympathetically. "I am gratified to know all this, Nephew. I feel quite warmly toward the girl, and shall do all I can to ease her life."

"I am glad to know that. I must leave, but . . ."

"So soon?"

"I must be about my Prince's business," replied Michael, with a touch of irony.

"You told me it would not be necessary to leave for two or three days. What has changed your mind, Nephew?" She peered at him and under this steady gaze he looked away. "It is the girl, isn't it?"

Michael started to deny, but Lady Flora Jane would not be dissuaded from her conviction.

"She has a winning way, Michael. I will be the first to agree. But you mustn't think of involving yourself with a crofter's daughter. You have said yourself . . ."

He was suddenly irritated with the voluble old woman. "I am an adult male, Aunt; and I intend to provide my own counsel in the matter of Fiona Macleod as I do in everything else." His tone was harsher than he had intended, and Lady Flora Jane's eyes filled with tears. Michael was instantly remorseful. "Forgive me, Aunt, if I seemed unkind. My only excuse is a distracted mind. My leaving has nothing to do with Fiona. I tire of city living and the presence of this new Prince—this Gabriello Franco—disturbs me."

"Then he will go. Why didn't you speak up before, my boy? If I must choose between Prince Gabriello and my darling nephew, can there be any doubt as to my decision? Shall I have him leave today?"

"No, Aunt. Best to leave matters as they are for the moment." Now he chose his words with particular care. "But I must offer you this word of caution. These Italians are . . . not like us. Be careful."

"Now it is my turn to announce my independence," Lady Flora Jane said, a trifle archly. "You think because I am a maiden lady I am not to be trusted in the company of worldly folk, but that is not so. And I beg you to remember that Prince Gabriello is not the only Italian I have met. When I was a girl I spent a winter in Rome with my papa. I can even speak the language a little."

And then there was Abigail. "As for my cousin . . ."

Lady Flora Jane waved his concern away. "I tell you, I am well able to care for myself. You must serve our Prince in your way; I will do so in mine. And if Abi can be of service, then so much the better. It is a wonderful opportunity for her, you know, after all these years with that beast of a father."

Michael sighed. "Of course." He kissed his aunt on the forehead; then, in a rush of unexpected emotion, pulled her up from her chair and into his arms.

She patted his cheek. "You're a good man, Michael Cameron, and a comfort to your old aunty. Go with God, and hasten home to me as quickly as you can. If it is true that the British have made it virtually impossible to cross the Channel, then I shall worry about you constantly."

He shook his finger at her playfully. "That will never do. I have cautioned you to be alert; and if you are always worrying about me, then Heaven knows what might happen right in your own home."

"Don't make me cross, Michael! I am fully capable . . ."

"Of course, Aunt. Of course."

Muddy had packed and brought the valises down to the entrance. While he fetched the horses, Michael went in search of Fiona, and found her in the music room with Abigail. The older girl assumed that Michael had come for her, and was obviously put out when she discovered differently. She lingered, straightening the piles of sheet music on the harpsichord, fussing with the roses, keeping up an idle and—to Michael—infuriating chatter until, at last, he asked her to leave so that he might be alone with Fiona.

When Abigail had departed, the air in the music room still crackled with her hostility. Or was the atmosphere of tension the result of something else?

"I am for Campbelltown now," he told Fiona, standing some distance away. "I have come to say good-by."

Fiona, wearing a simple cotton morning dress borrowed from Abigail, was seated in the sunny window seat, a piece of embroidery in her lap. She wouldn't look at Michael at first, for fear he would see something in her eyes that she knew she must keep secret forever. She could not tell him that after he left her that night she had lain awake until almost dawn, staring at the ornate plaster ceiling over her bed, possessed by a feeling she had known before and had never expected to know again.

"I love him," she had confessed to herself as the tears began. No matter that a few months before she had sworn herself eternally to Owen Hamilton; no matter that Mathilda Duncan had forbidden her to love. "I love him," she had sobbed aloud. Though Michael Cameron thought her a superstitious peasant; though his love was utterly impossible, even more so than Owen's, she loved him and knew she could not stop herself. The feeling she had had for Owen was like a preparation, or practice, for this greater and more frightening emotion.

"I have come to say good-by." Michael said again, stepping closer.

"Campbelltown?" she asked rather stupidly. She could think of nothing to say; but she couldn't let him go.

"Aye," he said.

"You will have fine weather. The sky is cloudless." She looked at him finally. In his smart kilt of red Cameron tartan and tweed shortcoat, silver-buttoned and immaculate, he appeared the perfect example of Scottish manhood. Her heart raced when she looked at him, and the embroidery needle slipped between her damp fingers. "You may have rain later, of course." She cursed herself for an ignoramus. How could a man like Captain Cameron care for anyone whose conversation was so unspeakably silly? But she couldn't stop. "On Skye I could predict the weather hour to hour, but here in Edinburgh I am always surprised. You will not have rain today, though. The sky is clear."

She burst into tears.

Throwing down the embroidery, she ran into his arms.

He held her for a long time in silence.

"My aunt will care for you while I am gone, Fiona."

"The English may capture you. If they know you are attempting to run the blockade, there will be a price on your head. You could be hurt. Or worse."

"Don't fret about that. I know those waters better than any man alive, I think. The British will never catch me!" She heard the lightness in his voice and realized that he was eager for the challenge, despite his equally obvious desire to stay with her in Edinburgh.

What could she do? What could she say? He was a man and war was in his blood, both his torment and his triumph. For a moment, she felt herself to be part of a tradition as ancient as the tradition of love itself: the parting of lovers on the eve of war—the men trying to disguise their eagerness for the fray, the women ashamed of their tears, their doubts, their disbelief in any cause that makes men murder one another. She thought, in a split second, of all the women who had kept their silence at parting, and had died with their love unexpressed, burning their throats and lips and tongues.

"Think of me while you're gone, Michael," she whispered.

"Of course. And you will think of me. Please?"

"You promise to come back to me?"

"My darling." He buried his face in her hair and drank in the deep sweet aroma of her. Remember this, an inner voice told him. This is everything!

The door to the music room opened suddenly. "Forgive me," said Abigail icily. "I do not wish to intrude upon such a touching scene, but your man, Ezekial Mudd, is waiting, Captain. You must be about the Stuart business."

If he had not been a gentleman, Michael would have pushed her out the door and slammed it with a noise to rock the whole house. Instead, he kept his voice controlled. "Thank you, Cousin Abigail, I will be there shortly. When you leave us, pray close the door behind you."

Abigail's slam was almost as loud as Michael's would have been.

Fiona was wiping her damp cheeks, trying to be brave. Her tough Highland will, which had only a few days before seemed a definite liability in a woman, now pleased him. She would be all right.

"But there is danger here as well, Fiona. You must be careful whom you trust, whom you give your confidence to. I know Prince Charles has formed a special attachment for you, and that will make many people your enemies. You understand that?"

She nodded, wishing him gone as quickly as possible before her show of bravery exhausted her. It was all a ruse; she was not courageous at all. Her heart was breaking, and with each moment the pain grew worse. She told him yes, she understood that there was danger for her in the Stuart camp; but she didn't care at that moment. Compared to what she was feeling now, there could be nothing worse.

Someone pounded on the door of the music room. "Captain," Abigail called, "Mr Mudd is ready to depart."

Fiona and Michael looked at each other and each one, without premeditation, gave a little shoulder shrug. The harmony of this movement, as if they had been practicing together for the moment, came as a surprise; and they laughed aloud and held each other, whispering their farewells again.

On the other side of the door, Abigail heard the laughter and hated them both. For weeks, she had been doing everything in her power to win the heart of Michael Cameron. She had used every charm she possessed and would even have offered him her body had he shown the slightest interest. She would have been willing to risk her virtue for him, and to sacrifice her good name for a few such moments of shared laughter. In her heart something twisted and deformed itself, and the ugliness burrowed deep.

She was her father's daughter, and would be avenged . . .

Chapter 19

Late in September, Charles Edward Stuart ordered a blockade of Edinburgh Castle; nothing and no one was to be permitted in. Colonel Guest had threatened to bombard the city to rubble in retaliation, but so far had not kept his word. The blockade was risky, but Charles knew that his position in Edinburgh—in Scotland itself—would not be secure until the castle was his. He was willing to risk anything to galvanize the patriotism of the clans.

Chafing with inactivity, Charles ordered the army to Duddingstone and moved his own quarters to a village nearby. Now there was nothing more to do but wait for the English General Cope—and the battle that Charles trusted would establish him as the rightful leader of the Scots.

Though Prince Charles and Prince Gabriello Franco met at Lady Flora Jane Campbell's, it was several days before a private rendezvous on Arthur's Seat could be arranged. The autumn day was exceptionally bright and clear, with a flawless sapphire sky that domed the world from horizon to horizon.

The two men walked their horses side by side. Ahead of them rose the long sloping flanks of Arthur's Seat, covered in bracken and purple heather. In the distance, a lake shimmered under the intense blue sky. Behind them lay Edinburgh and the castle; before them stretched a vast unpopulated wilderness. Despite the nearness of the city, the two Princes fancied themselves deep in the reaches of the Highlands, far from castles, crowds and armies. There were no other human beings in sight.

"You are conspicuous in Stuart tartan," scolded Franco affectionately, admiring Charles's dark blue riding costume accented by a wide red plaid across one shoulder.

"And if I am?" laughed Charles, his voice trembling slightly from the excitement he always felt when he was alone with Franco. "Am I not the Prince?"

They laughed together and then, mounting their horses, raced for the lake. As they came near the edge, clouds of startled geese rose and wheeled against the sun, momentarily shadowing the land. Charles shivered, as if a wedge of ice had been held against his back for a moment. A presentiment of doom darkened his thoughts, but soon the deathlike chill was gone, and the day was bright once again. The geese screamed to one another, circled, then settled silently upon the waters of the lake, as if the men had not disturbed them in the first place.

They watched the graceful birds in silence. Charles cast a surreptitious glance at Franco, and the sight of the beautiful young Italian Prince stirred his blood to warmth. Gabriello Franco possessed a dark sensual beauty that left Charles breathless and disarmed, strangely helpless to resist him.

They had met in Italy, when Charles was only fifteen and Franco three years younger. The Italian Prince had been like a gazelle then, lithe and graceful and skittishly beautiful, with immense incandescent brown eyes, like chocolate warmed by generations of Neapolitan sun. His generous pouting mouth had seemed, from the very beginning, made for Charles's kisses. Although he was ashamed of his unnatural appetites, the Young Pretender could not deny his longing to stroke, caress and fondle Franco, as if he were some pretty pet brought to him for entertainment. Charles had not planned to consummate his unbidden passion, but Franco had encouraged him with teasing glances and quick forbidden touches. Though barely out of childhood, the boy seemed possessed by an ancient and cunning spirit. He had a knowing mouth and soft skilled hands that captivated Charles and made him forget everything but Franco. For ten years, Charles had been in a kind of bondage. The trap was set with Franco's wild beauty; the bonds were desire.

From the beginning, Charles had known that it was risky to bring Franco to Scotland. Although their relationship was tolerated in sophisticated European circles, the rough Highland army would quickly disband if the clansmen thought their Prince was unmanly. But more terrible to Charles than the thought of disclosure was the fear that he might lose Franco to one of his countless admirers—both male and female—if they stayed apart.

Edinburgh did not satisfy Franco, and this morning as they watched the last of the geese settle on the water he was petulant and complaining.

"I expected so much more! The city is hardly a capital at all. More like an overgrown market town, with livestock and dung in the street. And my hostess," Franco laughed disparagingly, "a dumpy old dowager if I ever saw one. Her niece is there, however, which relieves the boredom somewhat."

Franco glanced sideways to gauge Charles's response to his mention of Abigail Gunn. He was not disappointed. Charles's face reddened as it always did when he was jealous. It pleased Franco to see that his power over the Young Pretender had not diminished. "You're rather like her, Charles. Both of you so blonde and fair-skinned. Miss Gunn seems quite ethereal, precious as a pearl." Franco grinned. "Don't you agree, my love?"

Charles gritted his teeth. With a few variations, they had enacted this scene before. Charles knew that Franco was going out of his way to make him jealous; he knew he should play a role and assume a bland disinterest. But pretense was impossible. Thoughts of Franco in another's arms drove him almost mad with jealousy.

"Don't tease me, Gabi," he whispered. "You know how I feel about you."

"Tell me, Charles. I like to hear it." Franco leaned from his saddle and placed his hand on Charles's thigh. The slight pressure of his long tapered fingers quickly aroused his companion. Words gushed out of him.

"I love you, Gabi. And if you will just be patient a little longer, when I am King of England you can have everything you want. This Abigail is no one, no one. A squire's daughter. But I, I will be King of England soon."

Franco appeared to think a moment, pouted prettily and laughed; then, with a sudden movement, turned his horse toward the southern slopes of Arthur's Seat. As he galloped away, Charles cried after him, "Gabi, don't go! Stop! Wait for me!"

On the southern slope of Arthur's Seat, with the mountain between them and Edinburgh, the men found a secluded copse of dense scrubby bushes where there were still purple foxglove in bloom and the air was perfumed by heather. They dismounted and tethered their horses.

"I hope you brought us some refreshment," Franco said, as he spread his saddle blanket on the bracken and sprawled comfortably. "I find your Scottish air increases my appetite alarmingly. If I stay here long, I'll grow as fat and lazy as my grandmama." He lay back, stretching his well-modeled body luxuriantly. Across the sky, a lark dipped and turned to its own music.

"I have wine and bread and cheese." Charles spread these gifts before his friend, his expression hopeful as a child's. He wanted more than anything for Franco to be contented and share his fondness for all things Scottish.

"Santa Maria! What these people call bread!" Franco spat out a mouthful. "When you are King, I hope you will have the good sense to import an Italian baker. This glutinous mess makes my gorge rise." The shapely mouth curled disdainfully as he tossed the remainder of his bread into the high grasses.

"I did not think it was so bad," said Charles in half-hearted defense. Franco's criticism always made him doubt his own judgments.

"You were born to this kind of thing, my dear. You can't help it." Franco laughed, drank deeply of the wine Charles offered as appeasement, lay back again and sighed. His eyes closed.

But for the larksong and the brush of the wind through the high grasses, it was utterly silent on the hillside. A rabbit poked its curious head through the bracken, stared at the young men for an instant, then ducked back into hiding. Charles tried to relax but, for him, to be in Franco's company was to be constantly on edge with sexual tension. The truth horrified him, but he thought his love for the Italian Prince was as great as his love for Scotland. In the past, when Franco's perfidy was blatant, Charles had tried to imagine what it would be like to break off their relationship forever. He thought of loving other men, even women, but it was impossible to envisage his body responding to any touch but Franco's. In the end, he learned to tolerate infidelity and insult rather than face the prospect of a life without the beautiful young Italian.

So beautiful. Shyly—after many years Charles was still not sure how his overtures would be accepted—he traced the delicate profile where the heavy brows almost met. He ran his finger along the ridge of the gently molded retroussé nose. Kissing his fingertips, he touched them lightly to Franco's lips. The younger man did not respond.

"Gabi," ventured Charles softly. "We have a little time today and we are very private here."

Franco grinned, without opening his eyes. "Dear Charles, you are utterly predictable."

"Please, Gabi. It's been so long." Charles heard the pleading in his voice and despised himself for it.

With a show of reluctance, Franco sat up and began to remove his boots. "I find these passionate interludes in the wilderness rather tedious, Charles. You know that. You promised me a gala season in London. You said we would be there by Christmas. Are you backing away from your promise now?"

"It takes time. The Hanoverian army . . ."

". . . is mostly in Flanders. It seems to me you should be able to march your greatly touted Highlanders into the center of London without any trouble at all." Franco removed his lace cravat, silken shirt and cotton undervest, and folded them neatly.

"You are so brown, Gabi," whispered Charles, touching Franco's smooth hairless chest. His hand was brushed away.

"Well, of course I am. I told you I would spend the summer in Sardinia. La Contessa was a charming hostess and her palace utterly magnificent. You will excuse me, Charles, but in comparison your Holyrood Palace is quite a barn." He clutched his forearms and shivered exaggeratedly. "Must we, Charles? This climate is not made for . . ."

"Not long, Gabi." Lest his friend change his mind, Charles hurriedly assisted him in removing his fawn breeches. His hands were shaking and, absurdly, he wanted to cry. The tension was almost too much for him, and he was clumsy undressing himself. He was without pride where Franco was concerned; he acknowledged that. Swiftly, fearing the young man's mercurial nature, he embraced him. The smell of tobacco and sweat filled his nostrils; he was aquiver with appetite, scarcely able to control the trembling of his hands as he touched Franco's naked body: the narrow indented hips, the long hard thighs. His lips caressed the flat belly, slipping down to where Franco's manhood drooped unenthusiastically.

"I told you, Charles, it's too cold. One must be warm to be passionate, *caro.*" From his bantering tone, it was clear that Franco was enjoying the moment, challenging his lover to arouse him. Even as he said, "Perhaps another time. When we're in London," his own hands reached between Charles's legs and found him firm and ready. "What have we here?" He laughed, then playfully pushed Charles away. Franco was erect now, heated with his own desire.

Charles half sat up, reaching for Franco, to pull him close again. As he reached, the Prince's eyes stared directly into another pair of eyes only partly hidden by the scrubby bushes.

Charles scrambled up and parted the bush. Standing rigid, as if rooted to the spot by the unwelcome scene, was a Highland boy dressed in the colorful Ogilvy tartan. The boy, no more than thirteen or fourteen and no taller than the Prince's shoulders, carried a brace of rabbits strung together over his arm, and a slingshot rested lightly in his hand. His amber locks curled tightly around his head, and his cheeks glowed ruddy like fire.

His gaze locked with Charles's. The moment seemed to last forever. Charles remembered another such moment when the sky had opened, its flashes of lightning illuminating a lone woman on a knoll, her amber tresses and fiery complexion signaling to him, the Prince, their common bond, their destiny—His destiny, the destiny of the Highlanders.

The boy stared at the two Princes with a look of astonishment. The three of them—the boy and the lovers—stood paralyzed by shock.

"Highness," the boy uttered, and hung his head, his locks falling over his eyes as if to conceal the scene he had witnessed, and his tawny color deepening to a blushing red. Backing up, he turned to flee; the rabbits fell off his arm to the ground.

"Stop him!" cried Franco. "Damn you, Charles, get him!"

Naked, Franco leapt through the bush to give chase to the boy. Charles was the more nimble, and in two steps he was astride Franco, his arm snaking out and striking his lover across the chest.

"Franco, no no!" Charles wound his arms around his lover's lean body, holding him fiercely against Franco's writhings to pull away and give chase.

"That boy is a Highlander," the Prince gasped. "His peasant coloring proclaims him. He is one of Us! His being here is Our sign. It is Our destiny to rule. We cannot hurt Our cause!"

Struggling to get away, Franco scratched and clawed; but the Prince held him in a grip of iron. They swayed and shoved, their bodies glistening from the sweat of the encounter. Finally, panting from their exertions, the lovers fell to the ground together, the duel ending in an embrace.

Franco's eyes were bright with terror and fear and something else—desire. He stretched out his hand and began to caress Charles's manhood, making it hard in spite of everything. "We must not! We cannot!" Charles tried to pull away, but Franco's mouth was hungrily upon him and he swooned back into the bracken, delirious with shame and pleasure.

The Princes rode back to Edinburgh in silence. Charles was stunned by the passion that violence had aroused, first in Franco and then in himself. He tried to recall a time when he had felt the power of Franco's desire as strongly as in those moments after they had struggled together. His lover had been insatiable and, after a moment or two of reluctance, Charles had responded wholeheartedly. He still tingled with residual excitement, wanting his young lover more than ever.

At the pond, their horses standing head to head, they tried to say good-bye. Charles was tongue-tied.

Franco spoke sulkily. "You're angry with me, Charles. You are punishing me with silence. I thought you loved me."

"I do, Franco. But . . ."

"If you want me to leave Scotland, I will." Franco held his breath. It was risky, but he knew Charles's weaknesses well. "If I am to be blamed for loving you . . ."

Charles quickly assured him that this was not so. "I blame you for nothing. If it is my destiny by divine right to be King of England, then I must purify myself or God will not see fit to give me what is rightfully mine. When I have taken

London, I will send for you. We will again be as we once were."

Something new in Charles's tone stopped Franco from making a sarcastic retort. He sensed Charles's strength gained from their struggle on the hillside. Franco thought it best to coddle his lover a bit.

"Charles," he said sweetly. "You know my true affection for you, and my loyalty to the Jacobite cause. I will do whatever you wish. I am, though neither English or Scottish, your truest subject."

Charles's eyes filled with tears. "Ah, Gabi," he sighed, "a man could ask for no better friend than you. And when I am King, you will know what it is to be truly loved."

Chapter 20

The future King of England was coming to afternoon tea, and Lady Flora Jane Campbell's household was in an uproar. Toby ran from room to room, yapping furiously; maids and footmen scurried breathlessly about their tasks. It was not enough that the drawing room had been polished and shined so the surfaces reflected like mirrors the bowls and vases of huge-headed chrysanthemums, marigolds and snapdragons, the aromatic roses and stocks. It was not enough that the carpets brought from France to Scotland fifty years earlier by Lady Flora Jane's father were taken into the kitchen yard and beaten until the dust flew. The mistress of the house insisted that every room be cleaned, every surface oiled to glowing splendor, every pane of glass and mirror washed, rewashed, and then rewashed again, so not the slightest smudge of dust was present. The servants, who under normal circumstances would have complained loudly among themselves at all this labor, were as excited as Lady Flora Jane. The housekeeper roamed the house like a master sergeant, issuing orders and demands. The lower servants obeyed her without complaint, for among the working classes Charles Edward Stuart was a hero of more than lifelike proportions. No effort could be too great, if the Prince was to be the beneficiary of their labors.

Because Lady Flora Jane had decided that Fiona "had a way with flowers," the girl from Skye had been given the task of supervising the floral arrangements. She was in the small front drawing room, arranging stocks in a silver pitcher, when Abigail Gunn entered, a message in her hand.

"This just came for you," she said curtly. "It is from Captain Cameron." Flinging the sealed envelope on a table, she stormed from the room, not bothering to conceal her ill humor.

With trembling hands, Fiona broke the wax seal bearing the imprint of the Cameron crest. "My dear Fiona," the letter began. "Since leaving you, I have been deeply concerned that I in some way offended your sensibilities at our last meeting. Knowing the love you bore my ward, I fear that my affection for you may be burdensome. I would not have it so. Rather, I want you to understand that I will not press myself further upon you, but remain, instead, your sincere friend, Michael Cameron."

She read the note twice before she was certain she understood its full meaning. It became clear that Michael regretted their impassioned parting and wanted to make sure that she did not consider him bound to her in any way, despite his promise to return. A quirky little smile played at the corners of her mouth. How foolish I am, she chided herself. If the letter had not made her sad, she would have laughed aloud at herself for daring to think a man like Michael Cameron could care for her.

She read the note once more. The words were carefully chosen, just the sort of language a gentleman might use to cool the ardor of a girl far below him in station. I am a ninny! she thought. The past few weeks in the company of Prince Charles, living under Lady Flora Jane's roof, she had forgotten who and what she was: a crofter's daughter. A peasant more at home with sheep and wild mountain goats than with aristocrats and gentry.

She wandered aimlessly about the little room, picking up cushions and fluffing them, straightening figurines and other decorative ornaments, adjusting the fall of drapes; she didn't think about what she was doing. The tumult of emotions raised by Michael's letter had obscured everything else. She was a mass of trembling emotion, unschooled and uncontrolled. At last she sat, buried her face in her hands, and began to weep. Would it always be this way? Would her heart's desire elude her forever?

The door opened and Abigail walked in. She stared at the weeping girl, smiling slightly.

"Bad news?" she asked cordially.

Fiona looked up and hurriedly wiped her eyes. "No," she said, although everything about her bespoke the lie.

Abigail laughed. "You're not a very good dissembler, Fiona." She sat beside her and began to offer advice. "Now you know a girl like you doesn't belong here. You're sorrowing now, and it will only be worse the longer you mix with your betters. Know your place, Fiona. Go back to Skye and do whatever women like you do. But don't be foolish enough to think that a gentleman of quality like Michael Cameron could ever care for you." She laughed again, flippantly. "Oh, he may bed you. Or try to. After all, he is a man. But he knows the difference between love and carnal desire. Don't you be misled."

Fiona listened to the scolding prattle, thinking that Abigail was a woman of experience, who knew the ways of the world and the moods of men. Perhaps I should go home, Fiona thought.

The day before, Fiona had been visited by Lady Flora Jane's solicitor, Sir David Ross. He was a jovial old man well into his sixties, with a huge round belly accented by a drooping gold watchchain, who listened politely and attentively as Fiona explained what had brought her to Edinburgh. When she had finished, he stoked his long beard thoughtfully before replying.

"If the documents of ownership are in your name and here in the city, we should have no problem. However, I must warn you that since the document you speak of was filed many years ago, it may have become lost in the archives. I shall put my clerk to the task of finding it."

"And if he does not?"

"My dear, you must be prepared for that contingency. The law is clear that if the document states your ownership by inheritance, then the cottage and lands are yours. Without that document, however, you have no proof, and must depend upon your uncle for protection."

Sir David had patted her head then in a fatherly way. "You look downcast, Miss Macleod. Don't be. It may be that I anticipate a nonexistent problem. Remember, I am a solicitor and it is my role to be prepared for any eventuality."

"Go back where you came from," Abigail was saying now. "For your own good. If you are without funds for the trip, I am sure my aunt will assist you with a loan."

Yes, thought Fiona. She is right, I should go. I will only make myself miserable if I stay longer.

Then she recalled her dream.

"I must stay," she said quietly, brushing the tears from her cheeks. "I am needed."

"By whom?" Abigail demanded.

"Prince Charles needs me."

Abigail laughed, but without humor. "You do give yourself airs!"

Fiona's voice hardened with conviction as she spoke. Abigail listened, her expression gradually darkening until it was obvious she could scarcely suppress her rage. But Fiona was obdurate. "You speak of matters you do not understand, Miss Gunn. Though I am first to admit it is remarkable, it is nonetheless true that I am needed here. And I will remain as long as Lady Flora Jane and His Highness make me welcome."

Not bothering to reply, Abigail hurried from the room, slamming the door. The drawing room shook, and the windows trembled in their frames.

Fiona was shaking too. She had spoken with more conviction than she would have believed possible. A few months earlier, she would have been unable to speak to a lady of such elevated position without censoring every word for fear of discourtesy. What had happened to her since those days on Skye, what had made her bold and determined enough to cross Abigail Gunn?

The answer dawned on her slowly. A multiplicity of factors—the dream and the destiny she had learned to accept, the difficult days with Mistress Lejeune and her troupe, the affection of Lady Flora Jane and Prince Charles and even Michael Cameron—had conspired to make her stronger in herself than she had ever been. She knew that for the time being she belonged in Edinburgh, despite Abigail's taunts and her own yearning for the distant wilds of her island. She knew that fate had brought her to the home of Michael Cameron's aunt for a reason, just as she had met the Prince on the wagon track that stormy day for a reason, and that these reasons would, in time, be revealed.

Thinking of this, Fiona grew calmer. Though she dared not dwell on the substance of Michael's letter, she felt at peace with herself, and should it again be necessary, quite capable of defending herself against Abigail Gunn. She was even grateful to the older girl for not bothering to hide her animosity. It helped to know one's enemies, Fiona realized.

Of all the fine rooms in Lady Flora Jane's home, the large back drawing room was the most splendid of all. On the second story, its high bay windows overlooked the garden, and just beyond could be seen Kings Park and the stone towers of Holyrood House, where Prince Charles had been in residence up until a short time before. Indeed, from the windows of the drawing room one could see all the way to the rise of land called Arthur's Seat. What could not be seen was the castle, that towering edifice, gloomy and threatening and still very much under British control.

The room was decorated with several wall-sized panels depicting the hunting scenes Flora Jane's father had so enjoyed when his health had permitted. Though quite old, the colors in these paintings remained bright, and the gilding on the borders had not peeled. It was a room designed for comfortable elegance. Many dark velvet setees were arranged along the wall and before the immense fireplace. Along one wall was a heavy black walnut sideboard, intricately carved with animal heads. A set of three black marble side tables inlaid with mother-of-pearl were placed conveniently near the setees and chairs. For the occasion of tea with Prince Charles, a long rosewood table, dressed in fine lace and china, had been placed before the decorative panels. A silver tea service, etched and scrolled by craftsmen one hundred years before and inlaid with gold, had been set at one end of this table. While Lady Flora Jane poured for her important guest, Abigail directed a serving girl to load the Prince's plate with rich cakes and tarts, fruit compote and slivers of minted chocolate.

The party had just begun. Conversation was light and trivial; and the Prince, though distracted, appeared to be enjoying himself. Lady Flora Jane, fidgeting lest anything go wrong and spoil this important occasion, was continually up and down, seeing to one or another detail. Fiona was about to offer her help, when a great hollow booming noise was heard, then another and another. From some distance, Fiona heard screaming.

Everyone ran to the windows. But there was nothing to be seen—the drawing room faced away from the city.

"Guest! Damn his English hide!" exclaimed Charles, suddenly comprehending everything. Fiona was standing near him, and he turned to her. "It is Colonel Guest's response to my blockade of the castle."

"Someone will be killed!" cried Lady Flora Jane. Throwing her hand to her forehead, she sank into a chair.

"He threatened . . . I didn't think . . ." Charles looked from side to side. Fiona saw doubt and fear on his face.

"Lift the blockade!" she whispered. "You must not be responsible for . . ."

"Don't listen to her, Your Highness," interrupted Franco, pushing Fiona away roughly. "You are master here."

The more advice he received, the more difficult it became for Charles to do anything except stand in the middle of the room looking confused and frightened, his laden plate balanced on his palm.

"Stop the blockade!" Fiona cried again. She took the plate from the Prince, laid it on the table, and grasped his hands tightly. "You must not let him kill your people!"

"Don't listen to her!" repeated Franco, pushing Fiona away a second time. "You must show Guest you are too strong. He will not dare . . ."

"He is English! He will do anything!" Fiona was about to say more, but her words were stopped by the repetition of the booming cannon. This time the noise was much nearer.

"My God," said Abigail, "he wouldn't fire on the aristocracy, would he?" Fiona fell to her knees before Charles, clutching his hands. "The English have written the history of Scotland in blood! They mean to destroy us, if they cannot enslave us. They will stop at nothing." The eyes upturned to him were huge and hurt. "You must stop this, Your Highness. You are our Prince, do not be our destroyer!"

Charles found his tongue at last. "You're right," he said. "This is too much."

"But this is war, man!" Franco was almost yelling, and his face had gone white with rage.

Fiona turned on him. Before she spoke, it crossed her mind in a flash of prescience that, like Abigail Gunn, this pretty Italian was an enemy. "If we must fight let it be with armies, not women and children. Scotland has suffered enough!" Her final proclamation was a wail; in the silence that followed, everyone was looking at her. Embarrassed, half-ashamed, perplexed by the furious certainty that burned her heart and gave her courage when others would falter, she fled the room.

"I must go," said Charles. "Lady Flora Jane?" She was swooning and half-delirious. "Miss Gunn, tell your aunt how sorry I am. I . . . I . . ." He turned and hurried from the drawing room.

"What are you gaping at?" Abigail spun and confronted the servants, who were staring open-mouthed with astonishment. "Elspeth, take her ladyship to her bedroom. I'll be there in a moment." Since no one moved at her command, Abigail stamped her feet and screamed, "Do it now!"

When they were alone, Franco turned to Abigail. "Well, Miss Gunn. We seem to be the sole survivors."

His words were accented by the resumption of cannon fire from the castle. The crystal drops on the chandeliers rang nervously.

"At least we now have opportunity to speak in private. I had given up all hope of having a moment alone with you, away from your aunt." Franco, dressed impeccably in moss-green velvet, his wig powdered and curled perfectly, indicated a setee away from the windows. "Shall we sit down? Perhaps, if there is tea . . ."

"Of course. Let me pour you some. And will you have some of this blackberry tart? It is a shame to let all this fine food go to waste." She poured tea, liberally sugaring it as he suggested, and then cut a wide slice of the juicy pie.

"I must say," he commented when he had tasted the tart, "I have not been much pleased with the cuisine here in Scotland. This, however, rivals anything I've tasted on the Continent."

Abigail blushed the color of her rosy gown. "It's good of you to say so, sir. I prepared it myself from an old family recipe." As she poured her own tea, her hands shook slightly. The heavy booming cannonade enhanced the drama of the moment, and Abigail tingled with unaccustomed excitement.

"Sit here beside me and explain how it is that a woman of your quality is also a cook. In my country, a lady does not occupy her time with such mundane occupations as cooking."

Abigail sat as she was bidden, and with a little encouragement began to speak of the life of a "Scottish lady of quality." She didn't mention that her own family was impoverished, that if she hadn't cooked there would have been no food at the Gunn table. They had been in conversation long enough to feel relaxed with one another, when the door to the drawing room opened and Fiona appeared.

"Excuse me," she said hastily. "I thought Lady Flora Jane . . ."

"The servants took her upstairs," said Abigail coolly.

Before Fiona could escape the room, Prince Gabriello called her back. Using his most aristocratic voice of authority, he demanded to know what gave her the right to advise the Prince.

"I am one of his subjects. Like all good rulers, he is willing to listen." Fiona's experience with Abigail earlier in the day had given her a confidence that the afternoon's events had not dispelled. If anything, this confidence had settled in and become a part of her nature in only a few short hours. She was no longer a simple country girl, easy to intimidate, unsure of her rights. Her new authority was apparent when she spoke, and its effect on Franco was stunning.

"The arrogance! How dare you assume you have any rights at all? If it were up to me . . ."

"But it is not," she said, then turned and left the room.

Abigail and Franco stared after her. Abigail was the first to speak.

"There is something not right about that girl. My poor aunt is entirely under her spell, but I find her company disturbing, and I worry that our beloved Prince is too much under her sway."

"Who is she? How did she come to be here in the first place?"

"I know only what you know, Your Highness. She met Prince Charles and impressed him somehow."

Franco chewed his lip thoughtfully. "It seems unhealthy. A girl like that seeking to influence a great leader."

"Aye," murmured Abigail.

For a time, Prince Gabriello Franco and Abigail Gunn were silent, each thinking private thoughts.

"But was she not connected to this Captain Cameron in some way prior to meeting Prince Charles?" Franco asked, after some time had passed and the tea in his cup had grown cold.

As she poured another cup for him, Abigail related what little she knew of Fiona's history. "I will ask my aunt about her," she said, resuming her place beside him. "Perhaps Michael Cameron has confided some part of her story."

"Good. Good. It may be we will need to interfere slightly."

"For the good of Scotland."

"Yes," said Franco. "For the good of Scotland." Another silence ensued, interrupted only by the occasional bursts of cannon fire to which they were gradually growing accustomed, now that it seemed certain the homes of the Scottish aristocracy would not be hit. They began to speak of other things. Franco did not bother to conceal his admiration for Abigail; and she, in response, preened and fluttered like a dove. No man had ever looked at her as Franco did, and it was easy to lose herself in the dark brown depths of his liquid eyes. It was easy to accept his flattery, and when he touched her hand the flow of energy was noticeable to both of them.

"You are lovely, Miss Gunn. In my country you would be a Queen, while the red-haired one would be burned as a witch!"

Blushing again to the rose color of her gown, Abigail laughed prettily and looked up at him from beneath long silver lashes. Franco wasn't laughing. His expression was warm and serious, intense and thrilling. She thought of her father, then of Michael Cameron. Neither of them had made her body tremble in its most private places, nor had she ever been as conscious of the burning hunger of her womanhood for release and satisfaction.

Franco touched her shoulder with feather-lightness. He felt her yearning for him. His hands on her shoulders turned her round to face him.

"Abigail," he whispered and drew her to him.

"Gabi," she sighed, and opened her mouth for his kiss.

Book Six

THE TALISMAN

Chapter 21

Prince Charles sent word to Colonel Guest in Edinburgh Castle, and with the lifting of the blockade the English bombardment of the city ceased. But Charles paid a high price for his capitulation. The spirits of the Jacobite forces sank to their lowest point. There were few volunteers, despite Charles's repeated insistence that King Louis of France would soon provide the necessary arms for victory as well as a goodly number of French soldiers from the Royal Stuart Regiment. The people of the city were badly demoralized by the English cannonade. In the smoke-filled oyster cellars and public houses of squalid Edinburgh, the fate of the Stuart cause was argued vociferously over quantities of drink. A spirit of doubt moved through the city, troubling even the most loyal heart. Prince Charles had barely begun his campaign and already, when the doubters spoke, everyone listened.

Nevertheless, the Pretender's spirits continued to soar in contemplation of future victories. While his generals—Macdonald, O'Sullivan and Lord George Murray—argued among themselves, he put his faith in two things: the fighting will of the Highlanders and his own God-ordained right to wear the crown of England.

Two evenings before the Scots army was to engage General Cope on the field at Prestonpans, a gala assembly was planned at Holyrood Palace. It was the sort of occasion at which Charles felt most comfortable, most royal. There would be plenty to eat and drink; the music would be rousing and hearty. He had no doubt these influences would lift the Jacobite spirits and provide the necessary springboard to victory at Prestonpans.

Prince Charles was adamant: Fiona's presence at the assembly was not merely requested, it was required.

As she supervised Fiona's dressing late on the afternoon of the festivities, Lady Flora Jane assured the nervous girl, "You'll do fine, m'dear, just fine! No matter what you may think, no one there knows more of life than you do. Oh, they may try to make you believe otherwise, but you must not be fooled by all their folderol and affectation."

"But the dances, my lady!" Fiona had been told by Abigail that Edinburgh society was immensely critical of anyone who executed the intricate dance combinations imperfectly. "Miss Gunn told me . . ."

Lady Flora Jane waved Fiona's words away with a flip of her jeweled fingers. "Never you mind Abigail. You learned the basic steps I showed you, so there's nought to worry about. Besides, even if you had three feet, no one would notice. Beautiful women may do as they please in this world. Haven't you learned that yet?" Fiona looked doubtful. "You don't believe me! Well, just take a look at yourself, my girl."

Lady Flora Jane had seen to it that Fiona was dressed as elegantly and as properly as any Edinburgh aristocrat. She knew only too well that gaffes in dress were considered as unforgivable as bad manners and missteps on the dance floor by the tradition-loving Scots. Fiona's gown was of heavy white satin with a deeply sculpted neckline, and the hemline, over a hoop almost fifteen feet in circumference, was gracefully belled and gathered up in several places to reveal tiers of lacework. Across her shoulder, crossing her right breast as was proper for an unmarried woman, was a brilliant silk sash of Stuart tartan. Her costume was completed by high satin pumps and long white gloves. In only one respect did her appearance break with the style of the day. Though Lady Flora Jane tried her best to argue Fiona into conformity, the girl refused to wear a wig or powder her hair. After trying all her arguments, Lady Flora Jane had at last capitulated to Fiona's wishes. She knew that though some folk would be scandalized by Fiona's defiance of fashion, none would deny the magnificence of her long coppery-gold hair, particularly when it was arranged in a lofty style of curls and waves. With this crown of bright hair adding eight inches to her natural height, accentuating the shapely grace of her figure, Fiona was more than beautiful, she was almost regal.

Sedan chairs were waiting to take the women and Prince Gabriello to Holyrood Palace at four o'clock, the traditional hour for assemblies. Abigail, her pale hair richly powdered, curled and piled into a towering silvery headdress decorated with pastel rosettes, eyed Fiona's unadorned tresses disdainfully. To her it seemed the girl from Skye was trying to call attention to herself by breaking with tradition. She gloated inwardly, thinking how this independence would offend the Edinburgh aristocracy, for whom conformity was considered a sign of good breeding. In her own modish gown of white silk adorned by a sash of Gunn tartan silk, Abigail was confident of her own beauty.

When Franco joined the women on the outer steps, Abigail was stunned by his exquisite good looks. Her heart beat thunderously in her breast, her breath came short, and she did not realize that he far outshone her in his snug-waisted frock coat of royal blue brocade and tight-fitting paler blue stockings embroidered in gold thread. His wig hung almost to the middle of his back, framing his handsome face in curls. In the French style, a sparkling artificial birthmark in the shape of a butterfly had been affixed to his cheek, drawing attention to the limpid brown eyes that had the power to melt all of Abigail's natural reserve. As he helped her into the sedan chair, his fingers brushed lightly against her breast. Their eyes caught and held; a warm wave of yearning melted through Abigail as she bent to whisper, "Take care! Someone will see!"

Lady Flora Jane noted the interchange and, pursing her lips together, looked away. Despite her determination to think ill of no one, she daily grew more troubled by her niece's behavior. She resolved to have a little talk with Abigail on the subject of propriety. As for Franco . . . she preferred not to consider him at all. His vanity and obvious self-love offended her sense of what a man should be. She heartily regretted having brought him into her home but knew that, given another chance, she would do the same thing again; it was her duty as a loyal Jacobite to help Prince Charles in any way she could. In the privacy of her sedan chair en route to the assembly, she tried to set her mind on lighter matters. Usually, she delighted in galas and the opportunity to wear her finest jewels, but this evening was different. She was worried for Fiona, for Abigail and—though she could not imagine why—even for Prince Charles.

Lighted by hundreds of colored lanterns, the assembly rooms of Holyrood Palace were festively decorated for the evening with Stuart banners and streamers of Stuart tartan silk. Music for the evening was provided by harpsichords, violins and cellos; the musicians, seated on a slightly raised dais, played minuets and reels and strathspeys. The entire evening was directed by one of Edinburgh's most famous personalities, Miss Nicky Murray, a distant relative of Lord George's. Without the aged spinster's presence as directress, the assembly could be called neither fashionable nor proper. It was she who chose the dancers for each set; though the assembly rooms were long and wide, only three or four groups could dance at one time owing to the extreme width of the ladies' hooped skirts. Those not chosen to dance stood or sat in clusters along the walls gossiping among themselves about the other guests, taking snuff from tiny gold boxes, and sucking on orange sections for refreshment on this unseasonably warm evening. The tall French doors, which opened onto the terrace giving access to the palace gardens, were opened wide, and couples strolled in and out to escape the oppressive heat of the assembly rooms. Well-born, autocratic, the directress sat on the dais slightly apart from the musicians—the Queen of Propriety, surrounded by a court of obsequious admirers who, with her, kept a sharp eye out for any misconduct.

When Fiona and Lady Flora Jane entered the room, those near Miss Murray noticed the sudden rise of her eyebrows, the shocked widening of her rheumy eyes.

"Who is that one?" she croaked, pointing rudely.

" 'Tis said she is a special friend of our bonny Prince," someone volunteered.

Another added, "A country girl, I'm told, despite her affectations otherwise."

The word spread quickly around the room, and Fiona felt the barbed curiosity accosting her from every angle. Lady Flora Jane squeezed her hand affectionately.

"Never you mind, my dear," she whispered. "Wait until His Highness appears. They'll notice something else then!"

Fiona was presented to Miss Murray, who merely dipped her head in the most meagre show of hospitality. The dowager stared pointedly at Fiona's unpowdered hair, her lips twisted downward with obvious disapproval. Fiona could not wait to escape the ugly old woman's company. As she and Lady Flora Jane walked away, she felt the sharp eyes of tradition fixed on her, and the buzz of gossip tailed her to a settee along the wall.

Fiona blushed crimson and longed to escape the curious eyes that picked and probed at her. But as the moments passed and the curiosity did not diminish, she felt her temper rising and her eyes—formerly downcast in girlish modesty—flashed as if to signal the crowd she was not intimidated by their insulting looks and whispers. In her heart she was miserable, however, and longed to be far from Edinburgh.

The musicians began a sprightly reel and Miss Murray rose to identify the dancers who would execute the intricate ancient steps. Though she dreamed of the Highlands and Skye's misted solitude, another part of Fiona could not resist the merry music. In spite of discomfort, anger and a painfully acute homesickness, her foot kept perfect time to the engaging rhythms.

From the dimmest and most distant recesses of her memory, Fiona salvaged an old picture. She and her mother and her aunt Mathilda Duncan were in the cramped sitting room of Janet Macleod's cottage outside Dunvegan. Janet was singing a tune, clapping her hands and measuring time with her clogs on the beaten earth floor. Mathilda, her skirt held up above her ankles, was dancing, while Fiona tried to imitate her movements and only succeeded in making everyone laugh.

Though Fiona appeared to be watching the dancers at the grand assembly, her memory was so vivid that it took her entirely away from the room and back through the misted years to that long ago happy time. It seemed incredible that she, her mother and her aunt had ever laughed so joyously together. Yet the memory was so strong it brought a smile to her lips, and strengthened her so that she no longer cared what the aristocrats of Edinburgh thought of her.

Prince Charles wished to gauge the perfect time for his entrance into the assembly rooms. On a floor above, he paced the balcony, nervously sipping brandy, resisting the impulse to hurry down into the crush of admirers. It would not do for him to appear too eager; yet he longed for the praise of his people, and needed it like food and drink for the survival of his spirit.

O'Sullivan looked in on him, but Charles bade him go downstairs. "I will be along presently," he said, continuing to pace.

After a time, he stopped his restless walking up and down and leaned against the stone railing, gazing up toward the castle towering against the dimming sky. It was like a monster from another world, hovering over Edinburgh and threatening to engulf the city in blackness. He thought of Colonel Guest up there behind his mighty cannons, laughing with the satisfaction of power. He could imagine the Englishmen ridiculing him, calling him weak and unmanly.

His attention was taken by shadows moving in the garden. Then he saw a woman in white and a man bent in a passionate embrace. Charles could almost feel the heat of their attraction, though he stood high above them.

For the first time in many years, he wished that he could love a woman. Instead, he seemed to be enchanted by a dark-eyed fallen angel, who could love without emotion.

"Gabi." He whispered his beloved's name aloud with longing. "Will there never be a time for us?"

Once their future had seemed easy and assured. Victory against the English would come because it was ordained, and with that victory would come the certainty of kingship, which would tie Franco to him forever. Now—in blackest night or in the midst of wrangling war councils—he sometimes doubted his destiny. A fist of shameful lust twisted his entrails; his eyes burned with passion and self-loathing.

God forgive me, his agonized heart cried out. I love him. I cannot help myself.

At that moment, from the garden below came the sound of

laughter he recognized too well. The lovers were Abigail Gunn and Franco. Charles's face flared red with jealousy, and his breath came short. Fool! he thought of himself. He had dared to believe that, like him, Franco pined at their separation. Instead, he had wasted not an hour in finding female companionship. Charles began to tremble. Tearing his eyes from the romantic scene, he hurried off the balcony, slamming doors behind him, kicking aside tables and chairs that blocked a direct path out of the room. He yelled for a manservant to bring his coat.

The assembled guests—and most of all the unconsulted Miss Nicky Murray—were scandalized when Prince Charles, gloriously regal in red velvet and brocade, selected Fiona to be his first partner. The room was filled with the belles of Edinburgh. How dare he overlook them, and choose instead this flame-haired girl who was nothing and no one!

"But, Sir, I canna do these dances!" Fiona whispered in panic as he led her onto the floor before the staring crowd.

"Just watch and keep the time!" muttered the Prince between clenched teeth. "No one will look at your feet for long anyway!"

At first, Fiona thought she would collapse from mortification. So long as she had been seated on the sidelines with Lady Flora Jane, Fiona cared not what others thought of her. It was, however, entirely different to be one of half a dozen couples dancing in the center of a room lined by critical faces. The lighthearted music of the strathspey was irresistible, however; and after a little time she forgot her self-consciousness and began to enjoy the dancing. Though the steps were difficult, she had a natural ability that enabled her to master them quickly. The onlookers, despite their disapproval, began to whisper that there was something special, remarkable even, about the strange young woman from Skye.

Nothing would satisfy Prince Charles except that he monopolize Fiona for dance after dance. When he was engaged in conversation, he insisted that she stay at his side at all times. She seemed to sense his great need for her and flashed him a brilliant smile. He thought again of his destiny, and became more confident than he had been in several days. He became calm in Fiona's company; the pain of Franco's infidelity was less acute.

When supper was announced, Fiona and the Pretender led the partygoers into the long dining room where a half-dozen huge tables had been laid with damask, silver and the finest china. The tables were heavy with rich food: racks of venison and lamb, fricassee of rabbit, poached salmon, cod's head, crayfish in syrupy wine sauce and a ragout of sweet breads. For sweets there were tarts oozing gooseberries, raspberries and blackberries, as well as puddings flavored with rum and brandy. Fiona could not help thinking of the many nights when she had gone to bed hungry; and the bounty, the stew of opulent aromas, almost overcame her. She clutched Prince Charles's arm to keep from swooning.

"Are you unwell?" he asked, with real concern. Her face was ashen.

She shook her head but requested, "May I be excused a little time, Sir? The air in here is stifling."

"I will send someone with you. Lady Flora Jane perhaps. Better, let me attend you myself." He turned away from Lord Strathwaite and Lady Douglas, and put down his plate.

"No, no," she said hastily, placing her gloved hand on his. "I would prefer to be alone. With your permission, Sir?"

He let her go reluctantly, then forgot about her. He listened to the conversation around him, basking in the warm glow of adoration that engulfed him whenever he was among loyal Jacobites. But without Fiona beside him, he found his thoughts returning to Franco. He saw his lover across the room in laughing conversation with Abigail Gunn. Franco's hand was resting lightly, with easy familiarity, on hers; and from the way her head was tilted up toward his, Prince Charles could tell that already the Scotswoman adored Franco. Although the Italian Prince did not look at him, Charles sensed that he was flaunting this new attachment in order to arouse Charles's jealousy. At last, the Pretender could bear it no longer. He called a servant to his side, whispered directions to him and then suddenly left the room.

The ladies and gentlemen of Edinburgh watched him go, assuming he had a rendezvous with Fiona.

She was alone in the little garden gazebo filled with late blooming chrysanthemums. From the palace she could hear the dance music as it resumed after supper. But when she closed her eyes and inhaled deeply, the rich moist aromas from the garden filled her head with country memories, erasing the reality of the moment. She recalled the hours spent with Owen Hamilton on the high moor. Lying on their backs, hands at their sides so only their fingertips touched, they watched the clouds; and it was as if they felt the very movement of the world in their bodies.

Memories of Owen brought with them thoughts of Michael Cameron. Fiona's eyes filled with tears. If Owen watched her from the spirit world, she knew somehow he did not begrudge her love for Michael. It had not been in Owen's nature to deny happiness to anyone. Perhaps on the night he lay dying, he had even guessed that one day . . .

The cool finality of Michael Cameron's note came back to her, and she reminded herself that she had no right to think of him at all. But she could not help it. The music and the sweet night air conspired to wipe away all her doubts, and she was filled with a bittersweet longing to love and be loved.

Her attention was drawn by two figures approaching in the darkness. They stopped not far from her. In the shadowed gazebo, she could not be seen, but her view of Prince Charles and Gabriello Franco was clear. Their arguing drove all thoughts of Michael from her mind.

Charles's voice, though low-pitched, was strident and enraged. "You couldn't wait, could you? It has always been the same with you. Admit it! You betray me at the first opportunity!"

"Charles, you bore me with this jealousy." Franco spoke laconically, as if the conversation were unbearably tedious to him. "What do you expect me to do while you play at soldiering? Am I to sit like an old woman, with knitting in my hands? You expect too much!" Franco turned to go, but Charles stopped him with a hand on his arm.

"Admit it! You're glad, aren't you?"

"Glad?"

"That we must be apart."

"I remind you, Charles, that our separation is entirely your doing." There was silence from Prince Charles. "Well, am I correct?"

"Damn you!" hissed the Pretender. "Why don't you go back to Rome and leave me in peace?"

Franco's voice was low and caressing. "Is that what you really want, my love?"

There was a pause. "No. Of course I don't. But the way you philander. It is as if my affection were nothing!"

"That's about all it is, right now."

"What do you mean?" Fiona heard whining in Charles's voice. It made her angry, and she wanted to shake him as she might shake a small child.

"You promised me we would be in London for Christmas, Charles. Well, here it is autumn, and we are stuck in this cesspool of a city, surrounded by ignorant country squires who think they are the last word in society. I have sacrificed a great deal for you," Franco sulked; "and for what? For this?" He gestured toward Holyrood Palace.

"They are my people!"

"Nonsense! You're as French as I am Italian. We both know that. You have a very real weakness, Charles. You believe you own cant. But I'm not so easy to fool. If you will not make a life for me in London, then I have no recourse but to find other friends. I mean it."

"I must have time, Gabi. These things are not easily accomplished!" Charles reached for his friend and embraced him. Fiona could not hear what was said, but she saw Franco push him away roughly and brush himself off as if the Prince had dirtied him somehow.

"Please, Gabi. You would not desert me now, on the eve of battle?"

"Such melodrama! I am not deserting you, merely issuing a gentle warning in good time. Unless you keep your promises, I will leave you. It is as simple as that, *caro mio.*"

As she prepared for bed that night, Fiona wondered at the scene she had witnessed from the gazebo.

She had never heard men speak to one another as the two Princes had. Though she did not understand the full significance of their words, she sensed that she had been given yet another piece belonging to the puzzle of which she already knew the final picture: a bloody moor below steely skies, a dying soldier and his weeping lover.

The dream was a regular part of her life now, and she accepted it with something close to equanimity. It came to her every night. Only the amount of detail varied; the mood and tone of it were reliably leaden. Occasionally it was especially vivid, and she awakened screaming in the black room, clutching her bedcovers between her moist palms. On these nights she lay sleepless until dawn, tracing and retracing the details of the dream, always seeking a clue to its final meaning. She knew a time would come when all the pieces of the dream picture would fit. The doom foretold would become reality or be forestalled forever. Then she would sleep in peace, as she had before her mother's death, and her own bitter inheritance.

Early on the day following the assembly, a message arrived from Holyrood Palace requesting that Fiona Macleod attend the Prince immediately. Lady Flora Jane fussed about her, making sure her appearance was perfect for the honor of the occasion before finally seeing her off in a gilt sedan chair, dressed in velvet and furs. As the old woman watched the chair depart her outward appearance was calm, but her mind was deeply troubled. She liked Fiona, but she could not forget the halfling story told to her by Michael Cameron before his departure. She asked herself if it were possible that Fiona's beauty and poise disguised an unbalanced mind. If so, Prince Charles's dependence on her was certain to bring unhappiness to a great many people. Perhaps a whole nation . . .

Fiona was taken directly to the Prince's private chambers.

Though it was early afternoon, Charles was still in his velvet-trimmed brocade dressing gown. His normally rosy complexion was sallow, his eyes lacked their usual spark of animation. After retiring from the assembly the night before, he had drunk too much in the isolation of his chamber; now his head hurt, and his spirits were oppressed.

He had resorted to brandy to help him sleep, but repose had eluded him even so. He had lain on his chaise, one ear tuned to the music of the assembly many apartments away, the other turned inward, to the nagging concern that reverberated through his thoughts.

I should never have let Gabi come here, he told himself. The same thought recurred over and over, like a scolding from Sheridan or a lecture from his father. I should have left him in Europe.

Charles Edward Stuart, raised to be King of England, believed in his destiny with the totality of his being. Nothing could shake that belief in himself—nothing except Franco. The Italian Prince had the power to raise Charles's spirits with a simple smile—and to dash them with a sneering word. He was a manipulator; Charles had known it for years and yet was unable and unwilling to call for a separation. Franco was greedy and lacked nobility despite his ancient title, and yet . . .

He is nothing, Charles told himself again and again.

But the thought of permanent separation was too painful. For the thousandth time Charles told himself, when I am King it will be different.

That night, alone in the splendor of his echoing bedchamber, he was assailed by doubts. Will I ever be King? he wondered. The hour grew later, the carafe of brandy beside him was emptied and replaced by another; but neither comfort nor oblivion came to the Pretender. Indeed, the odds against his cause grew in his perception as the mist of drunkenness enveloped him.

He felt one of his black moods coming on.

And so he called Fiona to him.

Just the sight of her raised his spirits that morning. "You are Scotland," he whispered, taking her small gloved hands in his own.

She recognized the gray face, the lightless eyes, from a hundred mornings-after with her Uncle Rob Duncan. Curtseying deeply before him, she asked gently, "How may I serve you, Highness?"

"Come. Sit by the fire and talk to me. A chill is in my bones." He helped her to remove her cloak, then urged her toward a cushioned bench near the marble hearth. A servant entered discreetly with tea and bannocks.

The homely fare pleased Fiona, and she said so.

"Whatever you wish, it is yours. You need only speak." He stared at her, at the September-colored hair and the eyes to match, the delicate sweet curve of her mouth, the high intelligent brow. Yes, her presence was having the desired effect. She cheered him in an almost mystical way, and carried within her a contagious strength. In her presence, he felt cleansed of the perilous burden that infected his mind and weighed upon his heart.

"Talk to me," he said. "Tell me about your home on Skye, the Highland life."

She began haltingly, but gradually warmed to her subject. Homesickness gave a power to her words that was lacking in

179

her normal conversation. In nostalgia she discovered gifts of description and observation that she had not known she possessed. She saw that her words not only soothed, but also thrilled the young Prince. He became more animated, and when she described the way the lambkins gambolled over one another in their haste to suck, he laughed aloud and caught her hand.

"You have saved me, Fiona Macleod," he cried with a boyish laugh. "Sometimes the burden of royalty is heavy, almost too heavy to bear. But you have lightened it for me. I know now that our brave Highlanders will be victorious on the morrow. Once Cope is done with, we will be off to England and the throne!"

The color drained from Fiona's cheeks. "You must not go to England, Sir!"

He looked at her, too puzzled to be angry. "You told me that another time. When we were in the company of Captain Cameron. I don't understand it. You concern is appreciated, nevertheless . . ."

"I can't explain, Sir. I only know that you must not go to England." She spoke with certainty, her gaze unflinching.

"You want me to wait for more troops?"

"I only know you must not go to England."

He moved away, a trifle cross with her, and yet, knowing she was concerned only for his safety, appreciative as well. "You are my talisman, Fiona. With your spirit, the spirit of all that is strongest and most noble in the Scottish people to guide me, I cannot fail. It is my destiny!"

In another part of the city, in a pleasant sunny room at an inn called The Bull and Goose, Lord George was bidding a despondent farewell to his pregnant wife.

She had come down from the country to spend a few final hours with her husband. Cumbersome with child, suffering from swollen joints and shortness of breath, she had found the trip difficult. But she came when her husband requested, knowing that he would not have asked her had he not been greatly in need of her company. Now, despite the arduous journey, the fatigue she felt in every fiber, Lady Murray's strong-boned countenance, flushed with concern, was almost girlishly pretty.

Lord George was almost ready to depart. His horse was saddled and waiting; it was time to leave for Duddingstone. There would be a battle the next day, a battle he might not survive.

Lady Murray helped him buckle his kilt as he talked. He had been going on in much the same vein since she arrived that morning. Her heart went out to him for the despair she heard in every utterance, but she knew it was useless to ask him to leave the Prince and the Jacobite cause and return with her to their family and friends in the Highlands. Lord George was first and always a man of honor, and she loved and respected him for it.

Their tender farewells were interrupted by the arrival of a messenger, who talked privately with Lord George for some time.

"Perhaps we are not lost, Wife," he said, when he had sent the messenger away. He positioned his plaid across his shoulders. "The lackey brought me good news. A young fellow in our ranks, Robert Anderson by name, has intelligence of a secret track that may enable us to catch Cope unawares. Our Highlanders will have the advantage of surprise at Prestonpans."

"Still, I wish you would not go." She could keep silent no longer. Her concern was for her children as well as for her husband.

Lord George shook his head. "I cannot desert him. I have come this far, and must see the wretched business through until the very end." He went to his valise and withdrew a sealed envelope. "If I should fall in battle, I have written here the details of my will. I have also attempted some explanation for my actions, so that my unborn child will not think too harshly of me. Nor, I pray, will you, my love," he added softly.

They embraced passionately. "Stay," she whispered in spite of herself. "Stay."

"I cannot." He pulled away. Always a straight man, almost rigid in his self-control, these traits were particularly prominent now. "You know as well as I that British rule has been fatal for Scotland. The government of our poor land has been corrupt ever since the Stuart line was broken. The rightful King must rule before I can rest."

She hardly dared ask, but ask she must. "And if you suffer defeat?"

"I would rather die than see it," he answered.

Though the next day's battle was a nightmare, the Scots were not defeated.

Thanks to Robert Anderson's secret track through the bogs at Prestonpans, the troops—Lord George and the Duke of Perth leading the front line, Charles heading the second—swooped down on the English just after dawn, taking them completely by surprise. Intelligence about Cope's men had been incomplete; the Scottish generals did not know what raw recruits the Englishman called an army. When the Highlanders came upon them shrieking like banshees, their pipes screaming for blood, the young English soldiers knew nothing but terror. No amount of training could prepare them for the fury that motivated the Highland troops, so long denied a battle. The Englishmen were terrified by the kilted soldiers who threw away their firearms, preferring hand-to-hand battle with claymores and dirks.

Facing an army of blood-hungry madmen, Cope's uniformed boys turned and fled for their lives, despite their orders to stand and fight. Those who didn't escape were slaughtered, their heads, arms and legs severed so that portions of them littered the moor; the bogs and springs gurgled blood. Even the horses were not spared; gutted and mutilated, they lay with open staring eyes beside the mangled bodies of their riders.

The Battle of Prestonpans was over in minutes. Prince Charles had his victory. But it was gall in his throat.

Chapter 22

The Highland army left for England on the first day of November.

For a few days, life in Edinburgh was quiet.

But in the Campbell household, beneath a facade of calm graciousness, a conflagration was building, fueled by jealousy and ambition.

"Who is this Macleod girl?" Franco demanded. He and Abigail were alone in the small sitting room at the back of the house. While she sat despondently by the window, the Italian Prince paced. His handsome face was disfigured by petulant rage.

"I've no idea. Prince Charles brought her here only a few days before your arrival." Abigail stared moodily out the window at the gray November afternoon. She had just that day received a letter from her father, and its contents preyed on her mind. Aeneas Gunn asked why his daughter was taking so long to make a match. He threatened her. Without a wealthy husband, she need not return to Gunn Manor.

"She has some relationship to Captain Cameron, I thought." Franco, aware of Abigail's distraction, pursued his point relentlessly.

"I believe they lived nearby one another." She shrugged. "You know as much as I, Gabriello."

Franco watched her carefully, wishing he could read her mind. Though he found her blondeness appealing, he did not really care for Abigail in the least. Her conversation, limited as it was by her lack of experience and education, was tedious to him. He tolerated her only because he assumed that she was wealthy. He tried to imagine being married to her. It would be boring, but if Charles was going to be difficult, Franco knew it was just as well to have Abigail as insurance. That morning, he had found a gray strand of hair among the black ones; unwittingly, thoughts of old age and poverty had intruded.

"Bellissima," he said now, his voice a velvet caress. On Abigail's bare shoulder, his touch was warm and dry. "You are troubled. Can it be that you grow tired of me?"

"Oh, no, Gabriello," she said quickly. When he came near her, the air was charged with the currents of her desire. She closed her eyes. The feeling intensified, and she could not trust herself to speak.

"Then tell me . . ." He leaned close and his breath stirred the fine blonde hair on the nape of her neck. "Sweet Abigail."

When they kissed it was as if a ravening hunger possessed her. Gone was her cool blonde reserve, her ladylike demeanor. No sooner had his hands touched the swell of her breasts above the deeply cut neck of her dress than she was plunged into a pit of overwhelming desire, where animal cravings drove all reason from her mind. She craved the passionate fulfillment she knew should be hers.

"Yes, Gabriello. Now. I can wait no longer!" Her hands reached inside his coat and fumbled on the buttons of his vest as he undid the closure of her gown. A moan escaped her lips as his fingers touched her bare flesh and probed her hidden fires. She was ready for him, hot and ready, too swollen with desire to question what was happening. She gave in to the tides of her nature; she was an animal answering the ardent demands of her body.

Later, when she had composed herself, Abigail went in search of her aunt as Franco had requested. Lady Flora Jane was in the sewing room sorting silk stockings for dancing. Her aunt's affection for homely household duties appalled Abigail.

I will never be like that, she thought disdainfully. I will be an Italian Princess, and a dozen servants will attend me!

"Aunt," she said, her voice sweet with false concern, "you

really should let one of the girls do that kind of work. It is hardly becoming for someone of your position."

"La, Abi, what else would I do?" Lady Flora Jane laughed good-naturedly. Although she would have liked to scold her niece a little for her idleness, she tried to be tolerant. She sighed, regretfully admitting to herself that lately she had grown to dislike her niece.

The young woman's concept of good breeding carried with it no accompanying sense of duty or responsibility. Abigail was content to while away the time in daydreams and frivolous conversation with Prince Gabriello. Such idleness appalled Lady Flora Jane, who believed that luxury without labor was sinful and decadent.

"Well, my child, how have you entertained yourself today?" There was nothing consciously facetious in the question, nonetheless, Abigail shot her a quick suspicious look.

Had the old woman set spies on her?

"With this and that," she responded lightly. "To tell the truth, with His Highness gone the city seems quite drab." And ugly, she added to herself. A smoky fog hung about the many chimneyed rooftops, and from the sewing room window she could see only the vague outline of the towering castle atop the hill. "Still," she continued, "the sooner we have a new King, the better for Scotland. I suppose I should be glad he has gone."

"Well, of course, Abi. We're all glad."

"Except Fiona."

A frown creased Flora Jane's brow. "She is a different matter, of course. She can't be blamed for . . ."

"Who is she, Aunt?" Abigail came to the purpose of her visit to the sitting room.

"A friend of His Highness, and of your cousin Michael. A poor orphan girl with a sad history." Though Lady Flora Jane's instinctive fairness told her it was unkind to make comparisons, she could not help doing so where Fiona and Abigail were concerned. Much about Fiona perplexed her; nevertheless, she thought the girl was admirable. Beside Fiona, Abigail seemed pale and vapid, mean-natured, empty.

"If I may speak honestly, Aunt. It seems strange for you to open your home to a stranger. You must be careful. Not everyone is to be trusted."

185

Lady Flora Jane looked up from her sorting quickly. Was Abigail being sarcastic?

"Michael asked that I be kindly to her. And I find I have grown quite fond of the poor child."

"You keep saying what a poor child she is," said Abigail with a pout. "May I know what makes her so special? For I must say that to me she seems quite ordinary."

"No, I mustn't speak of it, Abigail. It wouldn't be fair." Lady Flora Jane searched in her sewing basket for her porcelain darning egg.

"Speak of what? Surely you can trust me."

Irritated by her niece's bickering questions, Lady Flora Jane knew the only way she would get peace was by telling Abigail something to satisfy her curiosity. At first, she only intended to mention that Fiona was prone to nightmares; but as she became involved in the tragic romance of Fiona's life, Flora Jane's natural garrulousness took over and she told much more than she had intended.

"Her mother was a witch?" Abigail's heart leapt. How Franco would love this news!

"It's all superstition, Abigail. Don't carry on so."

"Yes, of course it is." Abigail thought for a moment. Lady Flora Jane must not suspect her of more than natural curiosity. "Still, it is strange that her mother was stoned to death for witchcraft, and now she exerts some magical influence over our Prince."

Despite her fondness for Fiona, Lady Flora Jane had to admit that it was, indeed, a strange coincidence.

"She doesn't belong in Edinburgh. She should be sent back to Skye, where she cannot trouble the course of history." It seemed very simple to Abigail. Fiona would be told to leave and put in a carriage. That would be the end of her. But Lady Flora Jane thought otherwise.

"In the first place, she promised His Highness she would not leave until he had sent word. And in the second, she is here on business, and I have no intention of letting her go home before she has the papers she needs." Quickly, she outlined what had brought Fiona to Edinburgh in the first place. "Nevertheless," she added when she was finished with this portion of Fiona's story, "you are right that she does not belong in Edinburgh. She will be happier at home in Skye. I shall tell Michael that when he comes."

"My cousin is expected?" Although her body was still moist from Franco's passion, Abigail's heart fluttered at the sound of her cousin's name. "When is he coming?"

"I expect him tomorrow."

Abigail reported her findings to Franco with unconcealed glee.

"A witch!" he cried incredulously. Never in his wildest imaginings had he thought the girl part of such an incredible history. And yet, as he thought about it all that afternoon and evening, he realized it should not have come as such a great surprise. There was always something fey about Fiona, as if she were privy to secrets unknown to common folk. As the early twilight settled on Edinburgh, he paced his apartments restlessly. The room filled up with shadows, and with the encroaching darkness came a deep unease.

He was living under the same roof as a witch's daughter. Surely she was a witch herself.

She had cast a spell on Prince Charles, and in this way attached herself to him. It perfectly explained his compulsive devotion. Charles thought she was his talisman; in fact, Franco realized, she was a curse upon the whole Jacobite cause.

Franco remembered the reports following the Battle of Prestonpans. He recalled the brutality of the Highland soldiers—even he had been appalled by the holocaust. Like the local gossips, he had believed there was something tainted about the victory. Cowardly English soldiers, savage Highlanders: the Battle of Prestonpans shamed Charles's cause rather than otherwise. Now Franco knew why it had happened. He breathed a heavy sigh and sank thoughtfully into a chair before the fire. So many things had suddenly become clear! Franco had always concealed the fact that he was a superstitious man. He had been raised by an ancient grandmother, who had passed on to him her deep belief in demons, devils and witches, spirits of Hell that could invade a mind and take it over completely. Evil was seen as something that could, by its own choice, become human for a time and wreak havoc in the process.

Fiona, with her talk of defeat, was a corrupted soul, an evil that must be destroyed if the Jacobites were to have a chance of victory. But how was this to be accomplished? He considered and then immediately discarded the idea of murder. It would do no good. Death would liberate the evil spirit and free it to find another host. Better that the girl be driven away somehow, her credibility destroyed. He wondered if he could appeal to the part of her that was still human. Could he terrify her into leaving Edinburgh?

Fiona awoke the next morning when a shaft of yellow sunlight warmed the satin coverlet on her bed. Without opening her eyes, she turned and stretched luxuriously. So warm and safe she felt, so brimming with happiness.

Lady Flora Jane had told her just the night before. Michael was coming. He is coming, her heart cried. He will be here! Against her closed eyelids she saw his image clearly: the strong, slightly craggy profile, the broad shoulders and chest. Eyes still closed, she imagined how it would be when she told him that despite everything he was her own true love. Though Mathilda Duncan's warning rang clearly in her memory, she shunted it aside. The whole of her young being cried out for ardent love.

She opened her eyes and screamed.

The head of Toby, Lady Flora Jane's darling pet, lay on the pillow beside her. Blood had soaked through the satin cover and formed a sticky mass just inches from her eyes.

She screamed again and again.

The door opened. "What is the matter, Fi . . ." Lady Flora Jane's eyes widened with horror as she took in the scene. Then she too began to scream.

In a moment, the room was full of servants. Abigail and Franco were there also.

Fiona was speechless. Even the screams had frozen in her throat.

"My lady," she cried, throwing herself at Lady Flora Jane's feet, "I don't know how this happened. I simply awoke and there . . . there . . ." Fiona covered her face and sobbed.

As a servant removed the remains of the poor animal, Franco searched the room for some clue to explain what had happened. Abigail held her aunt in her arms, letting the old woman sob against her breast. The dog had been with Flora Jane almost ten years. He was a trusted friend, her dearest companion. The tears would not stop; she felt she had lost a part of herself.

"I found this," said Franco, emerging from the dressing room. He held up a bloody knife.

"What? Where?" Lady Flora Jane looked about her in confusion.

"And this." In his other hand Franco held Fiona's satin wrapper, a new one recently provided by the generosity of Lady Flora Jane. It was drenched with blood.

"I don't understand," Fiona cried, stumbling to her feet. "I told you what happened. I simply awoke and found that . . ."

Abigail sneered at her. Lady Flora Jane, her eyes wide in hurt and confusion, choked back her sobs at last.

"You killed my dog? You killed my Toby-Boy?" Even as she asked the question she was shaking her head, unwilling to believe what seemed conclusive evidence. The bloody knife, the stained clothing: was it possible that the girl she had befriended from the goodness of her heart had betrayed her in this horrible way?

"My lady, I would never . . ." Fiona reached for her hand.

Abigail pushed her away. "Haven't you done enough?"

Fiona would not be kept away. She grabbed for Flora Jane's hands, but the older woman shrank from her touch.

"How could you?" she whispered. "How could you?"

"I didn't! I swear . . ." They were gone from the room before she could repeat her denial. Only Franco remained. A shroud of cumulus cloud obscured the sun. The fireless chamber was icy as death.

The Prince and the halfling girl stared at each other.

"I heard you last night," he said coolly. "You were ranting in your sleep. At least, I assumed you were asleep and dreaming. I heard . . . other sounds. I could not identify them at the time."

"It's not true," she whimpered, throwing herself on the chaise. "It's not true, not true."

As Franco watched her sobbing, a small satisfied smile played on his lips. He saw how easily she was defeated simply by cunning and imagination, and his fear of Fiona's haunted nature subsided. As she sprawled on the chaise in deshabille, with her radiant amber hair falling about her face like an aureole, Franco saw only a woman: a beautiful woman but still a commoner, his inferior in every way.

With a snort of disgust, he left her alone.

Fiona took no notice of his leaving. As she wept she

wondered: was it possible she had done such a nightmare deed in her sleep, while under the influence of her terrible dream? Had she slaughtered an innocent creature and lain beside it all the night long?

She was faery kin. A halfling. Anything was possible.

Chapter 23

Michael refused to believe it.

He arrived from the west coast late in the afternoon and found the Campbell household still reeling from the events of the morning. His first concern was for Fiona. After hearing that Lady Flora Jane was sleeping fitfully, he went to Fiona's room. He found her packing to leave.

"I've come back to take you to Blair Castle," he said. "You and my aunt are in danger here."

Fiona shook her head. She refused to look at him as she folded her pitifully few belongings and placed them in a traveling box. There could be no thought of love between them now. She was a halfling and possessed by evil.

"Don't argue with me, Fiona. Colonel Guest and his men are preparing to retake the city. It won't be safe here for anyone connected to His Highness, but you'll be all right at Blair Castle." He grabbed her shoulder and turned her around to him. Only after a long minute, did she raise her eyes to look into his. Her lovely face showed the ravages of the day as a road shows the ruts and digs of harsh travel. "My God, Fiona, what has happened here?" The sight of her so terribly changed by grief and fear was like a mortal blow struck to his heart. Forgetting his intention of discouraging their love, he longed to carry her away with him, to shelter her forever in his tender embrace.

"Abigail told me you killed the dog. That moronic Toby."

"I don't know." She could think of nothing else to say. Truly, as the day progressed, she had grown more and more confused, until at last it seemed possible that she had done the terrible deed of which she was accused.

"What do you mean you don't know?" He shook her hard; her gold-flecked eyes shimmered with tears. "Don't cry! Just tell me what you know." Michael began to pace before her.

She sat on the bed. With faltering words she described the scene that morning, but would not look at him.

"That Italian found the knife, the wrapper?"

She nodded.

Michael laughed bitterly, pulled her up to him and embraced her tightly. He held her against his body as if he would make her part of him and of his strength, if only it were possible.

"You didn't kill that dog, Fiona. I don't know who did, but I can make an excellent guess." He held her away from him and scolded paternally. "You foolish girl. How can you believe such a thing of yourself? I know you would never kill a living thing. Why must I know you better than you know yourself?"

"I am a halfling," she uttered, her voice barely audible. She was still unable to meet his gaze.

He shook her again. "Don't believe that nonsense. You're just Fiona Macleod. Just Fiona Macleod."

"But my dream . . ."

"Damn that dream to Hell! It means nothing. Certainly it has nothing to do with that poor animal. For godsake, Fiona, take control of yourself. Believe in yourself or they will destroy you." He had a good idea who was trying to terrify Fiona, and he had a good idea of the motive as well. In any case, his Fiona was threatened and he must help her. Pulling her to him again, he buried his face in her opulent hair. He knew she loved him. Her young body yielded to his embrace, melting with softness and love.

"Thank God I came back," he murmured over and over again.

He remembered Campbelltown, when he went about the

business of preparing his ship and obtaining intelligence from France. He had tried to put Fiona from his mind; he believed her loyalties were torn between her love for Owen and the new feelings she was experiencing for him. But he was not a man to deny himself pleasure, and the thought of Fiona was a pure and bounding joy to him. Just the memory of her made him feel like a boy, and not the man of nearly thirty-six that he was.

Now he was furious with her for having so little trust in herself. He wanted to shake her until she cried for mercy. "Damn you, Fiona! Don't you know how good you are?"

She sobbed against him. He was saying what she had tried to tell herself all day. She wanted to believe in herself, but in the face of the evidence—the knife, the gown . . .

At last she controlled herself and dabbed her eyes with a handkerchief tucked in the long sleeve of her simple dark green voile gown. She tried to compose herself, sitting like a prim little schoolgirl on the edge of the bed. "Then who . . . ?"

"It doesn't matter who!" he interrupted, beginning to pace the room. "What does matter is that you did not do it! You could not do it. Never! Do you understand?"

She nodded and did, at last, begin to believe in her own innocence. Looking up at last, she saw herself mirrored in his loving eyes, and knew that she was good and kind and strong.

"I will speak to my aunt when she awakens. I will also attend to another matter, though I don't expect . . ." He cut off his sentence. There was no reason to speculate aloud on what had happened; it could only give Fiona greater pain. In the meantime, there were important matters to attend to. "The news from abroad is excellent. I have already sent a message to Prince Charles that Maurepas has arranged for men and arms to be shipped from France. King Louis is pleased with the victory at Prestonpans. Still, you cannot stay here any longer—Guest will have you and the rest of this household in prison by tomorrow night if he has his way."

"How do you know this?"

He laughed. "I played cards with some English soldiers last night, and besides taking all their silver I learned that Guest has heard of you. He thinks that if he captures you, Charles will be demoralized."

"Me?" Fiona almost wept again. She was threatened on all sides by forces far greater and more vicious than she would have believed possible. She wanted to go home to Skye, but knew it was an idle yearning. She could not go. Another force—as strong or stronger than all those pitted against her innocence—compelled her to remain where Prince Charles could find her.

It was the dream. It was her destiny.

Michael found Franco in his apartments, where Abigail had been with him a moment before. They had been gloating over the complete success with which he had sprung the trap on Fiona.

"We'll be rid of her soon," Franco had assured Abigail.

The Italian was alone when Michael entered. He heard the door slam and turned from the window. "Cameron!" he said in surprise.

Michael didn't bother to speak. He strode purposefully toward Franco. Sensing trouble, the Prince stepped back against the wall.

"Wait a minute," he cried, putting out his hand. "I don't know what you want, but . . ." His beautiful face was spoiled by a grimace of fear.

Michael's first blow hit him across the right jaw, the second across the left. Before Franco could defend himself, Michael's fist slammed into his stomach. He bent double, holding his forearms up to protect his face; Michael's hand came down across the back of his neck. The Prince sprawled on the floor and rolled, clutching his belly and moaning. With a savage jerk, Michael grabbed him by the collar and pulled him up. They were eye to eye, their faces only inches apart. Blood streamed from cuts near Franco's mouth and nose.

"I can't prove anything, Franco. But I want you to know I'm not as easily fooled as the women in this house. I'll be waiting for you—another false move and I'll cut you from ear to ear." Michael threw him down and strode from the room as suddenly as he had entered it.

Late in the day, after he had bathed and dressed in a kilt and short coat, Michael spent a long time with his aunt in her rooms. She was deeply shocked by the morning's event, and seemed frailer, older and more vulnerable than she had a few short weeks before. At first, she was unwilling to discredit the horrible lie that Abigail and Franco had convinced her was the truth; but at last Michael Cameron made her see that there was no motive for what Fiona was accused of doing.

"Why would she put the thing on the pillow beside her bed, Aunt? How do your friends explain that?"

"The girl is mad. You said yourself she was nervous. And her mother was a witch. She was, Michael! Don't deny you told me so yourself!" Lady Flora Jane was sitting up in bed dressed in a frilly bedjacket of lavender satin with a lacy beribboned nightcap on her head. Her eyes were red from weeping and she held a fragile china tea cup that trembled violently in her hand.

"I only said she was stoned as a witch. I did not tell you that she *was* one. Surely you don't believe this superstitious gabble. I would never have spoken so candidly, had I thought you could make such a mistake." Michael was almost as angry with his aunt as he had been with Franco, but he could hardly fight with a woman. Instead, he controlled himself and repeated over and over that she was an old woman and easily influenced. She should not be blamed.

"Who would have done it then?" Putting the cup on a silver bedtray, she began to weep again. "Oh, Michael, if I have maligned that poor child, I will never forgive myself! How can I make it up to her?" She snuffled noisily and searched for a fresh handkerchief.

Michael handed her a dainty square of embroidered linen and lace. "You will find her forgiving. She has known little enough of kindness in her life. If you show her that you are sorry for having misjudged her, she will be quick to respond."

Lady Flora Jane blew her nose noisily. "You care for her so much?"

"I do, Aunt."

"But Michael, she is a peasant. A crofter's child. You must remember who you are!" A new worry brought fresh tears to her eyes.

"I am a man and she is a woman. That is all that matters." The simple response embarrassed Michael, but it was the truth. Nothing else was important.

Lady Flora Jane looked into the distance and was silent. "I

wouldn't know about that," she said finally. She was silent again, this time for several moments. Then she reached for the crystal bell on the table beside the bed and rang it sharply several times. When the maidservant entered she said, "Send for my solicitor. Tell him to come immediately, there isn't much time."

Michael eyed her curiously. A moment before she had seemed like a hopeless invalid. Now she suddenly appeared years younger. A bright color had come to her lined cheeks, and she was smiling cheerfully as she said to him, "Well, what are you looking at?"

He laughed, observing the metamorphosis. "You are amazing. Wonderful and amazing!"

"At last the appreciation I deserve," she clapped her hands together and giggled coquettishly.

Some new inspiration had enlivened her, but Michael could not guess its origin. "What has come over you, Aunt Flora Jane?"

"A fit of sorts. What some call a minor madness." A devilish light sparkled in her eyes. "Between the two of us, I have thought of a way to show Fiona I am sorry and keep you from loving a penniless nobody. But it is our secret. You must promise not to tell anyone that I am making Fiona my heir."

Chapter 24

"I've ordered the carriages for just after dark," Michael told his aunt as he left her boudoir a little later. "I don't want our departure to attract attention."

"I will need to bring a personal maid and a gentleman for Prince Gabriello."

Michael's hand froze on the doorknob. "I'd prefer we left him behind."

Lady Flora Jane was shocked. "I never heard of such a thing, Michael. He is my guest. And more important, he is Prince Charles's friend. We may not care for him, but I will not hear of leaving him behind."

Michael considered for a moment. He could tell his aunt his suspicions about Franco's involvement in Toby's cruel death, but he knew this would only further upset her. She was a wise woman, and he knew that in time she would see the situation clearly without his help.

"Very well, Aunt. But I leave it to you to tell him. I can't trust myself where he is concerned."

"Why, Nephew, whatever . . . ?"

He closed the door softly on her question.

They left after dark that night in the bitter cold: two carriages accompanied by two riders, Michael Cameron and Ezekial Mudd. A persistent wind, bearing ice on its breath, drove across Scotland from east to west, bending the trees and bushes on the plain to almost horizontal. It moaned its warning at every hut and cottage door, and on the great plain neither man nor beast abandoned shelter to peer at the dark carriages as the speeding horses snorted clouds of vapor for the wind to carry off.

In the jolting carriage, Fiona slept as best she could. Sharing the coach with her were Lady Flora Jane and Abigail Gunn; Lady Flora Jane's personal maid and Franco's man rode behind them. Awaking from her fitful doze, Fiona was aware of Abigail's eyes fixed on her, darting acrimonious sparks. When she drifted into sleep again she dreamed of Abigail floating lily-pale on a dark pond, her silvery hair twisted about her neck. She awoke with a start. Abigail was still looking at her, but now her expression was horrified as well as hateful. It was as if—Fiona shuddered, trying to shake off the superstitious thought—the older girl could read her mind.

By morning, they had traveled some distance from Edinburgh. Keeping to the less busy tracks, they avoided the English. As the carriages shot through villages—mud tracks frozen hard with the early cold, thatched cottages shuttered and dark—not a soul greeted them. It was as if the countryside had been abandoned for the season.

They skirted Dunfermline, Kirkaldy and other villages where English sympathizers were thought to abound. Swathed in wool and furs, Lady Flora Jane shivered and complained of being faint with hunger. Abigail was sullen and angry by the time Michael found an inn he deemed safe for them; and the meal there was unsatisfactory. While Michael and Muddy changed the horses, the women, Prince Gabriello and his valet ate a tasteless mess of vegetables swimming in a greasy broth. Franco had nothing to say, and neither did Abigail. Even Lady Flora Jane did not try to make conversation. A black and icy mood was upon them all, and would not lift until they reached Blair Castle.

It took them more than two days, despite day and night travel and the best horses money could hire. During the daylight hours, Fiona busied herself with needlework. Under normal circumstances, the simple satin stitching—monotonous yet strangely satisfying—eased her mind no matter what concerned her. Yet on this trip she covered a square of linen with dozens of pastel flowers, and still peace did not come to her.

She was with Michael. Wasn't that enough?

She tried to make herself believe it was sufficient, but could not. She knew that he would be leaving her again soon; once more she would be caught between Abigail and Franco, the focus of their greed and envy. The only difference would be geography. She tried to distract her mind with pleasant thoughts. Late on the afternoon of their escape, Lady Flora Jane's solicitor had brought copies of the documents of ownership she needed to make the Skye cottage her own. When the rebellion was over and her destiny fulfilled, she could go home to her own land and find the peace that she longed for.

But thoughts of Skye and distant tomorrows were like faery tales to her. She kept returning to the terrors of reality. Prince Gabriello—hating her for reasons she could only dimly perceive—had killed Toby and blamed her; and his lies were so convincing that she had believed herself the villain he made out. And the other reality: Abigail hated her as much as Franco and for reasons equally incomprehensible to her. Together they were willing to say and do anything to disgrace her.

Believe in yourself, Michael had demanded. Yes, she would try to do this and yet . . . The odds against her were frightening; if she thought too much about them, she would give up all hope.

As the carriage rolled and jolted along the track, Lady Flora Jane thought her teeth would be dislodged, her bones permanently misplaced in their sockets. Her back ached, her ankles were swollen, her head drummed painfully with each beat of the horses' hooves. But she could have tolerated all this and more, if she were not so concerned about Fiona and Abigail. A nagging inner voice told her she had made a mistake in disinheriting her own niece. She thought how great would be her father's disapproval, if he were living. To his mind, the ties of family were the strongest bonds of all; to deny them was worse than treason. Still, Lady Flora Jane knew she could never bequeath her money to Abigail Gunn feeling as she did about the young woman. She was greedy, and driven by her mercenary nature to behave most improperly. She was family, true enough; but a distant blood relationship couldn't blind Flora Jane to the truth. Abigail was using her, played the role of devoted niece only so that she might one day be a rich woman.

Fiona Macleod, on the other hand, seemed genuinely fond of Lady Flora Jane. Though the girl must have been suffering as much discomfort as the rest of them, Fiona maintained a stoic calm that Flora Jane admired, and could not keep from contrasting with Abigail's general bad temper. True, between the two of them the young women had more than their share of problems. Lady Flora Jane did not imagine either of them should be lighthearted, like girls untouched by life. But unlike Abigail, Fiona seemed able to deal with the vicissitudes of life without sacrificing herself. She had an inner core of strength that enabled her to accept with dignity Lady Flora Jane's abject apology for having accused her unjustly in the matter of Toby's death. She had a goodness that prevented her from bearing a grudge.

But she wasn't family.

Do I have any right to make her my heir, Lady Flora Jane wondered again and again. As the miles of drab scenery passed by, it always came back to this: was she being a traitor to her family?

As they approached Blair Castle, the runaways from Edinburgh knew themslves to be in friendly territory, and everyone's spirits began to lift. Even Fiona forgot her fears for a while in the excitement. This was Stuart land.

They approached the castle—the finest in all Scotland and easily the rival of any in England—along a driveway almost a mile long, running through heavy forest.

Before the castle came into full view, its pristine white turrets and castellated towers could be seen above the mighty elms that guarded the track. The excitement in the carriage continued to build. Flora Jane chattered snatches of Blair Castle history, repeating several times that the Murrays were one of Scotland's first families, while Abigail twisted her handkerchief in damp-palmed anticipation. She had heard of Blair Atholl all her life, but had never expected to be a guest within its fabled walls.

All at once, they were out of the forest and there was the castle, so sparkling white it seemed to brighten the day itself. The heavy skies, the scouring wind tearing cruelly across the broad strath, even the bitter cold, became insignificant. With its acres of manicured grassland and formal gardens, the perfection of its angular crowstep roofs and shimmering whorled-glass windows, Blair Castle seemed to epitomize the pinnacle of strength and beauty.

The weary travelers knew they had come home to safety at last.

Lady Murray was there to greet them. Upon word from Michael Cameron, she had willingly delayed her departure for her parents' home to the north so that these unforeseen guests could be made comfortable. She was as gracious as Lord George was honorable, as sweetly thoughtful of their needs as he was loyal and brave to Prince Charles. For Michael she had a special fondness.

"Coz," she said, kissing him with obvious affection. "How many years has it been?"

"Too long," he replied. "I only wish the occasion were more pleasant, and that I had the time to stay here with you and renew our acquaintance." By way of explanation, Michael said to Fiona, "Lady Murray is a cousin, distantly removed, on the Cameron side. We played together as children."

"Do you recall the time I knocked you off your pony?" Obviously he did, for he laughed with her at the memory.

After introductions, the travelers were shown to their apartments. A bevy of servants hurried through the halls of the immense castle carrying hot water and fresh clothing, trays of tea and savory morsels. At supper time, they were reunited in a pretty feminine sitting room overlooking the wide deep pond behind the castle. In the last hour the skies had cleared. Now, standing near a window facing north, Fiona could see the shadow of the Highlands rising against the moonlit sky, in which danced a myriad of stars made especially brilliant by the icy cold.

"You're homesick," whispered Michael coming up behind her. He longed to touch her, but there were others in the room and he was conscious of propriety.

"Aye," she replied. "Those are the Highlands."

"You'll be home before long, Fiona. Only a little longer."

She looked at him strangely. "Do you know something? Is there news from England?"

Lady Murray, who was supervising the laying of the supper table, answered Fiona's question.

"The intelligence we have is not good, I'm afraid. I have just this morning heard from Lord George. His message bodes ill for us, I fear." She related her husband's news quickly and calmly.

Prince Charles's entry into England had been by way of Carlisle, where he expected hearty support from the country-folk whom he had been raised to believe were harshly put upon by the government and eager to take arms against the Hanovers. To the contrary, there had been little or no support. Instead, the Prince's arrival had been met with *ennui*. Lord George, Lady Murray told her guests when the servants had departed, threatened to leave the army because the seige of Carlisle had been so mismanaged.

"And to make matters worse, the winter there is as frightful as here. Already there is snow on the ground, and our poor soldiers are ill-equipped for it." She shook her head and raised her eyebrows. There were heavy sighs.

Supper that evening was pleasant despite the gloomy news and the mismatched company. Lady Murray's sitting room was decorated in French chintz and polished wood, with large many-paned windows lavishly draped in velvet, the parquet floors laid with Persian carpets in warm reds and blues. It was luxuriously comfortable after the jogging discomfort of the carriages. Lady Flora Jane drank several cups of claret, and was chatty and lighthearted despite her fatigue. Even Abigail and Franco managed to be pleasant. Franco, especially, exerted himself. He seemed to know how little affection he inspired in the group, and was trying to overcome his disadvantage by showing his most Continental charm and good manners.

Lady Murray had spent a summer in Rome before her marriage, and was delighted to have the opportunity to refresh her memories of the place. Abigail listened raptly, thinking that—with good fortune to assist her—it might not be long before she too saw the fabled city. Princess Abigail. Her attention drifted off and dallied with this thought.

Since meeting Franco she had confessed to herself how dull, how gray and cold and unappealing, she found Scots life. She knew that she was meant for romance and adventure. A time or two she had asked Franco about his life in Naples, but his answers were unsatisfactory. She took his reticence for good breeding. Having no clear image of the family palace or the royal way of life, she had fabricated a dream of the Italian aristocracy that satisfied her own imagination. If the dream had been exposed, she would have defended it as truth rather than admit her ignorance and the emptiness of all her hopes.

We are lovers, she reminded herself as if this were some guarantee for the future. A Prince—the title assured her he was a man of honor—would not seduce an innocent young woman unless he intended to make her his wife and Princess. She repeated this assurance to herself several times in the Murray sitting room that day, but a part of her remained unconvinced. Watching Franco in animated conversation with Lady Murray, her whole body tingled with longing; he had educated her in the ways of love and she was eager to resume her lessons. Wasn't this feeling a guarantee that she would one day be his wife? But the master seemed to lack the enthusiasm of his pupil. Suppose he tired of her altogether; suppose he abandoned her? The idea was intolerable. If Franco deserted her, she would have nothing. Even her father would forbid her return to Gunn Manor.

She glanced at Lady Flora Jane. The old woman's face was droopy with fatigue and she was half asleep. Die! thought Abigail venomously. Make me rich and I don't care about anything, not even Gabriello. She craved love and royalty, but what truly mattered was that she be saved from a life of poverty. In the end, it didn't matter whom she married or where she lived, so long as she was not poor. Though spinsterhood was a mortification, poverty was the greatest shame of all. In a moment of unusual self-honesty, Abigail looked into herself and knew she would do anything to make her fortune. Even if she had to kill for it . . .

Book Seven

THE HEIRESS

Chapter 25

The weary travelers went to their rooms early that night. Fiona had just shut her door and removed the pins from her hair when Ezekial Mudd knocked and presented her with a brief message from Michael Cameron. Michael wanted her to meet him at once in Lord George's small reading room adjoining the sitting room where they had all had supper a short time before.

With her hair dangling loose and free to the middle of her back, Fiona hurried through the darkened passageways of the sleeping palace, her heart beating madly. The reading room was dark except for the ruddy glow of the turf fire. Michael, dressed casually in dark breeches and a loose woolen shirt yoked and ruffled at the sleeves, stood with his head resting on the low mantel. Near his hand, an exquisite green china clock inlaid with porphyry chimed the hour of ten.

She cleared her throat. When Michael did not turn she said, shyly, "I am here."

He said something she couldn't hear. She took a step closer. "Michael?"

He laughed softly, turning to face her. "I hear my name,

Fiona, and yet I hardly recognize myself. What have you done to me that muddles my mind this way?"

"I?" Was he angry with her? His tone and the posture of his body—aggressive, accusing—perplexed her. She knew she was innocent—and hadn't he been the one to tell her so? "What have I done, Michael?"

Again he laughed. She was frightened by the sound and stepped back, almost to the door.

"Don't go!" he said quickly, stepping toward her, taking her hand. His grip was tight. It hurt her and she pulled away.

"You're angry with me."

"A little, yes," he confessed sadly. "I am a little angry with you."

"But why . . . ?"

"For being all you are: beautiful and strong and determined. It would be easier if you were like my cousin Abigail. Then I could dismiss you from my mind." He took her hand again, examining the palm in the dim red light. "You have worked hard in your short life, Fiona. This is not a lady's hand."

"I canna help that." She tried to pull away, but he raised the captured hand to his lips and tenderly kissed the palm, the inner wrist where the skin was blue-veined and silky. Compelled by the strength of mutual attraction, they moved toward one another; their bodies touched.

"I love you, Fiona, and I cannot rest unless you know it. When the rebellion is over . . ." She went rigid and pulled away.

"No, Michael. You must not speak of it."

"Why? Is it Owen? Did you love him so much?"

"I loved him when it was forbidden. I made that mistake once. I must not do it again."

The almost angry edge was back in his voice. "What is that supposed to mean?"

"I am forbidden to love, Michael. My blood is poisoned with the halfling taint. I can do nothing that will risk . . ."

He seemed to explode with rage. "That faery nonsense again! Damn you, Fiona. Damn all you superstitious Skye folk, with your witches and faeries." He grabbed her shoulders and pulled her up to him.

"You're hurting me!"

"I don't care. I would beat you if I thought it would make

any difference." His face was very close to hers. She saw the anger in his eyes and the steel-clenched jaw as he threw her aside with a bitter ugly cry. She staggered against a table, but he didn't appear to notice. "You are determined to make yourself suffer for this . . . this . . . myth?" He went on before she could reply. "Don't tell me you're not suffering, Fiona. I see it in your eyes; there's pain there. Pain that I can make go away, if you'll only let me."

"I deny nothing. I am not happy. But you canna make me blithe and bonny. No one can."

There was a long pained silence. Fiona tried to find the words to explain, but speech eluded her; her mind danced about with concepts and ideas too complex, too vaguely felt, for definition. Someday, she would understand her halfling nature; someday, she would know why she and her mother and generations before had been cursed with fey natures. There might even be a day—though she no longer dared to hope—when she would be free. The key to it all lay somewhere in her dream and in its connection with the Stuart cause.

"You have nothing more to say?" He did not disguise his anger.

"I would say a thousand things, but I have no words. Only feelings."

"Feelings!" He spun around and stared at her, then strode to the door. With a furious jerk he pulled the door open. "I have feelings too, Fiona. Do you care about those as much as you care about your own?"

"You think I'm heartless; I'm not." She ran her hand through her hair in frustration. "Don't you see? I would care for you if I could," she began to sob, "But I canna. I *dare* not."

He slammed the door on her tears.

She did not sleep that night. To fill the dark hours she invented chores to pass the time. She brushed her hair until it shone like golden treasure. She rubbed cream into the callouses and rough spots on her hands. She buffed her nails, darned a stocking and stitched on satin until her eyes burned and her fingers ached with cramp. Finally, she lay fully dressed on the bed and stared up, exhausted, into the quilted canopy.

From the moment Michael left her, she had regretted her decision.

"I love you, Michael," she said aloud to the darkness. The canopy did not collapse on her; the air did not crackle with heavenly fire. "I love you," she said again. No voice of doom demanded that she take the words back.

What if Mathilda was wrong, she wondered; what if she was not forbidden to love? The thought that she might be rejecting Michael for no reason except her old aunt's prejudice filled her with panic. How did Mathilda know what was right and wrong for her? She did not live with the halfling nature; she only feared it and knew the worst that it could bring. But might the curse not work differently in different subjects?

Fiona had loved Owen, and he had died. Who was to say that her love and his death were in any way connected? Might he not have been struck down even if they had never met? His parents had died young, and no halfling had caused their deaths. Mathilda had a way of blaming every evil happenstance on the faery curse, but the more she thought about it, the more Fiona realized that this was as simplistic as Michael's refusal to acknowledge the curse at all.

She was still awake when the first streaks of light invaded her bedroom. Her mind boiled with confusion and contradiction, but one thought rose more and more frequently to the surface. The dream and the Stuart Prince were her destiny. That had been ordained at her birth, and loving Michael could make no difference—except perhaps to make it all more tolerable.

"I love you, Michael."

In spite of everything, the simple phrase sounded right. It washed over her suddenly, an immense wave of truth that bore her up and out of the room, out of Blair Castle and down the drive to the crossroads where he would ride. The dream, the Prince—they were her destiny. But so was Michael Cameron . . .

He saw her as he came around the corner into the main road, Muddy riding beside him. Michael was grim and hard-minded that morning; he had spoken hardly a word to his man, afraid to risk himself. His anger—a bitter mutation of his love—was so near the surface that he had almost kicked the stable dog who yipped at his feet as he saddled his horse. Now, seeing Fiona there in the road, he wanted to hurt her rather than admit the ray of hope her surprise appearance once more cast into his life.

I'll ride past her, he thought.

But of course he didn't.

"Why are you here?" He saw the fatigue on her face and recognized her simple dark gown as the one she had worn the night before.

"I have decided . . ." She couldn't say more.

Words were unnecessary. In one strong gesture, he reached down and swept her off her feet and onto the saddle in front of him. Wheeling, they rode back into the Blair forest, leaving Mudd mystified in the empty track.

In the dark of an abandoned woodcutter's cottage, Michael made a place for them to lie with his saddle blanket. He did not ask for an explanation; her body, warm in his arms, communicated with its own eloquence. He was hungry, ravenous for her after weeks of waiting, weeks of imagining this moment of surrender. He pulled her roughly to the floor beside him and, taking her face between his hands, kissed her mouth long and hard.

He felt the tension in her body; then, gradually, he felt it dissipate. She floated against him, her arms entwined about his head, her fingers buried in his thick dark hair as his hands touched the length of her body. Soft and strong, the touch of her was like fire. She felt it too. By unspoken agreement they undressed each other lovingly, and lay naked in the dimness.

"You are magnificent, Fiona."

"Don't speak, Michael. We do not need words now."

His lips and hands discovered her nakedness, the skin smooth as sunlight, the hidden places moist with yearning. Fiona seemed to be riding a glowing cloud, which swooped and eddied as it rose, rocking her into a trance where sensation was heightened to the point of almost-pain. He caressed her belly and breasts, the soft pale skin behind her knees, between her thighs. Where he touched, the trembling warmth of her exquisitely alive. Her center pulsed with desire. Wrapping her long legs about his hips, she drew Michael into her.

A savage cry of joy escaped her lips as the cloud carried her breathlessly higher with the rhythm of their passion. His lips touched her throat, her ear, her brow; his mouth was wet and open on hers as his hands twisted in the amber coils of her hair. Fiona gasped. The cloud became a star, the star a constellation that broke into a million shimmering fragments and floated gently down. She was composed of light and magic, lucent with the radiance of love.

Afterward they dressed quickly, a little shyly. As he prepared to mount his horse, he said, "Is it all right, Fiona? You have no regrets?" He searched her face for the truth.

She smiled radiantly for an answer.

"I will be back as quickly as I can. Damn this Stuart Prince for keeping me from you. If I had my way I would take you back to Skye now, and close the door on rebels and soldiers."

"No, Michael. We're part of history, you and I. We canna have our way until this thing is done." She wished he would go quickly, before something happened to spoil the perfection of the moment.

"At least you understand there *is* a future for us. Last night I would have said that such a change was impossible." He pulled her to him, breathing deeply; he knew he must memorize the sweetness of her. "And there will be no more of this halfling nonsense, eh, Fiona?"

"I love you, Michael, and that is all that counts." She kept her head close to him, resting her forehead against the hollow of his throat.

But he would not be put off by her evasive declaration. He held her away from him. "No more of this halfling business, Fiona. Do you swear?"

There was a pause, a fraction of a second, and then she said, "I swear."

And knew that she was lying . . .

Chapter 26

At Blair Castle, Prince Gabriello Franco began taking long walks in the morning and evening. Though not a lover of either nature or exercise, he found that a strenuous walk—sometimes miles and miles over the rough Scottish countryside—calmed his nerves and helped him to think clearly.

On the morning of Michael's departure, Franco had been on such a walk; and he came upon the lovers as they were saying their final goodbys. A further step or two and he would have been noticed by them; but he kept to the darksome shadow of the woods and eavesdropped unobserved on their final bittersweet good-bye.

Instead of returning immediately to Blair Castle, Fiona walked through the woods and onto the open moorland. Franco followed her, keeping to the march of the woods where the gnarled old oaks provided cover. She walked to a high rocky promonotory, from which she could see for miles in a southerly direction. Blair Atholl Village and the ribbon of road leading south were clearly visible from this point. She saw the mounted figures of Michael Cameron and Ezekial Mudd, their backs to the Highland moor, galloping in the direction of Campbelltown. Her lovely face a mask of sorrow, Fiona watched them until they were hardly indistinguishable from the landscape.

Her head was swathed in a broad fringed plaid, which had protected her from the autumn morning chill. As the sun broke through the overcast, however, she let the wool slip to her shoulders, and her red-gold hair waved about her like a corona of flame.

Though not generally attracted to women of high coloring, Franco felt a surge of sexual excitement at the sight of her, wild and free as an animal. He recalled an incident from his youth.

He and Prince Charles had gone for a few weeks hunting in Brittany. Charles had soon tired of the recreation, but Franco went on alone. In an area of dense bushes, grass and wildflower-covered hillocks, he had surprised a fox and sent it darting ahead along the path. Though he had no fondness for wildlife, the beauty of the creature had stunned him almost as if a physical blow had been struck. So graceful and wild, it seemed to own the world.

Fiona was like that fox, but with the additional allure of witchcraft, which he found strangely tempting. This supernatural quality was part of her appeal. He wanted her, wanted the immense strength of evil that he imagined lay hidden beneath her innocence. He did not doubt that she was a witch like her mother. Until Michael Cameron's arrival, even Lady Flora Jane had recognized the force of evil in her. Like a corrupt goddess of Nature, she pulled at him with the promise of great power.

He left her finally, his body throbbing with the urgency of his hunger. There would be another time . . .

Fiona returned to the castle in midmorning.

"Where have you been, child?" Lady Flora Jane wanted to know. "A message has come for you from His Highness. We've been waiting for you in the sitting room. Come along quickly now!"

Morning tea was being served. A delicate teawagon—perfectly suited to the feminine taste of Lady Murray's little sitting room—had been wheeled into the sunny room, laden with plates of golden biscuits, bowls of clotted cream and raspberry preserves. Lady Murray was pouring tea as Fiona entered.

"My dear, you've come at last! Please sit—I'll pour some tea for you. Miss Gunn, give her the letter, will you? It's there on the table near your arm." Lady Murray's voice was high-pitched with nervousness; she had not heard from her husband. Even her unborn child was stirring restlessly, as if the mother's agitation were communicated to it. For a moment, she forgot her role as gracious hostess and stared—as did the others in the room: Franco, Abigail and Lady Flora Jane—while Fiona read.

> My dear Fiona:
>
> I write you from the depths of despair. I long to have you here beside me spurring my spirits and strengthening my will. Though I left you behind in the belief that war is no affair of women, I see now that you, as my talisman, are meant to ride at my side. Without you, Our cause does not go well. There is talk of retreat since Lancaster where I had been assured there would be enthusiastic support for Us. Instead the folk were openly hostile and ridiculed Our brave but shabby Highland army. The forces of both Cumberland and Wade are nearby, and yet we dare not meet them in our demoralized state. Send me your prayers, sweet Scotland. I suffer from a lack of men and arms. My generals are antagonistic, but with your prayers I yet believe we shall succeed.
>
> Your humble, Charles.

She read the letter twice, slowly, her expression reflecting the Prince's despair.

"Is it so bad?" Lady Murray whispered, still holding the teapot in midair.

Fiona nodded and handed her the parchment.

It was passed from hand to hand until each person in the room had read the desperate news.

"My poor George," Lady Murray cried. She labored to her feet and began to pace the floor, the high wooden heels of her slippers making sharp staccato beats on the parquetry between the carpets. "I must go to him. If there is to be a retreat . . ."

"That's not assured at all, my lady," interrupted Prince Gabriello. "It is unthinkable."

"He says the generals are antagonistic. That means my husband and he are in conflict. Oh, my poor baby!" She clutched her heavy belly.

Lady Flora Jane rushed to her. "You mustn't upset yourself

in your condition. His lordship wouldn't want it. Sit down and let me call your maid."

But Lady Murray would not hear of it. She had taken it into her head to go to the English border and await the retreat, and nothing would change her mind. Though Lady Flora Jane told her this was far from sensible in her condition, Lady Murray could not be dissuaded.

"You are my guests and I insist that you remain here in our home. But I cannot delay a moment longer." She bent to kiss Fiona's brow before she left. "You poor child. This talk of talismans is simply superstition, nothing more. Stay here, where His Highness can find you easily. And bless you for your loyalty."

No one spoke for several moments after she was gone. But all were deep in thought.

Least concerned were Abigail and Lady Flora Jane. Flora Jane had already survived one failed rebellion, and knew that defeat was not the end of the world. She would spend a little time at Blair Castle and then return to her home in Edinburgh. For a time the English would be rude to her and search her home; perhaps they would confiscate some of her property, although that was unlikely. Colonel Guest and his men depended on the goodwill of the Edinburgh folk, and would never press their role as conquerors beyond safe limits. In a matter of weeks, at most a month or two, Lady Flora Jane's life would settle into its old familiar pattern. She was sorry that the handsome young Prince was having difficulties, but she was realistic enough to accept the news with equanimity.

Abigail—though she pretended otherwise—hardly cared what happened to the Jacobites. Her own problems far outweighed political concerns. Her father had sent her to Edinburgh to find a husband and ingratiate herself with her wealthy old aunt. She seemed to be erring in both regards. She had not failed to notice that Lady Flora Jane had cooled toward her in recent weeks. She was not sure why this was, but suspected it was related to her *amour* with Prince Gabriello.

Abigail felt trapped. If she devoted all her time and energies to rewinning Lady Flora Jane's favor, Prince Gabriello would drift away from her, and he was the husband she craved. She glanced at him surreptitiously.

The handsome young Italian was standing at the window

staring out over the pond and high moorland. She could not read his expression. For a moment she forgot everything and simply enjoyed the pleasure of looking at him. Slim-bodied and tall, he wore his clothes with an elegance that she knew had spoiled all other men for her forever. Even her handsome cousin Michael Cameron seemed rough and overmanly by comparison.

What was Franco thinking? She would have given anything to know. She could only guess that the bad news from England had driven all thoughts of romance from his mind. Tossing her blonde head in determination, she vowed to make him declare himself before it was too late.

She turned on Fiona suddenly. "If you're so terribly important to His Highness, why don't you go with Lady Murray to the border? 'Sweet Scotland,' indeed!" With that she flounced from the room. Franco did not turn from the window.

"Do you think I should go, my lady?" Fiona asked Lady Flora Jane.

The old woman was quick to answer. Fiona was the woman her favorite nephew loved, and she meant to keep her safe and sound until he returned to claim her. "Certainly not," she said. "Prince Charles would have asked you to come had he so desired. Instead, he wrote that war is not a place for women. And I agree. If I could prevail upon Lady Murray to change her plans I would certainly do so; but she's a grown woman going to join her husband, and I would not presume to interfere."

Franco heard the women talking, but he paid no attention to their words. He was planning frantically. When he had decided on a course of action he left the room abruptly, without a word to Fiona and Lady Flora Jane.

He found Abigail in her suite. She was seated at the wide glass-topped dressing table, wearing a flimsy pink satin powdering gown, as three maids prepared her hair for the day. He ordered them out of the room curtly.

Abigail was pleased to see him. Dipping her head coyly, she said, "Your urgency takes my breath away, Gabi."

"I've told you not to call me that!" He was not entertained by her girlish airs, and could scarcely keep from showing the distaste he felt for her and all things Scottish at that moment. He had been an impressionable idiot to believe Charles's promises of London and the life of royalty awaiting him. He was trapped now—unless he could get out of the country. But he was penniless. He forced himself to be charming.

Putting his hands on her shoulders, he kissed Abigail's neck in the lingering way that he knew aroused her. "Forgive me, my sweet," he said. "The news this day has made me short-tempered."

She turned and embraced him, eager to forgive anything. "Of course it has, and I completely understand how you feel. His Highness is more than a Prince to you, he is your friend. Here, sit beside me on the bench."

"You'll get powder on my coat."

Again that coy movement of the head that struck Franco as amateurish and slightly vulgar. "Perhaps the bed would be less . . . hazardous?" The powdering gown slipped easily from her shoulder, revealing one bare breast, the nipple hard with anticipation.

He led her to the bed and removed her clothing. Her whiteness was suddenly rather disgusting to him. He recalled the tawny gold of Fiona's skin, like ripe apricots in the orchards near his home, and could hardly bring himself to caress Abigail as she wished.

"What's the matter?" Abigail asked. He could not quite disguise his dislike; she saw it in his eyes, but refused to recognize it. She covered herself hurriedly. "How foolish of me to think you could be so easily distracted at a time like this. Of course the news from England has distressed you terribly." She pulled him to her and he let himself be cradled in her arms.

She smelled slightly sour—a mixture of old powder and lavender water; but he urged himself to tolerance. She must not know; she must not guess his true feelings.

After a little while, he said, "I must ask a favor of you, Abi, dear. Dare I so presume upon your feelings for me?"

"But of course. What is it you desire? I will do anything to help you." She stroked his dark hair tied at the nape of his head with a sharply ironed ribbon. "You are so beautiful, Gabi. There is nothing I would not do."

"I need money."

She didn't answer right away.

"For what? All your needs are taken care of here. Surely there is time for you to write your family banker on the

Continent. Would he be in Naples or Paris? What is the urgency?"

"I want to go to France," he lied suavely. "I believe I can raise support for His Highness with the royalty there." Would she believe the story? He was counting on her naiveté. But she said nothing, and the stroking of his head had stopped. "Will you help me, Abigail?"

Her pale blue eyes were full of tears. "I haven't any money to give you."

"I can wait while you write to your father. Surely if you name the cause he will be eager to assist me."

She was shaking her head. "You don't understand. There is no money. None at all. I am impoverished."

He jerked away from her. When she saw the expression on his face—rage and loathing combined—she knew the truth at last. But still she wouldn't face it.

"I am to be my aunt's heir." Truth or falsehood didn't matter anymore; she must erase the hateful expression from his face. She would rather die than lose Franco. "I have no money now, but I will have. I will be very rich someday."

He was not appeased by promises of a better tomorrow. He had believed all that Prince Charles had promised—and had been bitterly deceived. "I need the money now, not some time in the future." He got an idea suddenly. "You must go to her, Abigail. You must borrow the money for me."

It was Abigail's turn to be calculating. "And if I do that?" She held her breath.

"I will make you my Princess," he said. Taking her in his arms he laid her back upon the bed and silenced her expressions of joy with kisses.

Chapter 27

The bitter weather relinquished its hold on Scotland for a few days in mid-December. It was as if a false spring had come extraordinarily early that year, and though a drenching fog covered everything in the morning hours, the afternoons were often clement and sparkling. On one such day, Lady Flora Jane suggested to Fiona that they walk together across the high moor.

"I am told there is a pleasant pathway leading to the village. I have need of some wool, and perhaps we'll find some in the shop there." She was not being entirely honest with Fiona. Her main reason for wanting a walk was a desire to be alone with Fiona, away from the castle. It was time for the lass to be told that she would one day be a rich woman. During their days at Blair Castle, Lady Flora Jane had watched both Fiona and Abigail carefully. Gradually, the doubts she had of Abigail's worthiness solidified into an irritable, rock-hard certainty. Abigail was lazy and obsessed with her own needs and wishes. Lady Flora Jane had no doubt that she was making a shameless fool of herself over Prince Gabriello.

She had decided that they were well-matched and deserving of one another. She no longer feared that Fiona was unworthy to be her heir, and she was highly excited, anticipating the moment when the truth would be revealed.

They left the castle in the afternoon after dinner, unaware that Franco followed them. Since the day when he had observed Fiona on the moor and likened her to a fox in his mind, he had often stalked her in a kind of unwilling fascination. Unwilling because at the same time he wanted her, he feared her magical influences. Influences that he was sure were responsible for the failure of the Jacobite forces in England, despite Charles's conviction otherwise. This mixture of attraction and fear perplexed Franco. Though he tried not to examine his emotions, on the fringes of his consciousness he understood that he wanted Fiona not simply for the pleasure of physically humiliating her, but also in the belief that through such a brutal conquest he could appropriate her strength and power as his own.

When the fog had lifted that morning, it had revealed a piercing cerulean sky, which stabbed the eyes with unremitting brilliance. Despite its beauty there was something cruel in that color, and Fiona was thankful when she saw the bruise-black clouds boiling up out of the Highlands to the north.

As they hurried over the stony path to Blair Atholl Village, muffled in heavy coats and long plaids, the women quickened their pace. Weather in the Highlands changed rapidly, and Fiona and Lady Flora Jane knew a storm would be upon them well before twilight. After half an hour's breathless hastening, Lady Flora Jane called a halt at last. Leaning against one of the hundreds of huge boulders scattered over the terrain, she put her hands to her heaving chest until the drumming of her heart slowed and she was breathing more easily.

"Are you all right, my lady? Perhaps we should return to the castle?" Fiona's flawless complexion glowed with good health. She tingled from the pleasure of exerting herself after so many weeks of ladylike ease. "Or shall you stay here and let me run ahead to the village for you? It's not so far, only beyond the ridge a mile or so." Concern for Lady Flora Jane showed in Fiona's expression.

"I'm all right, child. Truly I am." Lady Flora Jane was fibbing. Her madly beating heart frightened her; she could still hear it dinning between her ears. "I need to speak with you, and now is as fine a time as any." Lady Flora Jane was typically outspoken and direct. "I've made you my heir, Fiona. You will inherit all my fortune."

The girl stared at her in dumb astonishment. She was suddenly acutely aware of everything around her: the grouse skittering in the bracken, the rising wind smelling of rain and ice.

"I know you have not asked for anything. No doubt you feel you are undeserving. But I am an old woman, with little family I care for. There is no one I would wish to make rich save yourself."

"But . . . Abigail? She is your niece!" Fiona could not begin to think how this revelation would change her life. Her mind spun, unable to accept it, and her thoughts were all for the girl who hated her.

"La, Fiona, you are too good! That niece of mine is a mercenary little piece, and I decided weeks ago I would prefer to die intestate than see her made wealthy just to squander it on a drunken brute of a father and whatever Italina gigolo she finds appealing." Flora Jane continued along the path, picking her way carefully in high-heeled boots the same shade of brown as her heavy-skirted woolen walking dress.

Fiona walked beside her, her thoughts organizing themselves in rapid confusion. Her gratitude was almost impossible to express. Thanks to Lady Flora Jane, Fiona knew she would never again lack for worldly comfort. How ironic that this should come to her when she had never wanted very much in the first place: only her cottage on Dunvegan Head and freedom from the curse of the dream and her halfling nature.

"Bless you, my lady," she managed at last. Her hands were trembling in their muff.

Lady Flora Jane was immediately sensitive to Fiona's confusion. "It isn't necessary to talk about it, my dear. I didn't do it so you could thank me. I did it because you deserve it and because . . ." She stopped suddenly and turned around. "I have the strangest feeling. As if we're being followed."

Both women watched the path behind them for a moment or two; but nothing stirred to give them alarm and so they continued along as they had been. Lady Flora Jane talked about Michael Cameron and her affection for him. Though she never made the connection precisely, she gave Fiona to understand that it was in part Michael's influence that had decided her in favor of the unorthodox bequest. Having eagerly anticipated this moment of revelation, she was chattering girlishly as they reached a rocky swift-moving stream about six feet wide. A bridge of sorts had been laid between the banks; but during Lord George's absence from Blair Castle the groundskeepers had grown lazy, and the narrow plank crossing looked dangerously dilapidated.

"We should walk a little further downstream and find a place to cross on rocks," Fiona wisely suggested.

But Lady Flora Jane thought she was being coddled and wouldn't hear of it. Her heart was beating normally again; she could forget how aged and unfit she had felt a few moments earlier. She insisted on attempting the crossing despite the obvious danger.

"Let me go first then, my lady," said Fiona.

But the old woman was determined to have her own way.

"I grew up in the country near Inverarry," she declared with stubborn pride. "I'm not so citified as you think!" With that she placed her feet upon the plank, and stepped gingerly forward.

She had taken three steps when her heel caught in the rotting wood. Her hands pinwheeled frantically; her gay plumed hat toppled from her head as she fell into the icy water.

Fiona was beside her in a flash. With effort, she raised Lady Flora Jane's head out of the water. The old woman's face was ashen, and her eyes dulled by a glaze. A deep gash had cut her temple; it bled profusely, matting her hair and staining her skin.

Staggering, Fiona hooked her arms under Lady Flora Jane's and locked them in a firm grasp across her chest. She heard the old woman gag for air.

"I'll have you out in a moment, my lady," she gasped, struggling with the weight of the woman and her own sodden clothing. Once Fiona fell backward into the water, twisting her ankle under her. After that it hurt whenever she put her weight on it, but she dared not stop to pamper herself. Overhead the sky was fast clouding over. The rising wind launched her tri-cornered hat and sent it sailing over the moor. Fiona felt Lady Flora Jane shivering in her arms; her face was deathly white, the lips slightly blue. As she scrambled up the muddy bank, Fiona slipped again and then again, coating her gown and skin with dark slime. After what seemed like an endless time, she managed to lay Lady Flora Jane on the grass. Fiona sprawled panting beside her.

The old woman did not move. Her eyelids fluttered once or twice, but did not open. Only the labored rise and fall of her breast gave any indication that she was alive. The wound at her temple continued to bleed.

Fiona felt the inflammation from her twisted ankle pressing angrily against the snug boot. Quickly, she unlaced the boot and tore away her stocking. The skin was discolored and nasty. Though she believed she could never walk on it, she knew she must not rest a moment. A sickening intuition told her Lady Flora Jane was near death. Angry and impatient with the pain, she unlaced her other boot and removed that stocking as well. For years she had walked the Highlands of Skye barefoot. She would do it again.

She had gone less than a quarter of a mile, however, when the pain became acute; but then it seemed her luck was turning. As she came in sight of the castle woods, she saw a figure ahead.

"Help!" she cried into the wind. "There's been an accident!"

Franco was beside her in a moment. "What's the matter? What happened to you?"

"It's Lady Flora Jane," cried Fiona breathlessly. "She fell." She staggered and, putting her weight on the injured ankle, fell against Franco. She didn't have the strength to pull away.

"Where is she?"

"Back there along the path. I'm afraid she may be dying." Fiona looked up into dark eyes that were as cold as an arctic night. "Please," she begged, and then lost consciousness.

When she came to he was sitting beside her, leaning indolently against a large rock and cleaning his nails with a sharp stick. The temperature had dropped several degrees, and now the wind had ice in its bite.

"Lady Flora Jane! Where is she? Is she all right?"

Franco only shrugged and smiled at her. She tried to stand, but he pushed her down; her ankle hurt so much that she did not try again. Fear, like a poisoned tide, rose choking in her throat. She was drowning in it. She opened her mouth to speak, but nothing came out. Franco saw her discomfort and grinned.

"Why not use some magic, little witch-baby? You cast a spell on Prince Charles. Shall you do the same with me?" He threw the stick away, rose and stood over her. "Well?" He seemed oblivious to the harshening weather.

For the first time in her life, Fiona wished the stories of witchery were true. She longed for the kind of powers that could impress Franco and terrify him into going for help. But it was no good. She was not evil, and even for effect could not pretend to be. "Help her. She is old and weak. She will die if she isn't cared for. Help her!"

He ignored her words. Slowly, enjoying the fear on Fiona's face, he began to unbutton the front flap of his trousers. He was naked underneath, naked and big with desire.

Ignoring pain now, Fiona clambered awkwardly to her feet. She turned, but he caught her arm and pulled her close to him. His mouth covered hers as if he were trying to suck the strength from her; his tongue pushed deep into her mouth. The taste of him was like wormwood to Fiona. She beat against him with her fists, twisting and turning her head in a mad and futile effort to escape his kisses. But nothing helped. His grip on her arms was so tight that she felt her bones would crack.

Just when she thought she must succumb, when the pain was so great that she no longer cared for anything but a quick end to her misery, the image of Michael—strong, gentle Michael—came into her mind. It was as if he stood inches from her, his expression keen and vigorous. Over the wind and lashing sleet, he was yelling to her: Fight! You must fight and never give in. Fight, Fiona. Fight!

The Prince's hands shoved up under her wide skirts; his fingers dug between her legs, spearing her center. With a free hand, he turned her around and shoved her back against the rock where he had been leaning. She tried to kick, but the twisted ankle would not support her; though she snarled and squirmed, she was helpless as Franco ripped away the bodice of her gown, revealing honey-colored breasts and slightly darker nipples peaked in terror. His face had lost all semblance of dark beauty. Now it was twisted by rage, mutilated into savagery.

When he tried to put his mouth on her breasts she twisted like a serpent. Her elbow slammed into his chest, knocking the wind from him. He was caught off guard, and she slithered from his grasp and tried to run. Two steps were all she took before he brought her to the ground with a violent kick. She rolled away, the nettles stinging her bare skin.

She felt him invade her body while she screamed; but the anger and the pain coupled were too much to bear. Comets exploded in her head and, mercifully, she fainted.

Chapter 28

When Fiona regained consciousness, she was in her own bed at Blair Castle. A bushy-eyebrowed man she did not recognize was peering down at her with concern.

"You're feeling better at last?" He did not wait for her response. "I am Doctor Douglas. Miss Gunn and His Highness sent for me as soon as you had your accident. You've been a very sick young woman and gave your friends quite a turn, I must say." He smiled, showing ugly wooden false teeth discolored by pipe smoke.

"Lady Flora Jane. Is she all right?" It hurt to speak. She had screamed and screamed and screamed . . .

The doctor became instantly serious. "You mustn't worry about her ladyship. You've had a nasty turn yourself."

Fiona tried to sit up. "Is she alive?"

"Yes, yes, though only by the grace of God and good Prince Franco. Had he not found you there where you fell, I hate to think what might have happened."

She started to speak, to say that she fell because she was pushed, that Franco was a devil masquerading as a hero. But it all took too much strength, and she was so achingly tired that it hurt even to breathe. Adrift in pain, she slipped back into sleep.

Her dream was different this time. It seemed now to be set on a wheel, so that no sooner had she seen the last of it than it began again.

The moor was the same; so were the bloody stones that turned to heads. Even the gray quilted overcast was unaltered. But now the dream appealed to all her senses with urgent realism. She could smell the gunpowder in the air, the sickly sweet odor of decomposing flesh. She felt a buffeting angry wind that stung her eyes and tasted of the sea. But of all the sensations, the worst was what she heard: the banshee-moaning music of the pipes.

When next she opened her eyes, Franco was standing at the foot of her bed. It seemed to be the middle of the night, for he was wearing a red dressing gown of embroidered Chinese silk. In his hand, Franco held a candle; its yellow flame cast shadows that sharpened his features diabolically. Fiona had been given a sedative; she recalled accepting the cup unwillingly from the doctor's hand. Whatever it was, it had flattened her spirits, made her placid and unafraid even of Franco, who stood so near and stared at her with such malevolence.

It was raining hard. She heard the wind drive the torrent against her window. She looked at Franco, realizing dimly that she should fear him. But she hadn't the energy. Sickly calm, she drifted into sleep again.

When she awoke again her mind was clear. She heard Franco speaking to Doctor Douglas not far from her bedside. Pretending to sleep, she listened to their conversation. She knew she must get a grip on herself before Franco's advantage overwhelmed her spirit finally and forever.

"I beg to differ with your diagnosis, Doctor Douglas," Franco was saying smoothly. "I know this young woman better than you, and I assure you that though she appears to be healthy, her mind is confused. Terribly, pathetically so. She has a history of nervous disorders that makes continued medication an absolute necessity. I fear that without it she may become violent. God only knows what she might say or do!" Fiona heard the false concern in Franco's voice and wished with all her heart that she could leap up and expose him for the devil he was. But she would only fall into his trap. If she said or did anything out of the ordinary, the doctor would be sure to believe what Franco said was true. Helpless, unable to defend herself, Fiona was forced to listen to the lies in silence.

"Her mother suffered also, Miss Gunn tells me." No need to see Doctor Douglas's expression; his voice told Fiona that he believed all Franco's falsehoods. "She claims to have portentous dreams. Is that so?"

"Indeed. I'm glad you're an enlightened physician, Doctor Douglas. We are fortunate to have the services of such a man as you. But it distresses me that you must so frequently make the trip between the castle and the village merely to administer medication. May I suggest that you give me the belladonna? I will see to it she receives the dosage required."

For a moment the doctor sounded doubtful. "But what of Lady Flora Jane Campbell? She is far from well. She's had a terrible shock."

"And Miss Gunn is caring for her with all the love and skill of a devoted niece. You've said yourself that little can be done for her besides allowing rest and calm." Franco's heavily accented English soothed like music. The doctor was entirely deceived.

"Well, Your Highness, if I were a younger man I might contradict you. But to tell the truth, I suffer from the gout most painfully these damp days, and I would sooner keep to my room than traipse about the countryside when, as you say, there is little I can do that you and Miss Gunn are not fully competent to handle.'"

After a little more conversation, Fiona heard the men leave the room. The door shut; she sat up in bed. Not stopping to plan, she raced to her wardrobe and withdrew a wine-colored wrapper. She pulled it on as she opened the door; then, barefoot and shivering in the echoing corridor, she hastened to Lady Flora Jane's apartments. Pushing the door open a crack, she saw the room was empty but for the old woman, who lay in corpselike stillness in the middle of the huge bed. She seemed to have shrunk since her accident. Her face, withered as a fallen leaf, bore no expression. The tiny clawlike hands clutching the counterpane were the only sign of life. Fiona was horrified.

"What has he done to you?" she cried, rushing to the bedside and falling to her knees. She covered the gnarled hands with kisses.

Slowly, with an effort as great as any she had ever made, Lady Flora Jane turned her head and looked at Fiona. She opened her mouth, but could not speak.

"You are in grave danger and so am I," whispered Fiona, pushing her lips next to Lady Flora Jane's ear. "He's made the doctor think . . ."

She didn't finish the sentence.

"Speak a little louder, Fiona. I'd like to know what I am being accused of." Franco stood in the doorway, his beautiful mouth twisted in a deformed smile.

"You!" she cried out and ran to him, pummeling his chest with her fists. "Devil!" she screamed, the word scraping her throat like a knife's edge.

He only laughed as he held her away. "But you have it all wrong, Fiona. Have you forgotten? *You* are the Devil's child. You are a witch!"

Quick as a fox, she bit his hand.

Franco yelled and slapped her hard. His brown eyes had angry red lights in them.

"There'll be no fight left, when I get through with you." He started to drag her away.

"Lady Flora Jane!"

"The old crone is dying. Don't waste your breath on her!"

Fiona screamed for help: from the servants, from anyone. But he silenced her, shoving her against the wall and slamming his palm across her face so she could scarcely breathe.

"Keep your mouth shut, Fiona. Say one word and I'll kill you and the old one. I will! You know I will!"

The fight went out of her and she slumped against the wall. She put up no resistance as he drove her ahead of him down the hall. In her room, he forced her to drink something bitter; she could not summon up the strength to spit it out. The belladonna swam through her system, dulling every sensation. She was drowsy and thankful for the wide soft bed that held her like a cloud.

Since Lady Murray's departure for the south, Franco had appropriated Lord George Murray's small comfortable reading room adjoining his wife's sitting room. While icy rain continued to batter the castle, he sat before the peat fire feeling warm and mellow, like a weary traveler who has at last found his destination. He admired Lord George's taste;

though he knew the man to be personally somewhat cold and austere, his room was comfortable in the extreme, and the many bound volumes that lined the walls gave the place a richness that particularly appealed to Franco. There was opulence here, the discreet elegance of ancient wealth.

Long ago, Franco's family had owned palaces of incredible grandeur. There had been hundreds of servants at the command of his great grandfather, and in those days the family acreage stretched for miles beyond sight in all directions. But the house of Franco was noted for more than its wealth. Its cruelty was also widely recognized. There came a time when the peasants could tolerate the abuses no longer; and hordes of them, half-crazy from hunger and long suffering, destroyed the castle and grounds, burning and stealing and murdering as if empowered by righteous angels. After that the old Prince could not pay his gambling debts; his drunkenness was notorious. Somehow, the family had never recovered from the peasant uprising, but sank deeper and deeper into debt; until now, in Prince Gabriello Franco's generation, there was nothing left. Not one single acre of land belonged to him.

But all that would change as soon as Abigail had her legacy from Lady Flora Jane Campbell. Though hardly a Princess herself, the old woman was rich enough to insure a luxurious life for the Prince and his bride-to-be. The accident at the stream, though it further postponed his departure for the Continent, had proved to be a blessing. Not only did it bring much closer the day when Abigail would receive her legacy, it had also enabled him to satisfy his craving for Fiona Macleod.

He felt stronger for having forced her submission. Stretching his long shapely legs before the fire so the warmth of the turf toasted the soles of his boots, he thought how strange it was that he now felt no desire for her whatever. Nor for Abigail. This alternation of his lust from masculine to feminine was nothing new in his nature, but it was something he wondered at from time to time. He thought of it as great good fortune for him, since it enabled him to occupy a position of power with Prince Charles while at the same time securing his future security with Abigail.

His reverie was broken by an urgent rapping at the door. It was Abigail. She had a message in her hand.

"He's come back!" she said as she handed it to Franco.

"Who?" The note told him all he needed to know. For some reason Captain Michael Cameron had cut short his trip to Campbelltown, and had chosen to hurry back to Blair Castle. The note gave no clue as to what might have happened.

"What shall we do?" Abigail was so nervous she was almost in tears. She began to chew her nails.

"Stop that!" Franco was revolted by her. He needed time to think, and her presence—her near hysteria, adolescent mannerisms and chilly pallor—made it difficult. "Let me think. Get out!"

Abigail started to cry. "How can you speak to me like that after what I . . ." She wailed and ran into the adjoining sitting room, where she threw herself, sobbing, on one of the benches. This latest snub was just too much for her. When she thought of what she had given Gabriello Franco—her precious virtue, her woman's glory—she could not stop the heavy sobs that wracked her body. When she thought of all she had risked . . .

"Oh, God," she cried aloud. "Don't let it be!"

The truth was, she had not bled for more than a month. At first, she attributed this to the excitement of the Edinburgh life, the change of season. But just that morning she had checked a day book that she found in Lady Murray's desk, and discovered that not merely thirty days but considerably more had gone by since her last disability. And now—was it possibly only her imagination—she was nauseated and nervous; she even thought she felt a quivering in her belly as if some new life stirred there.

When Franco came back into the sitting room, she sat up quickly and wiped her damp red eyes with the back of her hand. She sniffled and saw him wince at the gross noise.

"Control yourself, Abigail," he ordered, cool and efficient. "There is absolutely no need to become hysterical. You and I have done nothing wrong, and if Michael Cameron doesn't like what he finds when he gets here, he can only blame himself for having abandoned his aunt and the inestimable Fiona Macleod."

"Why are you so mean to me?" Abigail wanted to know, the tears smarting anew. "Don't you love me anymore?" Compared to what concerned her, Michael Cameron meant nothing.

Franco sighed. "Of course I love you. You are behaving most strangely, Abigail. You are as irrational as Fiona!"

"But you never come to my room or invite me to yours." Do you take me for a fool, her thoughts screamed. I've seen the loathing in your eyes, the disgust.

"My dear, we must be discreet."

"We didn't think of that before. Before, you said you couldn't get enough of me, that you were hungry for me like a child for sweets. Those were your words exactly. What has changed?" She stopped crying, but her face was unattractively blotched.

"Nothing. Nothing has changed."

"It's the money, isn't it?" A new light flashed in her eyes. She jumped up and embraced Franco eagerly. "I'll go to Flora Jane now and borrow . . ."

"No. It's too late for that. You must get her to sign something. Something that says you will inherit everything." He narrowed her eyes at her doubtfully. "Do you think you can do that?"

"Of course." She pulled him close to her and covered his face with moist kisses. She began to cry, but now the tears sprang from joy. "I love you, Gabi! You'll see. It will be as it once was. I promise it will. Don't you know I would die for you?"

As he patted her back in pretended consolation, Franco's full lips twisted into a sardonic smile.

Chapter 29

Lady Flora Jane summoned her feeble reserves of strength to turn her head when her bedroom door opened. Just that slight movement caused the wound in her temple to throb agonizingly. She squeezed her eyes tight against the pain. When she opened them again, Abigail was beside her bed. The disappointment was sharp. She wanted to see Fiona and let her know that she understood. Though too weak to move or speak when Fiona had come into her room earlier, Lady Flora Jane had been conscious.

"You're feeling better, Aunty? That's good." Abigail drew up a satin-tufted hassock and sat down at the bedside. "We've all been so worried about you."

"Indeed?" Lady Flora Jane's lungs were congested from the exposure she had suffered during her long wait on the moor. Her voice was reedy, and the mere effort of forming words exhausted her.

"Of course we have. Why, if it had not been for Gabi," Abigail reddened, "Prince Gabriello, I mean, you might be much worse off."

Lady Flora Jane tried to laugh, which set off a spasm of coughing. She wondered if Abigail believed the lies she spoke.

The young woman fluttered about ineffectually, trying to make her aunt comfortable again. But her nursing was half-hearted, and Lady Flora Jane knew it. She wishes I were dead already, the old woman thought.

When Lady Flora Jane was resting easily once more, Abigail brought up the touchy matter of her will. "There's nothing really wrong with you, Aunt, that time and rest won't cure. I know you're going to be feeling better in just a day or two. Still, to be on the safe side, I believe you ought to write something down. Just in case."

A dry smile spread over Lady Flora Jane's face. Abigail was almost squirming in the awkward situation and that made her aunt happier than anything that day. The sight and sound of Abigail's greed actually made her feel a bit lively. "What's that you say, Abi?" she croaked.

"Uh, your will . . . Isn't it time you made your . . . wishes clear?"

The smile grew quite broad. For an instant, Lady Flora Jane's face was practically youthful. "I've already done that," she said.

"Oh?" Abigail looked confused for a moment. Then she gushed, "Thank you, Aunt Flora Jane. Thank you so much. I will always be grateful." She bent to kiss the gnarled old fingers.

"Grateful? For what?"

"Silly old dear! For the inheritance, of course."

"What inheritance?"

"The money. The money you've . . . given me . . ."

The truth dawned on Abigail very slowly. Clearly, it had never occurred to her that Lady Flora Jane would go so far as to disinherit her. Now the realization spread across her face like an ugly scar. Her mouth twisted in a grimace of pain and rage. "Who? If not me, who?"

"Fiona Macleod!"

"Who is she, when I am your flesh and blood? What about me? Me? Me?"

Lady Flora Jane was tiring. When it came right down to it, she was sorry to bring grief to her niece. At the same time, she knew the Campbell fortune would be wasted in Abigail's hands. It seemed cruel but it was necessary, and she no longer felt disloyal to her family. She tried to say all this, thinking that Abigail deserved some kind of explanation. But the effort of speaking was too much for her lungs, and she could concentrate only on the sound of her labored breathing as she strained for air. To Abigail's question, to her angry screaming demand, the old woman shook her head and whispered, "Fiona. Fiona. Fiona."

Franco was waiting for Abigail outside the bedroom door. "Did you get it?" he asked, reaching for the paper still clutched in her fist.

She pulled back.

"What's the matter?" He saw shock and horror on her face and knew something had fouled up the plan irremediably. "She didn't sign. Why?"

Abigail could not answer him. She needed time to think. Her imagination was playing a spiteful trick and she seemed to feel the new presence deep in her belly quivering with amusement, as if it were part of a conspiracy to make her miserable. She had to get away from Franco. She could not tell him, she would never tell him about Fiona. She knew him too well.

The revelation would spell the end of everything between them. Franco would drop interest in her immediately and do something to bind himself to Fiona's fortunes. She imagined the two of them as lovers. All her girlish fantasies of castles in Italy and a host of princely offspring were transmuted in her fevered mind. She saw Fiona as the reigning Princess, the mother of royalty. Never! She would die first.

She fled down the corridor. Franco hurried after her. At the door of her bedroom he grabbed her roughly. Shoving her ahead of him into the room, he demanded to know what had happened.

"There is no money."

"But the old *strega* is as rich as Croesus! you told me . . ."

"She's given it all away to . . . to . . . charity." Crazy silent laughter rocked Abigail's shoulders. In a way what she was saying was perfectly true. She wasn't lying to Franco at all. "She gave it away to the poorhouse women. There's none for us!"

"*Dio sudicio!*" Franco dropped Abigail's arm and sank into a deep cushioned chair near the window. The shutters were ajar and a stream of damp cold air grazed his neck and shoulders. He didn't notice. He was afire with frustration and anger.

"You promised me . . ." He wanted to kill her, to kill all the stupid Scots who were destroying his future.

"Don't use that tone, Gabi," Abigail whines. "You think I did this on purpose? I told you, I have nothing of my own. My father sent me to Edinburgh to . . ."

"May your father burn in Hell. May your whole family be doomed to penury. *Puta sudicia!*" He spoke between clenched teeth.

"Oh, Gabi, Gabi, it's not so bad. You still have your own fortune. We'll be all right with that and our baby . . ."

"Our what?" He screamed the question.

"That's right." She nodded her head many times and tried to smile. "Our child will be born in early summer. I don't mind going to Italy. I want to, in fact. I want to meet your family, and I just know I can adapt to life in Italy. I'll learn the language in no time, you'll see." She was pathetically eager.

He was too dumbfounded to speak. A baby! This was the last thing in the world he wanted. Never had he known such a murderous rage as that which threatened him now. His entire body trembled from the effort of repressing it.

She felt his displeasure, and a nastiness he had never heard came into her voice. "You are happy, aren't you, Gabi?" she asked almost shyly. "You will take me to Italy, won't you?"

He didn't answer right away. He didn't even look at her. She continued in the same unpleasant conniving tone.

"It wouldn't be wise to forget how much we've been through together. Apart from our child, there's all the talk and planning we've done. If Prince Charles or even Michael Cameron were to know your true feelings about Fiona . . . There is the matter of the dog. Prince Charles would . . ."

"Sweet Abigail, you have a viper's heart. Just because your aunt has betrayed you, there is no need to think I will do the same." The sound of his own voice calmed him. He waxed confident. "You do me an injustice. Of course we will go to Italy together. And of course you will be my bride." He pulled her to him so she would not see the expression on his face.

Miles distant on the road across the strath before the rise to Blair Atholl Village and the Highlands, Michael Cameron hunkered down in the saddle and pulled the collar of his greatcoat up against the wind and driven rain. He felt as if he had been a lifetime on horseback and regretted his decision to return to the castle by this means rather than hiring a carriage. Still, in the interest of speed, it had seemed the wisest course.

The news he carried was bad. Days before, the Jacobite army had begun its mortifying retreat from England. The army had been less than a hundred miles from London, yet could not go on. Clearly, there was no support for their cause in England; and to have continued on would have meant certain death for most of the valiant Highlanders and imprisonment in the Tower for Charles himself. King Louis, not wishing to be part of a humiliating and costly massacre, had withdrawn all his support: neither men nor arms would he send to Scotland. Disgraceful as it was, retreat was the only hope. There was talk of a spring offensive, but Michael had doubts that it would ever occur. He knew his Highlanders better than any francophile Stuart ever could. They would go home rather than make another foray into enemy territory. Proud men, they would try to forget their shame in the safety of their family circles and the comforting wilderness.

But it was not the retreat alone that had sent Michael Cameron hurrying back to Blair Castle. From several trustworthy sources he had heard disquieting news of Prince Charles. The Prince was said to be increasingly difficult, drinking heavily and alternating between moods of absurd optimism and abysmal despair. He was less concerned with the fate of his soldiers and the Scotsmen and women he claimed to represent that with his own public embarrassment. Hearing of the Prince's tantrums and diatribes, his growing obsession with himself, Michael had immediately been concerned for Fiona's well-being.

He hoped he had exorcised once and for all the supernatural fears that had obsessed her, but he believed the Prince might have the power to reinstate them. She might become convinced that she and her foolish dream had somehow figured in the defeat of the Highlanders. When he thought of her, Michael saw Fiona as beautiful and good, enchantingly desirable, but highstrung and not completely reliable. He couldn't trust her to withstand the influence of Prince Charles. He had to get her out of Blair Castle and back to Skye before it was too late.

Beyond these concerns, still another thought rankled and disturbed his peace of mind as he and Muddy swiftly covered the drab unfeatured winterscape. Though still a trader and an ardent believer in the value of the commerce of goods and ideas between nations, he had lately come to realize he wanted to fight for Scotland despite all his doubts and personal dislikes. Michael was a Highlander, and his attachment to that wild and open land was a thread that bound him to his forebears back through the centuries. He knew that if the Jacobites were overcome by the English once and for all, the conquerors would exact a terrible price from the rebels. It would mean the end of the clans and of Highland life as he knew it. It was time to put away personal preferences and heed the voice of his ancestors.

Michael shifted his weight in the saddle and hunkered deeper into the warmth of his greatcoat. Whatever else happened, he must see to it that Fiona was safely away from Prince Charles and the war danger. Then he, like all good Scotsmen in that year 1746, would take up his weapons and fight until the death for his Highland home.

Fiona awoke the next morning with her head clear of the belladonna. A nervous-featured little serving girl—no more than ten or twelve by the looks of her—brought a tray with a light breakfast and set it on a table before the fire in Fiona's room. From the half-scared half-curious way she eyed the girl from Skye, it was clear to Fiona that below stairs the servants were reveling in gossip.

The light meal refreshed Fiona and she was able to ponder her circumstances. She had poured herself a third cup of tea and was debating how and when to manage a secret visit to Lady Flora Jane's chamber, when the door of her room opened without warning.

"My dear," said Franco. "You seem to be feeling better."

"What do you want?"

"Come now, don't be so chilly. You and I should be friends. After all, our concerns are the same."

"Oh?" She could scarcely tolerate looking at him. The recollection of his hands and mouth were excruciatingly vivid, and raised a terrible anger in her.

"We both care about His Highness."

Fiona laughed bitterly. "You beast! You only care about yourself!" It was true. She recognized him as a man fighting for his life, for whom no measure taken toward self-preservation would be too extreme. Though she understood none of his motives clearly and knew none of his history, she could intuit enough to make her skin crawl with the certainty of his determination to have his way.

He eyed her speculatively. Idly, his manicured hand reached out to touch her flowing amber-colored hair, radiant in the glow of firelight. He was smiling. "Perhaps you are right, Fiona. My own concerns are foremost in my mind. That is what brings me to you this morning." He sat down near her. "We can expect a visitor a little later today."

"Who?" No sooner had she asked it than she knew. "Michael! When is he coming? Why?"

Franco waved her questions away. "I really cannot tell you why the man persists in traversing the country. Presumably," his voice was heavy with sarcasm, "he finds you irresistible. But never mind about that. Before he comes, I want to make several matters clear to you."

She stood up and walked away from the fire. "I have no interest in what you have to say, Franco. Get out of my room." She pulled her long Macleod plaid more tightly around her shoulders.

He darted up from the chair and grabbed her. His hand beneath her chin pushed her head back harshly. "Watch how you speak, *belissima*. I am not done with you and yours." He shoved back hard; she winced with pain and he smiled. "I think you will listen now." He released her and returned to his place beside the fire. As if nothing had happened, he poured himself a cup of tea and sipped it thoughtfully before continuing to speak. "So. When Captain Cameron comes, you will not mention what has . . . transpired between us. You will say nothing to arouse his suspicions." She didn't respond. "Well, Fiona?"

"And if I do not cooperate?"

"Then I will kill you."

"If I die, Michael will . . ."

"Stupid girl! If you die, it will appear to be an accident! Your beloved Michael will do nothing. Except have an accident himself, if that should prove necessary."

For a long moment, they stared at each other. Fiona did not doubt Franco's sincerity. Inwardly, she even found a little humor in her situation. There had been no need for Franco's threats. He might have known she would never tell Michael what had occurred on the moor that day. The shame was too great. Her scratches and bruises from that experience had mended will; physically she was in excellent health. She thought her personal pain and suffering were over now. And there was no need to call down punishment on Franco and thus reveal her own shame. Somehow, she knew Franco would suffer soon enough.

Fiona had her dream. She knew the future. Franco's time was drawing near.

Michael came to her late in the afternoon, as she was reading a book of verses near the fire. There were many words she didn't understand, but the discipline of reading helped to still her mind's unruly confusion.

"Fiona." Michael's voice, ringing with the cadences of Skye, made her heart leap. She ran to him, throwing her arms about his broad shoulders. His arms encircled her waist; their lips met. Time stopped.

"What's happened here?" He had to know at last. "How was my aunt taken ill? Are you all right?"

"Yes, of course. And now that you are here I am more than well, more than happy." In a prim afternoon dress of mulberry-colored wool, ornamented only by a wide white lace collar, Fiona looked schoolgirl-young and innocent as dawn.

"She . . . we had an accident. On the moor."

"I don't understand."

"We were crossing a stream on the way to the village. She . . . we slipped."

"Both of you?" He sounded doubtful. Holding her away from him he peered into her amber eyes. "You both fell? I don't understand how that could happen."

Discovering an artifice she had not known she possessed, Fiona laughed lightly and met his gaze full on. He must not guess what had happened. Apart from Franco's threats, she could not risk the loss of Michael's love. Better to lie, better to dissemble forever, than to have the love in his eyes change to loathing at the mention of Franco's name in conjunction with hers.

"It was a crazy accident," she chattered, pulling him toward the fire and urging him to sit. She tugged at the servants' bellcord. "We were on this little bridge and it collapsed underfoot. My lady's heel caught in the rotting planks and . . ." The servant entered. "Bring food and drink for Captain Cameron . . ."

"I'm not hungry, Fiona. I only want you!" He sounded almost angry but she melted at the love in his eyes, the desire he radiated. Blushing, she dismissed the servant.

The lovers looked at one another for a long time.

"Shall I lock the door?" she asked softly, blushing deeper at her own outrageous forwardness.

"I'll do it," he said.

When their bodies came together this time, in the comfort of the wide canopied bed, there was less urgency in their touching. Michael's hands caressed her silken skin—the soft mounds of her breasts, the swell of her hips and round feminine belly—lingeringly, wanting to prolong the moments when their bodies were new to one another. Some day, there would be no curve or swell with which he would not be totally familiar. They would love each other differently then. Now, while they were young and every touch was a discovery, he sought to make the moments last as if he believed he could cheat Time itself.

As his lips explored her slowly, delicately, she felt herself grow hot and wanton; meltingly, she submitted to the intimacies of his demanding mouth. Like blossom to bee, she opened for him. He sucked and licked the nectar of her body until she could wait no longer to feel him in her, completing her. With her legs wrapped about his hips she drew him into her liquid center.

"Love me, Michael," she moaned, losing herself in delicious sensation, "Love me."

"Forever."

"Forever and ever."

Afterward they rested. Then played like children, giggling and teasing one another lovingly. He held her down and tickled her, until she laughed so much she cried.

"No more, no more!" she spluttered, shoving him away with all her strength. "Someone will hear!" She jumped off the bed and picked up her shift, discarded in the middle of the floor. She slipped it over her head, then found her plaid and gave it to Michael.

"What's this for?"

"Cover yourself."

"Why?"

She couldn't think of why immediately, and that made him laugh at her.

"Ah, Fiona, you're a prim little innocent at heart, despite your womanly ways." He held out his arms to her.

Prim? she thought. Perhaps. But innocent . . . She turned away from Michael. Suddenly her merriment was gone, obscured by the unwanted memory of Franco. His hands and lips had touched her too. Was it possible that Michael did not taste him on her skin, when she could still feel him in her system like poison?

"What's the matter?" Michael asked, sensing her sudden change of mood.

She shrugged. "I guess I'm not completely recovered yet."

Instantly, he became concerned. "Lie down," he told her, helping her into bed and covering her well. "You will need your rest for the trip." He kissed her brow lovingly.

"Trip? Where are we going?"

"I'm taking you and my aunt back to Skye. Edinburgh is in English hands right now, and it won't be safe for her to return until . . ."

"What's happened?" She sat up and gripped his wrist urgently. "Michael, tell me. What of His Highness?"

"Retreat. It is all over in England."

She fell back upon the pillows. "Oh, God, no!"

"But there is no reason for you to be concerned. You have title to your cottage on Skye and you and my aunt . . ."

She was shaking her head from side to side. "I can't leave. He will need me."

"Never mind about the Prince. Be done with him! He's brought nothing but death and despair to Scotland."

"And there will be more," she whispered.

"No doubt. But it's not for you . . ."

"I must stay here, where he can find me."

A sudden chill ran through Michael and he shuddered. "Fiona . . ."

"It is the dream, Michael. The Prince and I are drawn together by destiny. I have no choice but to stay. I must . . ."

She saw his expression change from loving concern to disbelief and finally anger. "I thought you'd finished with that hocus-pocus! You swore you had! You lied to me!"

She tried to touch him, but he shrugged her off, disgusted and all at once eager to escape her. He was a man capable of violence when sufficiently prompted. He felt the rage of disappointment in him now, and knew that if he didn't leave Fiona he would hurt her no matter how much he loved her.

"I don't want to hear what you have to say. I don't even want to look at you." He pulled on his clothes in a hurry. She made no move to stop him until, seeing him at the door, she fully understood the finality of his words.

"You promised to love me forever. You said forever, Michael."

He stared at her for a moment, opening the door. "I lied, Fiona. Just like you, I lied!"

Chapter 30

Michael was with Lady Flora Jane when she died, just after dawn the next morning. The priest had come an hour before. She tasted the Host and her brow was crossed with the chrism of extreme unction.

In the moments before the end came, she enjoyed a lucidity that made conversation between them possible. Though she was very weak, she insisted on being helped into a sitting position with four or five satin-slipped pillows propped at her back, her face toward the window.

"Open the shutters for me, Michael. I would like to watch the dawn come one last time."

"Don't talk so morbidly, Aunt. I will open the shutters, but . . ."

"La, dear boy. So near the end, let there be no foolishness between us. Now is the time for truth. I am dying. There is not much time."

When she saw the sky change from black to gray, she sighed as if she had thought that on this, her final day, that change might not occur. It was the end of the world for her, why not for everyone?

Without taking her eyes from the window, she said, "So. Scotland is to remain in bondage to the English. Perhaps the Stuarts will give up trying now and let us learn to live in captivity without hope." She was quiet a moment, watching the sky, deep in her own thoughts. "Will you fight now, Michael?"

"Aye," he said.

"What changed your mind?"

"I think these Highlands may be worth dying for."

More silence followed. She lay so still upon her mountain of pillows that Michael would have thought her dead already had it not been for her shining eyes. "It will be a clear day," she said at last. "See I'm buried right away. I have a horror of graveyards in the rain."

He took her hand and kissed it. She was his mother's sister and always special to him. Even as a boy, he had known that she was uncommonly wise. Without her his world would be greatly diminished, and he told her so. She smiled her gratitude.

"But you have Fiona, my boy. She too is wise, and very strong. Strong, I think, beyond our knowing." She saw the shadow cloud his face before he looked away. "She will not always do as you wish, Michael. A spirit moves in her different from that in other folk. She will have to heed it no matter how she suffers. But even so, she will always need you, Michael."

The cloudless sky turned the color of cream. A gust of wind rattled the window panes.

"Let him in, dear boy," whispered Lady Flora Jane.

"You'll get a chill, Aunt."

She smiled tolerantly. "It hardly matters, does it? Let him in."

"Who?" He looked at the window where she seemed to see something or someone. "There's no one there." The sun's first rays turned the glass to gold.

Again she smiled. "It's Death, Michael. And of course you can't see him. I would worry if you could." She laughed and patted his hand. "Give me a kiss, then let him in. Be a good boy."

When he returned to her bedside, she was dead.

She was buried later that same day in the Murray family graveyard, under a blue and cloudless sky. Only Michael stood beside the grave and heard the priest offer up the soul of Flora Jane Campbell. Abigail refused to attend; Franco did not care to. Fiona, once more drugged and helpless, lay deep in sleep, oblivious to everything but her dream. Only when the sound of hoofbeats echoed up from the stone courtyard below her room, did she sit up and cry out. Once.

"Michael!"

But he was gone . . .

Book Eight

———

THE MADWOMAN

Chapter 31

At first Abigail refused any part in Franco's plan. Though she had once thought herself capable of anything, even killing, when her courage was put to the test; she quailed. Since she had become aware of the new life growing in her belly, she had changed somehow, grown softer, more fearful.

"Is this how you show your loyalty?" he asked. "If we were going to be husband and wife . . ."

So it was that she gave his plan consideration; and gradually, as she became accustomed to the idea of murder, it seemed less heinous to her. Franco was right. Fiona's death would be a blessing both to the half-demented girl and to Prince Charles. And, more important, to Abigail herself . . .

The morning after Lady Flora Jane's funeral, Franco had received a message from Prince Charles informing him that he and Fiona were to attend him immediately at the home of his old friend Sir Hugh Patterson, at Bannockburn. Reading the message in the privacy of his rooms, Prince Gabriello had winced at the tone of it: demanding, petulant, superstitious. Where Franco was more and more convinced that Fiona was the evil spirit damning the Jacobite cause, Prince Charles had moved further in the opposite direction. *I need the girl beside me. She is the spirit of my cause. Without her, I lose heart.*

Franco had seen the Prince in his periodic moods of black despair and knew that to go against his wishes, to leave Fiona behind, might be disastrous. It would be necessary somehow to disaffect the Prince from the pagan girl. Only if he rejected her himself would Charles be rid of her evil influence. Then, and only then, the Highlanders might have a chance against the English.

The oaken log burning before him settled, throwing up a cloud of sparks. Some were the color of Fiona's hair. He seemed to see shapes and supernatural forms within the caverns of glowing embers. A plan took shape within his mind, developed substance, and at last seemed perfect.

He had waited until that night when, sated with physical pleasure, Abigail lay warm and willing beside him. The softness of her white body horrified him now; he wondered that he had ever found her attractive. The thought of his child growing in her womb was almost physically nauseating to him. It made him feel unclean, contaminated. Now it required all his powers of self-control to conceal his disgust. He did so successfully, but no wonder. Abigail was sodden with love. He could have done almost anything, and she would have found a way of rationalizing it to herself.

Eventually, he had even made her accept the idea of murder.

Though Franco did not know it, one of the reasons Abigail could think of Fiona's murder was the legacy. If Abigail could not inherit from Lady Flora Jane, than neither would Fiona. A Highland peasant had no right to that money; and perhaps, if she were dead, a clever solicitor might convince the courts of Abigail's own rights. Abigail had been over and over this in her mind. She had only to convince the courts that Lady Flora Jane was senile at the time she made her will and, with Fiona dead, the legacy would revert to Abigail. Her child would never know poverty or fear.

The argument that she would be doing murder for the good of Scotland and Prince Charles was not compelling to Abigail. She could summon up the energy to care for little apart from herself at this time. She was obsessed with the child growing within her which must, at all costs, have a father and the advantages of wealth. She did not want to think what Aeneas

Gunn might do if she brought a bastard home to Gunn Manor.

Fiona lay dreaming of the holocaust as Franco entered her room after midnight. Though she had not recently been drugged, the cumulative effects of belladonna, coupled with despair at Michael's leaving, had induced a heavy slumber, which was not interrupted as Franco slipped the covers bacck and slid his arms beneath her body. She was light in his embrace, as if composed more of spirit than flesh and blood and bone. Abigail was in the corridor keeping watch for the night servants. At a tacit signal from her, Franco hurried down the back stairs with his burden. Three floors below, where the stairway ended in a heavy brass bolted door, Abigail stopped him with a hand on his arm.

"Are you sure, Gabi? Perhaps there is another way?" She had no intention of backing out of their scheme. During the last several hours, she had even become eager for the moment when Fiona would be dead. Still, at this last moment, she had to make sure that Franco was as enthusiastic as she. There could be no recriminations between them later. Again, she was thinking of their child; its parents must be united in their course or . . .

"Be silent, woman! Open the door before the whole house wakes up." She cringed at his tone, but obeyed his order.

A gust of cold night air redolent of the barnyard stirred Fiona's hair and brushed her lashes. She moved in Franco's arms.

"Hurry!"

Almost at a run, the two conspirators crossed the cobbled courtyard and hurried down the path between the bothy, where the field servants slept, and the duckyard beside the pond. Black night covered everything, and the wind howled with frustration as the castle's shuttered windows and barred doors denied it entry. Owls at nest in the eaves of the bothy queried them in passing. Rats fled away in front of them. Somewhere to the rear, nearer the castle, a dog barked sleepily.

A caretaker's boat was tied to a post set among the reeds at the edge of the pond. As Abigail fumbled with the knotted line, Franco laid Fiona across the aft seat. Then, angry at her ineptitude, he pushed Abigail into the boat, indicating the forward seat, and dug his nails into the icy knot. It came apart at last, and he leapt into the boat as it began to drift. Using an oar, he shoved out into the open water.

"Do it now," whispered Abigail urgently. "It's starting to get light."

Ignoring the demand, he rowed to the center of the four- or five-acre pond, where he knew the water must be twenty feet or more, with almost as deep a layer of mud below that. The pond was stocked with fish, which were used for the servants' dinner table. There were several large snapping turtles as well, and from time to time otters and muskrat had been seen swimming from shore to shore on warm summer nights. But on this frigid night in late December, nothing moved but the wind along the black surface. It seemed to be a lake of the dead, whose lapping waves beckoned eagerly.

"Here will do," cried Abigail impatiently. "Just push her in and be done with it. Hurry, Gabi." He stood up. As he stepped toward her, the boat rocked dangerously. "What are you doing, Gabi?" His bulk towered over her, and suddenly she knew the answer. His arm rose; in his hand he held the oar like a club. The only sound was the sweet slip-slap of water against the boat. In the instant before his hand came down, a dozen images flashed before her inward eye. She remembered Aeneas and how it had been with them before drink and gambling had mottled his spirit; she recalled their rides together when he held her before him in the saddle in princess finery: a cherry-red velvet riding habit with a white plumed hat. As the oar came down hard against her temple, she thought of the baby growing inside her. Instead of raising her arms to deflect the blow, she grasped her belly to protect it. Before she slumped back, her eyes were wide open. They stared at Franco in condemnation.

Quickly—he smeared blood from Abigail's forehead on Fiona's white nightgown. He tugged at the blonde girl's hair until several strands came loose. These he twisted in Fiona's hand. Then he dragged Fiona forward and sprawled her body across Abigail's, as if there had been a struggle between the two women and Fiona was the victor. Satisfied, he dropped the oars into the pond and then slipped into the cold water himself. Accustomed to strenuous sea swimming, he made it to shore easily and found the place where, the day before, he had hidden fresh clothing and a hank of rope with a stone.

Stripping, his teeth chattering noisily and the hairs on his arms and legs upright with cold, he bundled his wet clothes about the rock, tied the rope around the whole thing several times, then let it sink into the muddy goo at the bottom of the pond. In a few moments, he was dressed in riding clothes. Had any one among the servants been awake, he would have seen Prince Gabriello smiling as he strode to the stable to saddle his horse for an early morning ride.

At dawn, the night's overcast evaporated. Fiona awoke to the sun's pale rays slanting across her back. Her hands against something soft and cold, she pushed herself upright and looked around her. She held her hands before her face and saw the blood dried to brown and stuck all over with long blonde hairs. She saw Abigail, and began to scream.

Like the cries of an eagle scratched upon the morning's still surface, the noise carried for miles. Franco, grazing his horse beside a pretty stream, heard it, smiled and sighed contentedly.

The constable and Doctor Douglas were easier to convince then Franco had dared hope. He received the two sober-faced gentlemen in one of the many downstairs drawing rooms of Blair Castle. Equally sober, Franco put the situation to them simply.

"The story has several disturbing elements, which I would avoid speaking of if it were possible. However, there is a question of family honor here and . . ." Franco looked off into the distance, as if he wished he could be lost in the hunting scene depicted in the Belgian tapestry on the wall behind the doctor and the constable. He gave the appearance of a man of principle doing his utmost to be fair.

The law enforcement officer was a man of medium height, with a huge protruding belly and a face as uninteresting as a loaf of bread. He was a Murray, and proud of it. That day he wore his kilt as if to say to the Italian Prince, "I am a clansman and not to be taken lightly." In fact, he was easily convinced by Franco's story and contrived demeanor.

"You, doctor, will vouch for the fact that Miss Macleod has not been of sound mind in recent weeks." At a nod from Franco, the doctor almost preened, so pleased was he to be consulted at all.

"That's true. That's true," the weary old man said. He

could scarcely recall what he had said or prescribed for Fiona, but he took his cue from Franco. Though the agonies of gout had subsided for the moment, his arthritic hands and feet were an all-consuming agony. "Unstrung. A dream bothers her, she says. I prescribed belladonna for the nerves."

"The poor child has grown progressively worse. God knows why she did this . . . vile deed. I suppose we shall never know." Franco shook his head sadly.

"She should be put away then," determined Constable Murray matter-of-factly. "There is a place, Saint Dymphna's, near Inverness. Without a keeper, she's a danger to herself and others."

"I see your point, of course. Still, considering who she is . . ."

The constable looked baffled.

Franco explained. "She is a very special friend of His Highness, Prince Charles Edward Stuart. If any one is to determine that she should be put away, it is the Prince."

The constable was impressed, but still a little doubtful. "The victim, what of her? She had a family, I presume. What am I to tell them?"

Franco made a great display of being uncomfortable.

"Come, come, man. You can speak frankly to me." The constable thought he was being most clever, wooing the information from Prince Gabriello Franco. In the corner of his mind was growing the idea that if he did the right thing in this sensitive matter there might be an important advancement for him. He could always use the money, and he knew how much his wife would enjoy a bit of added prestige. "I'm used to these matters, Your Highness," he said, patting Franco's wrist in a comforting manner. "Just tell the truth."

"Well, the distressing news is that Miss Gunn was . . . with child. And—as you know—unmarried."

The doctor and the constable clicked their tongues in consternation. It was a full-fledged scandal!

"I believe the father was some young soldier boy. I really cannot say for sure. Miss Gunn did confide to me that the situation was quite hopeless, however. In light of this, it seems plausible that she might have tried to do away with herself."

The constable looked shocked. "What are you driving at? Would you have me lie?"

Franco smiled sadly. "Gentlemen, we are all three men of the world. I know I can speak frankly. Miss Gunn's father had but one child. A daughter who failed him miserably. Yet we may presume he loved her as fathers always do their foolish offspring. If we tell him she was murdered by a madwoman, he will surely demand justice. If we tell him of her embarrassing condition, he will defame her for the rest of his life. Is it not better to tell him she died accidentally, and let the matter rest?"

The constable's expression was both outraged and confused. "You said yourself that there was justice to be considered. What about the madwoman? What is to be done with her?"

"Hear me out, I pray you, Constable Murray. Doctor, would you be good enough to compose a letter to His Highness, Prince Charles, explaining Miss Macleod's unbalanced mental state? And you, constable, would you write another missive representing to His Highness that you believe he will know how best to settle the matter? Doctor, you might just mention this place . . . Saint Dymphna's, in Inverness." Franco looked from one to the other. They were obviously pleased with his idea, flattered that their words would be credited by Prince Charles himself. "There is another matter, which I'm sure you worthy gentlemen have considered. I need not tell you in what high esteem the Murray family is held. Surely we owe it to Lord George and his lovely lady to spare them the scandal." Doctor Douglas and Constable Murray quickly agreed. Franco's plan was adopted without further debate. The doctor even offered to write the necessary sad letter to Aeneas Gunn.

"May I suggest you wait until after the poor young woman is buried? Otherwise, the father might feel it necessary to fetch the body; there would be delays . . ."

"Of course, Your Highness," said the constable. "Your help in this delicate situation has been greatly appreciated."

Franco smiled sweetly. "It is I who am grateful. And I know His Highness will feel the same and will wish to show his gratitude in some way."

The doctor and constable almost fell over each other in their effort to out-humble one another. When they were gone, Franco rested his head on the mantel and laughed until the tears sprang to his eyes and his side ached.

Chapter 32

Fiona was under the heavy sedation when the servant carried her to the waiting carriage, and she remained unconscious for the first several hours of the trip to Bannockburn. When she awoke, her first memory was of Abigail's blood on her hands.

With a strangled scream, she sat upright in the carriage and stared at her hands. They were clean now, but she could imagine the stains as if they had made a permanent mark.

"Where am I?" She looked around her at the plushly appointed carriage. Franco was seated opposite her, with a look of wry amusement on his handsome face.

"Welcome to the land of the living, my dear," he said. He reached for her hand and kissed it lightly. She was very beautiful, disheveled and hot-eyed like some of the peasant girls his father used to throw at him to force him to prove his manhood. A time or two their charms had inspired him to satisfy his father's wishes. His nostrils flared. Licking his shapely sensual lips, he breathed deeply.

Fiona shrank back against the cushions; covering her face with her hands she began to sob. "I killed her! Why? I don't remember."

The repeated doses of belladonna made it impossible for her to recall anything clearly. She couldn't seem to concentrate as she once had, nor could she focus her attention beyond the fact that she had awakened to the pond and the morning and the blood on her hands and clothes.

Franco was chuckling with satisfaction.

She stopped crying and looked at him. As if he had spoken

the words—"You are innocent, I am guilty"—she knew it from the message in his eyes and the insulting curl of his lips. She could not know his motive, yet she knew his guilt as surely as she now knew her own innocence.

"I am innocent!" She spoke the words clearly and loudly.

"What? Would you deny the evidence of your own hands? You were, quite literally, caught red-handed, Fiona." Franco was amused by his clever English pun. He watched Fiona as the certainty of her own innocence grew. The constable and the doctor had been stupid and easy to deceive. He could not help appreciating Fiona's intelligence in contrast to their stupidity. He reminded himself not to take her too lightly. After all, she was a witch.

"I am innocent!" she said again, more to herself than to Franco. After she had repeated the phrase in her mind several times, the weight lifted gradually from her heart.

In Blair Castle, she had almost believed that she was mad, as Franco told her she was. Mad! The word itself terrified her. In Borreraig, there had been a raving wild-eyed old man who made his home in a cave littered with his own filth. A demented chatterer of gibberish, he had wandered from cottage to cottage on Dunvegan Head, begging crusts to keep him alive. Mathilda Duncan had said that once he was a young man of promise; but when his strange and terrifying seizures began, the townsfolk burned his cottage down to stop the spread of evil, and the priest had ordered that the man's tongue be cut out lest he choke on it. After that, no one spoke to him willingly, and even the village dogs went away from him with tails between their legs. To be mad, Fiona knew, was a living death. For those not tolerated by their communities there were walled places without windows, cages crammed with helpless men and women.

Franco was staring at her, a half-amused half-wary glint in his eyes. She squirmed uncomfortably, remembering the ugliness that had passed between them. Waves of evil seemed to emanate from the young Italian. She wondered how Abigail could ever have thought him handsome. Like a fallen angel, his beauty was poisoned by this pervasive evil. Poor Abigail . . .

She closed her eyes, but her mind continued to churn with memories of all that had occurred in the last few weeks; there was no hope of sleep. She thought of Michael, and her heart twisted with anguish and longing. She must survive somehow without him. She must find in herself the wisdom and courage to defeat Franco. What had Michael told her after Toby's death? "Believe in yourself or they will destroy you!"

I must be strong for myself and for Prince Charles, she lectured herself. The Prince needs me. Scotland needs me. I must be strong!

"I must be strong!"

Franco laughed. "You talk to yourself, Fiona. Another certain sign of madness."

"Liar!" In a rage she had not expected, she flew across the coach at him with her fingernails bared. The sudden attack caught Franco off guard; she had a chance to drag a nail across his cheek before he shoved her away.

"You whoring little witch!" The back of his hand slammed into her jaw, throwing her against the carriage door. Her forehead hit the brass door handle. For a moment, she was lost in stars.

She opened her eyes. He was almost on top of her. She could smell the sickly sweet odor of anisette on his breath. As she struggled he hit her again and again, until she lay back exhausted, weeping, terrified that he might kill her with his hands or—what seemed worse now—rape her again as he had on the open moor.

"Oh, Michael," she moaned, turning her head from side to side in near delirium. "Help me, Michael."

"No one will help you now, *strega*. I have you and I will do what I want with you. You will not be permitted to poison Prince Charles against me, nor hex the cause he believes in. He is going to see you for what you are—a crazy woman! A witch sent by Satan!" He pried her lips and teeth apart with his gloved fingers. She bit down hard, but he did not feel the pain. Against her will, she drank the potion of belladonna.

The carriage sped across the plain, stopping only to change horses and gather news. Even the village gossips knew the worst by now. Prince Charles and his generals—chiefly Lord George—were in constant conflict over tactics. At first they heard the Prince was in Glasgow, a Royalist town where he could not count on ten supporters in a hundred. They heard he was living in ostentatious elegance at The Trongate, planning sorties against the English that were doomed to failure from inception. He was often drunk, night and morning. And when he was sober, a raging black mood sent all who came in contact with him scurrying away, like crabs frightened by the fury of the sea. At each village stop, the reports grew worse; Franco's desperation deepened.

The information was so incredibly bad that only by blaming Fiona could he make himself believe it. Months before, in France, when the campaign was in the planning stages, everyone assured Charles, and Charles had assured Franco, that there was massive Jacobite support throughout the British Isles. It was said the Jacobites could not fail, that the English would need a miracle to defeat Charles, the rightful Stuart. Was Fiona that miracle? The superstitious core of Franco's personality grew more dominant as the miles between Blair Atholl and Bannockburn became less. He was— despite everything—frightened of her.

Chapter 33

Two days later, a few miles from the Bannockburn estate of Sir Hugh Patterson, a wealthy Jacobite, the carriage bearing Prince Gabriello and Fiona galloped through an encampment of Highland soldiers.

Her chin resting on her hand, Fiona stared from the window at a sight that brought tears of shame to her lambent eyes: tattered and bedraggled soldiers—some without brogues or pattens to protect them from the frozen rocky earth—huddled about their turf fires in disconsolate groups of four or five, their shoulders bent with weariness, their faces haggard from exposure, hunger and defeat. The glowing fires and the orange twilight sky lit the scene hellishly, and if Fiona had ever doubted the doom-message of her dream, she could doubt no longer. When the carriage halted at a stream where the bridge was out, Fiona heard a bagpipe's skirling dirge. The piper was playing MacCrimmon's lament. She recognized it as the same sorrowful melody that haunted her dream.

It is close now, she thought. After years of waiting, the moment of the dream was upon her.

His Highness must be warned. He must be made to believe in the dream, she thought. Perhaps the carnage could yet be averted.

Casting a furtive glance at Franco, she saw him watching her as if he hoped to read her mind. When he caught her eye, he turned away; and shaky movement pleased Fiona. She knew that he was afraid of her, believing her a jinx to the Highland cause, a witch of *oogly* powers. He had used up the drug supplied by the village doctor, and without it he was plainly uncomfortable in her company. She did not make the mistake of feeling confident, however. Once they were settled on the Patterson estate, Fiona expected Franco to find new means of incapacitating her. But she realized with surprise that she was no longer afraid of him. As the day of destiny approached, as the dream time came nearer, she felt herself grow adamant. Much would be required of her in the next few weeks, and she would not let terror weaken her. "Believe in yourself." Michael Cameron was gone forever, but his words remained to strengthen her.

The Bannockburn estate of Sir Hugh Patterson was traditional in architecture. A rectangular building constructed of rough stone with many large windows, it was fronted by a magnificent formal garden with large beds intersected by neatly graveled paths. Though winter was hard upon the place and nothing bloomed, it was still possible for Fiona to admire the clean symmetrical lines and the obvious care with which the garden was tended. Behind the mansion was a sloping of hill facing east. A terrace had been built around it, and in the warm months vegetables would grow there. Between the vegetable garden and the house was a cobbled courtyard, terminating at a stable and carriage house.

Prince Charles was not at the estate to meet them. He had ridden out with Patterson, Macdonald and O'Sullivan to examine his prize guns. They were arranged confronting Stirling Castle, in a battery designed and built by a young French engineer named Mirabel. As Sheridan helped Franco and Fiona from the carriage, he explained that His Highness planned to take Stirling Castle from Colonel Blakeney using the six cannon. What Sheridan did not mention was that Charles's concern with these guns bordered on obsession. He seemed to be concentrating all his hopes of victory on the big guns. Though his Scottish generals told him repeatedly that Stirling Castle was impregnable, he would not hear of it. Buoyed by his daydream of invincibility, Prince Charles's dark mood had disappeared for the moment.

Franco was cross and exhausted; the uncomfortable carriage had given him a backache, and his head was pounding.

"He might have been here to meet me!" he complained to Sheridan.

"But we didn't expect you until tomorrow or the next day. You have made a fast trip." Sheridan glanced sideways at Fiona. The girl gave him the cold shudders for some reason.

They entered the house through double shuttered doors. Though peat fires burned in every grate, the marble-floored vestibule was cold and gloomy. If Franco had not been impoverished and entirely dependent on Prince Charles, he would have turned and left Bannockburn immediately. He had seen enough of cold Scottish houses where the stink of defeat hung in the air like miasma.

Fiona was given a room adjoining Prince Charles. Sheridan indicated a pile of Stuart tartan clothing on the bed.

"You are to change into these," he said, avoiding her eyes. "His Highness would like you to stay near him now and feels it would be . . . easier, less noteworthy, if you appear as a boy."

Fiona nodded. She would have agreed to anything to regain her privacy. It had been days since she had enjoyed the luxury of solitude, and her soul hungered for it now. But before she could relax the door opened, and servants entered bearing bathtub, scalding water, and warm towels. After many days' travel, this intrusion was almost as welcome as solitude. Fiona relaxed in a leisurely bath, enjoying the vast amounts of hot water and perfumed soap; not until she was warmed throughout and totally relaxed did she step from the tub, dry herself, and dress in the required clothing. The Highland costume was complete, from the kilt and plaid in Stuart tartan to the linen shirt, brogues and knee socks. There was a handsome leather and brass sporran to hang at the waist and a vicious leather-sheathed *skene dhu* that slipped neatly into the top of the socks.

When she had finished dressing, she spent a moment admiring herself in the upright mirror. Apart from her incongruously long amber tresses, she made a perfect Highland boy! On the rosewood dressing table she found pins and combs, and with these she fastened her hair into a tight bun at the nape of her neck. With a bonnet banded by a ribbon of Stuart tartan and decorated with the Jacobite white cockade, her outfit was complete. Only a close observer would notice her feminine features.

A servant brought her tea and bannocks warm from the kitchen oven. Spread with jam and cream, they made a sweet and satisfying meal, washed down with the scalding drink. Afterward she sat by the fire, her eyes heavy, fighting off sleep. To sleep meant to dream, and she felt too comfortable, too cozy to risk the terrifying unbidden images. Her beleaguered mind and body luxuriated in the peace of the moment.

The door opened suddenly.

It was Prince Charles.

"Your Highness!" she cried, jumping up. She dropped to her knees before him. The gesture was automatic and showed the required respect; more significantly, it gave her a moment to compose her shocked expression. The change in Prince Charles was astonishing.

The golden young man whom she had bidden farewell a few months before had been transformed by defeat and disappointment into a petulant grayness. Though still brilliantly blue, his eyes were scalloped by pendulous flesh, and downward lines dragged at the corners of his mouth. His dress had become more dandified, and the contrast between the satin waistcoat, lacy front-ruffles, jeweled accessories and his altered appearance created an impression of decadence, horrifying in one so young.

"Get up, get up!" the Prince cried impatiently. "Let's see how you look." He gazed at the boyish costume Fiona had donned, and remembered the Highland peasant boy and the sign of destiny. "Wonderful! Thank goodness you've come, Fiona. Now," he put an arm about her shoulders and drew her beside him through the door, "I want you right beside me. We've lost some ground because you weren't with us, but I expect a change, a turnaround. The English think they have us now, but that will all change because you're here. I should have taken you into England, I know that; but never mind. Nothing is really lost. And no one said victory would be easy. Our doughty Highlanders know that. They're a bit depressed, but wait until Blakeney gets a taste of my guns. Everything will change then. From Stirling I can rule all Scotland!"

The Prince went on in this manner, clutching Fiona tightly about the shoulders as they entered his suite of rooms. Though addressed to her, Fiona knew his words were actually meant to cheer himself. She thought of what lay ahead for the Prince, and knew that the defeat to come would break his heart. She could see he was not a man equipped to deal with disappointment. Apart from his royal blood, he had nothing on which to justify his existence. Though he might escape Scotland uninjured, defeat would rob him of heart and soul.

The Prince's suite was crowded. Besides the regular court of hangers-on—Sheridan, Macdonald, O'Sullivan—there was Franco and the man introduced to Fiona as Sir Hugh Patterson, the master of the house. The mood in the room took its cue from Charles. He was cheerful and optimistic, so his companions pretended to be the same. As she watched the men and listened to them tell the Prince only what he wanted to hear, Fiona fought to keep her expression neutral. Inside, despair was growing.

Some time passed; after considerable drink the group was noisy. When Lord George burst into the room, he was hardly noticed at first. Then, as if he brought with him a perceptible chill, the tenor of the evening changed abruptly.

"What do you want?" asked Prince Charles, his voice slurred by drink.

"I'll deal with him," interrupted Macdonald.

"I'm here to speak with you, Highness!" Lord George stood with his legs apart, as if rooted to the spot. Clearly, he would not be satisfied until he had the audience he sought.

O'Sullivan stepped between him and the Prince. "I told you before, Lord George. If you wish to communicate with His Highness, you must do it through me!"

"Bugger you!" cried Lord George, shoving the Irishman

aside. "I'll have my words with you, Highness, and with no one else."

Macdonald was shocked. "You dare to threaten . . ."

"Will you hear me, Sir? Or do I leave and take with me what clansmen of mine have not been killed or maimed in this endeavor?"

Charles looked pitifully confused. Fiona knew if he could escape this confrontation he would do so. His boon companions looked at him expectantly. He said at last, "Very well. You others, go! I'll speak with Lord George alone." As Fiona followed the men out the door, the Prince stopped her. "I told you to stay beside me, Fiona. The others must go, but you are to stay."

For just a moment, Lord George glanced from his Prince to the girl disguised as a Highland boy. When he recognized her, his expression drooped miserably. Fiona—and in male attire yet—was the last straw!

"Well, speak up, Murray. What troubles you *this* time?"

"Sir, you know me to be loyal. You know I will die willingly if the cause requires it. But I cannot sit idly by and permit the death and defeat of all I believe in, when it would be so—if you will forgive me saying so—simple to see it otherwise." Lord George stopped, thinking how to say what must be said without bordering on insolence. Charles Edward Stuart was the Pretender, and loyalty demanded that George Murray serve him faithfully. If only he had been a wise and prudent Prince, a careful general, George Murray would never have been anything but scrupulously polite. Instead, he spoke forcefully. "You must call a council of war and agree to abide by the council's decisions. You do not know your army or their talents. They are Highland men for the most part, and fearless if permitted to fight where they have advantages. But again and again, you have placed them on the line like Hanoverians, and expected them to fight like redcoats armed only with knives and . . ."

"How dare you!" Prince Charles was purple in the face. Spittle shone on his lower lip and gathered at the corners of his mouth. "When I came to Scotland I knew well enough what I was to expect from my enemies, but I little foresaw this . . . this . . . treason . . ."

"Never, Sir!"

". . . from my friends! Do you forget I have the authority of my father, the King? Do you forget who I am?"

"Sir, no man can doubt the fealty I have toward you and your father. But I fear that only defeat lies in our path if we continue as we have. My men are exhausted and disheartened." Lord George seemed on the verge of breaking down. He looked at Fiona and smiled bitterly. "You. You are the talisman—and a Highlander. What say you?"

The unexpected question took Fiona by surprise. Perhaps with a moment longer to consider her answer, she would have chosen her words more carefully. Instead, she spoke what was foremost in her mind.

"His lordship is right, Your Highness. Defeat lies in the path of the Highland army. I have seen it in a dream."

"Shut up!" Sudden as a striking snake, his hand shot out and stung her face, knocking her backward into a table. "Get out!" he screamed. "Both of you, get out!"

Chapter 34

He came to her that night, half-drunk and abject.

Fiona was almost asleep when she heard the door between their rooms open softly. Instinctively, she reached beneath her pillow where she had hidden the *skene dhu*; the leather hilt nested in her palm. When she saw that it was Prince Charles, she relaxed.

"Highness," she whispered, sitting up.

He stood over the bed, staring down at her. He was disheveled. His wide lace and ribbon decorated shirt hung out over his breeches, his blond curls were unruly. She could smell the liquor on his breath when he spoke. "You shouldn't have said that, Fiona. That was wrong what you said, about the dream. I told you before, a long time ago, I don't want to hear anything about dreams."

It was best not to argue. She only nodded and said, "I know."

"I have generals and advisors to tell me how to fight. I don't want that from you. I don't want that." There were tears couched in his voice. Fiona's heart swelled with compassion; she reached for him, drew him down beside her on the bed. She cradled him like a little boy. "I just want you to be beside me," he said. "Support me and inspire me. You are the talisman I need. You can bring me victory. I know it. I've known it ever since we met that day on the road. It wasn't far from here. Do you recall, Fiona?" Transformed by the moment of closeness, once again Charles was golden and hopeful. The burden of generalship had lightened. "Do you recall?" he asked again.

"Of course." She had been thinking of what had passed between them, between herself and Michael and Franco, in the time since she left Lejeune's Diversions. In an instant, the faces of Willy and Manfred and Mélisande flashed in her mind.

"I knew when I saw you there on the Stirling Road that it was fated for us to meet, Fiona. It is our destiny to be together. You believe that, don't you?"

"I do," she answered sadly.

He stared at her. Their faces were inches apart and he took in each feature as if for the first time.

"You are very beautiful," he said softly, tracing the proud angular line of her cheekbone with his hand.

She felt the warmth from him and knew what might happen next. She thought of Owen and Michael, of brutal Franco; she even recalled Manfred Gott and the hunger in his eyes. What was she to do now that she saw the same expression in Prince Charles's gaze?

"I have never known a woman," he confided softly. "And you are a virgin." She did not contradict him. He leaned forward, tentatively, and put his mouth on hers. The rosebud lips tasting of brandy were curiously devoid of passion.

He pulled away and stood up.

"Perhaps when all of this is over, Fiona. When I am King . . ." Even in the candlelight, she could see he was uncomfortable, and tried to ease the awkward moment.

"You will marry someone of your own station, Highness. But," she added, "I will always be honored by your friendship. No matter what happens, you are my Prince."

When he returned to his own room, thoughtful and strangely sad, Charles found Franco waiting for him.

"Been visiting have you, Charles? I waited in my room for you to come. We've been apart a long time. I imagined you would be eager . . ." Franco sprawled indolently in a comfortable chair near one of the room's two fireplaces. The brocade dressing gown he wore was open to the waist. In his left hand, he held a tall goblet of ruby claret. "Well, what did little Fiona have to say? Or have you two dispensed with conversation?"

"What does that mean?"

"You have an unmistakably warm look about you, Charles. Can it be your sexual tastes are expanding to include the weaker sex?" Franco got up. Drinking the claret in one gulp, he refilled his glass from the crystal decanter on the sideboard, and lolled against the heavy maple cabinet inlaid with brass. "If you want me to go, I will. I don't choose to embarrass you."

Franco's heart was beating fast and his palms, normally kept dry by repeated powderings, were now sweating. For what seemed an interminable time, he had waited for Charles to come to him as he always had in the past when their apartments were adjacent. He had been excited at the thought of his lover's touch. He had been so long with women that he felt disgusted by the memory of their oversoftness. He was aroused by the thought of Charles's tight-muscled buttocks and slim hips, the way his lust empowered him with irresistible strength. Franco remembered the touch of Charles's hands on his hips and flanks, and finally could wait for his lover no longer. He had entered the room expecting to be greeted with passion; instead, the bed was empty and the door to Fiona's room ajar. Franco had not had time to eavesdrop, but he did not lack imagination. He could guess what had gone on between them.

"It's not what you think, Gabi," Charles assured him.

"Then why are you avoiding me?" Franco's claret-reddened lips pouted.

"I'm not. But I have much on my mind. Now that Fiona is here—and you, of course—I can begin to relax." Charles picked up the brandy decanter, started to pour himself another drink, then put it down. He looked at the dark liquid a second, turned away, turned back, and poured the drink he desired.

"I wouldn't relax with her around if I were you."

"What do you mean?" The brandy was half gone, and Charles felt more confident as the warmth spread throughout his body.

"Your talisman is a murderess." Franco told the story of Abigail, and was satisfied to see Charles deeply troubled. "She's mad, dear boy. Oh, she has moments of lucidity, but it's all part of the disease. I am convinced. That talk about a dream . . ."

"I don't want to hear about that!" Charles finished the drink and poured another. In his trembling hand, the decanter rang against the edge of the glass.

"Of course you don't, and who can blame you? That's why I can't understand why you keep her about. She isn't good for morale. Not yours or mine or anyone else's. Charles, I think . . ."

"I don't care what you think! I'm tired of being told what to do and say and how to act to please others. I don't think that girl is mad. If she murdered someone . . ." Charles looked at Franco and began to laugh. Franco stepped away from him, uneasy and conscious of the change in his formerly malleable lover. "I'll bet you killed her, Gabi! You are more capable of murder than that girl in there." The Prince laughed loudly and brokenly. The glass dropped from his hand, shattering and staining the carpet with brown. His arms went about Franco and he rested his head on his shoulder, sobbing.

"Gabi, Gabi, I have missed you so. Forget that Abigail. Lie with me. Let me love you as I used to."

But Franco could not resist the barbed question: "I thought you had vowed celibacy." With deft fingers he unlaced the front opening of Charles's breeches, and dropped to his knees.

"Never mind that. It doesn't matter now." Charles laughed for the first time in many days. Franco's mouth engulfed him hungrily; his body emanated rich musculine odors of wine and tobacco. For Charles, these were powerful aphrodisiacs. The Prince leaned against the sideboard, and his body seemed to melt into delicious sensations.

For a few hours, he was again the adored golden boy, born and bred to conquest and command.

On January 29th, in the cold and rain, Prince Charles gave orders for the battery of Stirling Castle to begin. Certain of glorious victory, the Prince had ordered that some of his Highland troops—chiefly those of the incorrigible Lord George—be amassed nearby to observe and spread the news to the other forces. Though he expected the British surrender to come quickly, Charles had taken the precaution of positioning himself, Fiona, Prince Gabriello, his generals and other advisors behind the safety of a bunker.

He gave the order to fire, and the monstrous cannon roar shook the newly constructed battery.

Behind the walls of Stirling, Colonel Blakeney permitted one round to be fired by the Jacobites before responding thunderously with his own weapons. Stirling had the advantages of height and protection; Charles's position was pitiful by comparison, and the rout of the Scots was accomplished in only thirty minutes. The sky cleared of cannon smoke and revealed the Highland army running in all directions like ants disturbed in their hill. Before Blakeney could reload, Charles and his comrades and colleagues were on horseback—Fiona jumped up on the saddle before Lord George when Charles rode off without her—galloping toward the safety of Bannockburn.

The humiliating defeat was more than Charles could bear. He retreated to his rooms, and did not emerge for nearly twenty-four hours.

He ordered the retreat to the Highlands to begin the next day.

Chapter 35

William, Duke of Cumberland, was on their trail.

A cousin of Prince Charles, Cumberland was England's ablest soldier, and was known for his cruel and unscrupulous tactics. Where Charles had been raised to wield the sceptre of leadership, William of Cumberland had been bred to the sword. As a boy, he had been given his own batallion of boy soldiers to act out strategy and play at killing in the courtyard of Saint James Palace. Unlike Charles, he was a quick student, avid for learning and with an ambition to succeed at whatever he set his mind to: languages, science, a military career. At the time he left Edinburgh in pursuit of Charles, William of Cumberland was about the same age as his cousin; but where Charles's life had been marked by the failure of his aspirations, William's had been singularly successful. As Charles's army, retreating to the Highlands in chaos, learned that Cumberland was pursuing them, there was widespread panic and desertion. They all knew Cumberland by reputation: a cold-minded professional soldier, he was respected by his army, disliked by the ladies—and feared by his enemies.

The Highland retreat was marked by tragedy and confusion. At Saint Ninians, the Jacobites blew up a church in which their own powder supplies were stored. Carts, cannon and weapons were dropped at the side of the road, as the undirected soldiers fled north. The spirit of the army was dying; the only medicine that could revive it was arms and men from France. But King Louis had abandoned the Jacobite cause.

While Lord George led his weary men through hip-high snow on the eastern road to Inverness, Charles and the remnant of the clans took the Highland road. Wherever they went they encountered unenthusiastic—and sometimes downright hostile—villagers. The word was out: Cumberland was coming. No one wished to be called a Jacobite collaborator. And so the army dragged north, hungry, dressed in rags, impoverished in spirit. Only loyalty, the clansman's noblest quality, kept them alive and moving. Though some deserted in fear, most remained; proud to the end of who they were, and of the cause that claimed them.

Charles and his entourage made their home at Thunderton House in Elgin, near Inverness, while they waited for Cumberland to force a battle. From her room overlooking the Lossie River, Fiona had more than enough time to think of what lay ahead; for Cumberland came slowly, almost as if he were taking pleasure in prolonging the agony of his enemies.

One day in late March, Lord George went to Fiona and sought her help.

He found her in the gardens of Thunderton House. The acreage, magnificently colored and manicured in the warm months, was now as drab and dead as Lord George's own spirits. Though spring had officially arrived, Elgin was too far north to benefit from the warming turn, and it would be May before the gardens brightened; June before they blossomed.

For a moment before he spoke to Fiona, he watched her secretly. Though he took her presence with the Prince as yet another indication that the young man was incompetent to rule, George Murray could not deny that she possessed a certain magical quality, which set her apart from the women who had courted Charles's attention so lavishly at the start of his campaign. Murray had visited Skye in his youth, and had been moved and disconcerted by this same uncanny quality everywhere on that misty island. Legend had it that when the faery folk retreated from the world of men, they went no further than Skye. There they still lived, and in their *oogly* way affected the affairs of the world, and the tides of human destiny.

Could Fiona be descended from those enchanted folk? Somehow, a story of this nature had begun to circulate among the army. Superstitious and ignorant as most of the Highland soldiers were, the talk frightened them—and further damaged morale. Lord George tried to dismiss the rumor as ludicrous; nevertheless, as he watched Fiona in the garden that day, he could not deny her strangeness.

She was dressed—as always now—in the Stuart tartan. Its brilliant red was the only spot of color on the otherwise dun and gray landscape of late winter. The wind off Moray Firth that hurried the layered clouds across the sky had tugged her orange-gold hair loose from its customary bun. It flew about her face, flamboyant and wild. Lord George was aware of the magic that drew the Prince to Fiona. It was nothing he could name or put point to directly; but it was there; undeniably magnetic and *oogly*.

She turned, hearing his bootstep in the dry leaves on the flagstone path. She had stopped at a stone bench on a little promontory that afforded a view of both Elgin and in the distance Lossie—the river's mouth and the firth.

"My lord," she said with surprise, dipping a curtsey.

"Did I frighten you? You were thoughtful."

Face to face, she was only a Highland girl; and he chided himself for superstitious daydreaming. He laughed aloud. In response to her questioning look, he explained, "I was only laughing at myself, miss. At how easily the mind plays tricks."

"I don't understand, my lord." The guarded expression in her refulgent eyes touched Lord George's kindly heart. She had been hurt by life.

He asked gently, "Have you heard the talk among the soldiers? They say our Prince keeps a halfling with him." When he saw her shocked expression, he wished he had kept silent. "It is nonsense, of course. But the Highland imagination is easily stirred by such ideas. I suspect some traitor has planted the idea to further demoralize our gallant men."

Fiona didn't answer. She looked away toward the misting horizon; silent and sorrowing, her peaceful expression belied her turbulent spirits.

A traitor named Franco, she thought. He hasn't done with me yet. He—and only he—could have planted the halfling rumor among the ranks.

Since Bannockburn, Franco had left Fiona alone. There had been no more talk—that she could hear—of madness or murder. She had been permitted to live quietly and undisturbed at Thunderton House. Occasionally, she noticed Prince Charles looking at her in a way that frightened her, as if some newly planted suspicion had taken root in him, and was slowly strangling out what remained of his reason.

As she stood beside Lord George her thoughts strayed to these matters, and to the laird her expression was clearly troubled. Again he thought, this girl has suffered. And wished with all his heart that time would mend the wounds inflicted on Fiona Macleod.

After a moment she said, with apparent calm, "Have you heard recently from your friend Captain Cameron, Lord George?"

"Nothing that will help our cause, unless the added strength of one good man can make the difference for us against Cumberland." They had begun to walk slowly along the path, with the River Lossie down the hill to their right, Thunderton House up the slope to their left. The great gray stone mansion lent an air of inescapable gloom to the bleak Highland winterscape.

"Captain Cameron intends to be a soldier?"

"What is so remarkable in that, miss? He is a loyal Scot."

Fiona was too frightened to reply. In recent weeks, she had taken comfort from the knowledge that whatever happened, her darling Michael would not be snared in the nightmare that lay ahead for the Jacobite army. Nightly the dream became more vivid and intense. Soon, she knew, it must burst into terrible reality. Her one consolation had been in knowing that Michael Cameron was not a soldier; his bloody face would not appear in her dream.

"He must not fight!" she cried.

"Nor should any of us," agreed Lord George. Ignoring her plea for Michael, he went on. "It is said you have great influence with Prince Charles. I know he regards you as some sort of talisman, with supernatural powers to assist his cause. Though this is superstitious nonsense, you must tell him what you know, what all save him know too well. We cannot fight. To meet Cumberland now will mean . . ."

"Annihilation."

Lord George nodded glumly. "He won't listen to me, or to Perth or to any of his Highlanders anymore. A manic blindness is upon our Prince. He seems to think that we can win by luck and . . ."

"Destiny." Fiona smiled sadly. "Prince Charles believes in those who tell him what he wants to hear: that he is destined for kingship; that nothing and no one can stop him. I have tried to warn him, but he will not listen. He hears only Prince Gabriello, Macdonald, O'Sullivan."

"Aye. That damned Italian has his ear, right enough. The sight of him, with his pretty-girl face and perfumed gloves, turns the stomachs of my men. Lady Macbeth, they call him. By God, I fear the appellation is truer than they know."

The allusion was lost on Fiona, whose familiarity with Shakespeare's ambitious villainess was limited to Cindy's brief rendition of the mad scene, but she understood Lord George's mirthless laughter. "I have no love for the Prince's friend and would oppose him if I could. But the Prince won't listen to me, not while Prince Franco's here."

"You must try again."

"It will do no good, my lord."

Lord George took Fiona's white-gloved hands and clasped them tightly. "Whoever, whatever you are, you are the Highlands' hope, Fiona Macleod. Persuade him to retreat into the wilderness. Later, when we are stronger, when our strategy is planned and King Louis is allied to us, we will demolish Cumberland and Wade and Hawley and all the rest of them. Tell Prince Charles this. Make him understand!"

Late that evening, Fiona knocked on the door to Charles's apartments. The sound echoed noisily in the hall and she almost lost her nerve, expecting all the doors along the corridor to open and accusing faces to peer out at her. She knew what she had to do; and although she did not expect to be successful, she had to make one last try. Before it was too late . . .

She heard sounds—laughter and footsteps—within the room. Too late, she realized that the Prince was not alone. Franco was with him.

The Italian opened the door. "What do you want?"

"I wish to see His Highness." Though terror gripped Fiona, her voice was firm and resolute. She stood very straight, refusing to be cowed by the cruel effeminate Prince. Her head was proud and high.

"Who is it, Gabi?" She heard the slur in Prince Charles's voice and knew that he had been drinking.

"No one. A servant who . . ."

She pushed roughly past Franco. Surprised by her temerity, he stepped back.

"Fiona Macleod!" cried the Prince jovially. "I salute you!" He raised his champagne glass. "Join us."

"Thank you, no, Highness, I do not care for strong drink. I will only take a moment of your time." She looked over her shoulder at Franco. He was barechested, leaning indolently against the jamb of the door. His dark hair fell in a wave across his forehead. But his relaxed posture did not fool Fiona. She could feel the tension about him; the air in the room fairly crackled with it.

"Of course you like champagne. Everyone likes champagne! Am I right, Gabi?" Charles poured a glass of golden liquid for Fiona. She took it unwillingly. "Drink!" he demanded.

Like drinking stars, she thought sipping tentatively. At another time, in different company, she might enjoy champagne.

The Prince insisted on filling her glass a second time. He was drunk and sloppy in his appearance. Like Franco, he was wigless and his blond curls were loose and untidy to his shoulders. His wide silken shirt hung loose outside his breeches, and she saw where there were spots on the lacy front-ruffle.

The Prince Charles she remembered from the days before the English campaign would never have let himself go in this way. But now his physical disorder seemed an appropriate mirror of the chaos within him.

"You must not stay here longer, Your Highness," she blurted out, realizing that there would be no better time, no perfect moment for what she had to say.

"What's that?" Prince Charles laughed. "Did you hear her, Gabi? Another Highland general!"

"But this one more dangerous than the rest," Fiona heard Franco murmur, as he came to stand behind her. She felt his hot breath stir the hairs at the back of her neck where her bun had begun to come apart.

"Your Highness, I am no danger to you. I am loyal, as are all your Highland generals." She was determined to ignore Franco. If she could cut the ties of influence between the two men, she might even be able to persuade Prince Charles to her course. "It is not we Highlanders who have endangered the cause. Hundreds of our men have died for you. Why do you refuse to listen?"

"Take care, Fiona, lest you go too far." Franco's whisper was the hiss of a serpent.

She turned on him. "It is you who go too far! It is you and O'Sullivan and Macdonald who jeopardize my land with your greed!"

"Fiona!" She turned to Prince Charles. He was staring at her in open-mouthed shock. "You dare to criticize . . ."

"I told you what she was. But you wouldn't believe me!" There was unmistakable excitement in Franco's voice. The moment he had patiently awaited had arrived at last.

Fiona fell to her knees at the Prince's feet. "Believe me, Your Highness. You must give up this plan of meeting Cumberland. Retreat to . . ."

"Retreat!" bellowed Franco. "Do you hear her, Charles? She's a traitor!"

She hugged the Prince's legs. "Never! I am your faithful Fiona. I am . . ."

Franco jerked her up by the hair. A dozen pins fell to the floor as the heavy amber waves dropped loose.

"You're a witch, a halfling from Hell sent to destroy the Jacobites!" Grabbing her by the shoulders, he held her facing Prince Charles. "Look at her, Charles. See her! Know what she is!" He shook her roughly.

"Let me go, murderer!" Fiona jerked free, turned and confronted Franco. In the power of her knowledge that what she said was true, she forgot her fears. "You care nothing for Prince Charles. You only wish for what can make you rich and powerful. You are using him, using Scotland!"

Franco shoved her and sent her reeling backward into Prince Charles. A paralysis of horror held him rigid in his place. His eyes were open, he was breathing regularly; yet he could not move to stop what was happening before his eyes.

"Please, Sir," she gasped, dragging at his shoulder. "Don't let him . . ." Another blow from Franco threw Fiona to the ground. She curled in a fetal ball, protecting her head in the crook of her arms. "Sir," she begged, "help me . . ."

The Stuart Prince, his brain numbed with drink, watched the girl crouched in front of him. This was Fiona, his talisman. She was a halfling, a curse; perchance a descendant of those three weird sisters whose fair prophesies had proved so foul for an earlier Scots King, Macbeth. And he had harbored her and given her a home; had even loved her in his own fashion. Now . . . She began to scream, "The dream, Your Highness! The dream!"

The cry beat against the walls of his shocked consciousness, before it finally broke through.

"Stop," he said in a whisper. "Enough. Franco, get rid of her somehow."

Franco threw a heavy cloth over the girl and grappled her to her feet. Fiona struggled but knew she was powerless to resist. She would be taken away. But she was alive. Alive.

Chapter 36

Saint Dymphna's Retreat lay in a low boggy area to the east of Inverness, where the River Ness opened into Moray firth. Its history was ancient, having been built originally by a small order of Roman Catholic priests devoted to the care and tending of the poor, the destitute, the criminal and the insane. Insufficiently supported, Saint Dymphna's was a filthy ramshackle place where men, women and children lived in their own filth like animals, crowded into a cramped tower of three stories connected by a narrow twisting staircase. The columnar edifice rose out of a boggy lowland. Even on clear days, a malodorous saffron mist hovered there. Abandoned to the company of their miseries behind a giant door bolted on the outside, the inmates of Saint Dymphna's were fed on slops. Those who were not mad in the beginning quickly became so, rather than face the horror of their captivity.

Franco's carriage entered the retreat grounds through a

massive spear-topped iron gate. This one gate, set in ten-foot stone walls, enclosed the tower, a dilapidated cottage and farmyard, and was the only way in or out of Saint Dymphna's. Fiona was drugged into unconsciousness as the carriage jolted down the rock-strewn track to the tower. She did not hear Franco explain her delusions to the keeper, nor see him give her ten gold pieces.

"She'll seem quite normal sometimes," Franco told the crafty old woman, who said her name was Pegan. "But don't be fooled by her. She's dangerous." He slipped another half-dozen gold pieces onto Pegan's filthy palm. Her twisted claw spasmed about the gold. She dropped the coins into the pocket of her soiled apron and smiled at Franco in a venal knowing way that made him physically ill. But the sight of Pegan—her hunched deformity, the rat's nest hair—and the rancid putrifying smell of her pleased him. Saint Dymphna's Retreat was worse than he had imagined. All his life, he would be happy knowing Fiona was Pegan's charge.

"You can trust me, master. Pegan's been here with the batties thirty years and more. The batties canna fool old Pegan!"

"I'm sure they can't." Franco smiled with what was, for once, genuine good humor. He felt immensely relieved as he watched old Pegan drag Fiona, still dressed in her Stuart tartan, into the tower. When she came out alone and the iron bolt dropped noisily, he laughed aloud. He had done with the halfling at last. And so had Charles . . .

Fiona awoke hours later in near darkness. Someone—or something—was sniffing at her. She heard the snuffling, and felt an inquisitive nose against her skin before her eyes became accustomed to the dim light provided by the half-dozen slits in the tower's stone walls. Calloused hands with long fingers and sharp curved nails prodded at her.

"Get away!" Fiona heard the voice, though darkness shielded the speaker. There was the sound of a kick, some grunts and a shuffling noise. "This one is mine!" The voice was French-accented, threatening—and strangely familiar.

In the dim recesses of her drug-clouded mind, an inner voice urged Fiona to action. But a lethargy like the weight of summer heat bore down on her, and she had neither the strength nor the will to fight. Her body ached in the dozen places where Franco's blows had struck. Gingerly, she touched her cheeks, then her eyes and nose. Where was she? She realized that she didn't care. She was exhausted through every fiber of her being; more dead than alive.

"I must sleep," she murmured aloud, cradling her head in her arms on the dank stone floor. "I have to sleep."

Gently, a hand stroked her forehead. "And I weel watch over you. I weel care for you!"

Much later she awoke again; something wet and cool was pressed against her poor battered face. She tried to pull away, but hands that were both gentle and strong held her. She submitted, realizing at last that this was no new assault. Someone was washing her.

Through the dozen narrow slit windows high up in the deep stone walls, Fiona could see strips of brilliant blue sky. Long slants of butter-colored sunlight, clouded by dust motes, brightened the center of the circular area, though it could not penetrate to the shadows near the walls.

Gray shapes, scarcely human, skittered away from the light as though they feared its touch. She saw a dozen bodies, clothed in filthy rags or entirely naked, their humanity disguised beneath tangled weeds of hair and layers of grime and filth.

The stench in the tower was overwhelming. Fiona could not control her nausea. Feeling her gorge rise, she tried to turn away, to stand and stagger to some place away from where she lay. But when she tried to move her legs they were numb with aching. She turned her torso and vomited repeatedly, her abused body shuddering convulsively.

The strong yet gentle hands she remembered from her last consciousness reached beneath her arms and tugged her to an area away from the foul egestion. But the tower room was nowhere clean. Beneath her hands, the floor of the place, clammy and cold, was slick with filth. The air was a stew of foulness: a fetid poison—contaminated, unspeakably vile—was everywhere.

"Breathe deeply," the French voice said. "You weel accustom."

Feebly, Fiona did as she was directed, turning her body to identify her speaker. The voice had been familiar . . .

Before she could be identified, the strange woman, her face

obscured by quantities of dark matted hair, skittered away to the shadowed obscurity of the tower's periphery.

"Who are you?" cried Fiona after her. Her voice, though she tried to make it loud and firm and demanding of response, came out as scarcely more than a whisper. She reached toward the shadows where the woman had disappeared. "Who are you?" she asked again. The only response was cackles of hideous laughter as the door of the tower opened.

"You've wakened then?" Old Pegan stood silhouetted against the afternoon light that suddenly drenched the tower room. From the shadows, she heard the mewling of fear and the rustling of bodies pressing further into the darkness, seeking to avoid notice.

"Here!" Old Pegan threw a crust of bread across the floor at Fiona. She grabbed at it eagerly, but when she saw that it was green with mold and covered with the filth of the tower floor, she gagged and dropped it. The old keeper laughed. "You'll be glad for that soon enough, batty!"

Old Pegan, hobbled and bent over a cane, came into the tower slowly, watching carefully from side to side lest any of the unfortunates in her care should try either to overpower her to make a dash for the open door. When she reached Fiona, she looked down at her with a glint of unmistakable madness in her eyes.

"Now your Stuart friends is done with you, ye won't be needing this." She reached for the closing of Fiona's kilt and ripped the warm wool garment off her. Fiona lay helpless. "And them fine shoes is just what Pegan needs." These too were removed, and though it occurred to Fiona to struggle against the attack, she was too weak. Old Pegan stared down at her—as if deciding whether to strip her entirely. Dressed only in her woolen shift, wide cotton shirt and high stockings, Fiona was already shivering with cold.

A sound near the door took old Pegan by surprise. She turned and screamed something foul and threatening. Hurrying to the entrance, she used her cane to ward away attackers, though as far as Fiona could tell the threats were only vocal.

At the door the ancient crone reached for something outside, then turned and tossed a bucketful of icy water across the stones. "There's water for them that's thirsty!" With a final lunatic croak of laughter, old Pegan slammed the door. The heavy bolt dropped with an echoing thud.

As Fiona watched in mute horror, the dreadful shapes took on human form as they crept from their dark hiding places toward the water that had pooled in the uneven floor. Deformed nocturnal creatures, dragged from their lairs by need, they lay or knelt on the floor and touched their tongues to the filthy stones, lapping the water avidly.

She had to look away. Squeezing her eyes tightly shut, she buried her face in her hands. The smell of Saint Dymphna's tower no longer troubled her. A new horror had overcome her. She knew where she was, and with the slamming of the door to the outside, she began to realize the utter hopelessness of her situation. Again she tried to stand, but could not. Instead she sprawled back on the stones and let the screams rise from her soul. Franco had won. She was defeated.

"No!" she screamed, drawing the sound out like a skirling wind across a high moor. "No!" she railed until she was hoarse and exhausted and could only lay her face upon her hands that touched the filthy floor and sob. Sleep came at last, but with it dreams . . .

The pipes keened across the shrouded heavens. A single man stood silhouetted against the gray skies. He held his hands aloft and they were dripping blood, blood that dropped to earth and became a stream, then a river that cut the broad swath of dream-familiar moor, and again Fiona saw the bloody stones turn to faces florid with gore. The man was laughing, and she knew his name was Cumberland.

Mist and clouds obscured the vision for awhile; then she saw Michael Cameron in kilt and bonnet. In his hands were smoking muskets.

The mist and clouds came again. Fiona awoke.

The tower was in complete darkness now. She heard the sound of sleep about her, muffled groans and snores and sobbing so pitiful that her heart wept for the unfortunate creatures with whom she shared the tower prison.

Franco had won. Saint Dymphna's was to be the fate of the halfling from Skye.

Even as she thought the words, Fiona somehow knew they could not be true. She had not been born and endured the hardships and sorrows of her nineteen years in order to die in a madhouse. Though she could not explain it, calm settled over her; she was able to think clearly of all that had happened, and she recalled details of her experience with vivid accuracy—and yet, miraculously, without passion or pain.

When Franco had finished beating her and had convinced Prince Charles that Fiona was a witch who cursed the Jacobite cause, he had carried her away to a room over the stables of Thunderton House. She had been in great pain, but her mind had been surprisingly clear. She had repeated one thought over and over, for it gave her strength: Believe in yourself or they will destroy you.

She had done something important in those short hours in the stable loft. Now, in Saint Dymphna's, she tried to remember what it was. Painstakingly, she repeated every move, every thought that had occurred to her before the time when Franco returned with the belladonna and she lost consciousness again.

Suddenly, she touched her breast. It was there!

Lying back on the stones, she began to breathe easily for the first time in many many hours. She had the *skene dhu!*

Had Franco been a Scotsman, he would have removed the tiny dagger from the top of her diced hose. No Scotsman would have missed this traditional weapon worn in its traditional place. But Franco, being Italian, was not familiar with Scottish clothing, and so had overlooked the deadly-edged knife. Fiona had thus had an opportuntiy to secure the lethal weapon to the inside of her bodice.

She touched her breast again. No, she had not dreamed it; the blade was cold against her skin. But it warmed her heart, because she knew it meant her freedom.

But how? Gradually, frustration began to build, as she realized that the blessed *skene dhu* was not enough. Without strength, she could not hope to overpower old Pegan and escape the madhouse.

Everything seemed hopeless again. Believing herself trapped for all time, she sobbed piteously.

A hand touched her hair. She screamed and hit out recklessly, imagining that one of the shadow-creatures was attacking her.

"I not hurt you. Hushaby. Mélisande weel care for you."

Mélisande? The French accent! It was the girl from Lejeune's Diversions.

"Mélisande? What are you . . ."

"Don't talk. I tell you everything but first we get away from dis floor, okay? You can walk eef I help?" Already Mélisande was dragging Fiona into a standing position.

"Where are we going?"

"Steps up here. You just hold to Mélisande, then we make eet fine." For one whom Fiona recalled as frail and helpless, Mélisande was extraordinarily strong; and Fiona found that with her help she was able to stagger across the stones to where a narrow staircase twisted to the next level of the tower.

"What is this place?" Fiona asked, as she took each shallow step in pain.

"I tell you after we get to top. Just keep walking and hold to me. I not let you fall, miss."

It took a very long time, and they had to stop several times before reaching the third and top floor of the tower. Here the window slits were wider, and the pale dawn sky had begun to cast its rosy fingers of light about the place.

"Why, there's hardly anyone up here!" cried Fiona. Here and there were ragged sleeping forms, but all in all the place seemed cleaner and less terrifying than the depths below.

"Not everyone has strength or mind enough to climb," said Mélisande matter-of-factly. She was spreading the tattered remnants of a blanket near the wall. "Here, rest against de wall. Soon do sun weel come here, make you feel better."

"Tell me why you are here. How?"

Mélisande silenced her with a finger to her lips. "No talking. Just listening and resting."

Fiona watched the Frenchwoman as she went to the window and, reaching far out, brought back a round object. It was a stone that had been carefully, crudely hollowed out in the center. In this small well was a cup or more of clear water. Thinking compassionately of the poor brutes below, who had not the strength to climb nor the wit to gather rainwater, Fiona blessed Mélisande and drank deeply.

"Don't take all. We need." Mélisande wrested the vessel from her before the water was gone. Then, tearing a bit of cloth from the hem of Fiona's shift, she dipped it in the water and began to gently bathe the injured girl's wounds. As she nursed Fiona, Mélisande told her story.

When Fiona escaped from the Lejeune Diversions encampment near Stirling Castle, Mélisande had told André, her husband—though she confessed no legal ties bound them—that she would no longer earn their keep by prostitution.

"André very mad. He go to Mistress Lejeune and tell her what I say, and she beats me many times hard." Rather than be beaten to death, Mélisande had agreed to resume her activities; but in her heart an anger was growing that could not be suppressed. Lejeune's Diversions moved north, then west again, revisiting Fort William, and then up to Fort Augustus. Both cities were crowded with soldiers, afire with anti-Jacobite sentiments and chafing at their comparative inactivity.

"Some dey beat me, others don't pay. They hate Mélisande because she French. Nothing good happen to Mélisande."

Eventually, she had determined that no matter what André and Mistress Lejeune did to her, she would give up prostitution before her life and youth were gone forever.

She had not expected the fury which her resolution met, but when beating and threats of worse did not win her compliance, Lejeune told her about Saint Dymphna's.

"This place?" Fiona asked, hearing the name of the tower for the first time.

"*Oui.* Dis place where dey put crazy people, sick people, any people what nobody wants. Mistress and André, dey tell me after six months here I be willing to do anything for dem."

"Oh, my God!" For a moment the full impact of what had been done to Mélisande affected Fiona so profoundly that she could say nothing. She thought of her own ordeal and realized that horrible as Franco had been to her, he was no worse than Mistress Lejeune and the scurrilous André. There would always be cruel men and women willing to exploit the weak and needy for their own selfish reasons.

Mélisande went on: after her first confused hours in the tower, she had realized that to survive she must use her wits. She had found the stairway and explored the second and third floors of the tower. For the most part, the worst cases remained on the lower floor. She pointed out the other denizens of the third story and described them to Fiona as either sick with sores or melancholy or—in one case—extreme old age.

"She help me," Mélisande said, pointing to a woman so wizened with age that she seemed more like a frail leaf than a human being. "She have no family and all her friends be dead. The priests put her here. They say it for her own good." Mélisande shook her head. "She tell me all about dis place, show me how to get water. Show me how to wait and catch birds, rats, quick!" Her hand darted out in example. "Got to be real quick." She had learned to eat these creatures uncooked, and the flesh of some had made her ill. But when Pegan didn't come with bread and the watery stuff she called soup, this meat had kept Mélisande and the old crone alive.

"How long until Mistress Lejeune comes back for you?" Fiona was sickened by the story she had just heard, but with her wounds cleaned and fresh water in her system, she felt alert and clear-headed for the first time in . . . how many days? She really had no idea.

Mélisande laughed at Fiona's question. "Dey never come back. Dey find some other girl. Mistress Lejeune like me catching birds. She move quick, surprise dem. Once girl go with Mistress Lejeune, she might as well be killed!" She looked at Fiona curiously. "You lucky. You escape. How you do dat?"

Fiona told the whole story. The sound of her own voice reassured her, and she spared no detail. She even spoke of Michael.

"You love him?"

"I do." And will forever, she thought. If I spend the rest of eternity in this Hell-tower, I will love Michael Cameron—until the dreams of what might have been drive me mad at last.

"Why you not stay wid him? Why go wid Lejeune?"

It was a question Fiona had never asked herself. That time—the years on Skye, her love for Owen and his tragic death—seemed so long ago, almost unreal. But meeting Mélisande had brought it back again and she asked herself the same question. Why had she not remained with Michael and gone with him to Edinburgh as intended?

"He seemed . . . different then. Cold and hateful. It was only later, when time had eased his pain from Owen's death, that he could see me as I was and love me." The words made sense, but she knew that they were only half the truth. The rest of the story she could not confide to Mélisande for fear the young woman would find herself believing in Fiona's madness. But, crazy as it seemed, Fiona knew the real reason she had left Michael in Mallaig and gone alone to Lejeune's Diversions: It was her destiny to meet Prince Charles on the road from Stirling Castle, with bruised mountains of cloud and an electric sky behind her. Perhaps it was even her destiny to rest now in Saint Dymphna's, awaiting the time when her dream would become reality.

As Fiona and Mélisande talked, the sun rose, was obliterated by dark clouds, and torrential rain began. Late in the afternoon, Mélisande went down to collect their ration of soup and returned with nothing.

"Old Pegan, she don't like rain. Say it make her bones ache. Dat mean no food. You want I try to catch you a pigeon, plump and sweet, eh?"

"No!" Fiona answered quickly. "I'm not hungry." Though she admitted to herself that anything was possible, still Fiona could not imagine a time when she would be hungry enough to eat a raw wild bird. She would sooner gnaw on the moldy crusts thrown at her by Pegan.

Though they talked on and off throughout the day, Fiona did not confide in Mélisande about the *skene dhu* secured in her bodice. She thought she could probably trust the French girl, but in this matter she did not dare make a mistake. Mélisande might be the collaborator she needed to make her escape; then again, she might go crazy with the hope of freedom and arouse suspicion. Mélisande might tell someone else about the *skene dhu,* and that person might in turn inform on them both to Pegan in the hopes of gaining favor with the evil old keeper.

Horrible as the tower at Saint Dymphna's Retreat might be, she must curb her impatience and await the perfect moment for escape.

Book Nine

———

THE END OF THE DREAM

Chapter 37

For the first time in many weeks, Fiona slept without dreaming and awoke refreshed and stronger on the morning of April sixteenth. The weather continued dark and overcast, and by midafternoon a cold drizzling rain had begun to fall. From the openings in the tower wall, Fiona beheld a landscape of gray and brown where even the evergreen plants appeared dead. Gradually, a sense of unspeakable doom settled over her. When Mélisande brought her water she drank it without speaking, and the Frenchwoman moved away from her, startled by the strange glaze that dulled Fiona's eyes, changing them from amber to a brown so dark that it seemed black. Her mouth fell slack, and she sank into a dream-filled stupor . . .

The dream had been transformed into scenes from a drama, separated each from each by a curtain of bloody mist. While Mélisande stared at her in fear, Fiona was oblivious, though her eyes remained open and her body erect. Her inward eye was focused very clearly on the landscape of her dream. Not a detail escaped her; not a death went unfelt.

The time had come at last . . .

Cullodin Moor: a wide barren stretch of heath, featureless but for an occasional tree or boulder, a stretch of open country covered with heather and gorse bushes. It is morning, and even in the gloom of early spring, the bedewed spider webs that lace the bushes glisten magically. A family of rabbits grazes in the dappled sunlight. From time to time, one of them looks up and turns his head to listen.

Something is coming . . .

To the west a long line of soldiers—clansmen in the tattered remnants of their plaids—approaches the blasted heath. A trio of rooks screams across the sky and the rabbits scamper deep underground. The soldiers walk with labored steps; some are barefoot, some unarmed. At the western edge of Cullodin Moor they stop, falling wherever the earth is least damp, and wrap themselves in what remains of their plaids. One, less exhausted than the others, passes among them with a canvas bag of biscuits. It is their day's ration: one dry biscuit washed down with water. Some fall alseep before the morsel is chewed, others lie awake and stare at the leaden sky.

No sooner are their eyes closed than Prince Charles is among them on horseback, urging them to stand and prepare to fight. In the distance, on the eastern verge of the heath, Cumberland's men are massing for war. Nine thousand royalist soldiers—trained and armed and fed and rested—face the five thousand exhausted Highlanders.

"Have at it, men! Rise up! Be strong!" The anticipation of battle is a tonic to Prince Charles's spirits. Never has he looked brighter, more hopeful, more the golden Prince. But his Highlanders are dispirited and bewildered by fatigue. They rise groggily, look about for their weapons, and wonder where they are. Across the moor, skirls of bagpipes come from Cumberland's ranks. Eight hundred Protestant Campbell pipers are preparing the British for victorious battle.

Behind the Jacobites are the Highlands, the brown bare hills one piled behind the other, mountains rising behind mountains, ridge after towering ridge. Ahead, across the plateau, is the long slow drop to the firth. To either side stretches the barren coverless heath. The Highland force is divided into two lines; to the rear of the first is Prince Charles, his generals and advisors. Prince Gabriello Franco wears the gaudy plumed cap of the Italian officer. Lord George is there and he is angry.

"We canna win this way, Your Highness. The men are tired and hungry. Cumberland has firepower that will mow us down unless we choose a more advantageous position. We must retreat, regroup . . ."

O'Sullivan is enraged. "Traitor!" he cries, raising his sword.

"Coward!" declares Prince Gabriello Franco. His face is hot and sweat streams from his forehead, although the afternoon is cold.

"You dare call me that? You!" For a moment it seems that the battle will begin here amid the Prince's war council.

"Stop it you two!" His Highness commands. "I know the men are hungry and tired, Lord George, but it cannot be helped. The time has come to confront Our destiny and seize what is rightfully Ours. We cannot retreat." The Prince is excited; his voice trembles with the eagerness he feels to do battle with his enemy. He despises Lord George and half agrees with Franco's accusation of cowardice. How else can he explain the laird's continued refusal to obey his orders to the letter? He tries to conceal his dislike, but it rings in his commanding tones. "I know my Highlanders. I do not doubt their bravery. I know they will fight like beasts when the charge sounds, no matter how their leaders feel."

Lord George cannot answer what is in his heart to say. He is too loyal. Instead, he wheels his horse and gallops to his men, the ribbons of his balmoral flying gallantly.

Cumberland's army announces its attack with the thunder of two hundred and twenty-five kettle drums. The wind is up; an ally of the English, it drives the noise toward the Highland army. The drummers are splendid in brilliant red and blue uniforms ruffled in lace, their stockings of the whitest white, their gaiters shining patent leather. Behind them, stepping quickly to the drumbeat, come the foot soldiers, resplendent in red and blue and white, their mitres blazing with golden coronets. Behind them are the big guns, more than twenty-four pounders aimed at the rear toward Prince Charles.

Bayonets, muskets, cannons, swords; the English are metal-heavy and eager. On command, wave after wave of fire is aimed into the Scottish ranks; the Highlanders respond, but their effort is pitiful. The clansmen, awake at last and ready to fight as Charles had said they would be, look to their leaders for the call to charge. The leaders look to Charles. But the Prince delays.

The English are four hundred yards away, and through the smoky air hailstones big as cherries bombard the Highland army.

Cumberland's connonade of grapeshot splatters mud on Charles's white horse. A little distance from him, a soldier screams as a ball destroys his face, throwing blood and gore across the Prince's cheeks.

The Mackintoshes can wait no longer. McGillivray of Drumglass raises the yellow Mackintosh flag. Roaring like savages, knives clenched between their teeth, swords and claymores held high, they charge the enemy guns. "Run, ye dogs!" they scream, as they hack their bloody way. A line of musket fire mows them down; but their comrades press on, vicious and desperate to die on the English bayonets.

All the clans follow.

Fiona saw them in her dream. The unbearded faces of the boy-soldiers blown away by musket fire; the reeking wounds of fathers bleeding into the soil that was their fathers' and grandfathers', but from which their children would be forever disinherited; the men in their prime who chose to die rather than be subservient to the Hanover King. She saw them slice and cut into the enemy until the mud was red. And she watched them fall until the heath was littered with the bodies of hundreds and hundreds of brave Highlanders.

There was no mist of unreality over any of this. She knew without understanding how, or questioning why, what she saw in her open-eyed sleep was happening just as she dreamed it.

Beside a little burn a wounded Highlander stoops to drink, raises his head and is felled by musket fire. His head drops into the water and the stream runs red to the sea.

A few paces away Lord George is thrown from his horse and loses his sword, looks about for it, then grabs another from a fallen kinsman. Shouting huzzahs to his staggering clansmen, he dives forward into the melee.

Michael Cameron is there. His hands and arms are bloody; his stockings and shirt are stained scarlet, the colors of his tartan are almost obliterated. He drags his sword from the body of a fallen Englishman, turns, and spies a riderless horse. All about him the carnage continues. Cumberland encourages his men to acts of savagery because he plans to teach the Scots a lesson they will never forget. Michael runs toward the riderless horse snorting in fear from the smell of blood that pools about its hooves. Grabbing the mane, Michael swings himself up and into the saddle, turns the beast and gallops back to Prince Charles.

"Captain! What is happening?" The Prince looks confused. He hears the skirl of pipes. "What's that?"

"Fraser is retreating."

"How dare they? Stop them, Charles!" cries Franco. His dark eyes are round with fear.

"All is lost!" wails Charles.

"Use the West Road, Your Highness. It is yet secure and will be for a few days. There is a price on your head of thirty thousand pounds—you dare not linger. Hurry!" Michael's tone is imperious. In Scotland he is just as much ruler as anyone now.

Charles casts a single look across Cullodin Moor where the battle is ending, then turns and gallops west with Sheridan, O'Sullivan, Macdonald and the rest of his entourage. When Franco tried to follow he finds that Michael blocks his way, his sword raised.

"Get out of here!" the Italian commands. "What do you think you're doing? How dare . . ."

In her dream Fiona hears Michael's voice, but his words are lost in the rolls of laughter from Prince Gabriello Franco.

"I won't tell you!" the man screams. "She'll rot and you'll never know. You'll never know!" Before he can say anything more, Michael dives from his horse onto Franco. The two men fall to the bloody ground, their hands on one another's throats. First Cameron is the aggressor, then Franco seems to gain the upper hand.

Franco sees a line of Cumberland's grenadiers approaching. He tried to run, but Michael has him. The point of his dirk presses the throbbing pulse on Franco's neck. Cameron seems oblivious to the nearing enemy; obsessed with wresting the truth from Franco, he ignores the fire about him.

In her dream Fiona cannot warn him, cannot scream that he must fly before it is too late. She watches helplessly as he abandons the Italian to the enemy and wheels into his saddle, the shot falling about him. She watches as he is hit, first in the shoulder, then in the head. The head-wound gushes crimson. He sways in the saddle.

Like the final curtain of a ghastly drama, a curtain of red drops on Fiona's dream.

Mélisande watched as the girl's eyes closed at last; Fiona's body drooped against the wall and she slept deeply.

She awoke aching and hungry, wracked by a dozen complaints. But the agonies of her body were somehow tolerable when she compared them to what others had so recently suffered. The details of her dream remained vivid in her mind—but now the Battle of Cullodin Moor was over. She had not been able to stop the carnage, and in the months to come she would be equally powerless against the vengeful English forces that would invade the Highlands, divide the land and the families, murder and steal, in an effort to break up the power of the clans. She knew now what should have been clear to her from the beginning. Though it had been her destiny to know the future, it had also been her destiny to be powerless.

She recalled Michael. She jumped up and ran to the window of the tower. For the first time, she saw the scrawny donkey grazing near the wall. It was light; the sky had cleared. She might still be able to get to him before it was too late. She remembered the way he had slumped in the saddle as blood ran from his broken temples.

"Mélisande!" she grabbed the girl and whispered in her ear. "I know how we can get out. Will you help me?"

A flicker of indecision showed in Mélisande's expression. She had seen Fiona in her dream trance and had become convinced that the girl from Skye was mad after all. She regretted having befriended her.

"I can't explain what just happened to me, Mélisande. I don't understand myself. But no matter how it seems, I am not mad! And I know how to get us out."

"How?"

"Can I trust you?" Did it matter? Fiona knew it was a risk she must take, before it was too late and Michael was dead. "I'll let everyone out, Mélisande. Even the old woman. You'll all be free."

Mélisande looked worriedly from side to side and placed a cautionary finger to her lips. "Say softly how dis will be done."

Fiona quickly told about the *skene dhu* hidden in her bodice.

"If you can attract old Pegan's attention, get her to open the door; I'll do the rest." Fiona did not know what the rest might entail, but she would stop at nothing to gain her freedom for Michael's dear sake. "Will you do it?"

Mélisande smiled and nodded. "Right now, *oui?*" She leapt to the window and clambered through the small opening so she was half outside the tower. She began to scream, until old Pegan emerged from her stone hovel nearby and looked up.

Meanwhile, Fiona raced down the dark steps, slipping and stumbling, still weak from Franco's beating. Before she reached the bottom, she was faint and fearful her strength would not hold. If Pegan struggled . . .

She just had time to make it to the shadows near the door. Twenty-four hours earlier she had been terrified by who or what huddled there, but now she was oblivious. Someone grabbed at her ankle, but she shook the hand away as if it were nothing.

Through the heavy door she heard old Pegan coming, muttering as she approached. The key was in the lock, the hinges squealed, the door opened.

Fiona grabbed Pegan from behind, pressing her *skene dhu* to the withered old neck as she had seen Michael do to Franco in her dream. The old keeper was extraordinarily strong for one so decrepit. Twice she almost slipped from Fiona's grasp. The girl screamed for Mélisande, who appeared beside her seconds later.

"I can't hold her. Take her, quick!" She shoved the knife into Mélisande's hand, then grabbed old Pegan's keys. "I must go. I'll throw back the keys when the gate is opened. Let everyone out and then lock her in."

There was a gleam in Mélisande's eyes. "First I hurt her, then I lock her in!"

Fiona wanted to argue. She did not care to be a party to murder, even indirectly. This was what Franco had accused her of: murder! But she could not blame Mélisande and she knew that if the French girl did not do it, another of old Pegan's tormented batties would. Like Franco, she had abused and manipulated the helpless. Perhaps it was fitting that her end be violent.

"Bless you for helping me, Mélisande," she whispered, touching the girl lightly on the shoulder. "Bless you a thousand times over."

With no further words, she turned and ran—toward freedom and Michael Cameron.

Chapter 38

Old Pegan's donkey was better fed than all the inmates at Saint Dymphna's. It carried Fiona back along the Cullodin Road with a sprightly step, as if it were happy to be free of its hateful mistress and the tower she controlled with cruelty and hate. Along the road, Fiona passed dozens of half-dead Highland soldiers going in the opposite direction. They eyed her as she passed; but they were too weak, too miserable in their humiliation to make anything of her peculiar state of semi-dress, or the fact that she was moving back toward the disaster scene they had just fled.

Fiona's heart ached for the poor men and boys who had sacrificed so much for a cause she had known was doomed at the outset. If only she could have stopped Prince Charles in his headlong rush to defeat. If only . . . It did no good to wish for what might have been. She knew that, yet could not stop herself. The donkey plodded east along the West Road, and Fiona wept until she had exhausted her grief and knew that she was cleansed.

She scrutinized the face of each passerby, looking for someone she knew who might also know Michael and tell her of his whereabouts. In the dream he had told Prince Charles to flee along the West Road; did it not follow that he also would escape by this route? But what if he didn't? She forced herself to consider this contingency.

If I cannot find him, she thought, I will return to Edinburgh somehow. I will go to Lady Flora Jane's solicitor. He will help me.

But she must find him! Without Michael, she knew that life would be empty for her. No amount of wealth could assuage the pain of his loss. She jabbed her bare heels into the donkey's flanks and urged it forward faster. Every moment was crucial, every second was a heartbeat.

She saw him first.

He was slumped over the mane of his horse, barely able to hold himself in the saddle. The mount was as exhausted as the rider. It plodded as if each step might be its final effort.

"Michael!" she cried out when she saw him. He didn't move. She thought the worst, that he was dead and held in the saddle only by some horrible fate that was determined to break her heart forever. "Michael!" She slipped from the back of the donkey and ran toward him. A special strength possessed her for a little while; she moved with speed and grace. In a moment, she was beside her lover.

His eyes fluttered open and he saw her. His expression was one of mystified confusion.

"It's all right, Michael. I'm here, I'm really here."

He tried to smile; the gallant effort brought tears to her eyes.

She led his horse off the road some distance to a hollow that could not be seen from the road. She helped Michael out of the saddle and made a place for him to rest where the bracken was thick. As if to celebrate this new beginning for Michael and Fiona, the first signs of spring had begun to appear in the countryside. The ground was dotted with tiny blue and pink and white flowers that sweetened the air. Heaving the saddle off the horse, she made a headrest, leaned Michael back against it, then covered him with the plaid she found in the saddle bag. Taking the animal by the reins, she led it to a little burn and tethered it to some low bushes. She brought water in a cup she had also found in the saddle bag.

When she returned, Michael was more fully conscious.

"How did you . . . ? I thought . . ." His head fell back against the saddle.

"Don't try to speak. You'll know everything soon enough." Dampening a bit of her underskirt torn from the hem, she washed his wounds. Though both had bled profusely, they were not life endangering. "Where is Ezekial Mudd?" She would find him and bring him back to assist her with Michael.

But Cameron shook his head. "Dead. All dead." His eyes widened and she saw in them the bloody memory of the Highland defeat. He struggled, as if in the grasp of some new madness. "Get away, Fiona. The English . . . Cumberland . . ."

"I know. I know," she whispered. Whatever was required to take them back to Skye safely, Fiona knew it was within her power even without the help of poor Muddy. The events of the last months, the fact of her survival against seemingly impossible odds, had given her a new and indomitable confidence. "Do not fear the English, Michael. They cannot hurt us now."

With eyes bleary from pain and fatigue, he gazed up at his beloved, his rescuer. Was it possible that this was the same girl he had thought helpless? "I thought you were gone forever," he managed to whisper, his hand reaching out to touch her cheek and make sure, once and for all, that she was real and not a death-bred hallucination. "How?"

"You told me to believe in myself and I did that. I did as you told me and they did not destroy me." She cradled him in her arms. "Now you must believe in *us*, Michael. Together we canna fail to find our way home. Together we are stronger than Cumberland, the Hanovers. They canna destroy us, or separate us ever again."

He marveled at her wisdom and at the remarkable fortune that had brought them together at last. There was so much he wanted to tell her, but he was too weak; he could not do as simple a thing as say how he loved her, how when he thought her forever lost to him, he had begun to die, had given up the will to fight for life.

Words were unnecessary. She understood.

"I saw it all, Michael. The battle, the blood. Even Franco's death was revealed to me." When he tried to shake his head in disbelief, she stilled him with her mouth pressed against his parched lips. The kiss was long and gentle, a refreshment to both their spirits. "It's all right, Michael. The dream is over now. It's gone, gone forever."

She had not known the truth before she spoke the words aloud. Once she had said them, their veracity rang unmistakably. She knew whatever power had forced the dream upon her was now gone. That part of her that was faery kin had been vanquished by the Highland defeat. Though Scotland would be in bondage to the English for centuries to come, Fiona Macleod was free at last.

Author's Note

Following the Scottish defeat at Cullodin Moor, Lowland law came to the Highlands. Highland families were burned out of their homes and shipped abroad to Australia, Canada and the United States. Thousands were imprisoned, hundreds murdered violently. The hereditary jurisdiction of the Highland chief was swept away. Until the time of Queen Victoria, the wearing of the kilt was forbidden.

Prince Charles Edward Stuart, Pretender to the throne of England, returned to France in 1746. He did not see the hundreds of brave Jacobites who were hanged for their loyalty to the Stuarts; he did not see them cut into quarters, their hearts and bowels removed.

Besotted by drink, bloated and debauched, Prince Charles died in Rome in 1787.

You Have a Rendezvous with Richard Gallen Books...

EVERY MONTH!

Visit worlds of romance and passion in the distant past and the exciting present, words of danger and desire, intrigue and ecstasy—in breathtaking novels from romantic fiction's finest writers.

Now you can order the Richard Gallen books you might have missed!

These great contemporary romances...

Continued next page

Dear Reader:

Would you take a few moments to fill out this questionnaire and mail it to:

Richard Gallen Books/Questionnaire
8-10 West 36th St., New York, N.Y. 10018

1. What rating would you give *A Dream of Fire?*
   □ excellent □ very good □ fair □ poor

2. What prompted you to buy this book? □ title
   □ front cover □ back cover □ friend's recom-
   mendation □ other (please specify) _____

3. Check off the elements you liked best:
   □ hero □ heroine □ other characters □ story
   □ setting □ ending □ love scenes

4. Were the love scenes □ too explicit
   □ not explicit enough □ just right

5. Any additional comments about the book?

   _____

6. Would you recommend this book to friends?
   □ yes □ no

7. Have you read other Richard Gallen
   romances? □ yes □ no

8. Do you plan to buy other Richard Gallen
   romances? □ yes □ no

9. What kind of romances do you enjoy reading?
   □ historical romance □ contemporary romance
   □ Regency romance □ light modern romance
   □ Gothic romance

10. Please check your general age group:
    □ under 25 □ 25-35 □ 35-45 □ 45-55 □ over 55

11. If you would like to receive a romance
    newsletter please fill in your name and
    address:

    _____

    _____

    _____